WILD
SHORES

Maria Adolfsson lives in Stockholm where she, until recently, worked as a communications director and now writes full-time. The Doggerland series has been sold into 18 languages to date, and has sold over 330,000 copies in Sweden alone.

Also by Maria Adolfsson
Fatal Isles
Cruel Tides

WILD SHORES

Maria Adolfsson

ZAFFRE

Originally published in Sweden by Wahlström & Widstrand in 2019
First published in Great Britain in 2021 by
ZAFFRE
An imprint of Bonnier Books UK
4th Floor, Victoria House, Bloomsbury Square, London WC1B 4DA
Owned by Bonnier Books
Sveavägen 56, Stockholm, Sweden

Translation by Agnes Broome

A CIP catalogue record for this book is
available from the British Library.

ISBN: 978-1-83877-612-1

Also available as an ebook and an audiobook

1 3 5 7 9 10 8 6 4 2

Typeset by IDSUK (Data Connection) Ltd
Printed and bound in Great Britain by Clays Ltd, Elcograf S.p.A.

Zaffre is an imprint of Bonnier Books UK
www.bonnierbooks.co.uk

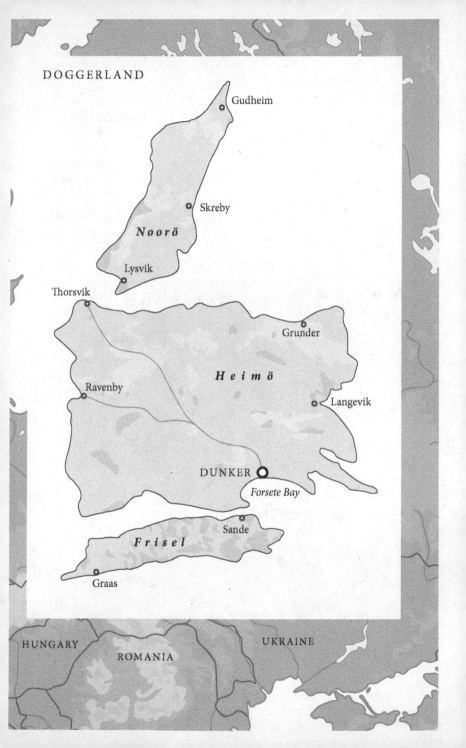

DOGGERLAND

Gudheim

Skreby

Noorö

Lysvik

Thorsvik

Grunder

Heimö

Ravenby

Langevik

DUNKER

Forsete Bay

Sande

Frisel

Graas

HUNGARY

ROMANIA

UKRAINE

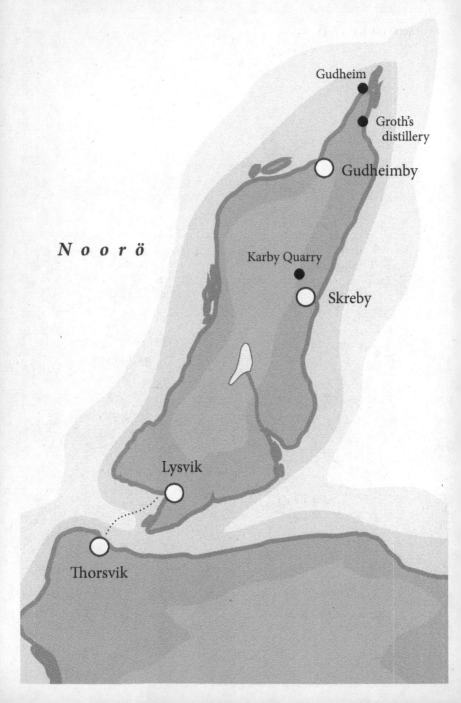

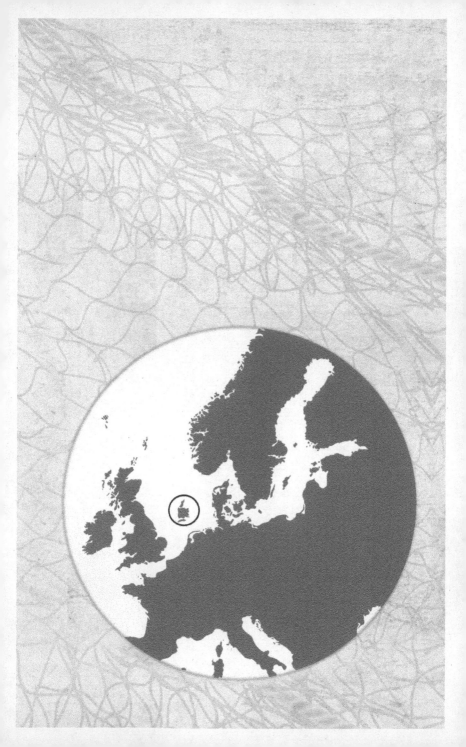

The meek pray in a dead calm,
sinners in a headwind,
fishermen in a storm.

Doggerian saying

PROLOGUE

She studies her phone with mild revulsion. Leans back, as though the mere sight of it constitutes a threat, gets to her feet and walks halfway around the kitchen table, where she pauses on the threshold to stare into the living room. Then she paces back the other way, avoiding the phone with her eyes when she passes the table again, pretending not to notice the black screen's mute entreaty.

Halfway to the hallway, she stops mid-step and gazes vacantly out the window. It would be so easy not to do it. To heed that seductive voice whispering that she doesn't have to, that she really shouldn't. That it would be wrong. The voice that takes on an edge now, urging her to keep her cool, reminding her that everything could fall apart if she doesn't.

She hesitates. Turns around and glances toward the pantry. So tempting to pull out a bottle of red, sit down in front of the TV and try to forget all about it.

It would clearly be the better decision. The right one.

And yet she knows she's about to pick up the phone and make that damn call. The call that will cost her her job if anyone finds out, the call that might cost her a lot more than that, if the person on the other end seizes their chance to get rid of an entirely different problem instead. Her.

No, this is wrong, Detective Inspector Karen Eiken Hornby thinks to herself – and picks up the phone.

Absolutely wrong. But the only way.

1

Four weeks earlier
Christmas Day

It's only a few degrees below freezing, yet the raw air rips at her lungs and she has to stop and breathe into her scarf. Horrified, Gertrud Stuub realises she just came close to cursing and hurriedly crosses herself with her hand. Her eyes dart around increasingly anxiously, taking in the copse of trees up on the mountain ridge and the narrow gravel path she is on. Quick glances in the other direction, toward the thing she is terrified of even thinking about.

You're imagining things, she tells herself and feels her airway slowly relax. He never promised to come, you just assumed he'd be there. And here you are, running around like a batty old lady. She forces herself to stand still and take a few more breaths through the woollen fabric before hurrying on, as quickly as she dares, along the craggy gravel path on which puddles of water have hardened into mirrors of treacherous ice.

On her left, bare trees dot the rise; between them she can see the blue silhouette of Goat Back Mountain rising up in the distance. Steep and inaccessible to a person her age. To a person Fredrik's age. He's not that stupid, she assures herself before suppressing the entire notion. The alternative on the other side is even worse. A few feet from the path on her right, the ground ends in a sheer drop.

She reluctantly turns her head. As long as she keeps her eyes focused on a point at the far end, it looks like a normal, pleasant lake, glinting in the first pale rays of the December sun. A lake in the middle of the woods, covered by a thin film of ice. But if you stray just a few steps from the path, crane your neck and look down, the quarry walls plunge precipitously into the black depths. Gertrud does not stray from the path. Nothing could make her approach that edge willingly.

'He walks by here every day,' she tells herself out loud and is frightened to hear her faint voice and the compact silence devouring her words. She can't bring herself to call out his name, doesn't want to know what that would sound like. If he's here, she'll find him.

He knows the terrain, she tells herself. Knows exactly where to put his feet, and so does Sammy. They're probably back home already; she wouldn't be surprised if he were snug in the warm kitchen, with a cup of coffee and what was left of the saffron pastry from yesterday, godless and completely unconcerned about heaven and hell. It would be just like him. No, I'm going to turn around right now and stop this nonsense, she decides and glances over her shoulder, back the way she came. On the other hand, she realises reluctantly, at this point, the walk back would take as long as completing the loop around the quarry.

With a heavy sigh, she presses on, crossing herself again while inwardly cursing her brother's lack of consideration in general and utter want of devoutness in particular. Fredrik doesn't often darken the church's doorstep, she is all too aware of that, but he normally attends the early morning Christmas

4

Day service, at least. For some reason, even the most irreverent of her neighbours, the ones who never set foot in the Lord's house except for weddings and christenings, tend to show up on Christmas. Maybe he just overslept.

Further down the path, she catches a glimpse of the turning area where the road leading down to the highway begins. Or ends. It's been years since the mining trucks stopped using it and the cracks in the asphalt are growing longer and wider every year. There's no point maintaining it; these days, the only people who use it are fly-tippers who can't be bothered to take their rubbish down to the recycling station in Valby. Stingy, dishonest people, who would do anything to save a shilling. But not even they would have the audacity to do their illegal dumping on Christmas Day, she thinks to herself. No one is stupid enough to come here, except Fredrik. Not even the height of summer seems able to draw the young people out here for forbidden swims in the unfit waters of the quarry. She instinctively touches her coat pocket to make sure she still has her phone. No one would find her here if she fell and hurt herself, especially not this time of year.

It would teach him a lesson, she muses, if he really had fallen and hurt himself. Not seriously, just enough to make him understand that he's too old to be scampering around all alone in the middle of nowhere. Her hand automatically reaches up to her chest to atone for the forbidden thought and this time, she calls out.

'Fredrik! Hello! Fredrik!'

Then she stops dead.

A wretched whining makes her head turn cold. And when she spots the black-and-white border collie further down the path,

5

she knows. Sammy's long lead drags behind him as he anxiously trots back and forth along the edge of the quarry, lying down for a few seconds, jumping back up and continuing his futile pacing, dangerously close to falling in. For a moment, it looks as though the dog is going to try to find a way down the sheer rock face, but the sound of someone approaching makes him prick up his ears and look around. Then Sammy spots Gertrud and races toward her, barking wildly. With his tail between his legs, the desperate dog dashes back and forth between Gertrud and the edge of the cliff, urging her on. She reluctantly follows, praying loudly to herself.

'Please, dear Lord, don't turn away from me now.'

There's no sign of her brother from where she stops on the path with her mitten pressed to her mouth. For a dizzying second, vain hope overcomes her – maybe it's not Fredrik down there. Maybe it's just the old tennis ball Sammy insists on carrying with him at all times. Maybe Fredrik threw it toward the quarry in a careless moment instead of up the slope the way he usually would. And when she moves closer to the edge, heart thumping, and cranes her neck, she still can't see him.

It's not until Gertrud Stuub gets down on her stomach and, with one last helpless prayer, carefully inches her way to the edge to look down the precipice that hope dies.

2

Karen Eiken Hornby pulls the door shut behind her and digs around her coat pocket for her packet of cigarettes. Leaning with her elbows on the cold railing of the front steps, she takes a deep drag and feels her heart rate slow. She stares blankly straight ahead.

It's already pitch-black outside, though it's only just gone half past four, but the December air is unseasonably mild. The light from the kitchen window pools on the ground around the large rowan tree. Only a few rapidly melting patches of snow remain of the four inches that covered the ground just a week ago. Anything that manages to freeze when the temperature dips overnight quickly thaws under the grey woollen blanket the sky has resembled over the past few days. The sounds of clattering china, laughter and yet another drinking song carry through the closed window.

Fisherman, take comfort,
The codfish is so cruel, so cruel, so cruel
Quench your thirst with spirits
It's yule, it's yule, it's yule . . .
Cheers!

Without turning to look, she knows the seven people around the table inside are raising their glasses to eye height before lowering them and drinking as one. She waits for the bang of their glasses being slammed back down. There it is.

How the fuck am I supposed to survive another two days of this? she wonders.

There's nowhere to escape for some alone time. Her mother and Harry are in the big bedroom – Karen had decidedly mixed feelings about giving up her double bed – and she has moved into the guest bedroom next door and will soon, for the third night in a row, do her best to ignore the noises on the other side of the wall.

It had seemed like a good idea when they planned the whole thing over a few glasses of wine at the Dunker pub, The Mine, a couple of weeks earlier. To have her closest friends come to stay with her over Christmas Eve and Christmas Day. Her mother and Harry were going to visit anyway and the more the merrier. Marike had assured her she was fine on the sofa in the living room and that she would bring both crispy pork roast and red cabbage. Kore and Eirik could take the sofa bed in the guest house with Leo and bring horseradish herring, gravlax and home-made mustard. Her mother had promised to bake both saffron biscuits and rye bread the moment she arrived, so Karen would really only have to make a big batch of juniper beer and season the snaps. Two days of good food, good conversation and long walks in the snow, because surely they'd get some snow soon?

Now, she listens to the laughter inside. Yes, everything is exactly as lovely as they planned. Everything is as it should be. Except that she wants to be alone. To hear, even if just for one moment, the sound of silence.

Just one more night, you can do it, she tells herself and takes another deep drag. Kore, Eirik and Marike will in all likelihood go home straight after breakfast tomorrow. But her mother and Harry are staying one more night, she reminds herself. They're not flying back to Spain until the day after tomorrow. Two more mornings of pretending not to see Harry affectionately pat her mother's bum, pretending not to hear the sound of stolen kisses every time she turns her back. Thirty-six more hours of biting back the caustic comments about to leap off her tongue every time her mother refers to the seventy-six-year-old Harry Lampard as her new 'boyfriend'.

And then there's Sigrid.

Why couldn't the kid just stay with her dad after finally reconnecting after years of estrangement? It's bloody Christmas, a time to spend with family, Karen grumbles inwardly and sucks so hard on her cigarette it burns her fingertips.

'I won't be staying long,' Sigrid had happily assured her when she turned up unannounced in the kitchen almost three hours ago. 'Just stopping by.'

And then that wave of warmth crashing over Karen before she could stop it. That unreasonable, frightening joy that rushes through her every time she sees Sigrid. All the things there is no room for in her life anymore.

I won't be staying long. How Sigrid had planned to cover the mile and a half to her own house at the other end of the village after two glasses of juniper beer and at least one shot of snaps is her affair. Karen is not on the job tonight. And besides, she's tired.

And then there's her damn knee. A constantly aching reminder of what happened, and what could have happened. Karen shifts her weight onto her right leg and feels a stab of pain in her hip. Over two months ago now, and still it's not back to normal. Four weeks at Thystedt Hospital and then rehab at home. Painful visits to the physiotherapist in Dunker three times a week. She has meekly done everything they've told her to, all the exercises, twice a day. And still she can't put weight on her left leg for more than a few minutes at a time. It's a strain, having to conceal the truth from the people sitting in the warm kitchen behind her, having to keep up appearances, to conceal the constant ache, to choose between yet another round of painkillers or a snaps with her herring, to keep the fake smile on her face: no, it doesn't hurt at all anymore, I'm just a bit stiff still. To pretend not to notice her mother's suspicious looks.

She is on sick leave until Twelfth Night, so just twelve more days, trapped in her house with far too many thoughts. She's going back to work the moment the holidays are over, even if she has to crawl there. At least she has managed to persuade her doctor not to extend her sick leave. If nothing else, I'm a good liar, she muses.

For a moment or two, the din grows louder as the door opens and then closes again, slightly too hard, making the kitchen window rattle. She knows it's Leo without turning around. She sees the flame of his lighter out of the corner of her eye, hears him inhale deeply, hold the smoke in his lungs for a second and exhale. He holds out his packet and she bums a cigarette.

'It'll all be over eventually,' he says. 'You have to cling to that thought.'

Am I that easy to read? she wonders inwardly. I thought I had a pretty good poker face.

'How philosophical of you,' she mutters. 'Any other words of wisdom for me?'

10

'Alcohol helps, obviously. And isn't drinking and knowing it'll be over eventually what Christmas is all about?' he replies with a grin.

She briefly meets his eyes and tries to stop herself from smiling.

'Well, you should know,' she replies drily. 'Was it alcohol and knowing it would all be over eventually that sustained you when you were living under that loading dock?'

'It certainly wasn't women and song.'

They continue to smoke in silence. Karen turns her head and notices that Eirik and Marike have started to clear the table, while Harry is using the unwashed pot to refill the coffee maker. She sighs.

'He's a good one,' Leo comments, 'your new stepdad.'

It stings when she snorts out smoke.

'Stepdad! Oh, come off it . . .'

'And Eleanor is happy,' he continues.

'Yeah, thanks, I've gathered. Thin walls.'

Leo takes a drag and stares mutely into the darkness.

'I guess you'll have to move in with me tomorrow after Kore and Eirik leave,' he says after a while.

'With *you*?'

'Sure, they claim the sofa bed is actually comfortable if you just use a few pillows to pad the steel beam poking into your lower back. And if worst comes to worst, I'm sure I could make room in my bed.'

Taken aback, she gives him a quick, sidelong glance; this isn't like him. Come to think of it, participating in a Christmas celebration doesn't seem like him either, singing drinking songs and listening to Harry go on and on about how converting the attic

11

or winterising the shed would give Karen more space. Completely oblivious to Karen's growing irritation, Leo and Harry had continued to make plans for her house while topping up each other's glasses. How she should go about it, how much it would cost, how much it would raise the property value now that the old fisherman's cottages in Langevik have become popular again. Especially houses like Karen's, with private jetties and boat sheds.

It's probably a train of thought that comes naturally to Harry Lampard; according to her mother, he ran a successful building company in Birmingham before retiring to Spain's Costa del Sol. But that Leo Friis would sit there and listen and take an active interest . . .

What the fuck does he know about insulation, roof shingles and loadbearing walls? Karen thinks to herself and grinds her half-finished cigarette out against the railing. On the other hand, what do I really know about Leo Friis? she thinks a moment later. Just a few months ago, he was homeless, tramping around with a trolley in Dunker, looking for glass bottles to recycle.

'So you're suggesting I move in with *you*?' she says. 'Last I checked, it was still *my* house.'

Leo shrugs as if generously allowing her point.

'Which I rent, yes. For a pittance, granted, though I don't recall being given a proper contract,' he adds. 'But I assume you don't want to get the revenue service involved . . .'

Karen inhales sharply.

'Oh, relax,' he says quickly when he notices her stricken look. 'It was a joke, Karen.'

And for a second, she's left wondering whether he's referring to what he said about the bed or the revenue service.

Then he puts his cigarette out in the upside-down terracotta flowerpot by the door.

'Ready to go back in?'

She reluctantly straightens up.

'It'll all be over eventually,' she says with a sigh.

3

Twenty minutes later, the dishwasher has been loaded, the coffee has been poured and the saffron biscuits have been set out on the living-room table. Kore and Eirik are back after a quick visit to the annexe and Marike says something about getting a room and being considerate of their less fortunate friends when she sees them canoodling.

Harry glances their way, a look that signals equal parts discomfort and curiosity.

Marike herself seems to be in fine spirits for once, and her Danish accent is barely noticeable tonight. And yet, Karen knows the only thing standing between this version of her friend and a scary harpy, hissing in an incomprehensible North Jutland slur, is a failed kiln firing. But tonight, Marike Estrup is radiant and there is no sign of the anxiety that will slowly but surely creep over her as her exhibition in New York draws nearer. Karen leans back in her armchair. Be present. It'll all be over eventually.

Someone has dug out a bottle of Groth's whiskey and another of rowanberry liqueur and everyone has managed to find somewhere to sit, on the green sofa, in one of the well-worn wingback armchairs or on the old hope chest, which she still hasn't found the time to lug up to the attic. Her first decision after taking over the house from her mother was to get that monstrosity out of the way: that's nine years ago now.

Sigrid has sat down on the floor with her legs crossed and her elbows on the coffee table. Karen studies her long black hair – dyed so many times it's completely lustreless – her tattoo-covered, skinny arms, the ring in her nose, which catches the light from the candles in the brass candelabrum when Sigrid nods eagerly in response to something Kore says. She and Kore actually look a lot alike, Karen realises. At least as far as their hair colour, tattoos and piercings go. Sigrid's father wouldn't like that comparison, Karen muses and smugly sips her drink.

Eirik, on the other hand, couldn't be more different from his partner. In honour of the festive occasion, he is wearing a pink sweater vest over a white shirt he has paired with a subdued grey-striped tie. The creases in his grey trousers are razor sharp. As ever. Good old Eirik, Karen thinks to herself, his sartorial choices are as dependable as his friendship – without him I wouldn't be here today. Her throat tightens and she lets her eyes move on. With a shudder, she realises her mother and Harry are wearing identical sweaters again, this time Christmas themed with juniper bushes. At least they look happy, she tells herself.

Her fit of irritation has subsided, replaced by some kind of resigned tenderness. Now, in the wake of the anger and frustration, here, warmed by the whiskey and with a limp cat on her lap, she doesn't have it in her to keep her guard up, doesn't have it in her to defend herself against all the things that will be her undoing unless she's careful.

She's not your daughter, don't ever forget that.

Susanne Smeed's last words are still ringing in her ears.

She silently studies the daughter that isn't hers, the girl she took under her wing just a few months ago. She had found Sigrid slumped, wet and feverish, on the front steps of the house that had unexpectedly been forced on the girl. Too weak to protest, Sigrid had let Karen take her home and ply her with hot tea, crackers and Tylenol until the flu had relinquished its grip on her.

And somehow, she had never really moved back out.

Granted, Sigrid's official address is still the house her mother left her, but she spends most of her time at Karen's. She's supposedly never staying long, but often ends up hanging around until late at night and stays over in the guest room as often as she dares to ask. Like a cat you shoo away, only to have it turn up on your front porch again the next day.

Just like you, Karen thinks to herself and strokes the grey cat's belly, absent-mindedly teasing out a knot with her nails. Rufus just turned up one day, too, and decided to stay. Leo, she had invited as a house-cum-cat sitter when she went on holiday. A holiday that had been cut tragically short. But he doesn't seem to be in a hurry to leave, either. On the other hand, he doesn't have a lot of options.

How had this happened? When did my house turn into to bloody homeless shelter? Karen wonders and takes another sip of whiskey.

She doesn't hear it herself. Instead, Marike, who had gone to the bathroom, comes back with Karen's phone in her hand.

'It was in your coat pocket. I figured you might want to take this particular call,' she adds with a significant glance at the screen before handing the phone over.

Karen just has time to see the words 'Jounas Smeed' before the phone falls silent. She heaves a deep sigh.

'Don't tell me it's Dad,' Sigrid says. Karen confirms with a nod.

'Has he tried to call you, too?' she asks.

Sigrid pulls her phone out of her back pocket and shakes her head.

'No, no missed calls,' she groans. 'What does he want *now*? I was there both today *and* yesterday!'

'Maybe he just wants to wish you a happy Christmas?' her mother puts in gently.

'He's supposed to be off to Thailand tomorrow,' Sigrid continues. 'He's been badgering me about going with him for three weeks! Isn't it *enough* that we did Christmas together? Am I supposed to sit on some fucking coconut beach, too? What's his *problem*?'

Sigrid spreads her arms and opens her eyes wide to further underline that she has done everything a daughter can possibly be expected to do to patch up her damaged relationship with her father.

She looks closer to eleven than nineteen, Karen reflects.

She stands up with another sigh and goes out to the kitchen, where she hesitates for two seconds before returning the call. If it's not about his daughter, there can be only one reason why the head of the Doggerland Police's Criminal Investigation Department is calling Karen Eiken Hornby on Christmas Day. And it's not to wish her a happy Christmas.

4

No, humble is overstating it, she thinks to herself two minutes later. Jounas Smeed has probably never felt humble in his life. But the voice on the other end of the line is slightly tentative and lacks the domineering tone she's grown so used to.

'Hey, Eiken, thanks for calling me back. I'm really sorry to bother you on Christmas Day and everything. Have you had any Christmas snaps yet?'

'Two glasses, actually. You?'

Jounas Smeed seems not to have heard her, or perhaps he doesn't consider the question worth answering.

'And your parents are visiting, I hear,' he goes on, and this time Karen definitely hears a strain in his voice.

'Well,' she replies wryly, 'Dad's been dead for years, but my mother's here with her . . . with a good friend of hers.'

'Aha, I see. Well, I realise you must be in the middle of your celebrations . . .'

Karen waits for him to continue, but her boss seems to feel it's her turn to speak.

'Well, yes,' she says. 'But I assume you're not calling to inquire about my alcohol consumption or my relatives?'

Jounas Smeed chuckles. Then he clears his throat and his voice regains some of its usual tone.

'Obviously not,' he replies curtly. 'There's been a murder. Up on Noorö of all places.'

'Noorö? OK, but isn't it just a case of alcohol induced manslaughter, as usual? Can't the local police handle it?'

'Apparently not. I'm given to understand the victim is an old teacher and the murder took place during the early morning Christmas Day service.'

Karen pulls out one of the kitchen chairs and sits down heavily.

'In church? How the fuck does that happen?'

'No, no, not *at* the service, but during it. Or sometime early yesterday morning, at any rate. And the local doctor apparently discovered something that made him call us. I don't have all the details yet.'

'And where do I come into this? I'm still on sick leave, as you know.'

She asks the questions even though she's pretty sure she knows the answer. She wants to make him squirm a little. Her reward is a heavy sigh on the other end.

'The thing is that we have an acute staff shortage. Half of my detectives are in bed with the flu and the other half are away over the holidays. I myself am getting on a plane to Thailand tomorrow. At least, I was planning to,' he adds in a resigned tone.

Karen stands up and stares out into the darkness on the other side of the kitchen window. Notes the sound of the rowan's branches scratching against the panes and makes a mental note to prune them before the next big storm.

'So you want to put me in charge of the investigation? You're asking me to cut my sick leave short and cancel the rest of my Christmas?'

Nothing in her voice hints at the relief spreading through her body. Let Jounas Smeed think she's doing him a big favour; it could prove useful down the road. For a split second, though, she wonders if she's taken it too far.

'Well, I figured it was worth a shot,' her boss replies, stiffly and with no trace of the warmth that suffused his voice earlier. 'But I obviously understand if you don't—'

'No problem.' Karen cuts him off. 'I'll do it.'

A few seconds of complete silence follow.

'Really? Are you sure? Because I can still cancel my trip and head up there myself.'

Of course you can, she thinks to herself, but you called me instead, even though I'm probably the last person on earth you want to beg favours from. He must be dying for a cocktail on the beach to think it worth being in my debt.

'You go,' she says. 'I'll deal with it. But are you seriously saying there's no one else available? I'm on my own?'

'There's no one from the CID, but I've obviously talked to Brodal and Larsen, who are thankfully both home and in good health.'

Karen sighs inwardly. Neither the coroner nor the head of forensic services is going to be happy at being ordered out to Noorö on Christmas. Especially not Kneought Brodal, she thinks to herself. He's going to be difficult.

'They're going up there early tomorrow morning,' Smeed continues. 'Not ideal, but it's dark now anyway and the crime scene is supposedly cordoned off and under guard. And the body has been taken to the local clinic in Lysvik; apparently, they have a freezer. Which is slightly odd, actually.'

'You think? Why? Surely it's for whenever the ferry's not running?' she says. 'I mean, they can be cut off for days at a time up there.'

'I suppose,' he admits, 'but it must have been ages since that happened. Don't you have family up there, come to think of it? I seem to recall you saying something to that effect once.'

'Yes, Dad was from Noorö and I spent a lot of time with his family as a child, but I haven't been there in years. Haven't seen them since . . . well, it's been a long time.'

'All right, well, this might be for the best, then, since you know your way around up there,' Jounas Smeed says, as if to convince himself he has once again made a rational decision. 'How soon can you leave?'

'Same time as Brodal and Larsen, early tomorrow morning, not before then. Unless you want to send a car and driver. Like I said, I've been drinking.'

So you had a reason for asking about the Christmas snaps after all, she muses. Bloody Smeed.

'Tomorrow's fine,' he replies quickly. 'The locals will have to hold the fort until then. Your liaison up there is a Thorstein Byle, by the way, regional commander of the Noorö Police. Call him tonight if you can. You're going to have to make do with Byle and his boys until I can rustle up someone from the CID to help you out – if it does turn out to be a murder, that is.'

'OK, anything else I need to know?'

'Yes, I may be on holiday, but it goes without saying I want you to keep me informed. My phone is always on and you can call any time.'

'OK, anything else?'

She can hear her boss take a deep breath, then a few more seconds of utter silence follow. In the end, Karen relents.

'Sigrid stopped by for a bit, but I think she's about to head home now,' she says. 'She says hi.'

Jounas Smeed exhales.

'Say hi back,' he says. 'And . . . thanks, Eiken,' he adds.

5

'Are you serious? Is there no one else they can send? Haven't they put you through enough? And on Christmas, too!'

Eleanor Eiken is sitting on the bed watching her daughter move a stack of dark blue T-shirts from her closet to a big cloth bag on the bed. Karen is working quickly and efficiently, her long dark hair, pulled back into a ponytail, whipping at her face every time she turns from the closet to the bed and back.

'Everyone's sick or out of town,' she replies and shoves bras and knickers in next to her toiletry bag. 'I'm the only one available right now.'

'Available!' Eleanor snorts the word derisively. 'You're not available, you're on sick leave. Don't you think I can tell you're still in pain?'

Karen freezes mid-movement and stares at her mother, braces to protest but is cut off before she can even start.

'Oh no, lambkin, this old ewe isn't so easily fooled. If you're not careful, you're going to throw out your back, always leaning on your right leg. Carrying you around on my hip all day long when you were little gave me a slipped disc, so I know what I'm talking about.'

Karen slowly sits down on the bed next to her mother.

'Fine; I'm still in pain sometimes,' she admits, 'but it gets a bit better every day. And you're going home the day after tomorrow anyway, so we only miss out on one day together.'

Eleanor heaves a heavy sigh.

'Fine. I'm not the kind to cry over a thing like that, but I'm worried about you being in pain. And you're looking far too pleased.'

Karen turns her head and looks at her with raised eyebrows.

'Pleased?'

'You know exactly what I mean. You can't get out of here fast enough, leave all the people who care about you and sit around in some hotel room, all alone.'

Karen shrugs.

'You know what I'm like.'

'Not what you're like, what you've *become*, you mean.'

'And you know why, too,' Karen retorts tersely.

'Yes, Karen, I know exactly why. But it's getting to be time to deal with that. You're not dead yet.'

No, I'm not, Karen counters inwardly. I was the one who lived . . .

She gets back up and resumes packing.

'Well, if you insist on going to that godforsaken place, at least make sure you visit Ingeborg and Lars,' Eleanor says after a while. 'She would never forgive you if you don't. Or me.'

'And since when do you care about what Aunt Ingeborg thinks? Unless I'm misremembering, you moved to the other end of the country to get away from Dad's Noorö relatives.'

'You know perfectly well that . . .'

'. . . you moved to Langevik because he inherited this house and the fishing rights from his grandfather. But admit it, you were relieved!'

24

Eleanor fails to supress a smile.

'My goodness, was it ever terrible up there,' she says. 'I don't know how I lived with it for as long as I did! Imagine, living in the same house as your parents-in-law and less than three hundred yards from your sister-in-law. You couldn't swing a cat without hitting an Eiken. Petty crooks the lot of them, and they made plenty of moonshine in those sheds of theirs, but everyone had to say grace and go to church every Sunday, without fail. I would probably have flung myself into the sea if we hadn't left that horrid place.'

Karen watches her mother with a smile. Eleanor Eiken, née Wood, three-fourths British and Scandinavian for the rest. As the daughter of a provincial doctor from Ravenby, she had probably never imagined the tribulations that lay in wait for her when she decided to marry Walter Eiken. And yet, Karen had never once heard her complain about her life as a fisherman's wife in Langevik. Eleanor had stoically endured the cleaning of fish and mending of seal-chewed nets. Neither autumn storms, icy winters, poor catches nor constant worry about the family's finances had prompted any expression of despondency. But the few years spent with Walter's paternal family up on Noorö had apparently been more than she could take.

'I'll send Aunt Ingeborg your love and let her know you'd love for her to visit you in Spain,' Karen says with a wide grin.

'Don't you dare! When are you leaving?'

Karen pushes down the contents of the bag and closes the zipper.

'Tomorrow morning, before you wake up. But let's go downstairs and enjoy what's left of Christmas.'

*

Several hours later, after one last cigarette, Karen pulls the front door shut and glances up at the clock to discover she won't get many hours of sleep. Her mother and Harry went upstairs almost an hour ago and Karen fervently hopes they're asleep by now. Leo, Eirik and Kore have retired to the annexe, but she can still hear faint voices and music coming from there.

She hangs up her coat, walks over to the sink and drinks a glass of water. Before turning off the kitchen light, she pops her head into the living room. The sound of even breathing and snoring in two different keys can be heard from the sofa. Sigrid has managed to persuade Marike to share the small space and is now paying the price in the form of a pair of feet with red toenails poking her in the back of her neck.

Karen lingers in the doorway for a moment before pushing the door closed. Carefully, so as not to wake anyone, she tiptoes up the creaking staircase.

6

Karen Eiken Hornby glances down at the dashboard and turns onto the motorway. Quarter to seven, an hour later than planned, but the extra sleep has made her feel surprisingly rested. The roads are dry after a week of mild weather, and this early on Boxing Day there's not going to be any traffic. Unless there's a long wait for the ferry in Thorsvik, she should be able to reach Lysvik on Noorö in time.

She turns the radio on and immediately changes the channel when the morning service theme begins to stream out of the speakers. It takes her few seconds to find a channel she can bear, but when she does, she turns the volume up and leans back. Drumming her fingers to the beat of the opening riff of 'Start Me Up', Karen accelerates, singing loudly enough to drown out Mick Jagger.

A feeling of freedom washes over her. Two months of imposed idleness, stuck at home with an aching knee and the aftermath of several broken ribs and a severe concussion has triggered thoughts and feelings that have bored her but also sometimes left her sleepless and afraid. In a matter of months her carefully controlled existence has been turned on its head. She has gone from leading a monotonous life of long workdays, the occasional visit to the local pub and solitary evenings, to dealing with the constant presence of others and a growing sense of being invaded. Sigrid hates her own house but pretends not to and Leo has never so much as hinted at when he might leave. She has avoided asking him because whatever the answer, she doesn't want to hear it. She's not alone anymore. She no longer knows if she wants to be.

For a few months now, her house has been filled with the sounds of other people. The clattering of plates in the kitchen, someone drawing a bath, music drifting across the yard from the annexe. Voices talking in the next room. And the smells. Fresh coffee she didn't make, shampoo from someone's newly washed hair. The presence of other people. Little pinpricks of joy. And then the crippling fear that follows. The constant reminder that she had all these things once before and lost them. That they can all be taken away again before you know it.

The call from Jounas Smeed had been a lifeline. Exhausted by her protracted confinement, she had welcomed the chance to return to work as though it were a sorely needed holiday. A concrete assignment, something she knows how to handle. She's not worried about the investigation yet. What little information she's been given about what has happened up on Noorö is too meagre to build theories or anxieties around. So far, all she feels is unadulterated, intoxicating relief.

The road curves gently, skirting the northern edge of Dunker. Karen catches a glimpse of the city lights before the view is blocked by the tall, barrack-like blocks of flats in Gaarda and Moerbeck. The photographs from the assault cases last autumn suddenly flash before her eyes. A series of rapes with sadistic undertones and one of the women died in the ambulance on the way to Thysted Hospital. No perpetrator has been arrested and no new attacks have been reported in the past two months, but the latter is probably

28

just a matter of time. The bastard will no doubt be at it again as soon as spring arrives, she muses. Jounas Smeed had said what they all knew to be true, 'Guys like this one usually manage to keep their cocks in their trousers so long as it's freezing outside.'

She hadn't been involved in that investigation. Instead, she'd almost died hunting down Susanne Smeed's killer.

The memory of those events briefly threatens to overwhelm her before she can push down the feeling that she had been seconds and millimetres from death. Her good mood takes another knock when she spots the sign marking the Glitne exit. Maybe she should have called her friend Aylin again, not left it at one attempt the day before Christmas Eve, when she'd been put through to Aylin's answerphone but hadn't left a message. Instead, she'd sent a text saying, 'Happy Christmas' and 'see you at Eirik and Kore's on New Year's'. She had deleted the last words 'Say hi to Bo' before sending the text. She doesn't wish him a happy Christmas, or a happy anything else, for that matter. Bad enough that I have to see the bastard on New Year's Eve, she grumbles to herself, that I'll be forced to just sit there and keep up appearances while furtively studying Aylin for signs of the thing she so strenuously denies.

'Of course he doesn't hit me.'

Maybe that's the truth. Maybe it isn't.

Karen glances over at another road sign announcing she has another 122 miles to go and forces her mind back to the task at hand. Late last night, she managed to get hold of the regional commander of the Noorö Police, Thorstein Byle, and they agreed to meet at the clinic in Lysvik around nine. As expected, he had sounded slightly guarded. Local officers' reactions to the CID taking over an investigation were usually characterised by a mix of irritation and relief. The decision to extend the National Criminal Investigation Department's jurisdiction to all serious crime investigations had been made eleven years ago. The media had, as usual, adopted a 'grassroots perspective' in their reporting, gleefully relaying an endless string of doomsday prophecies from aggrieved officers around the country. The local connection would be lost, the number of cases solved would decrease. The general view had been that it was a reform devised by bureaucrats who had never set foot outside the capital and cared only about trimming budgets.

In reality, the reform had been driven by a catastrophically low clearance rate for violent crimes. Granted, alcohol and drug-fuelled rows, assaults and killings were solved nine times out of ten, and in those types of cases the local connection was often critically important. But proper murders were so rare local forces lacked the experience to handle them. Besides – and this had been pivotal to the controversial decision – one of the regional police chiefs had been found to have withheld information in a case involving sexual abuse of three nursery aged children in Frene, just south of Ravenby. His nephew, it turned out, was the perpetrator.

The media outrage had died down eventually, not least when new statistics showed the clearance rate had gone up every year since the reform had been implemented. Unfortunately, the number of violent crimes had also doubled over the same period, which as recently as last week had prompted an article in the *Kvellsposten* newspaper about the number of criminals going unpunished in Doggerland. The article had inevitably implied a connection with the old legend that Doggerland had once served as a haven for escaped criminals from both the British Isles and

Scandinavia and the number of copies sold had probably contributed considerably to the newspaper owner's Christmas cheer.

But widespread resentment still simmered among local officers and detectives from the capital didn't often receive a warm welcome in the provinces. Karen has no illusions about this investigation being an exception. Had she been at work, she would have looked up Thorstein Byle on the intranet before going to Noorö. Now she has to make do with her own preconceived notions and the brief impression he gave on the phone: an old-fashioned type and a Noorö native, judging by his harsh consonants. He had been impeccably polite, but his voice had betrayed a level of unease.

Who cares, she thinks to herself, so long as he's up front with me?

Just then, her phone rings. Karen eases up on the accelerator and pushes the earbud of the hands-free into her ear without checking the display. Convinced it's her mother calling, she answers with her first name. But there is no trace of motherly warmth in the voice on the other end and it wastes no time on unnecessary pleasantries.

'This is Brodal. Where are you?'

Karen glances over at the sign she's just passing and replies without thinking.

'I just passed the Ferring exit. Why? Don't tell me you're already there?'

She instantly regrets not getting up an hour earlier.

'Well, you're going to have to turn around. I can't get my bloody car started and I need a ride. What's that damn racket?'

Karen turns down the radio and curses under her breath.

'What about Larsen?' she suggests. 'He's on his way up, too, you know.'

'He's already in Thorsvik. Do you know where I live?'

'Somewhere in Lemdal, right?'

'Fyrviksgatan 18, on the corner of Sandevägen. I'll be waiting outside.'

'All right, I'll be there in fifteen minutes,' she says through clenched teeth and turns the radio back up.

On the radio, Jagger howls about making grown men cry.

7

The suspension creaks and the car sways when Kneought Brodal climbs into the passenger seat next to Karen, grunting loudly. Muttering gruffly, he tugs at the seat belt, and Karen hesitates for a moment before leaning over to help him adjust the length. She can't remember who was last in the passenger seat, but whoever it was, they can't have been more than half his size. In the end, she manages to fasten the seat belt around the coroner's considerable girth.

'OK, here we go,' she says and hears the obsequious cheeriness in her voice.

Kneought Brodal makes no reply.

She keeps at it for twenty minutes before giving up. Karen normally has no trouble handling Brodal. Almost ten years of curt, snippy answers to questions about cases involving deadly crimes, have made her impervious to his terrible mood. There's nothing personal about the way he treats people; the coroner treats everyone, from the lowliest constable to the commissioner himself, like idiots. The only person Kneought Brodal seems to mildly enjoy discussing things with is the head of Forensic Services, Sören Larsen. No, she usually has no trouble with Brodal, but being trapped in a car with him for several hours is a different kettle of fish entirely.

After a few initial questions about how much he has been told about the suspected murder of the retired schoolteacher, Karen concludes he knows no more than she does and wishes he knew even less, because then – as he informs her grimly – he would be able to enjoy his Boxing Day lamb and bog myrtle snaps instead of running around the back of beyond.

'But I suppose that's my punishment for not being a weakling, unlike the young guns who slink off to bed at the slightest sniffle. Everyone claims to have caught the flu this year. Bloody convenient, if you ask me.'

Karen changes the subject, continues to make increasingly forced chitchat, doing her best to extract more than a grunt in reply from the cranky coroner. But nothing, not the unseasonably mild weather, nor the rumours of an imminent restructuring of the Police Authority seems to interest Kneought Brodal. And since none of it interests Karen Eiken Hornby either, she eventually stops talking.

As she glances at her watch and reaches out to turn on the news, while simultaneously bracing herself to ask Brodal whether he heard the previous broadcast, and if so, whether it contained anything about the murder in Skreby, she suddenly hears snoring coming from the passenger seat.

She grits her teeth and drives as fast as she dares, accompanied by the sound of the coroner sawing logs, interrupted only by fits of sleep apnoea serious enough to make her eye at him worriedly until he resumes rumbling. Kneought Brodal doesn't wake up until they bump aboard the ferry in Thorsvik, after Karen spent the eighteen-minute wait at the slip pointedly avoiding looking at the string of saliva dangling from the corner of the coroner's mouth, and eventually landing like a snail track on his seat belt. Now he makes a series of noises that seem to signal dazed confusion and a sore neck. He gingerly rubs the back of his head and yawns.

'This seat is bloody uncomfortable.'

'And yet you managed to sleep in it for over two hours,' she replies drily. 'But at least we're on board now and crossing the sound only takes fifteen minutes. I'm going to stretch my legs and get a bit of fresh air.'

Without waiting for a reply, she unbuckles her seat belt and climbs out of the car. She can hear Brodal open the passenger door, but gratefully notes that he doesn't seem to make any move to get out. I can't bear to buckle that giant baby in again today, she grumbles and slams the door shut behind her.

There are only two other vehicles on the ferry, a black Renault and a motorcycle. The driver of the hog stays seated on his Harley-Davidson with a firm grip on the curved handlebars. Karen recognises the logo on his black leather jacket: OP.

She knows the acronym is deliberately ambiguous, standing either for the Odin Predators or the One Percenters. Nor is it much of a secret that their headquarters are located on the west coast of Noorö. What's unusual is seeing one of them on their own, Karen thinks, studying the long grey plait hanging down the man's back.

Maybe he's returning from a solo mission, scaring the shit out of some poor bugger who had no real means of resistance. Or maybe he spent Christmas with his mum. Whether the bloke considers himself a predator with links to Old Norse mythology or is proudly announcing to the world that he belongs to the one per cent of bikers involved in serious crime, he probably does have a mother somewhere, someone who was happy to see him at her Christmas table. Maybe his mummy helped him plait his hair; it looks remarkably neat.

She walks up to the prow and leans against the yellow railing. The mountain ridges of Noorö rise out of the sea ahead of them, more imposing with every passing minute, but on the leeward side there's still open sea. The pale December sun has just pushed above the eastern horizon and seems to have already given up its struggle against the cloudbanks blowing in from the other direction. She resists the impulse to take out her cigarettes. It might not be immediately obvious, but she has quit smoking. In theory. At least during the daytime. But, Jesus, it would be just the thing right now, she thinks and sticks her hand in her pocket.

A sharp honking interrupts her and she angrily whips around to stare at the black Renault behind her. The driver spreads his hand to convey his innocence and nods toward her own Ford Ranger. She stomps over to it.

'What the fuck are you doing? Why are you honking?'

Kneought Brodal shrugs and points to Karen's phone on the driver's seat.

'Your phone beeped. And speaking of which, being a detective and all, shouldn't you make sure you have that with you at all times? It could be something important . . .'

The text is from her mother.

Told Sigrid she could stay in the guest room for a few days. Everyone sends their love.

She doesn't bother replying.

8

Everything looks much smaller than Karen remembers. True, she's been back here a handful of times as an adult, but even so, her childhood memories still firmly shape her idea of what Lysvik should look like: the fishing harbour with the Doggerian boats, the cutters, the trawlers and the smokeries. The freight ships and the big dusty coal piles up in the container port. No one smokes herring, haddock or eel in the harbour anymore, and all that remains of the coal piles is the black soot that stains all the houses a dirty grey, like they will never be clean again.

She drives slowly along the high street, which winds its way from the harbour all the way through the village. The provincial doctor's office has long since moved from the yellow wooden house on the square to a modern clinic, which turns out to be located in one of the village's two modern blocks, in the same building as Social Services, the Fishery Commission, the Planning Committee and, on the top floor, the Provincial Board. The local police station is across the street. Karen parks outside and turns with a sigh to Kneought Brodal, who is impatiently tugging at his seat belt.

Thorstein Byle lives up to all her expectations. A tall, balding, weather-beaten man in his sixties with a firm handshake and ice-blue eyes that dart irresolutely between Karen and Kneought

Brodal's imposing form as he lets them into the clinic's waiting room. Behind him, a slightly dumpy, greying man approaches. He is casually dressed in a blazer and is carrying a coffee pot.

'Welcome! Sven Andersén, provincial doctor,' he says with a smile and holds out his hand.

Karen introduces herself and, after a moment's hesitation, Kneought Brodal as well, since he doesn't seem inclined to speak.

They pass the reception where someone has tried to get in the Christmas spirit by decking the counter with hypo-allergenic plastic juniper garlands and continue into a small kitchenette. Four mugs and a plate of biscuits have been set out on a table with a red-and-white-chequered tablecloth and the chairs scrape against the linoleum floor as they pull them out and sit down in silence.

'Right, so how do you want to go about this?' Thorstein Byle says after a while and pushes the plate toward Karen, who takes a biscuit even though she would prefer to pass.

'Well, Kneought here is going to perform the autopsy and establish the cause of death,' she says with a nod to the coroner. 'I will be heading up the investigation, assuming the results of the autopsy indicate we need one. From what I understand, the body will be taken to Ravenby for the autopsy tomorrow?'

'Yes, that's right.' Sven Andersén nods. 'It will be collected tomorrow morning and we're scheduled for eleven o'clock at the Centre for Forensic Medicine. I say we, because I'm hoping to participate. With your permission, of course.'

Sven Andersén pours them each a cup of coffee while directing a querying look at Kneought Brodal, who after a few seconds delay appears to finally snap back in.

38

'Oh, right, yes, of course you can, if you want to,' he mumbles while reaching forward and grabbing a fistful of biscuits.

'You and I will be working very closely together,' Karen says, turning to Thorstein Byle. 'It'll be a while before we get reinforcements from the CID, so I'm counting on your help. How many officers do you have up here?'

'There are seven of us here in Lysvik, including me. There's a local station up in Skreby and one in Gudheim, each with a couple of lads, but they're closed for the holidays. Everyone lives on the island and everyone should be available, except one, who's jetted off to the Canary Islands. Two have been dispatched to guard the crime scene, or potential crime scene, I should say until we know for sure. It has been cordoned off – we've done everything by the book,' he adds. 'Your technician approved it when I took him up there about an hour ago.'

'And what about Fredrik Stuub's home?'

'I've put a man on that, too. Well, outside, obviously, we haven't entered.'

'Great. Why don't you tell us what you know and Sven can add his information as we go.'

Thorstein Byle clears his throat and starts speaking in a monotonous, tense voice, as though he were being quizzed on homework.

'So, the victim is Fredrik Stuub, a retired teacher and widower. He was found dead by his sister Gertrud around nine yesterday morning in an old flooded quarry in Karby. Fredrik Stuub lived nearby, just north of Skreby.'

He glances uncertainly at Karen. She nods to let him know she's familiar with the area.

39

'I have family on the island and I spent a lot of time here as a child, so I know my way around reasonably well.'

Something that might be surprise flashes across his face.

'Eiken Hornby, you said. So you're related to the Noorö Eikens?'

Karen nods and Thorstein Byle continues, in a slightly more relaxed tone.

'Right, so, Fredrik was found by his sister Gertrud Stuub, who became worried when she couldn't reach her brother on the phone. Apparently, he hadn't showed up to the early morning Christmas Day service, as he usually would have, so as soon as the sun came up, she went over to his house, which is not too far from her own. When neither Stuub nor his dog were to be found, she became worried he might have fallen and hurt himself walking the dog. Apparently, he walks the loop trail around the quarry every morning. At least, that's what I gathered from what she told us when we got to the scene, but she was very upset and we didn't want to press her for too many details.'

Thorstein Byle pauses to sip his coffee.

'Anyway, she set off and found first the dog and then her brother. Luckily, she had her phone with her, so she was able to call emergency services right away. The on-duty officer who took the call from them contacted me immediately. I live in Skreby myself, so I was the first person on the scene at twenty to ten. The boys from emergency services arrived right after me. And you, Sven, you arrived around ten, didn't you?'

'A few minutes past,' the doctor confirms with a nod and Byle continues.

'Fredrik Stuub had fallen over the edge and his body lay on a protruding rock just above the water. Had he fallen just thirty feet further along the path, he would have ended up in the water and sunk like a stone. The boys from emergency services went down there with a gurney straight away and winched him up. They have a lot of experience from the mountains.'

Karen hesitates a moment before turning to Sven Andersén.

'Was there no doubt he was dead at that point? Before they winched him out, I mean?'

'None whatsoever,' Andersén says emphatically. 'His skull was crushed and brain matter was leaking out of it. I could tell the second I got there. They'd just pulled him out when I arrived.'

'And how long had he been dead, according to your best judgement?' Karen asks.

'I would say two hours. Give or take half an hour. If he'd ended up in the water, it would have been harder to tell.'

'OK,' Karen says. 'That means he died sometime between half past seven and half past eight. So not long before his sister found him.'

Silence falls around the table as no one feels a need to comment further on the summary. Kneought Brodal grabs another handful of biscuits and shoves two into his mouth in quick succession before speaking.

'So what compelled you to tear us away from the joys of our Christmas tables?' he slurs with his mouth still full. 'Isn't it possible the bloke just slipped and fell?'

'Two things,' Sven Andersén answers. 'Do you want to take this or should I?' he asks the regional commander.

'Go ahead,' Thorstein Byle says.

'When he was brought to the clinic for a preliminary examination, I immediately noticed chafe marks on both wrists. The

41

next thing that stood out was that his left shoe was missing, which, granted, might have been explained by the fall; they weren't lace-up shoes, you see, but the kind with the elastic under the tongue. But I noticed his sock had come down past his heel, which had clear scuff marks on it as well.'

The others say nothing. They all know where Sven Andersén is going.

'There were also marks on his clothes and on the back of the shoe he was still wearing,' the doctor continues. 'You'll see for yourselves tomorrow, but my best guess is he was dragged on his back. Once I came to that conclusion, I ended my examination and called Thorstein.'

Byle nods.

'I'd already cordoned off the scene. Not that I suspected foul play, really, more because I wanted to set a good example. We have a couple of new guys at the station and they were on duty on Christmas Day. When Sven called a few hours later, we started looking for the other shoe and after a while, we spotted it on a boulder, not far from where Stuub was found. One of the guys managed to fish it out using a rope and piece of barbed wire from a fence down by the road. It may not be strictly by the book, but I was worried it might blow into the water if we left it there. Anyway, the back of it was scratched up, as Sven said the other shoe was. That's when I decided to contact the CID. Not sure if it was the right thing to do, but I go by the book.'

'You did the right thing,' Karen says with a reassuring smile.

He must have called the CID around two, she muses, but Smeed didn't call me until that evening. I really must have been his last resort.

'That means it's been more or less exactly twenty-four hours since Gertrud Stuub found her brother,' she says.

Once again, her statement is met with silence. The only sound is Brodal chewing. In the end, he is the one to break the silence.

'So,' he says with a dry laugh, 'how many curious locals have tramped around the potential crime scene by now, do you reckon? Sören Larsen's not going to be pleased . . .'

Nothing in Thorstein Byle's voice betrays the irritation hinted at by the tension in his jaw.

'None,' he replied. 'Though I suppose Gertrud Stuub might have compromised any potential evidence. And the dog, of course. And I'm bound to have left shoe prints, too. On the other hand, the body was impossible to see from directly above it, which is to say from where he fell. You had to walk off to the side a little to spot him, so that's likely where most of our footprints will be concentrated. And that's where the boys from emergency services went down, as well. They had to pull him up sort of sideways.'

'We'll see when we get there,' Karen puts in.

But Kneought Brodal refuses to back down.

'And you're certain the scene has been kept secure the whole time?' he asks. 'That your boys didn't sneak home to the missus to scarf down some Christmas lamb's head as soon as you turned your back?'

A flush of anger climbs up Thorstein Byle's neck to his cheeks; he stares down into his empty coffee cup in an attempt to compose himself before answering.

Karen decides to step in.

'Lay off, Kneought,' she says sharply. 'He has a unique sense of humour,' she adds, addressing Byle. 'Which is to say, no sense of humour at all. So, shall we take a quick look at Fredrik Stuub then, before heading up to the Karby quarry?'

Fredrik Stuub is covered by a thin plastic sheet. His body is still dressed and the only skin on display is on his face, neck, hands and one foot. His head is turned to one side and almost his entire face is covered in blood. Karen finds herself thinking of one of the plastic-wrapped lamb's heads in her freezer back home, probably primed by Brodal's words in the kitchenette. That association and the temperature in the cold room at the far back of the small clinic make the skin on her forearms pebble. The whole thing is a formality; coroners and lead investigators are supposed to perform a visual inspection of the body as close to the time of death as possible. From now on, the only person allowed to touch the body is the coroner. Kneought Brodal won't perform a full examination of the dead man until tomorrow at the Centre for Forensic Medicine in Ravenby, and he will be accompanied by the lead investigator then, too. Karen is not looking forward to it.

Sven Andersén carefully folds back the plastic sheet and nods for Brodal to come closer.

'What do you think?' he says once Brodal has made a quick visual inspection of the head and then turned Stuub's left lower leg over to study the parallel scratches running from the top of the heel toward the malleolus.

Brodal nods for Sven Andersén to cover the body back up and removes his latex gloves.

'Well, I don't know what kind of rambling you do up here, but marks like those usually mean one thing in my experience. We obviously can't be sure until we've completed the autopsy and the crime scene investigation, but I'm ready to bet a couple of pints that you're right. He was dragged.'

'So, murder,' Karen says and rubs her forehead with her wrist. 'Or at least manslaughter.'

And for the first time since Jounas Smeed called and freed her from her Christmas obligations, that familiar worry about how an investigation is going to turn out makes itself known to Karen. On the phone the night before, he'd promised to try to get her some reinforcements, but so far she hasn't heard anything to suggest he has succeeded.

'Well, happy holidays, Eiken,' she hears Kneought Brodal say with something awfully close to schadenfreude in his voice. 'Looks like you're going to be stuck out here in the middle of nowhere for a while.'

9

Road 12 cuts through all three of Noorö's counties, from Lysvik to Skreby and Gudheim in the far north. West of the road, the Skalvet mountain range rises up like a wall, sheltering the island from the winds off the Atlantic, while on the other side, the landscape climbs more gently toward another mountain range in the east. Not as imposing as Skalvet, but high enough to provide shelter for the villages scattered seemingly at random across the island's interior.

Having left Kneought Brodal in Lysvik, Karen is following Thorstein Byle's black Volvo in her Ford Ranger. Just north of the Skreby exit, they turn off the highway onto a paved but poorly maintained road and Karen only just has time to make out the words on the crooked road sign as she jangles past in Byle's wake: KARBY QUARRY. PRIVATE ROAD.

She has seen that sign before many times as a child and always thought there was something ominous about the name, something forbidden and fascinating. She heard her cousins brag about swimming in the quarry even though it wasn't allowed – and it may well have been true. Finn, Einar and Odd's social lives revolved around daring each other and their friends to do stupid things, the more dangerous, the better. Seeing who was brave enough to jump into the toxic and freezing quarry water would have been right up their alley. And they had done their best to raise her in that spirit, too, during those long summer holidays. Egged on by her wide-eyed admiration, and maybe because having no sisters of their own they thought of Karen as a cute little pet, they taught her how to shoot a gun using rusty tin cans for target practice, kill chickens and distract the tobacconist in Vesle while Finn snuck in behind the counter and stole cigarettes. They taught her to smoke and to touch cow dung with her tongue without throwing up and to stand look-out while they kidnapped the neighbour's ram. They taught her how to fight and how to take a beating without crying. She had loved them more than life itself.

And maybe it was because Finn was six, Einar four and Odd three years older than her, or maybe because she was a southerner, or maybe because she was a girl, or maybe simply because there were in fact some limits even in their confused boy brains, that they had never taken her to the quarry in Karby.

Thorstein Byle rolls into the turning area at the end of the road and pulls up next to a tumble-down barbed-wire fence with a sign that reads: NO FLY-TIPPING.

Karen parks right behind him and studies the piles of rub-bish behind the torn-down fence. Broken wooden boards full of rusty nails, cracked plaster walls, wet cardboard boxes, two old prams, empty paint cans, dirty plastic containers, a rusty bike, a pile of broken roof tiles.

'And it's looked like this since the recycling stations started to charge a fee, I assume,' she says after opening the door and walking up to Byle.

He nods.

'The provincial board approves a clean-up every year, but a few months later, it's back to looking like this. We drive past here sometimes, but so far we've only caught a handful of people red-handed. We have to go on foot from here,' he adds with a nod toward a steep gravel road on the other side of the turning area. 'We could drive a bit further, but the technicians wouldn't like it. Plus, the road's so overgrown up there, you'd have to reverse out anyway.'

'After you,' Karen says, for lack of anything more imaginative.

The gravel road turns out to be surprisingly wide but very steep, and the asphalt that had been sunken and occasionally cracked on the way up to the turning area, is little more than disjointed sheets joined together by slushy snow here. Karen grits her teeth when every step provokes a sharp stab of pain.

'The coal was transported in carts down this road from the quarry to be loaded onto lorries,' Thorstein hollers and strides on with his long legs.

'So, you have family on the island,' he adds after a brief pause.

Karen hesitates briefly.

'Yes, but I haven't seen them in years.'

He obviously knows exactly what blood flows through her veins. Unlike Karen, Byle has had plenty of time to look her up on the intranet. And he obviously knows that once upon a time, a couple of generations ago, the Eikens were a thoroughly respectable family. God-fearing and hard-working, her grandparents – or at least their parents – had gone out in their boats come rain or shine and humbly bowed their heads in church every Sunday. Their graves up in Gudheim are a testament to that, with their black iron anchors instead of headstones. Not the largest, granted, not the man-sized ones with chains, like the pilots', but nevertheless anchors instead of regular stones like farmers and such simple folk had to make do with for their final resting places. The Eikens had had that right once. They don't anymore.

'The Eikens, yes . . .' Byle says slowly, as though he's searching his memory, and Karen decides to come right out with it. With some of it, at any rate.

'I'm afraid some of my relatives have had rather a lot of run-ins with the police. I seem to recall hearing something about a jacklighting incident up in Gudheim a few years ago that earned one of my cousins a couple of months in the nick.'

The thought of large off-road vehicles roaring across the moors at night with powerful spotlights on the roof and bored men shooting anything on four legs that crosses their path revolts her. She doesn't mention the moonshine or the tax fraud. Byle presumably knows all about it.

Thorstein Byle turns around without comment. Mutely, he holds out his arm to support Karen past a patch of slippery exposed rock. She gratefully accepts his help, but even with the assistance of her colleague a jolt of pain shoots through her knee as she picks her way around it. When she lets go and looks up, she has to suppress a gasp.

So this is Karby. Once an inhospitable worksite for men with worn-out backs and aching shoulders, now it's a lake surrounded by pines, bare-branched deciduous trees, underbrush and a blueish-grey mountain ridge. It's a mysterious and dark and inappropriately beautiful place.

'Goat Back Mountain,' Byle offers, noting her gaze. 'You'll find Skreby Bay on the other side of it, but I suppose you know that already. Your boys will probably be done soon,' he adds after a quick glance at his wristwatch and nods down toward the old quarry.

Red-and-white striped plastic tape rustles faintly in the breeze. Two people are standing inside the cordoned-off area, talking to each other. They look like aliens in their white protective suits. Even though they have their backs toward Karen, she can tell one of them is Sören Larsen and the other is probably a bloke she believes might be called Arvidsen. Larsen barely reaches his shoulder. When not in protective gear, Sören Larsen enlists the help of heavy boots with thick soles – the thicker the better – to make himself a little bit taller. The soft shoes he's forced to wear in the new type of overalls don't give him the few extra inches he wants so badly. And overalls keep his hair from helping, too – the frizzy blond hair that normally forms a halo around his head is now flattened by the protective hood.

Two constables have made themselves comfortable on tree stumps outside the cordon. When they scramble to their feet to salute their superiors, Larsen turns around and spots Karen.

'About time!' he shouts with a smile, pushing up onto his toes.

Karen says a quick hello to the two uniformed officers, nods to Arvidsen and walks up to the police tape.

'Hiya, Sören, how are things? Found anything useful?'

'Less than you're hoping for, I'm afraid. Drag marks, but no clear footprints. It was a few degrees below freezing here yesterday morning, so the ground was hard, and then some sleet fell overnight, making it virtually impossible. Maybe if they'd called sooner . . .'

Sören gestures toward Thorstein Byle, who has joined to the uniformed officers.

'I think they did what they could,' Karen says. 'None of us would have made it up here before dark anyway.'

'Yeah, yeah. Anyway, we've secured some partial footprints in the mud right at the edge, but to be honest, it's mostly paw prints from the dog. Poor thing must have been frantic, judging from how it ran back and forth. But we can't secure any prints in this muck and the macadam up on the road is obviously no better.'

'What about tyre tracks?'

'None down here. Hundreds up by the turning area. Nothing to be done there.'

'Hair, skin, nails?' Karen smiles as she asks the question, well aware what the answer is going to be.

'*CSI Noorö*? Forget it.'

Sören Larsen gives her an inviting wave.

'Feel free to come in and scour the mud for hairs yourself. We're pretty much done here.'

'Thanks, I'll pass. But I wouldn't mind taking a look at where the body was found.'

'Be my guest,' Larsen says and chivalrously holds up the police tape.

She walks behind him, studying the drag marks and prints he points out. Without his guidance, she wouldn't have noticed them, or at least been unable to interpret what she saw.

'He fell here, but you have to go over to the side a little to see the spot where he landed,' Larsen says, pointing.

Karen has a brief moment of vertigo as she cranes her neck to look out over the edge. Her fear of heights is relatively new-found; at least, she has no memory of feeling her stomach flip when she was younger, of the fear of losing control and throwing

51

herself over. The remnants of blood and probably the brain matter Sven Andersén mentioned are still visible, like a dark shadow, against the grey rock.

'He was unlucky,' Sören says behind her. 'The murderer, I mean.'

Karen lets her eyes rove along the quarry walls. With a few exceptions, they are sheer and precipitous. From where she's standing, she can only see protruding rocks in a handful of places. Almost anywhere else, a person pushed over the edge would have fallen straight into the freezing water. The thin film of ice covering it would have cracked and the body would have sunk in minutes. It would probably have resurfaced eventually, but we would have had to drag the entire lake long before then, Karen muses.

'I guess so. Though Fredrik Stuub wasn't particularly lucky, either,' she observes grimly.

10

Fredrik Stuub's house is not unlike Karen's own. A two-storey limestone house with a black slate roof, the kind of house you find on all three Doggerian islands. Here, though, the exteriors are darker, stained by coal dust that still clings to everything on the island like a thin film. Even as a child, Karen noticed that everything was somehow darker on Noorö than at home, that the soot and dust and dark shadows from the mountains seemed to make it hard for Noorö to breathe. Back then, she'd found it exciting, almost exotic. Now, it makes her feel dull and heavy.

But there is lightness here, too, she knows that. High up in the mountains and in the bays below, there is none of that oppressiveness, and in the far north, around Gudheim, the landscape is spectacularly beautiful. But here, in the interior, where coal mines are everywhere and the sea nowhere to be seen, Karen is overcome with gloom. She forces out a smile and turns toward Thorstein Byle to shake off her dreary mood.

'How long had Fredrik been a widower, do you know?' she calls out and pulls a pair of latex gloves out of her coat pocket while shutting the car door behind her.

She and Thorstein have driven over to Fredrik Stuub's house after giving Sören Larsen their word 'not to touch so much as a flyspeck' before he can go over it himself. Now she nods for the two police officers on guard duty to stand down and walks briskly toward the house.

'Not off the top of my head,' Byle replies when he catches up, 'but it must be years. His wife passed away just a few years after their daughter died and that must be twenty years ago now.'

Karen's stomach flips again.

'How old was she? The daughter, I mean,' she asks as casually as she can manage.

'Just shy of thirty, I think. Hep C, or I've been told. She'd apparently been rather out of control in her youth and been sick for a long time. Ulrika was her name. Her son Gabriel went to school with my youngest girl, that's why I know.'

'So Fredrik has a nephew,' Karen says. 'And who's Gabriel's father?'

'That, I can't tell you. But she definitely wasn't married to him. I could try to find out, assuming she herself knew.'

'Hold off on that. Let's wait for the results of the autopsy before we start poking at old wounds.'

'So you don't think he was murdered?'

Karen pauses with her hand on the door handle.

'Most of the signs certainly point to it, but we can't be sure until we have the autopsy results.'

She pushes the handle down, opens the door and steps over the threshold. And as she does, she becomes sure.

When the black van carrying Larsen and Arvidsen turns into the driveway thirty minutes later, Karen and Byle are sitting on the stone steps in front of Fredrik Stuub's house.

'Did you lose the key?' Larsen grins as he climbs out of the van.

His frizzy blond hair has puffed up around his head once more. Without waiting for a reply, he and Arvidsen start unloading equipment bags, a camera and fresh protective suits. Karen waits for them to finish.

'We backed off right away,' she says when they join them. 'Didn't make it past the hallway. Look for yourself.'

'Well, either he has no talent for cleaning, or someone helped mess the place up,' Larsen says a minute later, after taking a quick look inside and discovering pulled-out drawers and books torn out of bookshelves. Sören Larsen steps out onto the front steps and squints at the pale sun.

'Hardly a regular break-in, looks more like someone searched the place, if you ask me,' he says. 'OK, we have our work cut out for us. You realise you can't come in, right?'

'Why do you think I turned in the doorway? This isn't my first day at the races,' Karen says tersely. 'How long do you think it's going to take?'

'No idea. Probably all day. They should pay me double,' he mutters, 'there's enough work here for four.'

'Take it up with Viggo Haugen, I'm sure he'd be happy to open his wallet for you,' she replies with a grin.

Sören Larsen gives her a dark look. The stinginess of the police chief goes well beyond what can be motivated by political limitations. To Viggo Haugen, the annual budget process seems more like a chance to beat his own personal record than anything else.

'Sure, or maybe I could try squeezing blood from a stone,' Larsen snorts derisively. 'I'll call you when we're done, but I don't think it'll be before evening. You'll have to find some other way to amuse yourself.'

11

As they start back toward Skreby, Karen is thankful for Byle's suggestion that it might be time to break for lunch. It's almost one and other than a dry biscuit, she hasn't had anything to eat since breakfast back in Langevik in the early hours of the morning. They drive at a leisurely pace, with him in the lead and her following. The Boxing Day traffic is still light and they are overtaken by the occasional car; she wonders if Byle is driving more carefully than he usually would.

Skreby grew up around the Firth of Skre, a long arm of the sea that cuts through Noorö's eastern mountain range along a natural fault line. The village is flanked by Goat Back Mountain in the north and Halfen in the south. And even though the mountains loom ominously over the town, compared to Skalvet on the west coast of the island, they appear no more imposing than two coal piles. Neither one rises more than 1,500 feet above the waves of the North Sea, while the highest peak in the Skalvet range is over 4,000 feet.

Karen relaxes as she follows Byle's car and takes the opportunity to study her surroundings. She absently notes that the sun has won its battle against the clouds and is infusing the December scene with a golden glow. They pass sleepy barns, frozen pastures, fallow fields and a petrol station.

As soon as they turn off the highway and onto Skrebyvägen, the farms become more numerous: cottages with narrow strips of land that once yielded a complementary source of food and income for beach fishermen and people who didn't own a boat, plots that were primarily farmed by women while their men – the men who only had tiny anchors on their graves – were at sea, toiling aboard other men's ships.

The road gradually takes on the appearance of a traditional village high street, with simple terraced houses from the 1920s and 1930s on either side, built during the golden age of coal mining. Karen glances down the seemingly deserted side streets. Half the houses are probably empty, she thinks and feels a pang of melancholy as she studies the stillness. There's something heavy and hopeless about the soot-stained houses. Granted, Noorö has always been the most sparsely populated island in the Doggerian archipelago, but she can't remember it ever being this desolate, not even on Boxing Day.

Rural flight. This is what it looks like, she thinks to herself. Unlike on more urbanised Heimö and picturesque Frisel, where the population decline has been successfully reversed in recent years and where Doggerian expats from Scandinavia, the UK and the continent are now settling once more, on Noorö, the trend has been the opposite.

They slowly follow the high street down toward the harbour, driving past closed shops, cafés and a pub with blacked-out windows. They pass an older couple walking arm in arm, a closed pharmacy, a man shutting his car door behind him and walking briskly toward a side street with a newspaper under his arm. He probably had to drive over to the petrol station to buy it. Nothing seems open. Only now does Karen start to have misgivings about finding somewhere to eat. Back home, Sunday trading has long since become the norm; these days you can go to the pub or buy pressure-treated wood even on Good Friday. Here, on the other hand, people seem to stay home on Boxing Day. Whether out of deep-rooted respect for the church or because of a lack of customers, she doesn't know, but whatever the reason, it doesn't look as if anyone will be serving lunch. Things are unlikely to look any better down in the harbour, she realises; there won't be any catches coming in until the day after tomorrow at the earliest.

Yet even so, Thorstein Byle's plan doesn't become clear to her until he turns on his indicator to turn down one of the residential streets.

The Byle family lives at the end of a side street lined with one-storey stone houses with wooden second-storey additions. Originally, these houses would have been pitch-black, but over the years they've acquired a silvery patina, houses and colours so typical of Noorö, Karen can once again feel herself being sucked back in time.

Solveig Byle greets them on the front steps. She's a greying blonde wearing sturdy clogs and a lovely smile. She extends one hand while holding the cardigan draped over her shoulders closed with the other. Thorstein must have called her from the car, Karen thinks as she takes the offered hand with a mix of gratitude and an urge to flee. She would have preferred to sit alone in a pub with a plate of lamb stew and a pint, going over her notes or simply flipping through a paper another patron left behind. Instead, she will now be forced to ask polite questions, listen with interest, compliment the food, be offered more – decline at first but eventually give in – and eat another serving. And remember to thank her hosts three times, as tradition dictates. Or even worse, answer questions about herself.

She couldn't have been more wrong.

'The kids and I already ate, so we'll leave you two alone,' Solveig tells them. 'I know you will have a lot to talk about. I left some things out for you in the kitchen, nothing fancy, just leftovers from yesterday.'

When Karen takes a seat at the Byles' kitchen table, it is with a plate heaped with parsley herring, creamed kale, clove-scented black pudding, thin slices of lamb steak and rowanberry jelly. Only on Christmas would it ever occur to her to mix all those things on one plate.

Solveig Byle has decorated the floor around the hob with juniper branches, laid the table with green cloth napkins and lit the seven-armed brass candelabra on the table, even though it's the middle of the day. Her thoughtfulness gives Karen a lump in her throat. The door to the hallway is open and she can hear jaunty music and the squeaky, contrived voice-over of a children's cartoon from another room. It sounds remarkably cosy.

'You have young children?' Karen asks, trying to hide her surprise. Thorstein must be past sixty and Solveig didn't look much younger.

Byle, who is pouring juniper brew from a pitcher, looks nonplussed, then he chuckles.

'You mean "the kids"? Dear me, no, she's talking about the grandchildren. Our daughter is working at the nursing home down in Lysvik both today and yesterday, so the girls are staying here over the holidays. Trine kicked her husband out last spring – and not a day too soon.'

He doesn't elaborate and Karen doesn't ask.

They eat in silence for a while. The leftovers Solveig dismissed as 'nothing fancy' were clearly cooked from scratch with a lot of love.

'This is really good,' Karen says after a while.

'Yes, Solveig knows her stuff.'

'Maybe we should sum up what we have so far?' she says. 'You talk, since you get to eat like this every day, and I'll keep chewing.'

Thorstein Byle takes a sip of juniper brew, leans back and wipes his mouth.

'Well, there are fairly clear indications of dragging on both the body and at the scene, so we can assume we're dealing with a crime. And the fact that someone seems to have turned Fredrik's house upside down supports that.'

Karen nods.

'Yes, it would take a lot to convince me otherwise at this point. So the question is: who stands to gain from killing Fredrik Stuub? Any theories?'

'None aside from the obvious one. I assume the grandson inherits.'

'Gabriel, was it? What's his surname?'

'Stuub. His mother's name, since she was unmarried.'

'Right, father unknown, you said?'

'Rumour has it his father is a certain Allan Jonshed, which I suppose would explain some things.'

'*The* Allan Jonshed?'

Byle nods. For whatever reason, Karen has never worked a case with direct links to Noorö's criminal motorcycle gang. But she obviously knows Allan Jonshed is the President of the OP.

'Where exactly are the OP headquartered?'

'They have a farm up by Tyrfallet, near Skalvet, on the other side of the island. Why? You're not thinking of going up there, are you?'

Karen shrugs.

'Not this second, but Jonshed has been convicted of manslaughter at least twice, and if he has a connection with our victim, interviewing him will be hard to avoid.'

'If it weren't for the fact that Jonshed is behind bars again since a few months back,' Byle retorts wryly. 'And I hear he's seriously ill, too, so I think it's safe to assume we're in for a messy war of succession soon.'

So Jonshed is in prison again: that piece of information had not made its way to Karen.

'What did you mean when you said Gabriel being Jonshed's son would explain things? Is he a member of the OP?'

'Not officially. But they do work with "civilian" associates of various kinds.'

Brodal uses air quotes and Karen suppresses a shudder.

'Is that a verified fact, or just rumours?'

'The latter, I'm afraid . . .'

'And Gabriel is supposedly one of those civilian associates?'

'Either that or a hanger-on. There are always young men hanging about up there, trying to get in good with the leaders. I hear Gabriel's embroiled in a custody battle, so he's probably trying to keep his links to the OP on the downlow, at least until the divorce is final. But both the boys and I have run into him up at the OP headquarters more than once, so he's got at least one finger in that pie.'

Karen wipes her mouth, leans back and studies her colleague.

'My goodness, do you know everything about everyone on this island? You're a virtual goldmine.'

Thorstein Byle tries to hide a pleased smile.

'Well, I've lived here my entire life, and as a police officer you do get a measure of insight into the less flattering side of people's lives, as you know. But I'm only good for this kind of gossip when it comes to people who live around Skreby. And, like I said, Gabriel went to school with our Trine.'

'What does he do for a living?'

'He works at Groth's. I think he's in charge of bottling or something along those lines.'

Karen smiles inwardly. A visit to Groth's whiskey distillery sounds a lot more tempting than driving up into the mountains to talk to men with long grey plaits.

'How the Huss family has fallen,' Byle says thoughtfully and gets up to fetch them each a coffee cup. 'Old Albin wouldn't have been pleased to know a descendant of his worked for the Groths.'

Karen searches her memory.

'Albin Huss, the mining baron?' she asks.

Byle nods and pours the coffee.

'So Gertrud and Fredrik are related to Old Huss?' she says thoughtfully. 'Am I right in thinking that means there's money involved?'

Thorstein Byle shakes his head and smiles ruefully.

'He was their grandfather. As for money – not as much as you'd think. Huss made his fortune in mining, but he had no sons to take over the company. Huss ran everything himself with an iron fist until the day he died. And when his poor nephew Ivar finally took over in the mid-seventies, the golden age of coal was a distant memory. Within a decade, time caught up with the Huss mining empire and things went south fast. The company was done in by a weak economy, soaring import prices and exhausted coal seams, but Ivar Tryste was left to personally shoulder the blame for the closures.'

Ivar Tryste. Karen vaguely recognises the name from interviews and newspaper articles from the mid-eighties. An image of a harassed-looking man with sad eyes suddenly flashes before her. But the image is fuzzy; she would have been in her twenties at the time and busy with other things.

'No, there's no fortune left, I don't think,' Byle continues. 'They do still own fairly large tracts of land, but it's neither close to the sea nor particularly fertile. They've probably sold some for pasture, but the prices up here aren't like down on Heimö.'

'When did the last mine close, do you remember?'

'Both the quarries were still open in the early nineties, Karby and the one up in Hovnes, but the last mine closed in 1989, I remember it very clearly. Half the people around here lost their jobs; it was a bad time. Divorce and all kinds of trouble followed in the wake of the closure. My sister and brother-in-law were affected, like so many others. He lost everything and took to the bottle when the mine closed. Killed himself four years later, forty-six years old.'

'I remember hearing stories about people trying to break into the owner's house to give him a thrashing. So that was Ivar Tryste, Old Huss's nephew?'

63

Byle nods.

'Yes, it must have been terrible for Ivar. He's still alive, by the way. If you can call it living. He's in a nursing home in Lysvik, apparently gone with the fairies. Alzheimer's, or so I'm told.'

She notes that Byle has become considerably more talkative in the short time they've spent together. Kneought Brodal's foot-in-mouth tendencies this morning seem forgotten and Karen gratefully notes that Byle's extensive local knowledge is going to come in very useful. She suppresses her frustration at his habit of sounding like what he's telling her is general knowledge. She supposes it is, if you live up here.

Just then, a memory flutters by and Karen laughs.

'Is the house still standing? "The Complex", I mean. Isn't that where the Huss family used to live?'

Karen hadn't caught the double meaning of the name the hard-to-impress locals had given the mining magnate's residence. As a child, she had been fascinated with the extravagant building, which looked more like a castle than someone's house. Instead of the usual limestone other islanders made do with, Old Huss had had yellow sandstone brought up from Frisel. A fairy-tale castle, Karen had thought, pressing her nose against the car window to admire the thing. She had secretly found the scornful laughter the house always drew from her aunt and uncle completely inappropriate. That The Complex was a reference to Albin Huss's need to flaunt his wealth, rather than to the magnificence of the building itself, had only become clear to her many years later.

'Sure, still standing, turrets and all. But it's pretty dilapidated, I think. The upkeep must be astronomical.'

That the victim, Fredrik Stuub, was the grandchild of the man who had once ruled half of Noorö is clear enough, but

Karen realises she has become lost in the tangled branches of the Huss family tree and decides to drop the subject. Should the convoluted family relations become relevant to the investigation, she'll have to ask Byle to go over it all again. Right now, they have more important things to think about.

'OK, the first thing we need to do is talk to Fredrik's sister,' she says. 'Does she live far from here?'

12

The answer turns out to be a fifteen-minute drive away. After thanking Solveig Byle and accepting a dinner invitation for some time later in the week with genuine enthusiasm, Karen climbs back into her car. They drive back up to the highway, turn north and make a right after crossing the Skre River viaduct. As they slowly pull into Gertrud's driveway, Karen realises it must be the roof of Fredrik's house she can glimpse on the other side of the river. The two properties are probably connected by a footbridge.

Gertrud Stuub's house turns out to be a copy of her brother's; Byle explains that the two plots were once part of the same estate.

'As you know, Old Huss owned more or less everything north of Skreby, all the way up to the Gudheim country border,' he says as they walk up the gravel path. 'Huss's daughters inherited half each so Gertrud and Fredrik eventually inherited half of their mother's half each and the other half went to the Trystes. Both this and Fredrik's house were probably workers accommodation once. Not for the miners, mind, for the overseers.'

Gertrud Stuub doesn't come to the door herself. Instead, they're greeted by a man in his seventies, with a thick mop of grey hair hiding a receding hairline. His furrowed face might have been the result of a hard life at sea, if it weren't for the white dog collar peeking out of his black shirt. Karen instinctively straightens up when she introduces herself.

'Karen Eiken Hornby, Doggerland CID, I'm leading the investigation into Fredrik Stuub's death,' she says and holds out her hand.

'Erling Arve,' the priest replies and takes her hand in his much larger one.

His handshake is firm, verging on crushing.

'Hi, Thorstein,' he says as he turns from Karen to Byle. 'We've been expecting you.'

He steps aside to let them in.

'How is Gertrud holding up? She was pretty upset yesterday when I met her up by the quarry,' Byle says after Erling Arve shuts the door behind them.

'I think the shock is wearing off, but as I'm sure you'll understand, she is grieving and I don't think she's slept much.'

'Has she been seen by anyone from the clinic? Maybe she needs something?'

Arve shakes his head.

'She says she doesn't want to see a doctor, just me. She's looking to God for help. Sometimes, brother, I think her faith is stronger than yours or mine.'

Erling Arve leans toward Byle with a small smile when he says the last part. Karen, effectively sidelined, discreetly clears her throat.

'We need to talk to Gertrud,' she says. 'I know it will be difficult, but it's important that we speak to her while her memories are still fresh.'

'Like I said, we've been expecting you,' Arve says and leads them through a hallway where a tall mirror has been covered with black cloth. On the accompanying side table, a vase with three white roses sits next to a wooden crucifix. The priest pauses in front of a door and seems to take a deep breath, then he knocks gently on the doorpost and slowly pushes the handle down.

A black-and-white border collie is waiting on the other side, his head defensively lowered.

'There now, Sammy,' Arve says. 'Settle down.'

The dog backs away and walks over to lie down with his head on his paws next to a woman with a slate-grey bob and red-rimmed eyes. Gertrud Stuub is perched on the edge of an armchair, one hand clutching a balled-up handkerchief, the other gently placed on an open Bible. Karen walks over to her and extends her hand.

'Let me start by saying how very sorry I am for your loss,' she says after introducing herself. 'Losing a loved one is always difficult, and I know having to relive what you went through yesterday will make it even harder. Are you getting all the help you need?'

'Yes, thank you,' Gertrud says and pats the Bible. 'I find consolation in the Lord. And in Father Arve,' she adds with a tired smile in the priest's direction.

'Our Gertrud has always had a direct link with God,' Arve says. 'I'm afraid my most important contribution here has been to make tea. Can I offer you a cup?'

Karen accepts the offer so they can be alone with Gertrud for a while and Erling Arve disappears off to the kitchen. They squeeze into a small, uncomfortable sofa, and after apologising for intruding on her grief and explaining how important it is that they go over the details of the day before, Karen asks

Gertrud Stuub to tell them everything that happened in her own words.

'Start with what first made you worry,' she says.

'The early morning Christmas Day service,' Gertrud says without hesitation. 'Fredrik didn't go to church as regularly as he should, but he never missed the early morning Christmas Day service. And besides, he told me he'd be there.'

'He did?' Karen asks.

'Yes, or at least I assumed that's what he meant. It was the last thing he said to me, "See you tomorrow" . . .'

Her words fade into a whisper and there is suddenly confusion in her eyes, as though the unfathomable fact that she is never going to speak to her brother again has only just sunk in.

'And when was the last time you saw Fredrik alive?' Karen asks.

The question seems to pull Gertrud back to the fathomable.

'Christmas Eve. He stopped by around midday and we shared a meal, like we usually do. Nothing fancy, just regular Christmas fare.'

'Just you and Fredrik?'

'No, Gabriel and the children came over, too. Well, not Katja, of course, I've hardly seen her since they . . . since they separated.'

Gertrud Stuub crosses herself as she says the hateful word.

Karen searches her memory for what Byle told her. So Katja is the name of the woman Gabriel is involved in a custody battle with. She makes a mental note to talk to her, too.

'No one else?'

'William and Helena popped in, of course – they're such sweethearts – but they didn't stay for the meal. Just wanted to

69

wish me happy Christmas and bring me flowers. I believe they were having Helena's sister and brother-in-law over.'

Karen shoots Thorstein Byle a quick glance. This time he makes no move to jump in to help.

'William and Helena, are they neighbours or relatives?'

Gertrud gives Karen a surprised look.

'Both, of course. Cousin Ivar's son and daughter-in-law. Their house is up the hill a ways, so they drove here. People are so lazy nowadays.'

Karen decides to skip ahead.

'Did Fredrik seem troubled in any way?'

Gertrud Stuub ponders that for a second.

'No more than usual,' she replies. 'Fredrik wasn't the cheerful type. Always fretting about one thing or another. But then, that's bound to happen, when you don't have faith in the Lord.'

Just then, Erling Arve returns with a tray of rattling teacups. After setting it down on the table, he takes a seat in the armchair next to Gertrud's.

'We're talking about Fredrik. I was telling them he always found something to be upset about. Didn't he?'

Erling Arve nods, leans forward and starts handing out cups and saucers.

'I suppose you could say that. But I'm sure some people would tell you he just cared deeply about things.'

'Like what things, for example?' Karen asks and takes the cup she's handed.

'Certainly not the church,' Gertrud says with a hard edge of disapproval in her voice. 'But other than that, all kinds of things, big and small. The environment, of course, pollution and such, the fish dying. And what happened up in Gudheim. Fredrik was very upset about that.'

'Gudheim?' Karen says. 'What happened there?'

Gertrud waves her hand dismissively, as though she can't bear to talk about it, and the priest puts a reassuring hand on her arm. Karen looks at Byle who answers for her.

'The ship setting,' he says. 'Apparently someone's been amusing themselves by drilling holes in several of the stones. Kids, probably. And it's hardly the first time the place has been vandalised. Last spring, a group of local lads tried to tip one of the stones, drunk out of their wits, of course. Some tourists stopped them. And we've had a fair amount of graffiti, unless I'm misremembering.'

There's a difference between tagging and drilling holes in two-thousand-year-old stones, Karen reflects, set in the ground in the shape of a ship around a burial or cremation site. It would have required an impact drill.

'If we could get back to Christmas Eve,' she says. 'How long did Fredrik stay?'

Gertrud Stuub seems to ponder the question.

'I'm not sure exactly, but it was probably three, half past three, no later than that, when they left. Like I said, it was lunch. Gabriel wanted to get home early with the children, he said, but I know it was the liquor that beckoned. He can't get enough of it. And he offered to give Fredrik a ride. Probably didn't want him wandering about alone with dusk falling, old man that he was.'

At this point, Gertrud is overcome at the memory of her brother's very last walk and she lets out a sob and seems to deflate in her armchair. There is a clattering of china as everyone fumbles for their teacups.

71

'Can you keep going?' Karen asks after a few minutes, looking Gertrud in the eyes.

She wipes her nose and nods.

'Thinking now about Christmas Day. You mentioned you went to the early morning service and were worried when Fredrik didn't turn up.'

'To be clear, I wasn't entirely sure he wasn't there. He liked to arrive at the last minute which meant sitting in the back. Isn't that right?'

She looks at Erling Arve, who nods confirmation.

'Yes, we usually have a full house at the early morning Christmas Day service, if at no other time,' he says, and Karen picks up on a hint of bitterness in his voice.

Apparently, church attendance is down even on Noorö. And yet, Arve probably has a larger congregation at his services than the priests on Heimö, she muses, remembering her mother's words. *They made plenty of moonshine in those sheds of theirs, but everyone had to say grace and go to church every Sunday, without fail.'*

'And after the service, when you realised he wasn't there, you decided to try to find your brother?'

'Yes, I tried to call him from home more than once. I suppose I figured he'd just overslept. To be completely honest, I was mostly looking to give him a piece of my mind about missing the service. But when he didn't answer, I started to feel worried and decided to go over on my bike.'

'Your bike?' Karen says, unable to hide her surprise.

The broken-down creature sitting in front of her now apparently has unsuspected reservoirs of strength when not devastated by grief. She's probably considerably younger than she looks.

'Well, there's hardly any snow, you know, so it was no problem, otherwise I would have taken the kicksled. Straight across the fens, it's just a few minutes, though you do have to get off and walk it across the bridge.'

'And you got to Fredrik's house. Did you go inside?'

'Of course I went inside,' Gertrud says, seemingly baffled by the question. 'I knocked first, of course, but then I entered. That's how we do things around here.'

Out of the corner of Karen can see Byle leaning forward, as aware as she is of how important this question is.

'Was there anything different about his house?' Karen asks casually. 'Did you notice anything unusual?'

'No, like what? He hadn't tidied up, of course, never did; a used coffee cup on the kitchen table and the butter was still sitting out on the counter, but there's nothing unusual about that. Fredrik was like that.'

'Did you look for him in the house?'

Gertrud looks puzzled.

'No, why would I have? I could tell straight away he'd gone out; the lead wasn't on the hook in the hallway.'

She turns to look at the dog still sitting by her feet, reaches out with her free hand and strokes its silky fur. The other hand stays on the Bible.

'Besides, Sammy here would have come running if they'd been home,' Gertrud continues. 'So I knew Fredrik must have taken him for his usual walk.'

'And that made you worried? What did you think could have happened?'

'I can't really say what it was that made me go looking for him. Just a feeling, as though I could sense there was something wrong.'

73

Gertrud Stuub looks down at her lap as though the open Bible might be able to give her the answer. Then she frowns and gently strokes the close-written pages and Karen notices a small smile on her lips.

'It hadn't occurred to me until just now,' Gertrud says, looking up with a dazed expression. 'But it's clear to me now – the Lord spoke to me. *He* was the one who made me go looking for Fredrik.'

Her grief-stricken expression has been replaced by something akin to calm certainty. Karen has often noted, not without envy, that a strong faith can be a comfort to people in dire need. But she has also seen that same faith instil a deluded sense of righteousness in people, selfishness disguised as virtue. Gertrud Stuub's faith doesn't seem feigned. If anything, she might start speaking in tongues any moment, Karen thinks to herself, watching the smiling woman with some concern.

The question is whether Gertrud will be able to hold on to that blissful serenity when she realises how close she came to running into her brother's killer.

13

Karen's lower back is aching when she finally turns into the car park next to the ferry port in Lysvik. There are probably places to park closer to the town centre, but here, she knows, the ferry operator's staff who work shifts around the clock in a building nearby, keep a bit of an eye on the cars.

She climbs out slowly, reaches into the back seat and pulls out the large bag she packed the night before. Then she puts her hands against the door, stretches out her back and feels pain shoot down her right hip. Hours of driving, coupled with favouring her right leg whenever she was on her feet, has left its mark. She had been particularly bothered by her knee on the slippery cliffs up by the quarry, clumsily trying to avoid putting too much weight on it. She glances at her watch and starts walking toward the high street. When she and Kneought Brodal drove through town in the morning on their way to the clinic, she'd noticed a pub on a corner. It had been closed then, but she's hoping it'll have a longed-for pint for her now. Or two.

A faint smell of cooking grease greets her when she opens the door and looks into a large, almost perfectly square room. About twenty men are standing at the bar or sitting at tables, some alone, others in groups. Everyone is staring intently at a TV mounted on the wall. Karen walks over to a free table by the window, puts her bag down on the floor and glances over at the TV. Manchester United versus Sunderland, she notes, so a home side victory is unlikely. She walks over to the bar and pulls her wallet out of her coat pocket.

The woman behind the bar looks to be in her late sixties. A faded beauty of the bombshell variety, she radiates warm motherliness. Her platinum blonde hair is set in perfect curls, her lipstick is meticulously applied, and nestled in her ample cleavage is a gold cross on a thin chain. When Karen approaches, the woman's face breaks into a smile so lovely not even the small spot of hot pink lipstick on her right front tooth can spoil the effect.

'Hi, lambkins, what can I get you?' she asks and Karen can feel herself beaming back. Even with the pain and exhaustion, it's impossible not to.

'A Spitfire, please,' she says. 'Oh, I'll have a glass of Groth's as well,' she adds.

Just a bit of research in case I do end up having to stop by the distillery, she tells herself. I should really let Smeed pay.

'Which one, love? I reckon we have every kind there is.'

The woman makes a sweeping gesture toward the shelf behind the counter where a handful of different bottles with the familiar logo are lined up.

'Wow, I'm not sure,' Karen says, studying the selection. 'Actually, strike that, I'll have an Old Stone Edition.'

Definitely research, she muses with a glance at the picture of the Gudheim ship setting on the label.

'You have a seat and I'll be out in a minute.'

Karen gratefully limps back to her table. Ducks her head a little when she passes between the men and the TV so as not to deprive them of a second's game time.

She wearily lowers herself onto her chair and looks around the room. A typical Doggerian pub, unabashedly inspired by its British counterparts. But here, the paintings on the walls are of maritime scenes and fishermen's tools rather than horses, hunting horns and hounds. The obligatory wooden rowing boat is suspended from the ceiling while its crossed oars adorn one of the walls and the equally obligatory fishing net with glass floaters hangs in its usual place above the bar. It could have been the Hare and Crow back in Langevik, or any other of the thousands of pubs still operating in Doggerland.

'By far the Britons' most important contribution to this country,' her father had liked to say.

He hadn't been alone in that opinion. Even the most reactionary codgers from the old Scandinavian families, grumbling about the strong Anglo-Saxon influence, tend to cherish their local pubs. Some of them stubbornly insist on using the old name for Doggerland – West Mark Land – while knocking back another pint of ale and shot of whiskey.

But the pub culture is under threat; in Dunker and Ravenby, pubs are now in direct competition with wine bars and local microbrewery outlets that are less dingy and free of that characteristic mouldy carpet smell. And yet, it's in pubs like these Karen feels most at home. Surrounded by old men who barely look up when you enter. Where you can sit in peace without constantly having to rebuff lonely men who sidle up to your table with a hopeful, 'Are you here all by yourself? Mind if I join you?'

Karen pulls out two notebooks. The small, thin one that fits into her jacket pocket and the large moleskin one she carries in her handbag. Just then a tray with a pint of ale, a small glass of light yellow whiskey and a bowl of fried red algae lands on her table. Karen looks up.

'Thank you. Can I ask you something? Is there a hotel in Lysvik, or could you recommend a good bed and breakfast?'

'Sure, there's Rindler's up on Lotsgatan, but if all you need is a comfortable bed with clean sheets, I have a room free – 300 marks and breakfast's included. You'd have to pay at least three times that at Rindler's.'

'Deal,' Karen replies. 'I may be staying a few days, if that's OK. Karen Eiken Hornby,' she adds and holds out her hand.

'Ellen Jensen. That absolutely fine. Can I ask what you're doing up here? I can tell you're from the south.'

'Work,' Karen replies tersely, but changes her mind and adds, 'I'm a police detective and I'm here to investigate a death.'

'Fredrik Stuub, yes, I figured. I heard about it this morning. So it wasn't an accident after all?'

'It's too early to say. We always investigate unexpected deaths, just to make sure.'

'That makes sense, though I really can't imagine who would want to kill that sweet old man.'

'Did you know him?'

Ellen Jensen shakes her head.

'He used to stop by after work sometimes. He would come back on the five-thirty ferry and pop in for a quick drink on his way home, like so many others.'

'I've been told he was a retired teacher,' Karen says. 'But I guess he didn't work at the school here in Lysvik, then?'

Ellen Jensen tilts her head back and laughs loudly.

'He wouldn't have liked to hear you suggesting it,' she said. 'His honour would have been impugned – he was a Huss by blood, after all. No, he taught at the university in Ravenby. Chemistry or biology or something like that. He certainly didn't teach the local nippers to read, that's for sure.'

She laughs again and picks up the empty tray.

'Let me know when you want to see the room. Would you like me to put everything on one tab?'

'That would be great,' Karen replies.

She'll deal with Smeed later.

When she sits down on the bed in her room about an hour later, Karen notes that, as promised by Ellen, it appears to be comfortable, and the room is neat and clean. And shockingly ugly. In addition to the brown carpet, the medallion wallpaper and the avocado-green kettle, there is bric-a-brac on every available surface. Fake flowers, a couple of porcelain dogs on the minimal desk, something that looks like an old hunting horn next to a painting of an exceedingly brash sunset, so hideous she has to avert her eyes. The wall above the head of the bed is adorned with what used to be a virtually mandatory ornament in all Doggerian businesses: a heart flanked by an anchor and a cross, here cast in plaster with a pinkish tint. Faith, hope and love. Right now, Karen doesn't feel much of any of those things. I should have gone to Rindler's, she berates herself.

She stands up and walks the three steps over to the window. It's already dark out, but the lights from the ferry terminal reveal that at least the room has a sea view. She pulls out her phone and dials her mother's number. Eleanor answers after four rings, sounding cheerfully winded.

Karen doesn't ask why.

After being updated on the situation at home – no, they're absolutely fine, they ate the leftovers from yesterday; yes, everyone left, except Sigrid and Leo, of course. No, it's no problem, Sigrid has a car and has promised to give them a ride to the airport. What was that, sweetheart? Oh yes, Harry sends his love. How are things going up there, will you be staying long? – Karen ends the call and pulls up Jounas Smeed's number. Just as she's about to dial it to report on the day's progress and ask about the prospects of reinforcements, an incoming call makes her phone ring. *Sören Larsen*, the display reads and Karen feels a pang of guilt as she answers. It's only half past six and she has already clocked off, and without letting Larsen know.

'All right, Eiken,' Sören Larsen says cheerfully, 'where have you disappeared to?'

'I'm in Lysvik. I just checked into a room above the pub on Skepparegatan. Where are you? Don't tell me you're still at Stuub's?'

'Hardly. Kneought and I are in the hotel restaurant, just ordered. Why are you staying at the pub? Rindler's isn't too shabby, actually. Apparently, they have both a sauna and one of those jacuzzi tubs. We're actually considering having a soak after dinner.'

Karen curses her fate with a heavy sigh. Not that the idea of sitting in a jacuzzi with Laurel and Hardy holds much appeal, but her back could definitely have done with thirty minutes in a hot sauna. Instead, she's trapped in a floral prison, gazing out at the flickering lights of a deserted ferry port.

'I took the first room I came across.'

'Too bad, but at least join us for dinner,' Larsen continues. 'You deserve a decent meal.'

*

Fifteen minutes later, Karen sits down at the table where Larsen and Brodal have just been served a piece of steaming turbot each. Next to them, bowls of boiled potatoes and grated horseradish are set out along with a gravy boat filled to the brim with melted butter. Her favourite dish. But with Solveig Byle's lunch still heavy in her stomach she opts for something lighter.

'Prawn toast for me, please,' she tells the waitress.

'And to drink?'

'I'll have a glass of theirs,' she says after a glance at the bottle of wine sitting in an ice bucket, wrapped in a towel.

'If that's the case, bring us another bottle,' Kneought Brodal adds.

'I assume you've discussed this with Smeed?' Karen says, gesturing at the plates, gravy boats and wine coolers.

'No, it'll be a lovely surprise,' Brodal replies sarcastically. 'It's bloody Christmas, we're not supposed to have a decent meal?'

While she waits for her food, Karen listens to Larsen and Brodal's contented chewing and pours herself a glass of wine. It's not until a mountain of freshly peeled shrimp, presumably hiding a slice of toast in its midst, is put in front of her that she realises she's actually hungry again.

'So, what have you learnt?' she says, washing down the first bite with a sip of the wine.

Too late, she realises it's a nice Chablis, probably incredibly expensive. Smeed is definitely not going to be happy. She decides to let Kneought Brodal handle the cheque; even Smeed knows better than to pick a fight with him.

'Well,' Larsen says. 'Someone has unquestioningly searched Fredrik Stuub's house, but then, you knew that already.'

'Can you tell if anything's missing?'

'Nope.'

'What do you mean? Surely you can tell me something?'

'Sorry, I meant to say nothing's missing. Or maybe things *are* missing, but if so, we don't know what. What I can say is that whoever did it wasn't interested in antiques, silver or art. And just so you know, there's plenty to be had of all three of those things in the house. The bloke seems to have been something of a collector, or he inherited some nice stuff.'

'You didn't find a mobile phone, did you? According to his sister he did have one.'

'It's not in the house. He probably had it with him when he took the dog out and then it fell out when he was pushed into the quarry. If that's the case, it's at the bottom of the quarry now. But we can at least get the call lists.'

'I'll talk to the prosecutor's office about requesting them from TelAB,' Karen says. 'But it's not going to be easy getting hold of people.'

'It's incomprehensible to me that the entire country seems to have gone on holiday all at the same time,' Larsen says.

Brodal mutters something that sounds like agreement and reaches for the gravy boat.

Karen puts her cutlery down with a sigh.

'You didn't find a computer?' she asks. 'If you didn't, someone must have taken it.'

'No, and sure, I suppose that could be what they were after. If he had one, that is.'

'I think we can assume he did. Fredrik Stuub was a lecturer at Ravenby University, or so I've been told.'

Kneought Brodal lets out a snort of derision.

'You think too highly of the natural scientists, Eiken. I've met people from Ravenby University who barely knew how to use email. Not the young ones, obviously, but Stuub had been retired for years. A man of the old school, according to Sven Andersén, but a bit doddery in recent years. Nice bloke, actually.'

'How do you know? Are you talking to the corpses now?' Sören Larsen says with a grin.

For a moment, Brodal looks confused.

'Andersén, obviously. We spent several hours together. Not so bad, actually, for a northerner.'

Sören and Karen exchange a look. It's highly unusual for the coroner to have anything positive to say about another human being. At least the living kind.

'All I mean to say,' Brodal continues, 'is that even if Stuub held a senior position, that's no reason to assume he had a computer at home. In the olden days, people got by just fine without staring at an LED screen 24/7.'

'So what do you think they were looking for in his house, then? Since nothing seems to be missing?' Karen says and takes a sip of her wine.

'How the hell should I know. Isn't finding that out your job?'

She turns to Larsen with a weary sigh.

'You know I have to ask. Nothing else in the house you haven't already mentioned? Fingerprints, shoe prints, hairs? Anything?'

'All of those things. Lots and lots.' He smiles around a mouthful of fish. 'If you're lucky, not all of it belongs to Stuub or his mutt. And there's always a chance the autopsy tomorrow yields something useful. You're going, I assume?'

Karen pulls a face.

'Don't have much of a choice. So, you don't have anything for me?'

Larsen wipes a trickle of butter from the corner of his mouth and reaches for wine bottle. Then he stops mid-movement, resting the bottom of the bottle against the tablecloth.

'No technical evidence, but I did get this feeling,' he says. 'I'm not even sure I should mention it.'

'Oh, come on,' Karen coaxes. 'Just tell us.'

Sören Larsen takes his time topping up their glasses. Karen impatiently watches him carefully push the empty bottle back into the cooler.

'I had a feeling, just a vague feeling, nothing else, you under-stand, that the whole thing was a bit too . . . neat.'

Karen lets the word sink in while listening to the sound of Brodal chewing. Neat wasn't the word she would have used to describe the chaos she'd glimpsed when she opened the front door.

'Put on?' she says. 'Is that what you mean?'

Larsen shrugs.

'Look, I don't know. Everything was pulled out, knocked over and in a bloody mess, as you saw. But I got the feeling whoever did it wasn't really looking for anything. More like someone had tried to stage a break-in, without having a clear idea of what that usually looks like.'

14

She lets the door slide shut with a click. Doesn't leave a small gap so Mikkel can see the light from the landing if he wakes up, the gap she's promised will always be there. The act of betrayal draws a gasp from her that she does her best to muffle with her hand. She stands stock-still with her forehead against the closed door, silent, resting her head against the drawing Tyra made that morning. Her little brother had howled with envy when it was put up with four drawing pins, so when they were done they'd gone down to the kitchen so Mikkel could make his own drawing to hang on the door. But as soon as crayons and paper had been set out on the table, he'd lost interest and run into the living room to watch TV.

She knows she has to go downstairs now, not make everything worse by delaying the inevitable. But she stays where she is, with her forehead against Tyra's drawing of a pink house, a green lawn and a yellow dog. She can feel one of the pins pressing against her hairline and fights down the thoughts of the black crayon swirl above the pink house, the dark cloud that has featured in every last one of Tyra's drawings for the past six months.

She swallows hard and focuses on slowing her breathing while her cramping throat begins to relax, expertly squashes pointless thoughts and the voice in her head whispering she has to leave him before it's too late. It's persistent this time;

the words creep up her spine, burrow under her skin, pushing almost all the way inside. She indulges it until the noises from the living room downstairs jerk her back to reality.

He has turned off the news and put on music. The gentle first notes of Schubert's eight symphony waft up from the ground floor. He chose it deliberately, she thinks to herself. Soon, the orchestra will be drowning out all other sounds.

Her inner voice has gone silent, given up and left. Her job for the next two hours is simple. To not provoke, not 'bicker'. Just endure until he's done for today.

And to not let the children hear.

She takes a deep breath and runs the numbers. Half a bottle of wine with dinner and the whiskey he was pouring himself when she went upstairs to put the children to bed. He probably had time for at least one more while she worked on getting them to go to sleep. Tyra had been fussy, had wanted Mummy to stay, to climb into bed with her.

Half a bottle of wine, a couple of glasses of whiskey, maybe three. Not enough to make him unsteady, not enough to make the blows slow and unfocused. Just enough for the silent rage that has been building since the moment he came home to require venting, releasing the wordless hatred that has grown stronger with every second he has spent in the house. The looks he gave her when he realised the children were still eating in the kitchen, even though it was seven o'clock, that she had bought the wrong wine, that she hadn't tidied up the toys in the living room. Not a word, just that sound when he kicked one of Mikkel's cars so hard they could all hear the plastic cracking against the wall. Then he'd come back into the kitchen and tousled his son's hair with a smile.

'You have to remind Mummy to keep the house neat and tidy, sweetie,' he'd said. 'She keeps forgetting things.'

She'd seen the confused mix of worry and relief in her son's face, had tried to catch Tyra's eyes to give her a reassuring smile, but her daughter had stared at her plate. He has never raised a hand to the children, she had reminded herself. They don't know.

Now she repeats that comforting thought inwardly, like a mantra, while she slowly starts walking down the stairs.

The children don't know.

15

The new university campus in Ravenby on the west coast of Heimö was built high up on the slopes of the mountain that gave the town its name. From Raven Mountain, scholars from every science discipline can look down on the less gifted – or at least less fortunate – Ravenby locals. In the eleven years since its opening, the campus has been in a state of constant transformation. The guiding principle of Doggerland University's expansion to a second campus was the division of labour: the science departments relocated and are now concentrated in the country's second largest city, Ravenby, while the arts and humanities departments stayed on the old campus in the capital, Dunker. These days, in addition to facilities for education and research, Ravenby is also home to the Doggerland University Hospital and a forensic medicine unit.

The address, Karen notes, is, unsurprisingly, 2 Analytics Drive. She parks outside the entrance, dreading what's coming.

Half an hour later, dressed in green protective gear and a white net cap, Karen studies the row of stainless-steel tables and instruments under the large overhead surgical lights and steels herself. The rules only stipulate that she be present, she's not required to be enthusiastic about it or even participate.

Fredrik Stuub's body is laid out on the table farthest from the door.

Kneought Brodal and the Head of Forensic Services, Sören Larsen, are going to be assisted by an autopsy technician. Karen and Sven Andersén are only there to observe and, unlike Andersén, Karen decides that means keeping a respectful distance between herself and the autopsy table at all times.

As usual, Karen is able to get through the first part, when Fredrik Stuub's clothes are cut up and put in plastic bags for further analysis and samples are taken from his nails and mouth, without too much distress. She spends the hours that follow trying her best not to hear the grinding of saws cutting through ribs, sternum and skull or the sucking sound of organs being lifted out and put in kidney dishes. Instead, she tries to make sense of what the two doctors are talking about and what Brodal is saying into the recorder. A year of criminology studies in London and ten years as a detective inspector has made her familiar with the most common Greek and Latin terms, but she would never presume to draw any conclusions from her own interpretations. When he's done, Kneought Brodal will summarise his findings in the condescending way he considers necessary to make even a police officer understand.

This time is no different.

'All right, then,' he says, after ordering the young autopsy technician to 'stuff the giblets back in and stitch up the steak'. 'Let's take this somewhere else, so Eiken can get some colour back in her cheeks.'

They sit down in an adjacent conference room with a panoramic view of Ravenby Bay. No one wants coffee, but the water pitcher is passed around the table and Karen watches Brodal pop a sugar cube in his mouth, for lack of anything better. She waits in silence.

'OK,' he says at length and turns to Karen, 'let me lay things out in plain terms, so everyone can understand. The bloke was murdered. You need more?'

She forces out a smile but says nothing, thinking to herself that she's had about as much as she can take of the coroner in the past twenty-four hours. After pausing for effect, Brodal continues.

'OK, everything points to Stuub having been given a powerful blow to the left side of his jaw. If I had to guess, I'd say by a fist. His head was then subjected to further violence, most likely a good kick. I say kick, because at that point, Stuub would have collapsed onto the ground. Agree?'

Sven Andersén and Sören Larsen nod. Brodal sucks loudly on his dissolving sugar cube and crushes it between his molars before continuing.

'Then he was dragged on his back, based on haematoma in both armpits in addition to the injuries we've already discussed. And then, well, he was probably simply rolled over the edge; there are faint bruises on his right upper arm and hip indicating as much. He was most likely unconscious, or at least very dazed when this happened, but the cause of death is that his skull was crushed against a protruding rock when he landed. Are we still in agreement?'

'Completely,' Sören Larsen says. 'Judging by what I've seen so far of his shoes and clothes, that's exactly what happened. Exactly like we thought yesterday. So, nothing new.'

'And no signs of a struggle,' Brodal adds, 'which suggests he was probably caught off guard. In other words, don't expect any useful skin scrapings under his nails.'

'All right,' Karen says, slightly disappointed. 'And what can you tell me about his general health? No obvious problems?'

'I suppose his liver was a bit worse for wear, but that's pretty much true of most men his age in this country. Nothing particularly serious. No infarctions and surprisingly healthy vessels. I've sent some samples off for analysis, but with everyone on sick leave I wouldn't hold my breath. And I wouldn't expect exciting results, either. He might have had fifteen, twenty more years in him, if he'd eased off the sauce and not been pushed into that quarry.'

'And what about you?' Karen says to Sören Larsen. 'Did you find anything potentially useful?'

'Like Brodal said, nothing under his fingernails. Some stains and hairs on his clothes, most of them probably his own and the dog's. But . . .'

'. . . it's going to take a few days. I know.'

'Even longer, likely as not. Everyone taking annual leave over the holidays really gums up the works and we have several people in bed with the flu at forensics, too. I wouldn't count on any definitive answers before New Year's.'

'Bloody hell, just have people work overtime!'

'You'll have to take that up with Viggo Haugen. Not convinced he feels it's worth loosening the purse strings for this case. That lunatic in Moerbeck has already eaten up most of the overtime budget.'

Karen sighs. The effort to catch the serial rapist terrorising one of Dunker's northern suburbs has rightly been allocated a lot of resources. Unfortunately, without result. There's no reason to believe they will be luckier with the technical evidence in this case. True, the fingerprints from Fredrik Stuub's house can be run quickly, but they won't be of much help unless they belong to someone who's already in their database.

'Well then,' Brodal says and slaps the table with both hands, as though to underscore that as far as he's concerned the meeting is over. 'You're on your own, Eiken. I, for my part, am packing up and heading back home. Can I hitch a ride with you, Sören?'

16

Karen looks around the living room and feels exhaustion hit her like a cudgel at the sight. Drawers have been pulled out and over-turned, piles of books and newspapers knocked over, pictures pushed askew. The floor is littered with things that probably used to be filed away in boxes: receipts, paid bills, photographs. The kitchen and bedroom are more of the same – everything not nailed down has been pulled out and thrown about, as though a bulldozer had been let loose in Fredrik Stuub's home. Sören Larsen might be right, she muses. There's something exagger-ated, almost theatrical about the mess.

The technicians are done; fingerprints, hairs and shoe prints have been collected from the house and its immediate sur-roundings. Before they parted ways in Ravenby, Larsen gave Karen the key to the new lock and the all-clear to enter.

'We've done what we can, now it's your turn to see if you can find something exciting. Knock yourself out!' he'd said.

Cheers, she thinks sourly and prods a pile of circulars with the tip of her shoe. I'll have to have a couple of constables come and collect and catalogue this crap. And I need reinforcements from the bloody CID. Thorstein Byle is sweet and helpful, but so damn polite and deferential. I need someone who'll stand up to me and have an opinion of their own.

She knows she's being unfair. Without Thorstein Byle's local knowledge, they would be nowhere right now, even if every single detective at the CID came up to help with the case. Byle has been nothing but helpful and has even opened his home to her. To atone for her mean thoughts, she turns to her colleague with a smile.

'Right, I guess there's no point putting this off. Ready to have at it?'

Byle nods, but stays where he is, looking around indecisively.

'We're just going to do a quick overview to see if anything jumps out at us; we'll map everything out more methodically later,' she says.

'In all honesty, it's probably safe to assume nothing we find in this mess is of any interest,' Byle says. 'If it was, it wouldn't still be here.'

'True. But there might be something that indirectly reveals something interesting about Stuub's life. Larsen had the feeling this break-in was staged. What do you think?'·

Byle sits down on a brown sofa, leans forward and glumly picks up a stack of papers.

'Maybe,' he says. 'Hard to say.'

Of course, Karen thinks.

With no idea what they're looking for, they start searching the house. Papers, bills, letters. They silently pick up, read, skim, put aside.

'Do you think they checked the concealment?' Byle says after a while.

Karen looks up from a pile of bills, uncomprehending.

'The concealment?'

94

'Yes, you know, a secret cupboard or drawer, could be either. Old houses like this one always have concealments, usually in the kitchen. Don't you have them down on Heimö?'

A vague memory from her childhood flashes past; her cousins showing her something behind the wainscoting in her aunt's kitchen. A secret, forbidden storage cupboard that a conspiratorially solemn Finn had presented to her while Odd and Einar kept watch at the door. Without touching anything, Finn had let her glimpse the hidden treasure: a brown envelope, a wad of notes held together by a thick red rubber band, a pair of gold earrings and a handful of rings. Excitement at being let in on the secret had set Karen's arms and legs humming, aided by the certain knowledge that Aunt Ingeborg would have their hides if she found out what they were up to.

One time they'd shown her the secret treasure trove, never again. It had never occurred to her other houses might have similar secret compartments.

'No, not that I'm aware,' she replies. 'Are you telling me everyone on Noorö has a secret stash?'

Byle laughs.

'Not everyone, obviously, but they're fairly common, though I doubt they're much in use nowadays. They kind of stopped serving their purpose once the police and customs agents found out people had them. But older people like them because they think they'll be more difficult to find for a junkie scrambling for something to sell.'

Or for a forensic technician from the south, Karen adds inwardly.

*

Ten minutes later, Byle has tapped walls, inspected floorboards, palpated dado panels, opened cupboards, traced joints with his fingers and compared inner and outer measurements with Karen watching in fascination from a kitchen chair.

Now he turns to her and sighs.

'I'm sorry if I promised too much. Either there's nothing here or it's too bloody well hidden.'

This is the first curse word she has heard escape Thorstein Byle's lips; she immediately feels her shoulders relax. Their meeting with the local priest, Erling Arve, made it abundantly clear that Byle's not only a colleague she has to stroke the right way to ensure local cooperation, he's apparently also a dedicated churchgoer. It's tiring enough to be polite in general – to always have to guard her tongue to keep the cursing to a minimum is enough to make her face feel stiff. The next moment, she is snapped out of her reverie.

Thorstein Byle is down on all fours in front of a large oakwood cabinet full of plates and glasses. He has already searched it once, but now he has pushed his hand in under the base and pressed something.

'Bingo!'

The entire front of the base pops out, revealing something that looks like a mix between a pastry board and a shallow drawer. Karen jumps up too quickly, causing jolts of searing pain to shoot up her thigh and through her hip. Together, they stare down into Fredrik Stuub's concealment.

For several seconds, the ticking of the clock on the wall above the kitchen table is the only sound, then Karen breaks the silence.

'Don't touch anything,' she says, putting a hand on Byle's shoulder. 'Can you fetch an evidence bag from my car? Make it a large one.'

Then she pulls a pair of disposable gloves out of her coat pocket and gently picks up the laptop.

17

She considers calling first. To say she's on Noorö and ask if it would be OK for her to stop by. She decides not to. Giving her aunt advance notice of her coming would inevitably turn a simple visit into a full-on family get-together. The moment they hung up, her aunt would start to summon every single one of Karen's blood relations on the island: first cousins, second cousins, third cousins, and probably their spouses and children, too. But going by Ingeborg and Lars' house is something she can't put off any longer. It's only a matter of time before they catch wind of the fact that she's on the island and they would never forgive her if she didn't visit.

Besides, she has to admit she's looking forward to seeing them and the farm again. After all, she did spend large parts of her childhood there.

And maybe, precisely because she hasn't been back since, her memories are unvarnished by time. She can take each one out and study its pristine details, turn them this way and that without the contents changing. In her memories, everything is still the way it once was: the sheep, the regular grey ones and her favourite black-and-white ones with their soft, curly fleeces; the lambs she was allowed to help bottle feed – at least one ewe always died during lambing and every year her cousins would find at least one scrawny, abandoned, starving little thing in the fields.

Then the nights when Uncle Lars and the cousins took her out with them in the boat. Her own father, who unlike his brother-in-law lived off what the sea provided, never took her out. But here, she was allowed to come along when they went snag fishing among the skerries outside Gudheim. Only many years later had she realised snag fishing was illegal.

And Ingeborg, her dad's stern sister, whose looks could kill if you started in on your food before grace had been said, or if you helped yourself from the berry bushes. Aunt Ingeborg who would also stroke your cheek with her rough hand and say, 'Tell you what, Kay-Kay, why don't you and I bake a really tasty sponge cake? If you fetch four eggs from the henhouse, I'll get the flour. Four of the smallest now, mind!'

The eggs. She can still practically taste them. Just ordinary eggs, straight from the nest. And then the ones from the ducks, as big as her fist. She was allowed to help collect them, but can't remember anyone ever eating one because the duck eggs and the large chicken eggs were sold in the marketplace in Thorsvik.

The marketplace. Not the local one in Lysvik, the big one, held every Saturday down in the harbour on the other side of the sound. Taking the ferry across, wind in her hair and admonishments not to climb the railing. The long trestle tables where farmers and fishermen lined up their wares and tried to outshout each other with unbeatable offers to coax southerners and gullible tourists to open up their wallets. Shouting and hollering, always in an exaggerated Noorö dialect with consonants as sharp as razors. For some reason that helped move the goods, or so Finn had told her.

The coolers full of cod, wolffish, herring, halibut, haddock, ling and cusk. The yarn dolls made of carded and spun wool in grey, black and almost pure white. The knitted socks and mittens, the cured leather. The bottles of cordial, the punnets of berries and mushroom fit to sell: raspberries, blueberries, blackcurrants and chanterelles. Gooseberries and sheep polypore for their own consumption. And the things that weren't put on display, but rather sold furtively from boots and flatbeds: car parts, 'antiques' and at the far back, white plastic containers full of special Noorö cordial that had nothing at all to do with blackcurrants.

And the smells. All her memories seem suffused with the smell of tar, diesel, fish, sheepskins and warm raspberries.

Driving through the gateposts and seeing the farmyard is like meeting an old childhood friend and realising the years have not been kind. Over by the barn, an old banger has been left to rust next to a tractor that looks as though it hasn't been used in years, a pile of timber and junk. The grass around the junk pile is so tall you'd need a scythe to get to it. The only things that look exactly as she remembers are the main houses: a long two-storey building of grey stone flanked on either side by a smaller detached house of the same height and material, all three topped with red-brick roofs rather than the traditional black slate.

As a child, the farm had looked imposing to Karen, almost like a mansion, with its detached wings and unusual red roofs. Driving up to them now, she realises several of the roof tiles are missing and a number of broken ones are stacked next to the water barrel by the corner of the main house. And there's nothing mansion-like about the root cellar with its grass roof, the outbuildings, the henhouse, the barn or the sloping plot. And then there's Skalvet, looming up ominously behind it all, like an impenetrable wall against the sea beyond. She never liked the mountains, not even as a child, especially not during thunderstorms. And looking up at them now, she realises she still finds that monumental immovability unsettling.

She already regrets coming . . .

Just then, the front door is thrown open and before Karen has made it halfway up the driveway, a large German shepherd is racing toward her, barking loudly. Without thinking, she sinks into a squat.

'Calm down, Heisick,' she says, realising her mistake the moment the words leave her lips.

Of course it's not Heisick. He would be forty by now.

The voice from the house is like the crack of a whip.

'Lie down!'

The big dog obeys instantly, lowering itself onto its belly with its head pushed forward. It growls deep in its throat with its eyes fixed on her. Karen gets up slowly, her heart pounding, watching those bared teeth out of the corner of her eye, careful not to stare the amped-up shepherd in the eyes.

'What do you want?'

The voice from the house sounds suspicious and hostile. And unmistakeably familiar.

Karen, who has pushed herself back up, momentarily takes her eyes off the dog and squints up at the house. The man standing in the doorway has one hand on the door and is using the other to shield his eyes from the powerful light above it. In the window next to the entrance she can just about make out the outline of another person who seems to be taking an interest in the goings-on outside.

Karen hesitates. If she shouts back, she risks setting off the dog. The shadow in the window disappears. Moments later, the man is pushed aside and a gruff woman's voice barks, 'Get out of the way, Lars, don't you see who it is? Come here, Jacko! My goodness, Karen, dear, is it really you?'

A few minutes later, Jacko has slouched away and Karen has been embraced by strong arms and ushered into the kitchen.

'How long are you staying? Why didn't you call first? I would have made you dinner. My goodness, it's lovely to see you.'

Ingeborg has both of Karen's hands in a firm grip and is studying her with concern in her eyes. Karen anxiously wonders what she sees. Ingeborg isn't one to pull her punches. But instead of pronouncements and questions, a quick series of commands follows.

'Lars, go down to the basement and fetch some hoggva from the freezer and call the boys and tell them to come over. Karen, you take off your coat and have a seat at the table and I'll get you something to drink.'

Lars obediently shuffles off and Karen has to press her lips together to hide a smile when she sees the light from the basement stairs like an ellipsis between her uncle's bowed legs before he disappears in the direction of the chest freezer.

No point resisting, she thinks to herself, sneaking furtive glances around the kitchen while pulling off her coat and handing it to her waiting aunt. To her relief, she finds what she's looking for. Not proof time has stood still in the large kitchen, not sentimental reminders of baking or cooking on the old Aga stove. What she was hoping to spot was a means of getting out of here before too long. A microwave.

Defrosting hoggva without a microwave would take forever and Ingeborg would flatly refuse being denied the opportunity to feed her niece a proper meal.

Karen gratefully accepts the glass of blackcurrant cordial and leans back. The first sip whisks her back to her childhood as Ingeborg pulls out a chair and sits down across from her.

'Now, then, lambkins, tell me. How are you doing? I don't think we've seen you since . . . well, sweet Jesus, how long has it been?'

Karen doesn't need to search her memory. She knows exactly when she was last here. On 16 June, eleven and a half years ago. She knows it was a Thursday. It had been almost noon when she and John and Mathis had arrived in Ravenby on the Harwich ferry and decided to swing by Noorö instead of driving straight to her mother's house in Langevik.

It had been a spontaneous decision. Karen had wanted to share at least a small part of what her own summers had been like with Mathis, if only for a day. The last time they'd visited, he'd been two years old and too little to remember any of it. Now, having turned eight, the memories would stay with him. She wanted to carve out a space for her own childhood in her son's memory bank, a small counterweight to all the summers spent in Surrey with John's parents and their trips to Italy, Spain and France.

She wanted Mathis to touch the soft fleece of a lamb, taste an egg that wasn't several weeks old. She wanted him to take off his socks and shoes and let his feet forget the hard streets and school-yards of London for a day. And she wanted both him and John to meet her relatives so they could see for themselves that she was telling the truth about Aunt Ingeborg's hands, so chapped they looked like fish scales, and Uncle Lars, so bowlegged he couldn't herd pigs; Einar with the improbable gap between his front teeth, Odd with hair so red the locals not only doubted his paternity, but also wonder if the black-haired Ingeborg could really be his mother.

And Finn. Her oldest cousin with shoulders like a barn door and eyes as piercingly blue as her own. She wanted to show them the mountains, have them look up at the highest peak and then take them to down to the bay, make them understand why she sometimes found London too confining.

She has more memories of that summer than of the rest of her life put together. The visit to Noorö and Mathis's smile when he finally did touch that soft lamb. She remembers calling her mother and Eleanor being in a huff when she realised they were putting off seeing her to visit the Noorö relatives first. She remembers her joy when they pulled up to her house in Langevik, one day later than planned. She remembers Mathis's tears when he was stung by a hornet behind the annexe the next morning and holding him in her arms while John called the medical helpline and Eleanor calmly went to pick marigolds and fetch a sugar cube to put on the swelling.

She remembers their trip to Crete the week after. Mathis discovering olives for the first time and eating so many she and John couldn't help but wonder if it might be bad for him. The sound of cicadas outside their open balcony door as she and John made love as quietly as they could so as not to wake Mathis. And she remembers the beach where they had fallen over themselves laughing, that day that's still preserved in the photograph on her nightstand back in Langevik.

Every moment is still there, seared into her very core. Her last, most precious memories.

She doesn't want to remember the autumn that followed, the nagging and the video games, the sleet and slush of the first weeks of December. Or the row with John that morning when she was angry with him for being hungover after celebrating yet another high-profile win in court for Gallagher, Smith & Hornby. His insistence that he hadn't forgotten, that he was fine to drop Mathis off at the dentist on his way to work like he'd promised, so long as he was allowed to finish his cup of coffee first, and couldn't Karen just please shut up until he was properly awake at least, and where the fuck was the paracetamol?

She doesn't want to remember snarling that he wasn't in a state to drive their son or himself anywhere. Or getting into the driver's seat with a sense of self-righteous resentment at having to chauffeur her hungover husband around, instead of enjoying the lie-in she'd been looking forward to for two months. Or ignoring John when he put his hand on her knee in a gesture of conciliation at the Waltham Abbey exit on the M25. Or how the world ended three seconds later . . .

The sound of Uncle Lars puffing and panting his way up the basement steps calls her back to the present. Dazed, as though only just returned from a long journey, Karen meets her aunt's eyes.

'How are you holding up?' Ingeborg asks and puts a hand, coarse like fish scales, over her own.

18

One after the other, they show up, as she'd known they would. Thirty minutes later, the kitchen is full of people hugging her or shaking her hand, depending on whether they've met before or not.

Finn is the first to arrive. He still lives on the farm, in one of the detached wings, and has just returned after celebrating Christmas with his in-laws in Lysvik. Now he strides up to the kitchen table and spreads his arms wide. Karen stands up and disappears into a bear hug.

He's still good-looking, she notes. Older, but as attractive as ever, despite grey hairs at his temples and the fact that he seems to be sucking his stomach in a little when he pushes her away with his hands on her shoulder and slowly shakes his head.

'My God, Karen. You're supposed to be ten, not an old bag,' he says with a grin.

'Finn!' exclaims a blonde woman standing behind him.

'This is Jannike, my wife,' Finn says. 'Well, you've met before. And this is our little Trailer. Or the runt, as Mum puts it. Turned up just when we thought we were done.'

He pulls a grumpy boy of about thirteen over. Karen searches her memory and is relieved to come up with a name.

'Jesper, right? And your two oldest, Daniel and Andreas, my God, they must be close to thirty by now. Are they here, too?'

'Thirty-one and thirty-three. No, they're out on the rig over the holidays. Einar, too. The money was too good to turn down, but are they ever going to be miffed when they find out you were here. They were already fuming about missing Christmas when they left.'

'The rig', NoorOyl's oil platform north-west of Gudheim. A lifeline for families lucky enough to have secured an income from another energy source after the last mine closed.

'Sounds rough,' she says.

'Not a lot of options up here anymore,' Finn replies. 'You work on the rig or up at Groth's or you go hat in hand to the government, like me.'

'Is it your back, still?'

Finn nods.

'And Odd, how's he doing?'

'Why don't you ask him?' Finn says with a nod to someone standing behind her.

She turns around and disappears into yet another embrace.

'Would you look what the cat dragged in?' Odd hollers to his brother over her head. 'I almost thought this was another one of Mum's tricks to get us over here.'

When he relaxes his grip after a few long seconds, Karen tilts her head back to look at his face. The fire has gone out; only a few faint streaks of red are left in Odd's greying hair, which is slicked back from a high, furrowed forehead.

'Damn it, Kay-Kay, it's good to see you.'

'Good to see you, too, Odd Boy,' she replies.

Without taking his eyes of Karen, he shouts to the side, 'Gunnela, damn it, come say hi already!'

Odd's wife leaves her spot by the door, saunters over and extends her hand.

'Hi, Karen, long time no see.'

Gunnela's dull, platinum blonde hair is pulled up into a high ponytail and she's wearing leopard-print tights. Karen notes that, for some reason, she has had the names of her children, grandchildren and husband tattooed across her ample décolletage.

'Hi, Gunnela, yes, it's been too long.'

There's a pause; to fill the silence, Karen reads the ornate script out loud.

'Odd, Tina, Kevin, Liam. That's very convenient – I have a hard time remembering names, too.'

She instantly regrets the joke, but her sarcasm seems to have gone over Gunnela's head.

'I've become a grandmother again, actually, so I'm going to be adding another name soon,' she says with pride. 'Tina just had a girl. They're naming her Jasmine.'

Of course they are, Karen scoffs inwardly and tears her eyes away from Gunnela's bosom.

The next moment, she stiffens.

And with her eyes fixed on Odd's back as he lumbers over to the fridge, Karen curses softly under her breath. The realisation is as instantaneous as it is unwelcome: this isn't the first time in eleven years she's seen her cousin. She saw him yesterday morning, on the ferry from Thorsvik.

With mounting dismay, she stares at the long, thin, grey plait hanging down her cousin's back.

*

It's twenty past nine when Karen turns back onto the highway. Blackcurrant cordial, coffee, half a beer and big helping of hoggva – which only needed an hour in the microwave before it was defrosted enough to fry – have left her stomach more than a little upset. Granted, she had been reminded of how much she liked the traditional Doggerian mix of lamb's liver, pearl barley, onion and cloves, but there's a reason a plate of hoggva is usually washed down with a strong shot of spirits to aid digestion. Today, she had to refrain from such aid, despite her relatives' coaxing. When it comes to blood alcohol levels, she holds herself to a stricter standard than the law does. A considerably stricter one than her relatives seemed to think reasonable.

'Bloody hell, Kay-Kay, drop the police crap already, will you? Without a proper stomach scraper, you'll be chewing the cud all night. It's not like you're going to crash and die . . .'

Ingeborg had come to her rescue.

'Give it a rest, Odd.'

He had closed his mouth with a snap. Karen is still unsure whether he realised he'd put his foot in it, or if Ingeborg still holds the authority to force obedience. If that's the case, it will hardly come as a surprise to her that her youngest son is a member of a criminal motorcycle gang.

She hadn't wanted to bring it up with Odd. She will probably have to eventually, but not tonight. Instead, she had asked Finn when they stepped outside together for a cigarette.

'How long has Odd been a member of the OP?'

He had replied without any sign of surprise.

'Since they moved to Tyrfallet, I assume. You didn't know?'

She had seen the flash of mistrust in his eyes.

'No, how could I have? I know some of the names, obviously, at least of the leaders, but they hardly keep a public website with a membership list. Besides, I've never worked a case with links to the OP,' she'd added.

'Why are you really here?'

Finn's voice had taken on an edge of something she couldn't quite put her finger on. And for the first time since she arrived, she'd felt a chill break through the warmth.

'I told you. To lead the investigation into Fredrik Stuub's death.'

'Nothing else?'

'Nothing else. What, a murder case isn't enough?'

'Well, I certainly can't see what the OP would stand to gain from doing away with old man Stuub, if that's what you're thinking.'

'I never said they did. I was just asking when Odd joined.'

'If you're here on police business, I think you should talk to my brother.'

'I was asking as your cousin.'

'No, Karen. You weren't.'

When she climbed into her car not long after, after much protest and a promise to come back soon, everyone had come out to see her off. And as Finn raised one arm to wave, he had put the other around Odd's shoulders.

19

The buzzing of her phone wakes her. A glance at the screen tells her two things: it's twenty-two minutes past five in the morning and it's her boss calling. It only takes Karen a moment to realise both those things were predictable. She briefly considers not picking up. Then she slowly pushes herself up into sitting position, clears her throat and says as clearly as she is able.

'Hi, Jounas.'

'Did I wake you?'

'No, why would you ask that? You wouldn't have called if you thought I might be asleep, would you?'

The sarcasm is wasted on him. Jounas Smeed's irritation is palpable just from the way he inhales through his nostrils.

'Why haven't I heard from you?' he asks bluntly. 'Didn't we agree you were going to keep me informed?'

Karen rubs her eyes and peers over at the tray on the desk. With a resigned sigh she gets out of bed, picks up the kettle and walks over to the bathroom.

'We did, and I was planning to call you later today.'

With the phone wedged between her ear and her shoulder, she turns on the tap, splashes some cold water on her face and fills the kettle.

'What the fuck is that noise? Are you peeing?'

'I was going to make myself a cup of tea, unless you mind. Because you were right, you see, you did wake me up. It may be well after lunch where you are, but it's twenty past five in the morning here.'

As you are well aware, she adds to herself.

'You only have yourself to blame. If you'd been in touch like we—'

'OK,' she cuts in. 'I don't have much to tell you yet, so I was going to hold off until tonight. But I can go over what little there is if you want.'

'Go.'

She turns on the kettle and sits down on the edge of the bed. Then she reaches for her notepad on the bedside table.

'I don't know how much you know, so I'll go over the facts first. Fredrik Stuub, seventy-two years old. Found dead in a water-filled old quarry in Karby, just north of Skreby. Clear signs of Stuub having been dragged to the edge were found, both at the scene and on the body. According to Brodal, he was given a powerful blow to the chin before that, a proper wallop, to put it simply, and he was likely subsequently kicked in the head, before he was dragged about twenty-five feet. Then he was rolled over the edge and cracked his skull open as he landed on a protruding rock shelf. And that was where his sister, Gertrud Stuub, found him.'

'Keep going,' Jounas Smeed says tersely.

So this is how it's going to be now, she thinks. Until a few months ago, his tone had been very different. Mocking and provoking but at least informal. Too informal even, especially after that drunken night they'd spent together in a hotel room. A big mistake on every level, as she had made clear to him afterwards. But then a grave error in judgement on his part almost

112

cost Karen her life and, in the wake of that, Jounas Smeed had showed her a different side of himself. The constant sarcasm and needling had been toned down and when he came to visit her in the hospital, there had been glimmers of regret and a wish for conciliation. And Karen's plan to ask for a transfer, or to simply quit, had in the end turned into a decision to return to service at the end of her sick leave.

She'd spent her convalescence fruitlessly pondering how they were going to work together again after everything that had happened, wondering how Smeed would ever be able to assert his authority over someone he'd not only slept with but was now beholden to. Someone his own daughter prefers over him.

And here's my answer, Karen realises. He's going to be looking over my shoulder. Checking every single thing I do. Demonstrating his power by demanding reports every step of the way, never waiting until I feel I have something to tell him. That's going to be his little revenge. Fine, let him have it his way.

She consults her notes and resumes her summary, adopting an exaggeratedly formal tone.

'Both Thorstein Byle and the emergency services arrived on the scene within minutes. Byle resides in Skreby and was personally contacted by the on-duty constable. The doctor, a Sven Andersén, arrived just after ten, at which point Stuub had, according to his preliminary assessment, been dead for approximately two hours, give or take thirty minutes. This means the murder took place sometime between—'

'Half past seven and half past eight,' Smeed cuts in.

At least he's quick, she thinks to herself and gets up to pour the boiling water over a teabag. Two plastic-wrapped oat biscuits are sitting on a small plate; she carefully opens the packaging with her teeth.

'I already know all that,' Smeed continues. 'I spoke to Larsen last night. His account is relatively similar to yours.'

Fucking prick, she grumbles inwardly. Having me sit here, at half past five in the morning, going over facts you already know. Out loud, she says, 'Just relatively, sir?'

'Yes, he told me Stuub's home has been searched as well. Apparently, the technicians found a laptop. But I guess you didn't find that little detail significant . . .'

Karen's already low early morning blood-sugar level plunges further. She briefly considers telling him it wasn't Sören Larsen who found Fredrik Stuub's laptop, but she decides against it. She's not going to give Smeed the satisfaction of dismissing her corrections as petty. Besides, it's not like she was the one who found it either.

She takes a bite of her biscuit and chews as quietly as she can.

'And I would have given you that information, too, if you had let me continue,' she says, forcing herself to stay calm. 'The laptop has been sent to forensics and I've talked to the on-call prosecutor, who has requested call lists for Fredrik Stuub's mobile phone. But as you know, because it's a holiday, getting hold of the right people can be a challenge. A lot of people are on holiday . . .'

Silence on the other end. Me – one, Smeed – zero, Karen notes and continues.

'The real question is whether the perpetrator was looking for the laptop or something else entirely. As soon as we have an answer, or at least a theory—'

'And what do you have for me on potential motives and per- petrators?' Smeed breaks in, as though he wasn't listening. 'Are you *eating* now?' he adds, sounding annoyed.

Karen squashes the impulse to hurl her phone at the wall. Instead, she puts the biscuit down and decides to give him a taste of his own medicine. She takes a deep breath and resumes in a monotone drone, 'Thorstein Byle and I have spoken to Gertrud Stuub. The conversation took place yesterday afternoon between 1.45 and 2.25. Also present was local priest Erling Arve.'

She continues to give a thorough account of every detail of their conversation with a meticulousness she knows must be enervating, and then moves on to inform him of her other activities.

'The autopsy was performed yesterday. I have already conveyed the preliminary results and will, as usual, be given the complete report by coroner Kneought Brodal in due course. Today, I am meeting with the local constables and then Thorstein Byle and I are speaking with Stuub's grand- son, Gabriel, same surname. As the victim's heir, he is a key person in our inquiry and even if he has nothing to do with the murder, we do, as I mentioned, know he saw his grandfa- ther as recently as Christmas Eve. The outcome of that con- versation will determine how I proceed.'

She pauses and throws the cup of tea a longing glance, but Jounas Smeed remains silent, so she continues in the same formal tone.

'We are, of course, also awaiting results from the crime scene investigation, which may take longer than usual. Sören Larsen has warned me not to expect a full report until after New Year's.

But I am certain you have already been told as much by Larsen himself, sir.'

'Lay off the "sir" nonsense, Eiken. I assume you have no problem with me wanting to be kept abreast?'

'Of course not. I will summarise every detail of the investigation in a daily report. You will find it in your inbox no later than eight o'clock every night. Was there anything else?'

Apparently, there wasn't, because Jounas Smeed ends the call.

Why the hell did I have to go and sleep with the bastard? Karen laments inwardly.

20

Three sceptical faces turn to her when she clears her throat and takes a deep breath. Thorstein Byle has done his best, introducing her to his team and emphasising the importance of cooperation and teamwork going forward.

It's a few minutes past eight and they have gathered at the police station in Lysvik for a first meeting. Judging by the blank looks around the table, 'close cooperation based on mutual trust' is not what the local officers have in mind.

'OK, so, Thorstein has already told you most of what needs to be said at the moment,' Karen says. 'I'm aware some of you may not be thrilled about the CID swooping in and taking over the investigation, but I also assume everyone in this room knows that's just procedure when dealing with a serious crime.'

Karen pauses and looks around the table.

'The autopsy was performed yesterday in Ravenby and the coroner is all but certain Fredrik Stuub was murdered,' she continues.

'All but certain? So we're not even sure about that, despite all the wonderful help we've had from the capital?'

The voice belongs to a man of about thirty-five with a shaved head, seated at the far end of the long conference table. He has crossed his muscular arms and is leaning back with his legs stretched out in front of him. Someone chuckles, but a look from Byle quickly turns the mirth into a cough. Karen sighs and has to briefly search her memory for his name. Police Constable Robert Röse, Byle had said.

'No, we're not, but as I'm sure you know, in reality these things are rarely as straightforward as TV makes them out to be. That being said, we do have enough to classify Fredrik Stuub's death as suspicious and continue our investigation.'

Karen outlines Kneought Brodal's preliminary conclusions based on the victim's facial injuries, the drag wounds on his feet and the bruises in the armpits. She passes around a stack of photographs, some from the crime scene and some from the autopsy table.

'The crime scene investigation also supports the theory that Stuub was murdered,' she continues. 'We probably won't have any lab results until after New Year's, but the technicians were able to identify drag marks that closely match the injuries on Stuub's body. Officially, this is only a suspected crime, but in practice there can be no doubt this is murder, or at the very least, manslaughter.'

'Were there any footprints or tyre tracks?'

This time, the question comes from a man who could be Röse's younger brother. The same shaved head and oversized arm muscles. There is none of his colleague's arrogance in his voice, however. Once again, Karen struggles to remember the name Byle gave her. It might have been Andersson. Röse is the arsehole, Andersson seems fine, and what was the name of the quiet woman with the ponytail? Ella . . . Svanberg? No, Svanemark. Well, she seems conscientious, at any rate, Karen muses, glancing at the woman's comprehensive notes.

'According to Larsen we shouldn't get our hopes up about the forensic evidence,' she replies, turning to Andersson. 'In addition to a large number of paw prints from Fredrik Stuub's dog, several sets of shoe prints were secured. Some of them are likely to belong to Gertrud Stuub and as soon as we know the size and type of the others, we can start looking for matches. I'm hopeful those results will come back sooner rather than later. Unfortunately, as far as tyre tracks go, there are far too many of them down by the turning area – from locals dumping rubbish – for there to be any point analysing them. And aside from all the ones that were there already, now there are obviously tracks from the first responders, which is to say emergency services, the doctor . . .'

'. . . and my car,' Thorstein Byle finishes the sentence for her. 'I parked up by the rubbish heap. Some of the footprints are likely mine, too. I'm afraid I didn't pay any mind to where I put my feet . . .'

He trails off, sounding despondent. Chairs creak and eyes are lowered to coffee mugs and water glasses. Clearly, having their superior admit to blundering makes them all uncomfortable.

'But thanks to Thorstein's efforts to quickly establish and guard the perimeter, the crime scene remained as uncompromised as the situation allowed,' Karen says with emphasis and notes a small twitch at the corner of Byle's mouth.

'What's more,' she continues, 'Fredrik Stuub's home was also secured early on. That has turned out to be particularly valuable, as we discovered that the house was searched, presumably by the perpetrator. Before or after the murder, we don't know yet. Nor do we know what the burglar was looking for, or what may be missing. On that, too, we're waiting for answers from the forensic investigation. What I can tell you is that Thorstein and I went to the house yesterday and that Fredrik Stuub's laptop was still there. It's on its way to Dunker as we speak.'

'So I guess that wasn't what the killer was after,' Ella Svanemark puts in. 'But why didn't the technicians take it?'

Karen contemplates how much to reveal.

'It was hidden in a secret compartment in the kitchen. Thorstein found it.'

There is scattered laughter around the table and Karen hears Röse say something about 'southerners'.

She checks her watch.

'Well, as you can tell, we have a lot of work to do. Your job will be to go door to door and check various information and alibis. Thorstein will be giving you your individual assignments and you still report to him. Your local knowledge, experience and contacts will be of crucial importance to this investigation. We will solve this together.'

Something has changed in the small room. Granted, Röse still looks sceptical, but the others seem to have at least temporarily forgotten that the woman in front of them is not only a southerner but an agent of the hateful police headquarters in Dunker. Sadly, that small victory is instantly undone when Röse pipes up once more.

'And what about you?' he demands insolently. 'What are you going to be doing?'

Karen pulls herself up and fixes him with a firm stare. Turns her head slightly to let the light from the window bring out the piercing blue and golden rims of her irises as she gives Robert Röse the look that has been known to make harder men than him back down.

'I will be determining how to proceed,' she says. 'I will lead and delegate. In short, I'm in charge. And you may address me as Detective Inspector Eiken Hornby. Or ma'am – your choice.'

21

'Blimey, how much land do they own?' Karen asks looking out the passenger side window.

They are once again driving the twenty-five miles from Lysvik to Skreby, through barren heathland and past frozen peat bogs. In the distance, the island's two mountain ranges rise up beyond stands of dark green gnarled juniper trees; these, and painstakingly constructed stone walls, are the only breaks in the flatness. Thorstein Byle turns off the highway, westward this time. Gabriel Stuub's house is on the same side of the Skre River as his grandfather's, but on the opposite side of the highway.

This time, instead of driving their own cars, they're in a patrol vehicle. Karen's question is rhetorical; Byle has already told her the Huss family used to own land from Skreby all the way up to the Gudheim county border. And she knows the land has since been divided up into smaller plots, but that most of those are still owned by the mining baron's descendants. Instead of answering, Byle nods toward a house on their right.

'Well, that's Gabriel's house. Unexpected, isn't it?'

The yellow wooden house looks at most ten years old. The white picket fence enclosing the garden seems a bit unnecessary considering that there's at least a few hundred yards to the nearest neighbour. It's hardly the only wooden house on Noorö; in the larger towns – Lysvik, Skreby and Gudheimby – old stone houses coexist with modern wood and brick ones, but in this rural location, Gabriel Stuub's house looks profoundly out of place.

'Why in God's name . . . ?'

'Don't ask me,' Byle says and pulls the key out of the ignition. 'There used to be a lovely old stone house here that they tore down to make room for this monstrosity.'

They open the gate and walk up the gravel path toward the house. Karen notices a small covered swimming pool, two plastic flamingos and a swing set on one side of the house and a two-door garage with something that might be an adjoining workshop on the other. Everything looks neat and well-cared-for. And completely incongruous. As though someone cut out a plot out of suburban Dunker or Ravenby and hurled it out into the middle of the Noorö countryside.

It takes almost four minutes and as many rings of the doorbell to get Gabriel Stuub to the door and another three seconds for Karen to conclude that the man standing before her is not just drowsy but also tremendously hungover. His strawberry blond hair is flat against one side of his face and sticking straight out on the other, his eyes are swollen and squinting against the light. The stale reek of last night's booze wafts out of his mouth when he makes a half-hearted attempt at stifling a yawn. His chest is bare and clearly the result of hours of weightlifting. He tries to button his hastily pulled on jeans with one hand while clutching a mobile phone in the other.

'Good morning,' Karen says with a broad smile. 'We're from the police. May we come in?'

Gabriel Stuub turns without a word and leads them into the house. Byle closes the front door and they follow him through the hallway to the living room in silence. It looks much as Karen expected. Two black leather sofas, a glass coffee table and a recliner with a footstool, bookshelves filled with knick-knacks and model cars, boats and aeroplanes next to a handful of books and photographs. Karen and Byle choose opposite ends of one of the sofas.

Gabriel is just about to slump into the recliner when he changes his mind and instead walks quickly back toward the hallway. Byle is about to follow, but Karen stops him with a shake of her head. Even if Gabriel is planning to make a run for it, at this particular moment, he clearly has more pressing concerns.

She pulls out her notebook, rolls her eyes at Byle, studies her cuticles and bites off a hangnail while they patiently listen to the retching coming from the bathroom. After a few minutes they hear the flush of the toilet, a running tap, a door opening, heavy steps, the sound of the fridge door opening followed by the hiss of a bottle cap, and then Gabriel Stuub appears in the kitchen doorway, now with wet, slicked-back hair and a can of sports drink in his hand.

'Can we start?' Karen asks with a smile.

Gabriel slowly lowers himself into the recliner and puts his feet up on the footstool. Leans back and takes a sip out of the can.

'Sure,' he says. 'What do you want?'

'As I'm sure you've figured out, we're here in connection with your grandfather's death. Let me start by offering my condolences.'

Gabriel nods mutely.

'First, we need some information about you.'

She quickly runs through the initial questions and Gabriel delivers his answers with a look of bored resignation. Thirty-five years old, two children, Loke and Lava, six and four years old, separated from his wife Katja since a few months ago. She has moved back in with her parents in Thorsvik down on Heimö. No, she's not originally from Noorö. Why did she move out instead of him? Because this is all his, obviously. He inherited the land from his mother and built the house himself. Katja didn't put a penny into it. He has no bloody idea what her plans are and he doesn't give a toss so long as she doesn't try to screw him out of seeing the kids. He wants every other weekend, no more, no less. Yes, he was informed about his grandfather's death the day it happened, by both the Noorö Police and the local priest. Yes, as far as he knows, he's Fredrik's closest living descendant; no, he doesn't know whether Fredrik left anything of value, they weren't particularly close. Why not? Well, he supposes Fredrik didn't consider him an ideal grandson.

'And yet you did see him the day before he died?' Karen says, fixing him with a firm stare below raised eyebrows.

Gabriel hesitates, as though he's actually searching his memory.

'Right, but that was bloody Christmas Eve, for crying out loud,' he says, spreading his hands.

'So you did see both Fredrik and Gertrud from time to time?'

'Well, not normally, I mean; not on an everyday basis, but of course it happened on occasion. Mostly on the holidays. I mean, we're bloody family and live just a few miles from each other.'

'So you went to Gertrud's house on Christmas Eve. Had she invited you?'

125

'She called that morning and the kids were here, so . . . yeah, I popped over. Figured they should meet my side of the family, too, not just Katja's. I was supposed to drive down to Thorsvik and drop them off with her the next day.'

'And did you? Drop the children off with Katja, I mean?'

Gabriel Stuub takes a deep swig of his sports drink and wipes his mouth with the back of his hand.

'Yep,' he replies.

'And what time was that? When you left home, I mean.'

'I don't know. Just after eight, maybe quarter past. I managed to catch the nine o'clock ferry, I know that, but I was in for it anyway.'

'What do you mean?'

'Katja. Or her parents, actually. I'd promised to drop the kids off no later than nine and I was thirty minutes late.'

'Has there been a lot of conflict? Since they were so upset, I mean?'

'Why? What's that got to do with anything?'

'What do you do for a living?'

Her tactic works. For a moment, Gabriel Stuub looks completely bewildered by the sudden change of subject. His eyes dart back and forth between Karen and Byle, as though looking for a fixed point.

'Up at Groth's,' he replies weakly. 'Bottling and shipping.'

'And who's your supervisor?'

Gabriel seems to ponder that for a moment.

'I suppose that would be Jens. He's some kind of sales manager, or whatever title he's given himself, but we all work pretty independently.'

'Surname?'

126

'Groth, obviously. Jens Groth. He's the son of Björn, the owner of the whole thing.'

Karen makes a note.

'What time was it when you left your grandfather?'

This time, the change of focus has a physical effect. Gabriel Stuub's cheeks take on a slightly green tinge and he clutches the recliner's armrests, as though trying to steady himself. For a moment, Karen is concerned he might throw up again. Then he runs a hand across his forehead and slowly shakes his head.

'Honestly, I don't know what you're getting at. Which time are you bloody talking about?'

'Christmas Eve. You drove your grandfather home unless I'm mistaken. Or did you see him after that?'

Karen notices the colour returning to his face with a measure of relief. Gabriel meets her eyes.

'No, I didn't. I left him in the driveway and went straight home with the kids. No idea what time it was, but my best guess would be around half past three. And no, I haven't seen him since.'

'And you haven't been back to his house? To look for something maybe?'

'Look for something? What would I want from his house?'

'A laptop, maybe?'

Gabriel chuckles. Maybe a bit too loudly, Karen muses.

'Are you sure he even had one? He still had an old-style TV and a transistor radio.'

'Sure, but your grandfather did teach at the university. Apparently did research as well. Are you telling me he used pen and paper?'

'I'm sure he had a computer at work. And probably some old doorstop at home, too.'

127

'Any idea where we might find it?'

'I didn't bloody steal his computer! The old git probably hid it somewhere. Honestly, I think he went a bit senile after Mum died.'

'How did that manifest itself? Your grandfather's dementia, I mean.'

Gabriel shoots her an annoyed look when he picks up on the discreet correction.

'I don't know. I guess it's just that he seemed completely obsessed with this fucking island and all kinds of historical crap. Going on and on about the olden days and that now all people want is to make money and they don't care about anything else. All I'm saying is that he was a bit doddery.'

Sounds more astute than doddery, Karen thinks to herself.

'Did he direct his ire at anyone in particular?' she asks.

'I don't know, I stopped listening whenever he got worked up. He wasn't stupid, though,' Gabriel adds suddenly, 'just old, OK? Let's be bloody clear about that.'

Noting his tone and look, Karen feels her spirits sink. Could this man, likely candidate that he is, at least on paper, really have killed his grandfather? Well, maybe, but if so, he killed someone he liked more than he cares to admit, even to himself.

She decides to change the subject.

'Your mother passed away early, I've been told?'

Gabriel lets out a bitter laugh.

'Yep, liver cancer caused by Hepatitis C. Turns out dirty needles are kind of frowned upon as far as causes of death are concerned. More like, she got what she deserved, if you catch my drift.'

'So your mother was a drug addict?'

128

A shrug of the shoulders to confirm and create distance.

'Heroin, rehab, relapse and all that jazz. She was clean for a few years before she died, but it was too late.'

He trails off and stares at the rug. Karen watches him in silence and feels a pang of pity. Behind the muscles and arrogance, Gabriel is the son of a junkie, the grandson of a disappointed grandfather. Could that be the motive? In the heat of the moment, triggered by his grandfather's indifference?

'And your father . . . ?'

'What about him?'

'I meant to ask who he is.'

'You've been listening to the local gossip and want to know if it's Allan Jonshed.'

Karen waits and notes out of the corner of her eye that Byle is shifting uncomfortably.

'Wouldn't that be convenient?' Gabriel says with a mirthless chuckle. 'If there was a connection to the president of the OP. But I'm afraid you're just not that lucky.'

Apparently not, Karen thinks to herself.

'Then who is he? Your father, I mean,' she says.

'Well, according to Mum, it was either a drummer from Newcastle or some bloke she met on the ferry. I don't fucking know. And I don't care.'

Karen shoots Byle a quick look to see if he has any further questions. As expected, he shakes his head. Karen sighs. Thorstein Byle may be affable and accommodating, but he clearly isn't equal to this challenge. I'm going to need someone else from the CID soon, she muses. Karl Björken, Cornelis Loots, Astrid Nielsen . . . Anybody, even that damn Johannisen would be better than nothing. Well, no, maybe not Johannisen.

'All right,' she says. 'One last question. Can you think of anyone who might have wanted to hurt your grandfather? Anyone who stood to gain from his death?'

'Other than me? No, no one.'

No surprises there, Karen notes. But shouldn't he have assumed his grandfather's death was an accident? As though he can read her mind, Gabriel suddenly adds, 'Wait a minute, what do you mean? I thought the old man slipped?'

'I think we need to stop by the distillery tomorrow,' Karen says ten minutes later when they're back in the car.

'To talk to William Tryste?'

'Exactly. They're distantly related somehow and he saw Fredrik at Gertrud's house on Christmas Eve, too. William and his wife Helena stopped by to give her flowers, according to Gertrud. And I would also like to talk to someone who works with Gabriel up there. Something about that guy bothers me.'

22

The post-Christmas slump envelops the local Skreby pub, The Lantern, like a soft blanket when Karen sits down at one of the free window tables. She looks out at the crowded room where about forty men of varying age are enjoying a moment of relaxation after fulfilling their Christmas obligations. The relief of getting away from wives, children, grandchildren, in-laws and relatives you now won't have to see for another year – unless a wedding or a funeral spoils that plan – is palpable in the quiet din. A handful of women have also found their way to The Lantern tonight for some sorely needed downtime. Or two, to be exact, Karen herself included. Probably single, she thinks, studying the middle-aged woman in the corner, who is reading a book in the company of a bottle of red wine. Christmas may be non-stop joy for children and non-stop work for women, but holiday exhaustion and the need for recuperation are apparently exclusively male.

An uninvited memory of celebrating Christmas in the Hornbys' posh residence in Surrey intrudes on her thoughts – stiff and groaning under the weight of tradition and no expense spared. So different from her own childhood Christmases in Langevik. So different from how she, John and Mathis celebrated by themselves on Christmas Eve, according to Scandinavian custom. Karen's mother was always invited – and always declined.

'I'm not going to *England* for Christmas, now that I'm finally free to put my feet up. But I'd love to visit in the spring.'

Karen had done her best not to feel hurt by the fact that all the traditions, which she was trying to keep alive, had apparently been nothing but chores for her mother, obligations she seemed relieved to be free of. Eleanor Eiken had never been nostalgic and was definitely not religious.

So Christmas Eve in London had been just theirs, Karen's, John's and Mathis's. And over the years, they had created their own traditions: a long, late breakfast, a Christmas Eve walk during which Karen would complain about the lack of snow, John about the lack of sun and Mathis about having to go for a walk at all. Herring in all its forms, smoked lamb ribs and red cabbage for dinner. No Heimö liquor – that's where John had drawn the line – and Karen had secretly been grateful she had to wash the lamb down with a nice red instead. Gifts in the evening and then a big jigsaw puzzle on the kitchen table (while Mathis furtively played on his Game Boy under the table), big cups of hot chocolate, a healthy splash of rum in hers and John's, a fistful of marshmallows in Mathis's. Christmas Day and Boxing Day belonged to the Hornbys, but Christmas Eve was theirs.

John's parents were never anything but welcoming. And yet, Karen had never felt as though she fitted in fully, had always known she probably wasn't the daughter-in-law they'd hoped for from the tolerant smiles at her strange accent, which became more pronounced when she felt nervous; the polite questions about Doggerian Christmas traditions and the nods and comments along the lines of 'how wonderfully quaint' or 'so delightfully rustic' when she described them; the discreetly exchanged glances that made it clear that what they really meant was 'simple and unsophisticated'.

'You're imagining it,' John had said, and she'd let him believe he was right. Not to spare him, but because she knew there was nothing else he could say.

The first few years had been the most difficult; eventually, her in-laws' love for Mathis had eased the worst of their stiffness. John's father had turned out to possess a dry wit Karen had learnt to appreciate and, as a retired prosecutor, he had shown a genuine interest in her criminology studies. Unlike John's mother, he had been supportive of her decision to resume her studies once Mathis was old enough to go to preschool, and Karen suspected he had put in a good word for her when she applied to join a research project about the potential impact of economic factors on verdicts in rape cases. They had rarely agreed on anything, but their discussions had been genuinely interesting.

But afterwards, not a word. Not even their deep-seated instinct for propriety had been able to induce Richard and Theresa Hornby to look the woman who they felt had robbed them of their son and grandson in the eye. Not even at the funeral.

Karen is grateful and annoyed in equal measure when she is snapped out of her reverie by her phone. She checks her watch: ten past seven. She had promised Smeed he would have his daily updates by eight. Or had she told him seven? If this is him calling to demand it, I won't be able to keep it polite, she has time to think while digging through her coat pocket. She is relieved to find that it's not Jounas Smeed calling.

'Hi, Aylin!' she says and leans back. 'You have no idea how happy I am it's you.'

A chuckle on the other end. A small one. Hesitant.

'Really? Well, I'm actually not sure why I'm calling. Just had a minute and thought . . .'

Sadness suddenly washes over Karen. It feels like something she wants to hold on to is dissolving and slipping through her fingers. Is this what they've come to? Do they need a special reason to call each other now after being friends for ten years? They first got to know each other when Karen had just moved back to Doggerland, crippled by grief. Aylin had just divorced Eirik's brother. After four years of unsuccessful attempts to conceive, Aylin had found out that her husband had fallen in love with a Norwegian flight attendant whom he'd managed to knock up on the first try. And Eirik had fought a three-front war, determined to both bring Karen back from the dead and console his ex-sister-in-law, while struggling with his parents' revulsion at what they called 'his choice of lifestyle'. Battered and broken, the three of them had supported each other, like a rickety three-legged stool.

A couple of years later, Marike had joined their group and, soon after, Kore had turned Eirik's world upside down. And then Bo Ramnes had done the same to Aylin's. But rather than bringing a new friend into their circle, his appearance had led to Aylin drifting away. Bo Ramnes turned out to have no interest in socialising with a couple of gays, a Danish art hag and a copper. And the feeling was mutual.

Maybe I should have tried harder, Karen thinks now and presses the phone to her ear to shut out the pub noise.

'Good thinking,' she says, 'it's been too long. I don't think we've seen each other since my birthday, have we?'

'Just once. I actually visited you in the hospital, but you were pretty out of it.'

'Oh, right. I do remember you coming to see me. That was a good book you gave me, by the way.'

'I know I should have been in touch more, but things have just been so . . .'

Aylin trails off again.

'Don't worry about it, I know you have a lot on your plate. Because you were going to back to work, weren't you, now that the kids are both in nursery?'

'Yes, that was the plan, but then we decided I should stay home a while longer. At least until the end of the summer.'

'We', Karen scoffs inwardly, remembering how happy Aylin had looked when she told her she was finally going to be able to go back to work. Clearly Bo prefers to keep her chained to the stove while he transitions from law into politics. As a newly minted candidate for the conservative Progress Party, he can probably get more votes with a stay-at-home wife who dedicates her life to her husband and children.

Karen hadn't been surprised in the slightest to learn about Bo Ramnes' decision to get into politics, or his choice of party. But the risk of him quickly rising much higher than she would have ever thought possible has suddenly become a distinct possibility. After two terms of strained Social Democrat-Liberal coalition government and a media scandal involving both the Minister for Justice and the Fisheries Board, the Progress Party smells an opportunity.

And, Karen reflects dolefully, enough Doggerians are probably willing to ignore what the party's message of 'sound values and law and order' is really code for.

'Yes,' Aylin says, 'I wanted to ask if you're going to be home tomorrow morning. Could I maybe come by?'

Karen is so taken aback by the question it takes her several seconds to respond. It's been years since Aylin last suggested they meet up for coffee. An eternity since they got together just to talk. Do we even have anything to say to each other anymore? she suddenly wonders. Then joy crashes over her. Aylin is calling, asking to see her; of course they have all kinds of things to talk about.

'That would have been lovely,' she says truthfully, 'but I'm actually up on Noorö. There's been a death here that needs investigating, so I had to drop everything.'

'You're working? But I thought you were still on sick leave?'

'I was, but I was honestly kind of relieved when I got a chance to escape all the Christmas stuff. Though I'm starting to regret it, things are less than cheery up here.'

'I can imagine.'

There's a pause.

'Was there something in particular you wanted to talk about?' Karen asks. 'You don't have time to stop by a lot these days,' she adds, instantly wishing she hadn't.

She doesn't want to sound accusatory now that Aylin has finally made some time away from her husband and wants to see her. Aylin's next sentence explains the situation.

'Yes, I know, but Bo is away for a few days, so I wanted to seize the opportunity. Like I said, I really just wanted to have a cup of coffee and see how you're doing.'

'I'm fine, aside from my knee still hurting sometimes and my boss having decided to demand daily written reports. But how are you? You sound a bit down.'

Aylin lets out another chuckle.

'Just tired. Both the kids have the flu and I have a headache and chills, so I'm worried I'm next.'

'Oh dear, well, I've been lucky enough to—'

'Actually,' Aylin cuts in, 'Bo is calling, so I have to hang up now. But I'll see you at Eirik and Kore's on New Year's Eve.'

Before Karen can tell her they probably won't be seeing each other on New Year's, Aylin has hung up.

New Year's Eve. The first big party Eirik and Kore are throwing in their enormous new house in Thingwalla. The party she spent weeks of mind-numbingly boring physical therapy looking forward to. Now, there's a real risk she may be spending New Year's alone in a hotel room on Noorö. And of course Bo has to interrupt when Aylin finally calls.

Karen puts the phone down with a deep sigh and opens her laptop. She wouldn't have had time to talk to Aylin anyway if she wants to send her damn report off before eight.

23

'If you have time, I can give you a tour after you've asked your questions? I'm afraid the place is a bit dead between Christmas and New Year's, but I'd be happy to show you around.'

The man standing before them extends his hand and looks at them with an expectant smile. His long, slightly gawky body is casually dressed in jeans and a blue jumper, which with notable exactness matches his eye colour. His hair is cut very short, in a style that often hints at the onset of male pattern baldness, but a dark blanket of hair covers every square inch of William Tryste's head. He is unreasonably good-looking, Karen muses.

Groth's distillery is located in Gudheim County, at the eastern tip of the narrow promontory that juts straight out into the sea. Karen passed it many times as a child. Every summer when she went with her relatives to the large cemetery by Gudheim church, the Eikens would also swing by the ship setting at the island's northernmost point. As a child, she thought of the two events as inextricably linked. Now, she realises, with a forty-year delay, that the visit to the ship setting must have been for her benefit. The place might be a draw for teenagers, new age types and the occasional tourist, but hardly for locals. She been impressed by the distillery's large red-brick buildings but stopping for a closer look had always been out of the question. At least with her in the car.

'That sounds interesting, but I'm afraid we don't have time for that today. Maybe some other time,' she adds with a smile.

William Tryste leads them through the wide double doors into a large lobby with a reception desk, display cabinets and brochure stands, past a narrow hallway with closed doors on either side and through the heart of the distillery with its enormous, pear-shaped copper stills. Eventually, they find themselves in a room that looks like a conflation of a conference room and an office. On their right is a long table surrounded by twelve chairs, two of the walls are covered in floor-to-ceiling bookshelves and the space between the two tall windows is occupied by a massive antique leather-top desk.

Why would anyone choose to sit with their back to that view? Karen wonders, gazing out at the unbroken horizon. Maybe so they can get something done, she answers her own question.

Prompted by a welcoming gesture from their host, Karen and Thorstein Byle sit down at opposite ends of a long, dark-brown leather sofa. William Tryste politely waits until they are seated before hitching up his trouser legs and sinking into one of the two large Chesterfield armchairs across from them. The coffee table is made of a thick slab of glass set on top of two old oak barrels and resting on it is a tray with three cups, a teapot and a plate of shortbread.

'Maybe you've visited the distillery before?' Tryste asks.

'I haven't,' Karen says and looks around. 'But I'm not unfamiliar with your products,' she adds with a wry smile. 'Have you been here before?'

She turns to Thorstein Byle, who nods.

'I have, but it must be ten years ago, maybe fifteen.'

'Oh, a lot has changed since then!' William Tryste exclaims and leans forward to fill their teacups. 'And there's more to come. Milk?'

Karen's eyes are drawn to the windows once more. No curtains to obscure the view and the sea is so close it feels like sitting in the prow of a large ship. Not too shabby for an office, she thinks enviously, picturing the Dunker police station where the Doggerland Criminal Investigation Department is headquartered. The building, an architectural fiasco from the seventies, is as menacing on the outside as it is dull on the inside and the locals have appropriately taken to calling it The Bunker. William Tryste's office at Groth's distillery is the very antithesis of The Bunker.

'This is as far north as you can get in this country,' Tryste says, noticing Karen's gaze. 'Well, with the exception of the ship setting, of course. But this is the northernmost building on the island. The northernmost building on *any* of the Doggerian Islands, in fact,' he adds with poorly concealed pride.

Karen tears her eyes away from the view and turns her attention to their host.

'Have you worked here long?'

William Tryste shakes his head.

'Just over a year. I've spent most of my career at various Scottish distilleries and I did a stint in Japan, too, but then I was offered this opportunity and it was too good to turn down.'

Japan, Karen thinks to herself, but before she can express her surprise, Thorstein Byle pipes up.

'From what I gather, hiring you was a bit of a coup for the Groth family,' he says with a smile. 'You're known as one of the industry's top noses.'

William Tryste spreads his hands and returns the smile.

'Let's just say everyone's happy,' he replies. 'For me, it's a chance to move back home and be part of an exciting process. Groth's distillery is obviously very small compared to most of its competitors, but quality has always been its watchword. And now, like I said, we have big plans.'

'Oh?' Byle says and leans forward.

Karen studies him with surprise. He hasn't been anywhere near this engaged before. She would never have guessed whiskey would be what finally brought him out of his shell.

'Oh yes,' Tryste replies. 'We're going to take the fight to the Scots and the Japanese.'

'I hear they make good stuff over there now,' Byle says with a nod. 'But personally, I would never buy Japanese whiskey. Or Taiwanese for that matter, I don't care how good they say it is.'

'You're not the only one who feels that way. A lot of whiskey connoisseurs are conservative and would never buy a single malt from anywhere but Scotland,' Tryste says with a smile. 'But luckily for us here at Groth's, enough of them will go where the quality is.'

He sounds like he's reading a press statement, Karen thinks and leans back to wait for Byle and Tryste to finish their small talk. She doesn't want to interrupt, now that her colleague is finally talking.

'Yes, I've heard rumours about an expansion,' Byle says. 'Doubling your production, or was it even more? A lot of new jobs, they say.'

'That's not the half of it. I should really let Björn Groth tell you himself, but unfortunately he's not here today. If you're interested, I have some sketches and blueprints I could—'

Karen decides it's time to bring the conversation back around to the reason they came.

'Unfortunately, we're a bit pressed for time,' she cuts in. 'As you know, we have some other things we wanted to talk to you about.'

'Yes, of course,' William Tryste says, and his enthusiastic smile winks out abruptly. 'It's terrible, what happened. Erling Arve informed me on the day. He's the local priest,' he adds as an explanation for Karen.

'We've met,' she says. 'At Gertrud Stuub's house. And that's actually one of the two reason's we're here. According to Gertrud, you stopped by to see her and Fredrik on Christmas Eve. Is that correct?'

'Yes, that's right. My wife and I actually even managed to persuade our very reluctant son to go with us. But we didn't stay long, maybe half an hour. Helena's sister and her family were coming up to celebrate Christmas Eve with us, so we had to get back. I think I was the one who insisted we at least pop in to say hello. You know what it's like, Christmas is Christmas and family is family.'

Karen glances down at her notepad, which is covered with scribbled names and arrows.

'Your grandmother was Gertrud and Fredrik's sister, if I've understood things right. Were you close, you and Fredrik?'

William shakes his head.

'Not particularly. After my parents got divorced, my sister and I moved to England with our mum. She had family there, so it made sense. But Dad's family goes back generations on the island. My grandmother's father owned a lot of mines here and Dad was given the unenviable task of taking over the business

142

when he died. He tried to salvage whatever he could when the mining industry imploded, but it was a fool's errand, as I'm sure you know. My sister and I would visit on the holidays, and I've holidayed here quite a bit as an adult, but I didn't move back properly until a year ago. So, to answer your question, no, I didn't know Fredrik particularly well.'

'OK. Let's go back to Christmas Eve. Did you notice anything unusual about Fredrik? Did he seem troubled or worried at all?'

William Tryste's gaze drifts toward the windows, as though he's searching his memory.

'No,' he says slowly. 'I don't think so. Or actually . . . no, it's probably nothing.'

'Why don't you let us be the judge of that. What were you going to say?'

'I had the impression Fredrik and Gabriel had quarrelled just before we arrived. I didn't hear anything, but the mood was a bit strained between them when we got there. Helena and I actually discussed it in the car when we left.'

'But you don't know what they might have been quarrelling about?'

'No idea. Like I said, it was just a feeling I had.'

Karen sighs. She's going to have to speak to both Gertrud and Gabriel again.

'Gabriel works at the distillery, doesn't he?'

'That's right. Bottling and shipping. But if you want a performance review, you'll have to speak to Jens Groth. He manages the logistics, once I'm done with my sniffing. I think he's around today, but if he is, he's probably in the warehouse. That's where his office is.'

'And what exactly is your role?'

143

'Well, you might say I'm in charge of quality.'

William Tryste leans back and gives an enthusiastic and detailed account of his duties, which include overseeing the maturing process, determining which whiskeys to blend and which to preserve as single malts, and deciding when it's time for bottling.

'I'm also in charge of the industrial marketing of our products. I leave consumer marketing and sales to Björn and Jens. Björn Groth,' he adds. 'He's the owner, along with his children, Jens and Madeleine. Groth's is a family business.'

'OK,' Karen says when William Tryste finally stops talking. 'I only have one more question. Can you tell me where you were on the morning of Christmas Day, between half past seven and half past nine?'

It takes William Tryste a few seconds to grasp the implications of the question.

'Where I was? Are you serious?'

'I'm afraid so. But it's a question we're asking everyone we talk to. To rule them out, if nothing else. If Fredrik's death turns out not to have been an accident.'

William Tryste still looks taken aback.

'Well, I guess I'm lucky, then. Normally, I would have been asleep, but on that particular morning, I was in Lysvik.'

Karen raises her eyebrows as a signal for Tryste to go on.

'I wasn't completely honest before. One of the reasons Helena and I decided to move back to Noorö was that our son, Alvin, had started using drugs. We spent our last few years in Scotland and there's no shortage of them there, as I'm sure you know. We realised we had to take drastic measures before things got worse. So when this opportunity at Groth's opened up, we jumped at it.'

'And what does that have to do with Christmas Day?'

'The thing is that we've promised to pay for Alvin's driving licence and buy him a car if he can hold on to his job and stay out of trouble. We've given up on making him study, at least for now, and he works at the nursing home in Lysvik. He's just a care assistant; he cleans and helps with the heavy lifting and sits vigil when needed. Anyway, his shift started at seven on Christmas Day and there are no buses on the weekends, so I'd promised to drive him. Or rather, to let him practise driving with me. You can ask him.'

'His shift started at seven, you said? What did you do after dropping him off?'

'I visited my father. He has Alzheimer's and lives at the nursing home, so I wanted to stop by, even though he doesn't really know what day it is. And if you promise not to tell the staff, I suppose I could confess to bringing him a few treats.'

Karen ponders Ivar Tryste's tragic fate for a moment. A grandchild of the old mining baron, he clearly lacked his power and influence. Loathed by the locals and denounced by the media for failing to save the mining industry from its inevitable demise. Then his wife left him and took the children and now that his son has finally moved back, he's too senile to be aware of it.

'We've obviously tried to bring Dad home to visit,' William Tryste continues, 'but he's so far gone now the change of scenery seems to do more harm than good. But he's still my father and I figured the least I could do for him was to smuggle in a piece of herring and a stiff drink on Christmas.'

'Herring and snaps at seven in the morning?'

Karen regrets her comment. She sincerely doubts many people still have pickled herring and snaps for breakfast, even on Noorö, but it used to be common, she reminds herself, and pictures the

145

snaps bottle next to the milk pitcher on the breakfast table in her aunt's kitchen.

'Only for the menfolk,' Ingeborg would declare, slapping away her cousin Finn's optimistically extended hand.

'Yes, the older generation's breakfast habits can be a bit hard on the digestion,' William Tryste replies with a smile, 'but that's how they did things back then and I figured it couldn't do Dad any harm to have something to remind him of the good old days. Besides, when I arrived, he'd already been up for a couple of hours. He was awake when I left, too, in case you're wondering. Though I suppose you can't really ask him, more often than not he doesn't even recognise me anymore.'

'Did any of the staff see you?' Thorstein Byle puts in.

'Doubtful. I went in with Alvin, but then we parted ways. He works up on the hospital floor, but it's the same entrance. It's possible someone saw me, but I had no interest in broadcasting my presence. I don't think the staff would have been thrilled to see the snaps, even if it was just a tipple.'

'And how long did you spend with him?' Karen says and reflects that William Tryste doesn't seem to have any obvious motive for wanting his distant relative dead, but on the other hand, he doesn't seem to have an alibi, either.

'Maybe an hour. Yes, it was just about eight o'clock when I got back out to the car. I remember, because I'd promised to call Helena to wake her up.'

Karen's heart sinks.

'You called home from Lysvik? From your mobile?'

William Tryste looks genuinely nonplussed.

'Yes . . .' he says slowly, then the penny suddenly seems to drop. 'Oh, right, of course, I guess you can check things like that.'

24

Aylin Ramnes opens the lid of her round concealer palette. The bottom is already showing in the green section and she's almost out of the skin-coloured one. Maybe she should buy a separate jar of each colour, but having all of them in the same kit is so convenient. Especially when she has bruises at different stages of healing. I have to remember to buy a new one before I run out completely, she reminds herself, adjusting the angle of the mirror and leaning forward.

The thumbprints on her neck are almost gone now, but the bruise on her cheek is proving stubborn. Instead of fading, it seems to have drifted south, creating the illusion that her right cheekbone is higher than her left. She contemplates the concealer wheel, pondering which shade to use while doing her best to ignore the sound of her heart thumping in her ears. One of the light pink ones on the blue, probably, and the green one to hide the red crack in her lip. Or is it the other way around?'

Focus. You know how to do this.

A sudden weariness makes her arms feel heavy, as though she won't be able to lift them. For a moment she considers not bothering since she's not seeing Karen anyway. She puts the round palette down on the edge of the sink and stares blankly into the mirror's magnifying glass, at a blurred kaleidoscope of different shades of beige, blue and yellow.

Was it really yesterday I talked to Karen? she marvels. It feels like a dream now. Or at least like it was weeks ago. I remember how happy she sounded when she heard it was me. Surprised at first, but then . . . yes, happy.

Her throat feels tight when she swallows and she wonders dully whether it's because she's about to start crying or if it's the pressure from Bo's thumbs against her larynx still making itself known.

Why on earth had she called? So pointless. So risky. She had known it when she started going through her contact list looking for Karen's number: if I do this, there's no way back.

Now, she can't recall what they talked about. Just that her disappointment at learning Karen was on Noorö and couldn't meet up had been accompanied by an equal measure of relief. No, she corrects herself, her relief had by far outweighed her disappointment, why lie about it? She can't remember anything after that. Karen had prattled on and she had probably said things, too. Set her mouth on autopilot, maybe adopted that carefree tone she has become so good at, while waiting for the phone call to be over. And she'd kept a firm grip on one of her thumbs the whole time as a reminder to erase Karen's number from her call log before Bo could have a chance to go through it. She hadn't completely lost her mind.

What was I thinking?

Karen would have made her tell the truth this time if they'd met up. Granted, Aylin had known as much when she made the call, but she had ignored the alarm bells going off in her head. She had sat with her phone in her hand for almost an hour, hesitating and reconsidering until she finally gave in to a longing that was too overwhelming. A longing to hear a voice from her past, from before. A longing to spew out the whole ugly truth about her failure and humiliation. A longing to let Karen's fury take over and carry her, since she's unable to summon any anger of her own. To let Karen cry her tears.

But then . . . ? Nothing. No thought, no plan, no strategy. No strength. Not anymore.

Karen has all those things, she tells herself. At least when it's about someone else. She has never been good at dealing with her own problems. And that thought grants her a moment's relief; she's not the only one with problems; everyone has their cross to bear. Then reality catches up with her. Not like mine.

Normal people don't have to deal with this.

Normal people would never end up in this situation. What happened to Karen ten years ago wasn't her fault, but I have only myself to blame. Karen would never understand. She would think there's a way out, a solution, deliverance.

As though anyone anywhere could ever win against Bo Ramnes.

That thought snaps her back to reality. Aylin quickly glances at her watch. She has to start dinner in half an hour. She leans closer to the mirror and expertly assesses today's make-up needs. Maybe things would heal faster if I didn't cover them up with creams and powders. But even as she allows herself to toy with the idea, she realises she can't do it; the children would ask, at least Tyra would. Or even worse, they might just look at her with those silent, frightened eyes. No, for their sakes, she has to make the best of the situation. Besides, Bo

149

would be furious if she forced him to see what she really looks like without make-up. Especially now that he's going through such a difficult time, with so much stress at work and all that pressure from the party, too.

Provoking him is the last thing she wants to do.

25

'OK, well, at least that's easily checked with his service provider,' Karen says quietly to Byle ten minutes later as they're walking five paces behind William Tryste on their way to the warehouse. 'He talks a lot, doesn't he? Chattering away like a street vendor on speed, hawking his wares.'

Thorstein Byle smiles.

'I suppose,' he says. 'But, then, I probably would, too, if I had his job. I assume sipping single malts all day is more fun than writing tickets for home distilling and speeding. And in this place, too,' he adds, nodding at the view.

As they follow William Tryste across the yard, he continues his enthusiastic monologue, frequently hollering back over his shoulder to make himself heard over the wind and the crashing of the waves:

'We make everything on site here at Groth's, from grain to loaf, so to speak. Or in our case, from barley to bottle. A lot of distilleries buy their malt these days – there are even some who call themselves whiskey makers despite not even making their own mash. But we have everything we need here on Noorö, barley, water, peat . . . Did you know we still use old-fashioned yeast logs? As far as I know, we're the only distillery that does.'

When Thorstein Byle starts to ask follow-up questions about fermentation effect, Karen stops listening. Tryste's enthusiasm is both endearing and exhausting.

William Tryste leads them at a brisk pace toward the warehouse where Jens Groth is supposedly to be found. As they pass a long two-storey building, he stops and turns around.

'This is the malt house, by the way. I started out in one of these, but in Scotland, obviously. Checked the temperature, turned the wet barley, opened and closed the windows to maintain a constant temperature. You want the barley to germinate, but you have to stop that process at the exact right moment for drying and smoking. Are you sure you don't have time for a proper tour?'

'I'm afraid not,' Karen says quickly. 'At least, not today, but some other time would be great,' she adds.

Next, they stop outside a big brick building. Large sections of its exterior are stained black by the coal soot that seems to cover everything on the island like a film. Up here, it looks as though any attempts to remove it have long since been given up. When they enter through the big double doors, Karen lets out an involuntarily gasp. Looking down the long, narrow aisle, flanked on either side by oak barrels all the way to the ceiling, makes her feel suddenly dizzy. For a brief moment she's convinced the racks are about to collapse and bury them under tonnes of whiskey-scented oakwood, but she has no time to indulge that thought. Tryste finally seems to have abandoned his role as their guide and is hurrying further into the warehouse. The air is damp and raw and they pass countless perpendicular aisles, each flanked by floor-to-ceiling racks holding large oak barrels full of maturing whiskey. Eventually, Tryste stops outside a closed door and

Karen realises with some surprise they haven't run into a single one of the distillery's employees.

'Most people are on leave until after New Year's,' Tryste says as though he could hear her unspoken question. 'But Jens is supposed to be here.' He taps a quick tattoo on the door and opens it without waiting for a reply.

'Hi, there, Jens,' he says. 'The police are here to ask some questions. Is it OK if I abscond now?' he adds, addressing Karen. 'The wife wouldn't be best pleased if I was late coming home again . . .'

'Absolutely. We'll be in touch if there's anything else.'

Behind a large L-shaped desk sits a blond man with glasses pushed up to his forehead. His unkempt hair is standing straight up, as though he has been frantically running his hands through it. He gets up and extends his hand with a friendly, slightly quizzical smile. Even though the room is cool, there are dark pit stains on his grey T-shirt. His stocky build hints at an impending transformation from what might still pass for a thickset young man into a fat old codger.

'Jens Groth,' he says. 'You're welcome, of course, though I'm not sure how I can help.'

Jens Groth may be one of the distillery's owners, but his office is considerably less grand than William Tryste's, Karen notes while she and Byle sit down on chairs in front of the desk, which is almost hidden under countless stacks of paper. Jens Groth carefully pushes two of the stacks aside, as though to create a corridor for communication with his visitors.

'There's a lot of paperwork in this business,' he says with a weary smile. 'So, what can I do for you?'

'Gabriel Stuub,' Karen says and pulls out her notepad. 'He works here, doesn't he?'

'Yes, that's right. Aha, I heard about his grandfather. Is that why you're here? But that was a tragic accident, from what I've been told.'

Karen doesn't answer the unspoken question.

'Can you tell us a little about Gabriel?' she says and notes that Jens Groth's eyes turn to Thorstein Byle, as though looking for an explanation.

'Gabriel? Is he in trouble?'

'We're talking to everyone who has a connection to Fredrik Stuub's family,' Byle replies evasively.

The absurdity of his statement seems not to register with Jens Groth.

'Right, I see,' he says. 'Well, what do you want to know?'

'How long has Gabriel worked here?' Karen says, clicking her pen and smoothing the page of her notebook with her wrist. She probably won't make more than a handful of brief notes – she rarely does – but she knows from experience that the sight of the notepad tends to sharpen people's recall.

Groth shrugs.

'His whole life, I imagine. Well, his whole adult life, I should say,' he adds with a smile. 'No child labour here.'

Karen smiles back without comment.

'I would think,' Jens Groth continues, 'that he was about seventeen or eighteen when he started. I was away at university at the time, but if it's important, I can check.'

They must be about the same age, Karen muses. One went to university, one went straight from school to working in the warehouse. That means Gabriel has spent half his life working

154

for the Groths, and it's probably going to be as long again unless he leaves the island for some reason. In the olden days, the mines provided jobs, now all that's left is Groth's or the oil platforms, and something tells her NoorOyl with their rigorous safety protocols would think twice about hiring Gabriel Stuub.

'No, that's fine. But given that he's been here so long, I assume you're happy with his work?'

'Yeah, sure ... It's not exactly qualified work, but yes, Gabriel knows how to do it. He and another bloke are in charge of bottling and shipping, but they're both off today.'

There's a hint of evasiveness in Jens Groth's reply, as though he has no specific complaints, but nevertheless wants to avoid saying anything good about Gabriel Stuub.

'What do you know about his private life?'

Jens Groth shrugs his broad shoulders again.

'Not a lot, I'm afraid. I know he's getting divorced. Two children, I think. Lives somewhere west of Skreby.'

'Come on, you must know more than that. You've worked together for years.'

'What can I say? It's not like we hang out after work.'

Karen can feel herself becoming annoyed. Jens Groth seems to have decided to give them as little as possible. She decides to cut to the chase.

'Does Gabriel Stuub have any links to the OP?'

Jens Groth's facial expression doesn't change, his gaze remains steady, not so much as a flicker of an eyelid. Instead, he goes rigid, as though a bucket of liquid nitrogen has been poured over him. For a split second, Karen ghoulishly imagines the man in front pulverised by the slightest gust of wind.

'OK,' she says. 'I'll take that as a yes.'

Still no answer. Only a slight twitch of the fingers of one of his hands. Then the paralysis seems to subside and Jens Groth slowly shakes his head. A second later, he inhales sharply.

'No!'

They study him in silence, waiting for more. In the end, he starts to speak again, now in a monotonous voice.

'I don't know whether Gabriel has anything to do with them or not, but I can tell you they make no trouble for us. Not ever. So, if there's nothing else, I'll be happy to walk you out . . .'

Jens Groth firmly puts both hands on his desk and stands up. Karen notes the pit stains on his shirt have doubled in size.

'What do you make of that?' Byle asks five minutes later while slowly pulling out his seat belt.

They've returned to the car and Karen has, without thinking and without asking her colleague, claimed the driver's seat. He drove them here, now he has climbed into the passenger seat without protest. He buckles himself in with a click.

'I think we should have another chat with young Mister Stuub,' Karen replies with her eyes fixed on a spot somewhere beyond the grimy windscreen.

'Yes, I suppose he's our most likely suspect. He does have a motive of sorts as his grandfather's heir, though he won't be inheriting any significant sums.'

'Any news on that?'

'Not yet. His lawyer is on holiday, but he responded to my email and promised to try to get the information from his assistant. The real question is whether Gabriel could have killed him. According to the port authorities he was in fact on the nine o'clock ferry from Lysvik to Thorsvik that morning, like he claimed.'

The fact that all registration plates are now logged by the ferry company has at least given them a quick answer to that question. Presumably by working his local connections, Byle had an almost instantaneous reply to his emailed query.

'Or at least his car was,' Karen says. 'We'll have to request the CCTV footage and make sure it was really him driving. On the other hand, he could have killed his grandfather and still made it down to Lysvik on time. At least in theory.'

'So you're saying he left the kids home alone, popped up to kill his grandfather, picked the kids up and drove to the ferry? Or are you suggesting he drove up to the rubbish dump and left the kids in the car while he walked down to the quarry and beat his grandfather to death?'

Thorstein Byle sounds as sceptical as Karen feels; she stares out the window without answering. She briefly considers telling Byle about something she saw as they left the warehouse, but then decides not to. Byle probably missed it.

She hadn't seen it herself on the way in. But while they were talking to Jens Groth, the sun moved, revealing a faint shadow on the wall by the door. Black spray paint that someone had done their best to remove. She'd noticed it when she turned around to shake Jens Groth's hand – and when he caught her looking, he'd made a clumsy attempt to block her view. But she'd seen it.

The number one and a per cent sign.

Odin Predators. Or the One Percenters.

Karen curses inwardly and turns the key in the ignition.

26

'I was wondering how long it would be before you came back. You're looking for this, aren't you?'

Ingeborg Eiken is holding a tartan scarf in one hand and the door handle in the other.

'Yes, perfect, thank you. I must have left it last night. Where did you find it?'

'Exactly where you put it, I'm assuming. Neatly hidden behind the wellies in the hallway.'

Karen accepts the scarf without argument. Arguing with her aunt is never a good idea. Especially when she's right.

'Any chance of a coffee?' she asks instead.

Fifteen minutes later, the coffee pot is on the table, along with two cups and a low birch-bark basket with what remains of the Christmas baked goods: lingonberry squares, saffron scratch biscuits and two balls of flaky puff pastry.

'I hope I'm not disturbing, turning up announced like this,' Karen says. 'Maybe this isn't a good time?'

'Don't be silly.'

'Are those apple turnovers?' Karen says, longingly eyeing the puff pastry. 'I haven't had one of those since—'

She breaks off and turns to her aunt, who has leaned back with her hands folded over her blue cotton apron and is making no move to pour the coffee.

'So, Karen,' she says. 'Would you mind telling me why you're here? And don't give me any foolishness about your scarf, or that you were just in the mood for apple turnovers.'

Mirroring her aunt's body language, Karen leans back with a sigh.

'OK,' she says. 'I need your help.'

At her words, Ingeborg gets back up, fetches a bowl of sugar cubes from the sideboard and an unlabelled glass bottle from the cupboard above it. No glasses, Karen notes and shakes her head when her aunt holds up the sugar bowl and the bottle with a querying look.

'I'm driving,' she says. 'And I'm on the job.'

'Since when has that ever stopped anyone?' Ingeborg Eiken retorts and pops two sugar cubes into her own mug. Then she pulls the stopper out of the bottle and pours a generous slug over the sugar before filling their mugs with coffee, Karen's first, then her own. She stirs hers, then leans forward and sniffs it.

'Are you sure you don't want some? No, of course, you probably don't drink karsk down on the mainland anymore. I suppose it's all expresso and cuppa-chino and whatnot these days.'

Karen smiles and refrains from correcting her about the names of the coffee drinks and from pointing out that Heimö can hardly be considered the mainland. Ingeborg already knows. It's just the kind of thing you're expected to say up here.

'So you want my help, do you? And what kind of help would that be, if I may ask?'

'Tell me everything you know. What people are saying about each other up here.'

'So you're looking for gossip? Fine, I figured. But I'm not going to say a word against my boys. Let's be clear about that.'

Ingeborg's eyes flash dangerously when Karen replies.

'No, what I need to know about my own relatives I'll find out for myself. I'm talking about the Stuubs, Trystes, Huss and Groths and all the rest of them. I can't keep track of all the names and who's related to whom.'

She decides to pretend Thorstein Byle hasn't already told her some things. She has trouble remembering what he said anyway.

'Well, start by narrowing your list down to two. Huss, Tryste and Stuub are all the same family. Old Huss had no sons. One of his daughters married a Scandinavian of Norwegian extraction called Tryste. The other married a Stuub. I think he was from Frisel. Apparently, a local man wasn't good enough for the Huss girls. They had to go find someone fancy.'

'Yes, I noticed The Complex is still standing,' Karen puts in and blows on her coffee.

Ingeborg makes a sound halfway between an amused chuckle and a snort of derision.

'Yes, that eyesore is probably going to outlast the Gudheim stones themselves unless someone takes it upon themselves to burn the dreadful thing down. But you liked it as a child, unless I'm misremembering. If you'd married William, you could be living there now.'

Karen picks her jaw off the floor while Ingeborg lets out a smug chuckle and reaches for her cup.

'Are you talking about William Tryste?'

'Of course, who else? He has moved back home. You don't remember him? He used to run around with my boys, causing mischief, until his mother put her foot down. The Eikens "weren't appropriate company", she said.'

Karen searches her memory. Nothing about the enthusias-tic man she met up at the distillery rang a bell. And apparently no penny dropped for him, either, or he would have been even more genial, she thinks wryly to herself.

'No, I suppose you were too little to remember all the children running about the farms around here. Besides, you only ever had eyes for Finn. My God, you worshipped that boy, and no wonder, he was handsome. Tall and wide like my father.'

Ingeborg's smile expresses a mix of nostalgia and pride at the thought of her eldest son. Karen clears her throat.

'So William used to play with the boys, you said? What was he like?'

'Like most boys his age. I remember him being very talkative and very polite. He hadn't been taught to say grace at home, but he always thanked me for the food. He could have grown into a decent man if his mother hadn't taken him and his sister away to England. I saw him in Lysvik the other day, pale and skinny. A proper mollycoddle, the very picture of a Briton.'

'Why did his mother move away?' Karen asks, picturing William Tryste.

Mollycoddle is not the word she would have chosen to describe the tall man with the blue eyes. Annoyingly loquacious, but there was nothing wrong with the way he looked.

'Well, I suppose being part of the Huss family wasn't so glam-orous once things started to go downhill,' Ingeborg Eiken says and pauses to slurp her coffee. Then she continues.

'Diana left her poor husband to face the music and ran back to her parents in Essex. British-born, she was, and always quick to point it out, too. I suppose the average intelligence went up significantly in both countries when she moved back home.'

She chuckles smugly at her own joke and Karen smiles politely.

'He's still alive, I'm told. William's father, I mean,' she says.

'Ivar, yes. If you can call it living; the poor sod was put in the Lysvik nursing home many years ago. Wasn't far past sixty when he started going doddery.'

'Sounds like Alzheimer's.'

'Yes, everything needs a fancy name these days. Softening of the brain is what they called it in my day. Though back then it only happened to the elderly. Now, I feel like I hear about it all the time, and with young people, no more than fifty.'

Ingeborg pushes the basket toward her.

'Don't be shy, Kay-Kay,' she urges. 'At least one of each.'

Karen bites into a saffron biscuit and licks a few stray crumbs from the corner of her mouth. She would have preferred to go straight for the apple turnover, but doesn't want to risk aggravating Ingeborg. You always eat everything you're served. And you don't ask the wrong questions. But the inadequacies of the Tryste family seem a safe enough topic.

'What kind of music was it? That William's mother left her husband to face, I mean?'

'The mining crisis, of course. Poor Ivar was the grandchild of Old Huss and was expected to take over when the old man died. But when they discovered oil, that was the end of mining subsidies and then there were the strikes. They lost everything in just a few years. All they have left now is the land, but apparently that's enough to justify putting on airs.'

Karen thinks back to her meetings with William Tryste and Gertrud Stuub. An enthusiastic whiskey connoisseur and a deeply religious woman mourning her brother. And Gabriel

162

Stuub, a hungover motorcyclist working in a warehouse. She certainly hasn't detected any airs in Old Huss's descendants so far. Her aunt's antipathy is clearly based on things that happened a long time ago, in previous generations, she concludes. And as though she can read Karen's mind, Ingeborg continues.

'Oh no, lambkin, that family's not so fancy if you bother to take a closer look. They've got shit in their arses, too, as the old saying goes. And I could tell you a thing or two to knock them off their high horses, if I wanted to . . .'

'Please, do,' Karen says quickly and is rewarded with a sharp look. 'I'm just trying to form a picture of all the people involved and their backgrounds, and there's no telling what might turn out to be useful. I figured you're probably the one who knows the most about all of this,' she adds.

Another sharp look lets her know her aunt isn't fooled by her flattery. A moment later, Ingeborg Eiken takes a deep breath, lets out a long sigh and continues.

'Well, I can't say I really *know* anything, and my father never wanted to speak about what he saw, not outside the four walls of his home, at any rate, but I heard him talk to Mother about it more than once.'

'What? Come on! I want to know everything.'

Ingeborg seems to hesitate briefly. Then her eyes flash.

'Father suspected Old Huss of doing business with the Germans during the war. He'd apparently seen something when he was out on the boat, or so he said. But he kept quiet about it, took it to his grave.'

Karen gives her aunt an incredulous look.

'How come? Grandpa hated the Nazis.'

163

'Probably because the whole island would have suffered if what Huss was doing had become public knowledge. We were completely dependent on the mines back then and if he'd fallen, he would have dragged us all down with him. He owned half the island and was on the county council and the fisheries board.'

'So Grandpa kept it to himself,' Karen says doubtfully. 'My God, that's bloo—'

'Now, now, don't take that tone, lass,' Ingeborg cuts her off sharply. 'They were different times, and if you think life is hard here now, you should have seen what it was like back then. Besides, this was right at the end of the war so it didn't make any difference.'

Karen makes no reply.

'But I think it weighed on him until the day he died,' her aunt says. 'And I can't deny it's made my tongue itch on more than a few occasions.'

Karen decides to change the subject.

'Fredrik Stuub must have been about your age, right? How well did you know him?'

Ingeborg freezes with her cup halfway to her lips. Then she continues the motion, takes a sip and slowly puts the cup back down. It clinks against the saucer.

'People talk too much. What have you heard?' she demands sharply.

'Nothing. At least, not about you and Fredrik Stuub. So you *did* know him?'

'Yes, of course I did, when we were young. It's a small island. Well, I might as well confess that we had a brief romance, but that was long before he married, of course. And before I married, too, for that matter.'

'Did you see him more recently?'

'Of course not! This is what I'm telling you, he was a Huss, born and bred.'

'I haven't had the impression Fredrik was much of a snob,' Karen ventures to protest. 'Nor his sister, actually; she's just very religious.'

'Pff,' Ingeborg snorts. 'Gertrud, she probably thinks she's closer to Our Lord than anyone else. That's how the high and mighty think. That they're wealthy because God favours them. Believe me, Kay-Kay, the women of that family have always strutted around with their noses in the air. The men were better, true, Ivar was always sweet, poor thing, and Fredrik was . . .'

She trails off; Karen waits.

'Fredrik was a good man,' she finishes curtly. 'I can't begin to imagine who would have wanted to see him dead.'

And something makes Ingeborg Eiken hastily turn her face away. Then she stands up and walks over to the kitchen counter.

'I think we've wasted more than enough time on idle gossip now.'

Ten minutes later, Karen glances down at the tinfoil packet on the passenger seat. Her aunt hadn't been in the mood to share any more information and Karen hadn't had a chance to ask any of her questions about Gabriel Stuub or the Groth family. Without another word, Ingeborg Eiken had cleared the table and pulled out a roll of aluminium foil from one of the kitchen drawers, wrapped up the untouched apple turnovers and handed the parcel to her niece.

'It's best to leave the past in the past,' she'd declared.

And it's probably best not to think too hard about what Karen now remembers hearing her mother say once.

God only knows where Odd got that red hair from. It certainly wasn't from Lars.

166

27

The organist has already struck the first blaring chords. Karen sits down at the far end of the backmost pew, quickly looks up at the hymn board and opens her hymnal to number 302. 'Come Let Us Give Praise'.

She dutifully sings along; unsure of the melody, she lets herself be guided by her neighbours while idly wondering why the key is always, invariably, inappropriate for her voice. And for virtually everyone else's, too, she notes, wincing as the congregation strains to reach the highest notes.

Once they've finally reached the end of the interminable hymn, Karen lets her eyes sweep over the assembled congregants. Skreby Church is full today. Custom dictates that all parishioners attend funerals, whether or not they knew the deceased. No one should have to meet their maker without a proper send-off: empty pews at a funeral service are considered sacrilege. It used to be the norm in every part of the country, but Karen doubts any of the churches on Heimö or Frisel would be able to drum up this kind of crowd. Especially on a Wednesday morning.

It had been the only way to get Fredrik Stuub buried within a decent time frame. New Year's Eve is tomorrow and waiting until after the holiday would have been severely frowned upon. The living accommodate the dead – not the other way around.

Fortunately, neither Kneought Brodal nor Sören Larsen had raised any objections.

'So long as they weren't poisoned, I don't care what you do with the corpses once I've stitched them back together,' as Brodal had so pleasantly put it.

After the one in Lysvik, Skreby Church is the largest of Noorö's houses of worship. It's imposing and richly ornamented, at least compared to the simple seamen's church in Gudheim and the many evangelical chapels that dot the island. Karen cranes her neck to find someone she knows. Her own relatives belong to the Gudheim congregation, but both Byle and Tryste's families live in Skreby.

It doesn't take her long to locate Thorstein and Solveig Byle a few pews ahead. If she leans slightly to the side, she can just about glimpse Gabriel's profile in the front row, next to Gertrud Stuub's slate-grey bob. And, unless she's mistaken, that's the back of William Tryste's shaved head right behind them. Between him and a dark-haired woman Karen assumes is his wife sits a scrawny young man who is just then being admonished by his parents. They probably told him to turn off his phone, Karen thinks as the guy sullenly shoves something into his breast pocket. Alvin? Was that what Tryste had said his name was?

Erlin Arve has climbed into the pulpit now and Karen notes that the inconspicuous dog collar he'd worn at Gertrud's house has now been replaced with the traditional ruff.

He's the person she's here to see. During a brief phone conversation earlier in the morning, Arve had promised to give Karen a few minutes of his time after the funeral service and the rectory is conveniently located right next to the church.

'I suppose the easiest thing would be to meet outside afterwards, then we can walk over together,' he'd said, 'and you can tell me how I did.'

And Karen, who had actually planned to study the arrivals from a safe distance, hadn't had the heart to tell him she had no intention of attending the funeral. And so, here she sits, listening to words about reflection and forgiveness.

The congregation bow their heads during the first prayer.

Fathur our, thu er i himla
Helgat er namet thit.
Let riket thit kom, let will thin råde
Her på yortha, sum i himla.
Give us bred, okk forgiv os sinnere ore
sum vi forgiver othre sinner.
Okk let us ikke frestes, men thet evle forsake.
For thin er makta okk thet gode, sum i himla
  okk på yortha.
Amen.[1]

After a seventy-minute sermon about time without end, atonement and hope in dark times, a few brief remarks about Fredrik's deep roots on Noorö and his passion for his homeland, a number of feeble attempts to sing along with the hymns selected for the occasion and finally the witnessing of the deceased's loved ones bowing and curtsying to the coffin, Karen is the first one out of the church doors.

---

[1] Lord's Prayer in Dogger

The sun is out and there's a real nip in the air now. Four below freezing, her car had informed her on the way here and according to the morning news, the temperature is going to plummet further over the next few days.

'We didn't get a white Christmas, but it seems we will have a cold and clear New Year's Eve,' the meteorologist had announced cheerfully and fired off a freshly bleached smile from the TV screen this morning.

Karen studies the parishioners who, after meeting their obligation, are now rushing toward the car park. There's not going to be a reception. True, such gatherings have become more common in recent years as a result of foreign influence, but in Doggerian tradition, wakes are held before funerals, which mark the end of the leave-taking. Unsurprisingly, Gertrud Stuub is a traditionalist.

Karen buttons her coat and is wrapping her scarf around her neck when Thorstein and Solveig Byle step out onto the church steps in the company of a tall woman of about thirty-five and two little girls. Karen recognises the children from her visit to the Byles' house. Only then, their faces had been covered in chocolate and their eyes glued to the TV. Now, they're neatly dressed in identical blue wool coats and obediently pull on the hats their mother holds out to them. Then Thorstein spots Karen and starts walking toward her with his family in tow. Karen thanks Solveig again for the lunch and shakes hands with their daughter Trine, who is almost as tall as her father and looks remarkably like him. They exchange a few words about how the cold has finally caught up with them, and about how Karen absolutely has to come over for dinner soon.

'Did you attend the service or are you just here to spy on the funeral guests?' Byle asks with a smile that fails to entirely hide an undercurrent of disapproval.

Karen is, and will remain, an outsider.

'Both, actually,' she replies. 'I'm meeting Erling Arve here in a bit. Thought I'd hear what he has to say about the Stuubs.'

Byle suddenly looks uncertain, glances over at his wife, daughter and grandchildren, who are now standing a little way apart, wrestling with their scarves and mittens.

'If you want, I could obviously . . .'

'There's no need for you to be there,' she assures him. 'I can probably manage a chat with the local priest on my own. But it would be great if we could meet up at the station tomorrow before I leave,' she adds.

'Of course. I take it you're going home for New Year's, then? Just as well, there's not a lot to be done here until we have the results of the forensic investigation. Any news on that, by the way?'

'No, I talked to Sören Larsen yesterday and he says we're probably not going to hear anything until after the holiday, so I'll be ringing in the new year at home.'

They arrange to meet at eight the next day and then the Byle family set off toward their car, leaving a shivering Karen to wait in the cold. She glances up at the church doors again; the last parishioners are leaving now, carefully negotiating the slippery stone steps. Some stop to chat while others walk briskly toward the car park. She smilingly watches the old men who reflexively doff their caps when they pass the large juniper tree at the edge of the church grounds. Paying their respects to the gnarled coni- fer with it healing powers and magical properties, as required

171

by their old-fashioned upbringing is a dying custom that has probably been temporarily resuscitated by the solemnity of the moment. The men are most likely unaware of the church's futile attempts to root out all the pre-Christian traditions linked to the prickly indigenous bush.

Noorö tradition dictates that the dead person's closest relatives be the last to leave the church after a funeral service; Karen looks on as William Tryste and his family are followed out of the open oak doors by Gabriel Stuub, pale and squinting in the light, to the sound of the mournful organ. Gabriel gazes out at the lingering funeral guests and stiffens when he spots Karen. Then he hurries down the steps and strides off toward the car park without turning around.

Last out is Gertrud Stuub, lightly supported by Erling Arve. They pause at the bottom of the church steps while Arve looks around. Then he nods at Karen and squeezes Gertrud's arm before parting ways with her. Karen watches the forlorn-looking woman in her black wool coat and beret slowly walk away and feels a pang of guilt. Maybe her request for a chat with Arve has robbed Gertrud of sorely needed company. She asks him straight out after exchanging greetings.

'Not to worry,' he replies with a reassuring smile. 'Gertrud wanted some time alone.'

'Are you sure? Because this will certainly keep until tomorrow.'

'There's no need. I'll be checking on Gertrud tonight. Truth be told, as soon as you and I are done, I'm driving straight to the Thorsvik mall to buy an electric screwdriver. They're on sale.'

He seems amused by Karen's surprised look.

'After I change my clothes, of course,' he says with a smile. 'This thing tends to get in the way at the petrol pump,' he adds, pointing to his large white ruff. 'But why don't we go over to the rectory and talk more there?'

Arve has a brief conversation with the church musician and churchwarden and then he and Karen walk over to the rectory, a two-storey limestone house which differs little from the other houses in the area and is smaller than Karen had expected. The only thing that gives away that this is the residence of the parish priest is the tithes barn. Like most other tithes barns, it's tall and narrow and comes with a heavy and intricately carved wooden bar, a massive lock and a wrought-iron cross. Karen wonders briefly whether the barn is empty or if Arve has managed to find some use for it. These days it's not exactly needed to hold the tithes the hard-working parishioners used to pay the church for the priest's services, she thinks while Arve climbs the steps to the rectory.

The interior proves equally lacking in the grandeur she would have expected in a rectory. Aside from a collection of portraits of his predecessors, which Arve has left up on one of the sitting-room walls, nothing in the room hints at clerical splendour. He leaves her in a comfortable red armchair with an assurance that he will be right back.

No crucifixes on the walls, no religious paraphernalia at all, except for a Bible on the coffee table. Other than that, it looks like a regular, modern living room, with a sofa, armchairs, a TV and a stereo. Karen glances over at Arve's collection of old vinyl records and CDs in the bookcase, but she can't make out any titles and she's not curious enough about his music taste to get up. Instead, she closes her eyes and leans back, feeling the pain in her knee slowly subside after their short walk from the church.

Five minutes later, Arve is back. Now dressed in light grey corduroy trousers and a matching cardigan. The ruff has once more been replaced by a small dog collar in his black shirt.

'Would you mind if I heat up some food while we talk? I haven't eaten since breakfast,' he says, gesturing toward the kitchen. 'Actually, maybe you're hungry, too?'

'No, thank you, I had a late breakfast,' Karen lies instinctively.

She follows him into a large rustic kitchen with old-fashioned and impractical but beautiful décor, pulls out a kitchen chair and sits down at the large oak table. She watches in silence while the priest takes out an enamel saucepan and fetches a glass jar from the fridge.

'Are you sure I can't offer you some lunch? They're just leftovers from yesterday,' he coaxes, 'but they're good. Venison stew from a deer I shot and chanterelles I picked myself.'

'No, thank you, but you go ahead.'

'Are you absolutely sure? There's home-made rowanberry jelly to go with it,' Arve says and turns around with the jar in his hand and his eyebrows raised.

Karen smiles. Some of the stiff wariness this man of the cloth initially inspired in her has eased since he changed out of his ruff and cassock. Besides, it's almost one o'clock and she really is hungry.

'Well, then how can I refuse?' she says. 'I have a weak spot for rowanberries.'

Erling Arve puts the pot on the hob and opens one of the cupboards above the kitchen counter.

'So what did you want to talk to me about?' he asks as he gets out two plates.

'I want you to tell me everything you know,' she replies calmly, 'about Fredrik – and above all, whether you can think of anyone who might want to see him dead. And I want you to tell me everything you know about his grandson.'

Arve puts the plates and two glasses down on the table. Slowly, as if playing for time, he lays out cutlery and paper napkins.

'You realise I'm constrained by clergy privilege?' he says.

'I'm just asking you to tell me what you've gathered as a private citizen, not to divulge any confidences given to you in your professional role. Though as far as I'm concerned, feel free to do that, too,' she adds with a smile.

Erling Arve returns to the hob. With his back toward her, he stirs the pot slowly and methodically, once again seemingly stalling for time.

'Start with Fredrik,' she says. 'Surely his priest-penitent privilege has expired?'

'Not at all. Death changes nothing as far as that's concerned. But at any rate,' he says and turns around, 'Fredrik was hardly the type to confide in me. Unlike his sister, he wasn't particularly God-fearing. I'm not even sure he believed in God. But I guess that's to be expected, given his profession.'

'As a teacher, you mean? Surely there are lots of deeply religious teachers out there. At least, my own memories from school would suggest there are.'

Unfortunately, she adds inwardly, recalling her class teacher in secondary school.

He lets out a brief chuckle.

'Sure, but Fredrik Stuub wasn't some village primary school teacher. He taught biology at the university in Ravenby and I hardly think what he taught was particularly compatible with Genesis.'

She makes no reply but returns his smile.

Erling Arve takes out a trivet and puts the steaming pot on the table.

'Please,' he says, 'help yourself.'

While they eat in silence, Karen marvels inwardly at the priest's many non-clerical skills: deer hunting, mushroom picking and jam-making.

'That being said,' Arve continues after a while and wipes his mouth, 'I don't think biology was really at the forefront of Fredrik's mind after he retired. What he did take an interest in was Noorö's history.'

Karen looks at him attentively and keeps chewing.

'But unfortunately, our paths didn't cross there either,' the priest goes on. 'The island's ecumenical cultural heritage held no allure for Fredrik; he was more interested in pre-Christian heritage sites. According to Gertrud, he studied old runestones and spent quite a bit of time at the ship setting in Gudheim. Highly impious, according to his sister.'

His words remind Karen of something Byle mentioned.

'Yes, I heard there was some kind of vandalism up there,' she says. 'Someone drilled holes in the stones?'

Arve nods.

'Yes, and Fredrik wasn't the only one who was upset, either. I mean, sure, there has always been a problem with young people congregating up there and sometimes there has been graffiti and attempts to tip the stones, but that was considerably more serious.'

'How long ago was this?'

'It was actually Fredrik who discovered the drill holes, the day before Christmas Eve, but there's no way of knowing how old they are. If you ask me, a few days at most.'

'What makes you think that?'

'Well, granted, the New Age types mostly congregate up there in the summer, but there's always a few hanging about during the winter solstice; they should have noticed the holes if they'd been there then.'

'Has it been reported to the heritage trust?'

'I assume so, but I can't swear to it. I do know Fredrik reported it to the Noorö Police, but I'm sure you're better placed to find out what they're doing about it than I am.'

Most likely nothing, Karen thinks bleakly, remembering how Byle dismissed the whole thing as a childish prank. The local police are unlikely to go out of their way to find the culprit. She decides to change the subject.

'And what can you tell me about Gabriel? I know that he works up at Groth's, is going to inherit whatever Fredrik left behind and lives in a modern house that looks like it's been randomly flung into the middle a barley field. And that he's getting divorced,' she adds.

'As a priest, I have nothing to tell you about Gabriel, either, but if the rumour mill is to be believed, it's a messy affair. A lot of arguments and quarrelling, according to the neighbours, and a while ago, Gabriel's wife took the children and moved back in with her parents in Thorsvik, leaving Gabriel in the house. I suppose one of them will have to buy the other out, and I assume they're fighting over the children.'

'And what else is there to say about Gabriel? Does he have any other ... interests?' Karen asks, scraping up the last morsels of venison from her plate. 'This was absolutely delicious, by the way.'

'Glad to hear it,' Arve replies with a crooked smile. 'Interests? I assume you're referring to that motorcycle gang?'

'I'm not referring to anything, just listening. What do you know about it?'

'Nothing, really, at least not from a police perspective. I have no proof, but the local gossip has it Gabriel is pretty chummy with those lads. Apparently, he spends quite a bit of time up at their clubhouse near Tyrfallet. I would caution you to take all of this with a grain of salt, though . . .' Erling Arve hesitates briefly then wipes his mouth with his napkin and continues, 'There are some who say he supplies the OP from the Groth's warehouse,' he says, fixing her levelly. 'But that's just what I hear.'

She knows he won't answer, but she asks anyway.

'And whom do you hear it from?'

As expected, Arve only smiles in response.

'Fine,' she says. 'Do you have any idea whether the Groths are aware of this alleged theft? Whether they've been threatened somehow?'

'I couldn't say, but if I were you, I'd ask them,' Arve says and gets up. 'Now, you'll have to excuse me, unless you have any more questions. Can I give you a ride somewhere?'

'No, thank you, I parked by the church. And thank you for the lovely food and for talking to me. I assume this conversation will stay between us?'

'Of course. And I hope you'll think about what I said about that grain of salt.'

*

178

On her way to the car park, Karen pulls out her phone and finds the number she added just a couple of days ago. She hesitates for a few seconds. Maybe it would be better to hold off on opening this particular door. No, she decides, she might as well get it over with.

With a heavy sigh, she presses the call button.

28

Neutral ground, Karen thinks, looking around the pub. Over by the bar, she catches a glimpse of Ellen Jensen's platinum curls and, at the tables closest to the TV, she sees the same faces as yesterday. Today, though, their attention is held by what appears to be some kind of Formula 1 race; the high-pitched whining of the cars blends with the old ABBA song coming out of the speakers. The likelihood of anyone taking an interest in her or who she's with must be considered extremely low, she concludes with relief.

When Karen finally spots her cousin at a table at the far end of the room, she waves and walks over to the bar to order before sitting down across from him.

'Thank you for coming,' she says, unwrapping her scarf.

Odd Eiken takes a sip of his pint, then leans back and studies her without responding. The warmth and elation she'd felt at seeing him again the other night is gone. The only thing she feels now is trepidation; this is clearly going to be exactly as difficult as she thought it would be. She decides to get straight to the point.

'You know why I want to talk to you?' she asks.

'Well, I assume it's not to reminisce about our youth,' he replies. 'Memories don't seem to mean much to you anymore. Or blood ties, for that matter.'

'If that were true, we'd be having this conversation down at the station, not in a pub.'

'Bullshit!' he snaps. 'You think you can lean on me because we're family, but you can forget it.'

Just then, Ellen Jensen comes over with Karen's drink. She puts her pint of Spitfire and a bowl of peanuts down on the table and leaves without a word. Karen takes two deep swigs.

'You're right, Odd,' she says. 'At least in part. As you know, I'm investigating the murder of Fredrik Stuub, and there's nothing to suggest there's any connection with the OP. At least not at the moment. What there does seems to be is a connection between you and Gabriel Stuub.'

'Is that so?'

'Can you confirm it?'

'Why would I?'

'So Gabriel's not a member of the OP? Is that what you're telling me?'

'Never heard of him.'

Karen sighs and takes another big sip of her ale. Then she leans forward and fixes her cousin with a firm stare.

'Fine, Odd, then let's do this. I'll tell you what I think, and you let me know if I'm on the right track. And the reason you will is that you don't want me to start making all kinds of trouble for you. One word from me and the island will be swarming with my colleagues. And they will bring in accountants and people from the economic crime unit to go over every last scrap of paper at your headquarters and your home and the homes of all the other members with a fine-tooth comb. Normally, they don't have the resources to pay that kind of close attention, but if a murder's involved . . .'

... it still wouldn't amount to much of an intervention, she finishes inwardly. But a shadow of concern crosses Odd's face before he can hide it behind a carefree smile.

'And I assume your standing in the club won't exactly improve when your mates find out that it was your cousin who made it all happen,' she adds quickly.

'Go on,' he says tersely.

'We know Gabriel steals from the Groth's warehouse.'

'Is that right? Well, I guess I would, too, if I worked there, but like I said, I've never heard of the bloke.'

'From what I'm told, alcohol isn't a primary source of revenue for the OP. I assume you prefer providing poor, innocent restaurant owners with so-called protection, assault, blackmail, laundering money through greyhound racing and whatever else. But I don't believe you have the logistical capacity to fence malt whiskey. Am I right so far?'

'I could possibly concede your last point,' Odd says and takes a sip of his beer. Then he wipes the foam from his moustache and grabs a fistful of peanuts. He tilts his head back, throws them into his mouth and wipes the salt off on his trousers.

'So Gabriel is stealing on his own initiative,' she says. 'And I'd wager he saves some for himself and sells the rest for what must be a decent profit. Maybe he even sells to some of the bars in Dunker and Ravenby. A way to make some extra money, simply put.'

Odd watches her with an amused expression, still chewing his peanuts, and Karen presses on.

'The mark on the Groth's warehouse wall does suggest, though, that the OP are involved somehow and that you had reason to make it clear to the Groths this isn't the time to start acting up.'

Odd Eiken stops chewing for a moment and gives Karen a look of what seems to be genuine surprise.

'What fucking mark?' he says.

'What do you think? The number one followed by a per cent sign. Even I know that's what you guys use to mark your territory. I've even seen it once or twice outside bars down in Dunker.'

Odd leans back, sighs and says in a tone a person might use with a small child.

'OK, Karen, let's say such a mark exists – which I'm not saying it does. It sounds like that would be used for territorial marking, as you say, something to encourage the Russians and Baltics to steer clear. How many of *them* have you seen up here on Noorö?'

'Let's say I buy that,' Karen says, firmly holding her cousin's gaze. 'That would hardly keep an individual member from using the mark to bully people. Maybe to warn someone who was onto him or making trouble. Maybe someone who was threatening to go to the police. Hypothetically speaking, of course.'

Odd Eiken raises his eyebrows and pulls the corners of his mouth down, making a face that suggests anything's possible. Karen takes a long sip of her ale.

'Shall we continue?' she says.

'Sure. Just don't forget that we're still talking hypothetically. The OP isn't involved in any criminal activities; we're just a bunch of guys who like hogs, that's it.'

Karen lets out a snort of laughter.

'Of course,' she says with a smile. 'But let's toy with the notion that someone in your group of saintly motorcycle enthusiasts had the idea of breaking the law and stealing from his employer.

Say he worked in a nursing home or at a library. No, hold on, let's make it a whiskey warehouse! Just as a "for instance".'

Odd stifles a yawn.

'Is this going to take long? I could really do with a fag.'

'Me too. I'll keep it brief.'

'Bit late for that, isn't it? You realise I'm only here for one reason, right?' he says and fixes her levelly.

She meets his eyes without blinking.

'That goes for me too, Odd.'

They stare at each other in silence for four long seconds. Then Karen takes a deep breath and continues.

'I don't know exactly what your role is in the club, but I assume your word must carry some weight after all these years. So I have a proposal to make.'

No reaction. Karen presses on.

'I won't bring in every single copper I can find, your homes and clubhouse won't be searched and I won't have to stop by your little philatelists' association. On one condition.'

Still no reaction.

'You tell me everything you know about Gabriel Stuub.'

'Forget it. I'm not snitching on a brother.'

'Of course. Aren't we lucky then that you just told me Gabriel Stuub's not a member and therefore not a "brother". You don't even know him, so I assume you'll have no qualms telling me everything you hear about him.'

Odd says nothing.

'And won't it be nice for me not to have to turn your club and maybe all your law-abiding little friends' homes upside down, not to have to drag my own family members down to the station to ask them what they know about the OP's activities? And won't it be nice for you that no one will need to know that the copper making your lives so difficult is your own cousin? We won't have to go through any of that, so long as you tell me what you can find out about any connection there might be between young Mr Stuub and the murder of his grandfather.'

She pauses.

'Do we have a deal?' she asks.

'You've turned into a real bitch, Karen.'

'I'll take that as a yes.'

29

Once she reaches the motorway, Karen turns the radio up and leans back with a sigh of relief. She watches Noorö's mountain ranges slowly recede into the distance in the rear-view mirror. It's only twenty past eleven. Almost forty-eight hours of freedom before she has to go back to those soot-stained houses and an investigation that has ground to a complete standstill.

The last report she sent to Jounas Smeed before leaving was dry as a bone and ended with a series of matter-of-fact statements: with no results forthcoming from forensics or IT, she wrote, the investigation is at an impasse. I consequently see no impediment to me absenting myself from Noorö over the New Year holiday with the intention of returning in two days' time. She had wrapped up by emphasising that Byle was a pleasure to work with, but that progress in the case hinged on reinforcements from the CID.

To her surprise, her inbox dinged just a few minutes later. *OK/Jounas*

The morning meeting at the police station had been so similar to the first one she'd almost regretted asking them to come in on New Year's Eve. True, Röse had toned down his insubordination ever so slightly, but he certainly wasn't doing anything to boost team morale. But then again, neither was she. She'd given them a brief summary of where things stood and informed them that all they could do was wait for the results of the forensic investigation, the call logs from Fredrik Stuub's phone and the analysis of the contents of his computer.

There had been one minor development. Unfortunately, it seemed to lead to a dead end rather than a break in the case. Just thirty minutes before the meeting, Karen had, to her surprise, had a reply from William Tryste's service provider. Yes, his phone had connected to the mast in Lysvik between 8.01 and 8.03 on the morning of Christmas Day. One of the care assistants at the nursing home had also confirmed that she saw William Tryste enter his father's room just after seven that morning. And later that day, the staff had found, to the intense annoyance of the ward manager, leftover herring, an empty beer bottle and a small bottle that smelled strongly of bog myrtle in a bin in Ivar Tryste's room.

'So, to sum up, William Tryste's information checks out,' Karen had told them, unable to completely hide her disappointment.

In her heart of hearts, having Tryste's alibi confirmed and thus losing a suspect, was not the outcome she had been hoping for. Karen had ended the meeting by stressing again that she had no doubt they would be able to solve the case together, then she'd wished everyone a happy New Year. She hadn't mentioned her meeting with Odd Eiken.

Driving at a leisurely pace toward Langevik and her home, Karen is overcome with the same feeling of relief she experienced five days ago going in the opposite direction. Her mood improves even further when she realises she won't have to sleep in the flowery hotel room for a couple of nights and that she is going to be able to go to Eirik and Kore's party tonight after all.

There's nothing more we can do until we get the results from forensics, she tells herself, suppressing a sudden pang of guilt. And I'll be back in – she checks her watch and counts in her head – just over forty hours. Besides, I'm technically still on sick leave. Smeed should be bloody grateful I stepped up so he can sit around on some beach sipping cocktails.

She can hear Sigrid's outraged voice now: *Am I supposed to sit on some fucking coconut beach, too?*

She turns the radio down, reaches for her phone and pushes the earbud into her ear. Leo Friis picks up after eight rings.

'I was in the shower,' he says. 'I think I might have used the last of the shampoo.'

'I'm on my way home. Taking a couple of days off.'

'Seriously? When will you be back?'

I've left you just enough time to tidy up, she thinks wryly.

'Couple of hours. I'm on the motorway now. Is everything OK with you guys? How's Rufus's ear?'

'Better. We did what you told us to but holding him still is a struggle. That cat doesn't like that ointment.'

'We', she notes. So Sigrid is still there.

'Do you want me to pick anything up on the way?'

'We went to the shops this morning, so we're good. We figured you might be back. But we forgot to buy milk.'

She can hear Leo talking to someone in the background. Then he's back on the line.

'Sigrid says we're running out of washing-up liquid, too.'

They finish the call and Karen turns the radio back up. The last notes of something she doesn't recognise are just fading out and the familiar intro to a Fugees song takes over.

Ready or not, here I come, Karen thinks.

Then she speeds up, just a little.

30

'What you need is a hideout,' Marike says and starts to pull on tights. 'Bloody hell, these are neat all of a sudden.'

They're sitting in the room behind her studio. Karen looks out the window at the silent snowfall and shivers. The temperature has dropped another few degrees and the kilns haven't been used in days. Or maybe she's feeling cold because she's wearing a sleeveless dress for the party. Fascinated, she watches the six-foot-tall Marike's futile attempts to make her tights reach all the way to the crotch.

She's a good listener, Karen thinks to herself. Marike has let her ramble on for forty-five minutes about how frustrating it is to have Leo and Sigrid on top of her. About how she wants them there one minute but then just wants to be left alone the next. About the thrill she'd felt a few hours earlier, coming home to the sound of voices and the smell of food cooking on the hob.

'Welcome home,' Leo had said and held out a bottle of beer.

She had stared at the floor to hide the mix of panic and joy that surged through her as she took the bottle. Life would be so much easier if they weren't there. So much quieter. 'Welcome home . . .' His words had been like a hockey puck to the gut.

And after dinner, Sigrid had asked the question. Would it be OK if she moved into the guest room? She's considering going to university and if she sells the house her mother left her she won't need to take out student loans.

'I'll pay rent and I'll be studying every night. You won't even know I'm here.'

She had just sat there, dumbstruck. And she'd seen disappointment take hold in Sigrid's eyes as she waited for the words Karen couldn't get out: 'I'd be happy to have you.'

Now, Marike pushes her dress down with a sigh and turns around. She continues, 'Like a secret lair. A refuge you can retreat to when things get overwhelming at home. An overnight flat. Here, in Dunker. *Comprende?*'

Karen responds with a grunt.

'That way you can spend more time with me, too, without having to drive home after one measly glass,' Marike continues.

'And where am I supposed to find an overnight flat?' Karen says gruffly. 'Practically all the buildings in this town are co-ops these days. I don't have the money to buy a second home. Or are you saying I should rent a studio up in Gaarda or Moerbeck?'

'Mm, I can see it now,' Marike says with a wicked laugh. 'Or right here's nice, in the harbour.'

Marike Estrup's ceramic studio is located at the western end of the promenade, where it occupies the ground floor of an old stone building that, in its long history, has housed, in chronological order: a smithy, a sheet metal company and a shop selling boat engines and parts. Previously a dingy neighbourhood full of derelict buildings, it has recently gentrified. Karen has made a habit of borrowing the keys to the studio whenever she's too tired or pressed for time to drive back to Langevik. The sofa bed is reasonably comfortable, and the fridge is always well stocked with gin, vermouth and olives. In the winter, the heat from the kilns is a welcome feature but in the summer you have to sleep with all the windows wide open to make it tolerable.

Marike herself lives in a house she's had built on a narrow strip of land just a few miles north of Dunker – land she'd purchased because it made her the owner of a rich deposit of the shimmering, supple, green clay she moved to Doggerland for. And it had been through her property purchase that she and Karen met eight years ago. Marike had announced that she would buy the plot *at any price*. Torbjörn, one of Karen's cousins on her mother's side and the owner of the worthless piece of land, had seen his opportunity to fleece the peculiar Danish lady. He hadn't been best pleased when Karen, who had happened to be present, had stuck her big nose in and pointed out that the muddy field wasn't worth anywhere near the ridiculous price Torbjörn was asking for it. But Karen had stood her ground and had also made sure a small adjacent plot of buildable land had been included in the purchase.

Granted, it had taken her over a year to repair her relationship with her cousin, but on the other hand, she'd found a new friend in Marike. And Marike had stayed in her new home, surrounded by forests and mosquitoes and with a muddy field as her closest neighbour. She digs the clay and processes it before bringing it to her studio in Dunker, where it's turned into the sculptures that have made Marike a world-renowned ceramic artist.

She's a good friend, Karen muses, but she has no idea what it's like to live off a police salary. She decides to change the subject.

'Are you almost done so I can call a taxi? Eirik will go nuts if we're late.'

She knows she sounds brusque. All the talk about an overnight flat, a place to retreat to, has ruined the festive mood, leaving her feeling despondent. Now she knows exactly what she needs and that she will never be able to get it. A hideout.

'Fine, go ahead and call,' Marike says and resumes tugging on her tights.

Half an hour later, they ring the doorbell of one of the biggest villas in Thingwalla. The house, built for a wealthy shipowner in the mid-Twenties, was, judging by the size, intended to accommodate both a large family and servants. Two foreclosures and sixty years later, it had begun to fall into disrepair, an eyesore in the otherwise posh neighbourhood. Over the years, buyers have come and then quickly gone again after realising just how much work it would take to bring the house back from the brink. Kore and Eirik had won the bidding process with alarming ease and, at almost twice the cost of the property itself, had replaced the plumbing and had the whole house rewired.

To the exasperation of Kore and Eirik's new neighbours, fixing the peeling exterior has been put on hold until spring, but on the inside, the house is already unrecognisable. A number of walls have been knocked down, turning the six normal-sized bedrooms upstairs into half as many of twice the size, each with its own opulent en-suite bathroom. On the ground floor, the result of the demolition is an open-floor plan with enough space to make the black grand piano in one corner look no bigger than a fly speck.

And just as their hosts look like they're from different planets, so the décor on the two floors differ so markedly it's hard to believe the same two people live on both. The bedrooms upstairs bear the mark of Eirik's conventional tastes, while Kore has gone all out on the ground floor with a clear nod to industrial design. Instead of plaster and wallpaper, the walls have been stripped to reveal the red brick underneath and the steel beams that had to be installed when Kore insisted on knocking down a loadbearing wall have been turned into permanent design features. A stainless-steel butcher's bench has been pressed into service as a kitchen island, the dining table is a one-hundred-square-foot behemoth made of thick oak boards and the twelve chairs surrounding it are cast iron, but surprisingly comfortable thanks to large white and grey sheepskins.

'The first half of the evening is mine,' Eirik had told them when they were first invited. 'Then Kore will take over and I'm not responsible for what happens after that.'

That's how they make it work, Karen thinks as she sits down on one of the sheepskins and studies the table décor. Instead of compromising, her two friends make sure they both get what they want. This part is Eirik's traditional New Year's soirée with folded napkins and a passed-down damask tablecloth to hide the rustic oak boards. An artful arrangement of white lilies and roses, which probably took hours to perfect, even for a trained florist like him, runs the length of the table.

Seated around the table are the usual suspects: Marie, Harald, Stella, Duncan, Aylin, Bo, Gordon and Brynn. The mandated dress code is lounge suit but Karen suspects a few of the men will be undoing their ties the minute dinner is over.

He looks stressed, Karen observes, studying Eirik's rosy cheeks as the first course is served and he raises his glass in a welcome toast.

'This is the first of many parties we will be throwing in this house and we wanted to start by inviting our closest friends,' he says.

'Unfortunately, none of them could make it, so we had to make do with you lot instead,' Kore adds.

Looking mildly annoyed, Eirik grudgingly joins in the laughter and the dinner commences.

As expected, the food is conventional and delicious in equal measure. The cheese soufflé is light as a summer cloud, the lobster thermidor a symphony of cream, tarragon and cognac, and the sun-yellow saffron panna cotta delightfully wobbly. The champagne is dry, cold and flowing freely and every time another cork is popped things get livelier. Even Aylin looks like she's enjoying herself, though her smile invariably winks out whenever her husband Bo leans over to whisper something in her ear.

Karen recalls Marike's words a few months earlier.

'I think he's beating her. She's always cooped up in that house. When was the last time she came out for a glass of wine with us?'

Karen had protested. Aylin and Bo had young children, of course she couldn't go out as often as she'd used to. And yet, she had felt the need to bring it up with Aylin. She had stopped by her house one day when she knew Bo wouldn't be home, posed the question point-blank and been laughed at in response. Sure, Aylin had said, Bo has his failings, but he doesn't hit me. Of course not.

Of course not.

And yet, on this festive occasion, Aylin is the only woman wearing a long-sleeved gown with a high neck. Karen turns her attention from her friend to her husband. When Bo notices her contemplating him, he raises his glass in a toast.

'Cheers, Karen,' he says, fixing her with a level stare. 'I hope you're not thinking about unpleasant things on a night like this? That just wouldn't do.'

'Go to hell,' she mouths with a smile and raises her glass back to him without taking a drink.

31

The rest of the night belongs to Kore.

Almost before they've had time to finish their coffee, the house is taken over by a second wave of guests. The moment the clock strikes ten, the elegant piano sonatas that accompanied dinner fade out and deafening rock music starts to blare out of the speakers instead. The living room turns into a dance floor. Karen looks on as Aylin laughingly tries to turn down a man who's insisting on a dance. In the end, she gives in and follows him out onto the dance floor, gesturing apologetically to Bo. He does not look pleased.

Apparently, there's going to be live music, too, Karen notes, studying the small stage installed at the end of the giant room. There's a drum kit set up there, and amplifiers, a double bass and two racks of semi-acoustic guitars.

All the lights have been turned off, even in the kitchen and the two bathrooms. Now, the only source of illumination is a couple of dozen large candelabra that set the brick walls aglow. Karen suspects electric lights would reveal things her hosts don't want her to see. When she was waiting to use the bathroom earlier, the man ahead of her had furtively run his index finger under his nose when he finally emerged. She had suppressed the impulse to run her finger across the closed toilet lid. She doesn't want to know.

Out in the garden, behind a lit bar, two young men in old sheep-skin coats and fingerless gloves are mixing drinks, their breath like clouds. Large infrared heaters are apparently making conditions tolerable out there, because some of the guests are lingering by the bar instead of scurrying back inside with their glasses.

Karen recognises several of them. Some she has bumped into at Kore's production company, KGB Productions, which he co-owns with the Swedish-Doggerian brothers Gordon and Brynn Englund. Others she knows from newspapers and TV. Musicians for the most part, but also an acting couple, the female half of which recently landed a roll in a big Hollywood production while her partner hasn't been cast in anything for years. The rising star, surrounded by of a gaggle of admirers, tilts her head back and laughs uproariously. The gossip rags have been speculating about the marriage being on the rocks and, judging by the looks the man is giving his wife, Karen is forced to conclude the rumour must be true.

She walks up to one of the sheepskin-clad bartenders, orders a gin and tonic and turns her back to the bar while she waits. Aylin and Bo are walking toward a dark corner of the garden. He has a very firm grip on her upper arm but removes his hand when he notices Karen watching. They stop and seem to be dis-cussing something. Bo is looking back and forth between the bar and Aylin, who is listening with bowed head. Karen turns her head but continues to watch them out of the corner of her eye. After a few minutes, they walk back toward the house. Bo has put his arm around his wife's shoulders and smiles when they pass Karen. Aylin looks away.

Further down the long bar, Gordon, Brynn and Kore have been joined by a newly arrived guest. Karen is startled to realise who it is. Apparently, there was more truth than Kore cared to admit to the rumour claiming a certain Los Angeles based band that had topped the charts two years previous are now working with KGB Productions. Karen has long since stopped paying attention to what's trendy in the music business, but not even she can fail to recognise Jason Lavar. There's no mistaking the tattoos that cover the singer's shaved head and snake down around his eye and across half his cheek. Come to think of it, she's not actually that surprised; in the past three or four years, more and more international artists have been seeking out Kore's remote production company with its growing stable of chart toppers. That success is what has made it possible for Kore and Eirik to buy and refurbish one of Thingwalla's largest houses.

She surreptitiously watches Jason Lavar and notes that although he's considerably shorter than she imagined, his charisma is palpable.

'Star-struck?'

The low voice and the puff of hot air against her neck makes her jump and whip around. Leo Friis holds up a bottle of IPA and clinks it against her glass with a mocking grin.

'By you? It's been years since you were famous, hasn't it?' she says with feigned surprise.

She instantly regrets the quip. The fact that Leo Friis was the frontman of The Clamp is something they never talk about. She was obviously aware of the Doggerian band's international success, even though she had lived in London back then and had other things to think about. She couldn't have missed The Clamp if she'd tried.

The band's abrupt breakup, the news of the rift between its members and the speculation about Leo Friis's sudden disappearance from the scene, on the other hand, had completely passed her by. Starting at the horrifying moment when her own life had been smashed to pieces, everything had passed her by. By the time she returned to the world of the living, the media had long since lost interest in the fate of Leo Friis. And it had taken her a long time to realise the filthy homeless person she'd come across while working on a case was *the* Leo Friis.

She has never pried into what happened to him after he disappeared from the spotlight and before he returned to Doggerland. What matters is that he has somewhere to live now and that he seems to be telling the truth when he says he's not doing drugs anymore. And Kore has arranged for him to fill in as a studio musician on occasion, which in turn means Leo Friis is able to contribute toward his room and board. What was supposed to be a temporary arrangement has, like so many other things in Karen's life, turned out very differently from what she planned.

'Touché,' Leo replies and shoots her a crooked smile. 'So what's your secret New Year's wish? Other than for me to finally move out, I mean?'

He holds out a packet of cigarettes and she takes one.

'Have I said that's what I want?'

'Not in so many words, perhaps, but I recognise a cornered woman when I see one. It's that look on your face, halfway between deer in headlights and chimp behind bars, that gives you away.'

'How flattering.'

'The problem is,' Leo continues, 'that half the time, you look like a contented pig. If it weren't for that, I would have moved out ages ago.'

Karen lets out a snort of derision.

'Where would you go? Back to your loading dock in the New Harbour?'

Leo shrugs.

'I'd sort something out. Seriously, Karen, if you really want me to . . .'

He spreads his hands and trails off. She opens her mouth, then closes it again. They stand there in silence, stomping their feet in the cold while they finish their cigarettes.

He should just move out, she thinks to herself. Just get out of my life, as quickly as he came into it.

'Want to head back inside?' Leo says and flicks his cigarette into the snow.

Nothing has been said, and yet, she knows. Unless she does something right now, he's going to be gone the next time she gets home. Things are going to go back to normal. She will have the whole house to herself again. Nice and peaceful. And quiet.

Before she can make her mind up, she hears herself say, 'I don't mind if you stay.'

But Leo has already turned to go back inside.

32

The first thing she notices is the smell of the rug. A stale, dusty whiff of wool finding its way into her mouth and nostrils. A familiar smell of sorrow and stillness, the unworldly calm after the storm. And then she realises there is no after, no reprieve. No time to relax, no tranquil cove or harbour for her to shelter in, no time to recover and mend what was broken. No after, just a before. Just the same deceptive calm that lasts only until the church bells start to toll for the next storm. It may be days or even weeks until the next one.

Or maybe just hours.

Without opening her eyes, she pricks up her ears. Holds her breath and prays not to hear the sound of one of the kids opening their bedroom door. The noise that reaches her instantly makes her pulse slow. Bo Ramnes has left their bedroom door open and his heavy snoring is a sure sign he won't be awake for hours yet.

The fringe of the tufted rug burns against her cheek. She opens one eye. The winter darkness outside the window tells her nothing, the middle of the night looks the same as eight in the morning. One of the kids could come skipping down the stairs any minute, wanting breakfast. Then her eyes find the digits on the DVD player: 04.43 and she suddenly becomes aware that she has held her breath for too long and her vision is getting blurred. She slowly exhales and takes a new breath. And as she does, the pain crashes over her.

With practised determination, she goes through the most important movements while she gingerly pushes up into sitting position, opening and closing her hands first, rotating her wrists, bending her elbows, shrugging her shoulders. There's a sharp new pain in her left shoulder blade and the usual jolt along the back of her ribcage, but nothing seems broken this time. Every inch of her feels battered and bruised, that's all, as though she's been tossed around a cement blender.

The world wobbles when she stands up and she grabs hold of the sofa for support. Its cushions have been knocked over and scattered across the floor. When she bends down to put them back, she finds her underwear. After straightening up the sofa, she goes out to the kitchen and drops the knickers into the bin under the sink, then makes sure to push them further down into the rubbish, hiding them under the brown grounds from a coffee filter. She knows Bo would fly off the handle if he realised she'd thrown them out and that she is never going to be able to make herself put them on again. He's right, she thinks, the problem is that I don't do what he tells me to.

A sound from above makes her freeze mid-motion. Please, don't let it be one of the children, not yet, dear Lord, please, I need more time. She instinctively holds her breath, every sense on high alert. Listening to the sounds as they change. Heavy footfall against the wooden floor upstairs, not Tyra's, not Mikkel's. His. She hears the bathroom door open, then the flush of the toilet and she closes her eyes and prays again. Please, God, don't let him come back down, I can't take anymore. Not now. Aylin doesn't let go of the kitchen counter until five minutes later when the sound of snoring once again drifts down to her from the first floor. Heavy, hungover snoring.

Five days. Just five this time. Early on, it had been weeks between incidents, months even, at first. Enough time to heal, to conceal. Time to come up with plausible excuses for the bruises and broken ribs. No lame clichés about walking into doors or slipping on the stairs – you had to do a lot better than that if you didn't want people to get suspicious. Patches of ice were good; people do slip on those. The slippery floors at the public pool, too. But never the same lie twice. She is good at remembering which ones she's told to whom. Good at making up new things and never repeating the same story. Good at hiding. She has bought every available shade of concealer, learnt how to turn a split lip into an ulcer, which colours camouflage blue and green and which ones are best for concealing the last yellow remnants of a bruise. She thought she was good at picking appropriate clothes, too. She has been so stupid.

Marike had smelled a rat. Last spring she'd asked why she was wearing long sleeves and high necklines during the May heatwave. Afterwards, she'd wished her careless laughter in response to her friend's question had sounded a little less convincing. That laughter had pushed the extended lifeline out of reach. Or was it that she had drifted away? She'd told herself she's a different person now, that she has made her choice, that it's too late to go back.

And he's right. Not about everything, but when it counts. He has given her everything she ever wanted, things she could never have had without him. Tyra and Mikkel. Last night he had bellowed it so loudly she'd been afraid he'd wake them up. It had started the moment their babysitter's taxi was out of sight.

'Without me, you'd have nothing. Do you hear me? *Nothing.* And this is how you thank me? By behaving like some fucking whore?'

She'd tried, even though she usually doesn't bother anymore. Stupid, of course, perhaps she hadn't been completely sober herself. That was probably why. She'd said it was a party, that it was just one dance, that she had tried to decline, but that she hadn't wanted to cause a scene and ruin the mood. Not at Kore and Eirik's. Not on New Year's Eve when everyone was having a good time, when everyone else was dancing. That's what she'd said.

So stupid.

He hadn't been able to control himself long enough to get her up to the bedroom. There had been no music to drown out the sound this time. Fear that the children might wake up had made the pain feel remote as she strained to detect sounds from upstairs. She'd barely felt the blows, just distractedly noted when he entered her and the relief when it was over.

The kids don't know, she tells herself and fills a glass of water from the tap. She drinks slowly to ease the constriction in her throat. They're too young to know what's happening. And then she tells herself she has to rinse off, quietly, quietly, so as not to wake him. Has to lie down next to him in the bedroom, be there when he wakes up. Comfort him when he's overcome with regret, prove that she's not thinking any silly thoughts.

Aylin Ramnes carefully puts the glass down in the sink and walks into the hallway. Before she can take two steps up the stairs, she knows everything has changed.

The white sheepskin teddy with red footpads and blue dungarees is propped against the banister. It almost looks like he ambled over there by himself and sat down. Tyra's teddy, which she would never leave behind, not for anything. Except maybe if she'd seen something so terrifying she forgot him ... Aylin knows what happened even before she discovers the small puddle of urine on the top step.

33

'Bloody hell,' Marike groans and puts her head down on the table.

Karen pours them each a cup of coffee, turns the coffee machine off with a click and puts the pot back.

'Drink this,' she says and drops a fizzy tablet of paracetamol into a glass of water. 'You're going to feel a lot better after you've had a slice of toast and some coffee.'

'I'm never drinking again,' Marike says darkly and downs the glass in four gulps.

'Of course you aren't,' Karen says and drops another fizzy tablet into a glass for herself. Then she downs the contents and wipes her mouth on the back of her hand, wincing at the bitter taste.

'What time is it?'

'Half past nine.'

Marike groans and reaches for the milk.

They eat in silence. The only sound is their determined chewing; neither one of them is in the mood to talk. Instead, they go over, each in their own mind, the events of the night before. Karen recaps in reverse. At quarter past three, a taxi dropped them off at the studio. While she paid the driver, Marike, who had apparently taken off her high heels, had tottered through the several inches of snow blanketing the pavement in her stocking feet. At the last second, Karen had remembered to pick up her friend's brand-new Louboutin pumps from the car floor. Then, despite being thoroughly hammered, she had managed to usher the considerably drunker Marike through the front door of the studio.

Now, her knee is throbbing and she can tell she has several big blisters on her feet. Had she danced? No, she assures herself, not a chance, I haven't danced in over a decade. Then it all comes back to her. Yes, she had danced. With Brynn, with Eirik. With the bitter actor whose wife is on her way to Hollywood. And then with Leo.

He'd performed, she suddenly remembers – against his will. He'd been talked into it by Jason Lavar, who had started the new year off by playing a few songs and then announcing that his big idol, Leo Friis, was in the room. He had then asked, in front of the entire party, if Leo would do him the honour of joining him on stage for a couple of songs. Startled and alarmed, Kore had tried to intervene, torn between a need to keep Jason Lavar happy and his instinct to protect Leo, who had made it perfectly clear he didn't want to play in front of an audience ever again. Not 30,000 people in an arena, not 150 people in a house in Thingwalla. But Jason Lavar had insisted.

In the end, Leo had reluctantly climbed up on stage, no doubt only because he knew he'd draw even more attention to himself by refusing. Karen had noticed his hands shaking as he picked up the guitar, his eyes darting nervously around the room, as though looking for a last-minute escape route. A deer in headlights, she'd thought. Exactly how he had described her.

But she'd also noticed that halfway through the first song, his anxiety had subsided a little. She'd noticed the corner of his

208

mouth twitching when he played the intro to the second. And she'd noticed his relief when it was over and he could get off the stage. But before then, something else. Another side of Leo.

Afterwards, she'd asked him to dance.

'Musicians don't dance,' he'd replied.

'Neither do I. And you don't have to move out if you don't want to,' she'd said.

'OK.'

Marike reaches for the coffee pot only to discover that it's empty. She slowly gets to her feet, holds the pot up with a querying look and receives a mute nod in reply. Ten minutes later, when Marike pours the freshly brewed coffee and registers Karen's absent look, she finally breaks the silence with the words:

'Oh, for crying out loud, will you just sleep with him already!'

Karen bangs her cup against her front teeth.

'Or are you only into shagging men you don't like?'

A familiar sound cuts the awkward pause that follows Marike's question short. Grateful for the interruption, Karen gets up quickly, locates her handbag on the kitchen counter and pulls out her phone. One glance at the screen and she's suddenly wide awake.

'Hi, Thorstein,' she says, knowing it's going to be bad news.

Byle's voice is tense, his Noorian consonants harsher than usual on the other end of the line.

'Hi, Karen, sorry to disturb you. I'm afraid you're going to have to come back sooner than you planned. Gabriel Stuub is dead. Murdered.'

34

This time, it's not with a sense of freedom Karen Eiken Hornby gets in her car. Aware that she shouldn't be driving for another few hours, she keeps a white-knuckle hold on the steering wheel and frequently checks the speedometer. She's grateful that at least the New Year's Day traffic is light and the roads don't seem too slippery, despite the heavy snowfall of the past twenty-four hours.

She raises her arm and sniffs her armpit. There had been no time to go back to Langevik to pack a bag. Her only chance of making it all the way up to Gudheim before nightfall had been to throw herself into her car, which was parked on the street outside the studio. After ending the call with Thorstein Byle, she'd pulled on the same clothes she'd worn when she left Langevik the day before. Thank God she'd brought her New Year's outfit in a bag and changed at Marike's. Jeans, an old T-shirt with a Ramones print and a much-too-thin suede jacket is hardly an appropriate ensemble for a detective inspector, she thinks ruefully and heaves a deep sigh. She probably has remnants of last night's make-up under her eyes, and if she's truly unlucky, pieces of the gold confetti that had filled the room at the stroke of midnight are still stuck in her hair.

Marike had, despite her fragile state, instantly grasped the situation and dug out a pair of muddy wellies and an old woollen cardigan, which she'd shoved in one bag along with a can of Coke and Karen's half-eaten slice of toast in another. That was all the studio had been able to offer in terms of clothing and sustenance, and Karen had no time to waste in any event. Another wave of guilt crashes over her. Why had she taken time off? She should clearly have stayed on Noorö over the holiday. And then that other voice, the one she prefers to listen to right now: it wouldn't have made any difference if you'd been up there; you're not a bodyguard.

Surprisingly, her boss repeats that sentiment almost verbatim when she gets him on the phone twenty minutes later. Karen realises it must be evening where he is. She can hear loud music and voices in the background and although Jounas Smeed sounds less than sober when he picks up, he quickly pulls it together and listens without interrupting.

'OK,' he says. 'I guess we know for sure what we're dealing with, then. Did you contact Brodal and Larsen?'

'Just now; they're on their way. Not best pleased, either one of them. Sören Larsen was the worse of the two, actually.'

'Probably hungover,' Smeed comments archly.

'Frustrated and tired, more like. The new year could hardly have come off to a worse start as far as he's concerned. We really need more technicians this time, even if that means paying them overtime.'

'I'll call Viggo Haugen as soon as we're done here and let him know what the situation is,' he says. 'And you? Frustrated and tired, too? Or just hungover?' he adds.

Karen sighs. She's used to her boss switching gears from chummy to bullying in the blink of an eye, depending on which best suits his needs in the moment. And she has seen both sides

211

too up-close. This time, Jounas Smeed almost sounds like he's genuinely concerned about her wellbeing. It must be the tropical cocktails temporarily mellowing his arrogance, she muses.

'All of the above, I'm afraid. I shouldn't have gone home for New Year's, I should have stayed up there.'

'Oh, get over yourself,' Smeed replies harshly. 'Your job is to investigate crimes, not prevent them. You're a copper, not a bodyguard.'

Just don't tell Viggo Haugen that, she retorts inwardly. The Chief of Police never misses an opportunity to underscore that the main mission of the police is, in fact, to prevent crime.

She gets lucky with the ferry. Just two minutes after driving on board in Thorsvik, the engines begin to rev up. The sky is leaden and a slow snowfall is blurring the edges of Skalvet in the distance. There are a lot more cars on the ferry today. She counts fourteen in addition to her own, but no one seems minded to leave the warmth of their vehicle for a breath of fresh air or a cigarette. Instead, Karen notes, some are using the crossing as an opportunity to nap. Several drivers have their eyes closed, the rest are on their phones. The only sound is the thudding of the engines and the occasional screech of a hopeful gull. The colour seems to have drained from the world; the sky is grey, the sea is grey and the only sign of life outside the cars is a handful of gulls that have settled down on the railing.

Karen turns the radio on and impatiently drums her fingers against the steering wheel while the ferry chugs through the slushy water. She glances at her watch and then at her phone. Just then, a familiar melody streams out of the speakers.

'It's one o'clock, this is your headline news. A man in his mid-thirties was found dead at Groth's distillery this morning. Thorstein Byle, commanding officer of the Noorö Police, confirms that an investigation has been opened, but declines to reveal the victim's identity or the cause of death.'

The newscaster pauses, then continues, 'New Year's Eve is reported to have been relatively uneventful in most parts of the country, with only a few cases of disorderly behaviour and assault. A knife fight involving five teenagers took place in the Dunker neighbourhood of Moerbeck. Two people were taken to the local hospital but are said not to have sustained life-threatening injuries.'

As the newscaster moves on to a car crash outside Ravenby and a collapsed scaffolding in Lemdal – neither of which caused any serious injuries – Karen stops listening. Apparently the only one who didn't have someone watching over him last night was Gabriel Stuub.

'And now, the weather. A low-pressure area moving in from the west is expected to reach the western parts of the country and Noorö tonight. DMI has issued snow and wind warnings. Conditions are expected to worsen over the course of tomorrow, before the storm moves on toward . . .'

Storm warning. Should have known, Karen mutters loudly to herself.

Indeed, storms are hardly unexpected on Doggerland this time of year and, normally, she would have come prepared. She turns off the radio and goes over what lies ahead. Wet trainers or Marike's wellies, which are at least two sizes too big. Those are her options. And then she has to assert her authority with colleagues and interviewees while wearing worn jeans and a knitted

213

cardigan that hangs down to her knees. Add to that a knee that's throbbing after last night's idiotic exertions on the dance floor and a pounding headache. She's patently not equipped to handle the weather or a murder investigation.

Byle had sounded tense and she can understand why. Fredrik Stuub's death had been largely overlooked by the media. Granted, the editor of a sleepy local paper had been in touch on Boxing Day night, but he'd bought her story about it probably being a tragic accident. Without lying outright, Karen had made sure to emphasise Stuub's advanced age and the treacherous terrain around the quarry, and the story had been limited to a brief notice in the newspaper's online edition. But the main reason the rest of the media had failed to take an interest in Fredrik Stuub had been the lack of witnesses calling them to tell their story.

It's not going to be as easy this time.

Byle's summary had been very clear on one point: more than twenty people had been present at the distillery when Gabriel Stuub was found with his throat cut.

35

The ferry docks with a shudder and the cars slowly start making their way down the ramp. Karen hesitates for a second in the roundabout that marks the start of the northbound motorway then decides to swing by the pub before heading up to Gudheim. Checking into the same place as last time, down here in Lysvik, forty miles from the crime scene, is far from ideal, but she's not going to take any chances. She definitely won't have time to look for accommodation up in Gudheim.

Ten minutes later, Ellen Jensen has confirmed that the same room is free if she wants it. As Karen climbs back behind the wheel, stress is pounding in her ears and she glances quickly at her watch. With a bit of luck, she will be there in an hour, but an hour after that, it will already be dark out. She reaches out and rummages through her bag. The can of Coke overflows when she opens it; she takes a sip of the lukewarm sugariness and forces herself to breathe deeply. In, out, in, out, in, then realises there's no time for that; the estimated sixty-minute drivetime is for when there's no snow.

She reaches for the slice of toast Marike tossed in the bag and turns the key in the ignition. Chews methodically as she makes a U-turn and drives back up the high street toward the roundabout. The snow is falling faster now, covering the windscreen like white lace between each sweep of the wipers.

She glances up at the sign with a sigh before turning onto the motorway:

GUDHEIM 39 MILES

She drives as fast as she dares. The wind is still relatively low and though there is snow on the road, it's not being packed into drifts just yet. Just south of the Skreby exit a car has broken down and she is forced to slow down until the resulting congestion clears up. After that, she sees no more than a dozen cars heading south, and she passes about as many going the other way. A combination of hangovers and bad weather is probably keeping people indoors, she thinks, and brakes hard when two deer bound out of the ditch and dash across the road. She continues at a slower pace, her heart pounding. She would hate to have to use the axe in the boot to kill an injured animal.

It's quarter past three when she reaches the end of the motorway and the sign that announces her three options from there:

GUDHEIMBY .7 MILES

GUDHEIM SHIP SETTING 1.2 MILES

DISTILLERY .4 MILES

Next to the bottommost signpost, someone has written in black paint: *God hears prayer.*

Karen turns right onto a paved road. The distillery comes into view after just a few hundred yards, dramatically set against its backdrop of sky and sea. Two cars and a van are parked outside by the low wall ringing the property. Karen drives past them up the narrow road as fast as she dares. When she reaches the gate, she rolls down her window and shows her ID to a uniformed officer. He salutes her and waves her through. In the rear-view mirror she can see the journalists climbing out of their cars to try to persuade the long-suffering constable to let them in. Or at least to let them talk to someone who knows what's going on. Karen noted the DTV logo on the white van and the *Kvellsposten* one on the green Saab. She suspects the third vehicle belongs to a very peeved local newspaper editor.

The small car park is full to capacity and about ten cars have lined up on what, during the other half of the year, is likely a lush lawn. Now, it's a frozen patch of mud covered in several inches of snow. Karen leans forward and peers out of the windscreen. She has to strain her eyes to make anything out. Granted, the snow adds light, but the sky is grey and dusk is falling, though it won't be fully dark for another hour. She sees three black-and-yellow police cars and, further up, Byle's Volvo, but there's no sign yet of Kneought Brodal, Sören Larsen or the white vans used by the crime scene technicians. She parks next to one of the police cars, reaches for the bag on the passenger seat and pulls out the muddy wellies. She's going to pass on the cardigan for now, she decides, and zippers up her green suede jacket.

Pain radiates from her knee to her hip when she slowly trudges through the snow in the direction of the main building. Light is streaming out through the tall windows and she can see a handful of men in orange high-vis vests stomping their feet to stay warm. Thorstein Byle spots her the moment she steps into the light and comes to meet her.

'Finally,' he says. 'Well, I obviously know you came as quickly as you could. Have you had anything to eat?'

Karen shakes his outstretched hand and then her head.

'Half a slice of toast.'

'There's plenty of food inside, lots of leftovers from last night's party. Maybe we should make sure you get something in you and I can fill you in while you eat.'

'Where's the body?'

'About five hundred yards that way,' he says, pointing. 'The scene has been cordoned off and I have two men guarding it. There's nothing we can do over there until the coroner and technicians arrive.'

Karen nods. Byle's right and she's definitely not about to try Sören Larsen's patience further by crossing the cordon just to satisfy her own curiosity.

'Sounds good,' she says. 'Has Sven Andersén been by?'

'Not this time. The cause of death is pretty apparent, so I called you right away. Besides, Andersén is ill and I figured there was no harm in waiting for the coroner. Like I said, even I could tell the guy had his throat slit.'

'Is there anywhere we can talk privately?'

'Yes, the Groths have been very accommodating. We have full use of the room where we talked to William Tryste last time we were here.'

'And where is everyone?'

'Björn Groth lives with his wife in one of the wings and their son Jens and his wife have the other. They're all in their respective homes. The daughter – Madeleine – and her husband live down the road in Gudheimby.'

'And the other guests? You said something about a big New Year's bash?'

'More like an office party. They're checked into the hotel by the golf course about half a mile from here. If you can call it a hotel, more like a boarded-up B & B, if you ask me. I have people over there, too, making sure no one slips away.'

'How many are we?'

'I have seven guys in the field. People, I mean. Two of them are women.'

'How did you get that many?'

'I called the station down in Thorsvik for backup and they sent three guys. I couldn't have got it done it without them, the flu has made it up here now, too.'

'Great,' Karen says, 'top-notch work, Thorstein, just like last time. Shall we go inside?'

Having decided to hold off on talking to their hosts, they walk through the lobby and past the large copper stills directly to William Tryste's giant office. Two uniformed officers are seated at the conference table when they enter, but they instantly spring to attention when they spot their superiors, wiping their mouths and saluting while discreetly trying to chew and swallow the food in their mouths.

'At ease,' she tells them and notes one of them eyeing her wellies and ripped jeans before sitting back down.

Byle hadn't exaggerated, she discovers. If these are the leftovers from the New Year's office party, Groth's must have pulled out all the stops. Large platters of charcuteries, cheeses, pâtés and shellfish cover most of the conference table. At one end there are baskets full of different types of bread and bottles of mineral water and low-alcohol beer sit next to two giant coffee urns.

Karen heaps a mountain of food on a plate and picks up two bottles of mineral water while Thorstein Byle takes a seat on the leather sofa at the far end of the room. When she joins him, he nods at the two constables, who are still chewing their food in silence, their minds seemingly elsewhere.

'Are you OK with them in here or would you like me to ask them to leave?'

'I don't think they'd be able to hear us from all the way over there, even if they were awake,' Karen says and spreads butter on a slice of black bread.

She pops a piece of lamb pâté into her mouth and pours herself a glass of mineral water. Then she pulls out her notepad and puts it down next to her plate on the glass coffee table.

'All right, let's have it,' she says.

Byle tells her the Groths had decided to throw a New Year's party for all their employees and their partners to kick off a year of significant expansion. Aside from Björn and Laura Groth, their two children Jens and Madeleine and their spouses and William Tryste and his wife, the guest list had consisted of eleven employees and six plus-ones. In other words, a total of twenty-five people, of which twenty-one were still present at midnight. Four people had left early, according to what he had been told so far, two after a call from a babysitter worried about the flu, the other two because the wife of one of the malthouse workers had had too much to drink before the main course had even been served, and had therefore been taken home by her husband. William Tryste's wife Helena had refrained from drinking and had driven her husband home just before one. The company's secretary, Eva Framnes, had gone with them, having been offered a ride to her home in Skreby. Madeleine Groth and her husband Elias had left the party around half past one and the rest of the family spent the night in their respective homes on the premises. The other guests had stayed at the 'hotel' by the golf course. This time, Byle draws air quotes around the word to underline the deficiency of the place.

'Aside from the foreman, Bergvall, it's all young men working in production and some of their girlfriends.'

From what Byle had been told, it had been a good party and the mood had been raucous. The Groths had spared no expense when it came to food, drinks or fireworks. Which was probably why no one had noticed one of the guests was missing.

Gabriel's absence hadn't been noted until breakfast the next day and at that point the general consensus had been that he was probably still sleeping it off. It wasn't until the cleaning crew arrived at about half past nine and started to pick up the spent fireworks and empty champagne bottles and glasses out by the lookout point that Gabriel Stuub's body had been discovered. A young cleaner had at first thought the man slumped under one of the gnarled Scots pines had lain down to sleep and been worried he might have frozen to death. She hadn't noticed the red snow around the man, or the fact that his throat looked like the throats of the deer her father used to hang in the woodshed after the autumn hunt until she got closer.

'OK,' Karen says when Byle is finished, 'so some of the guests are still at the hotel. We're not going to be able to keep them here another night.'

'No, I was just on the phone with Röse. He's over there with Svanemark and tempers are apparently starting to flare.'

'You haven't started taking statements?'

Byle looks uncomfortable.

'We've collected everyone's information. I wanted to wait for you, to make sure there's no trouble down the line. My understanding is that our role is mostly to stand guard.'

Karen sighs inwardly. This is the downside to having the national CID head up all serious crime investigations; you take away people's responsibilities and authority and the result is anxious officers who are scared to put one foot in front of the other.

'And you have done that wonderfully,' she says. 'Just one thing, Thorstein.'

She pauses, searching for the right words. Stop being so fucking passive, she growls inwardly. Out loud, she says, 'I'm never going to complain about you taking the initiative, so long as what you do makes sense and isn't in breach of established police regulations. You're an experienced officer and I need your help. OK?'

'OK.'

'So, starting right now, your men are going to take down very basic witness statements and then we're going to let the guests go home. I want to know the last time each and every one of them saw Gabriel Stuub and whether there were any arguments during the course of the evening. I also want them to ask open questions about Gabriel Stuub, coax out any other observations anyone might have about last night. And I want all the guests swabbed.'

'Of course. I'll tell them to get going straight away. But I need to keep a couple of my guys at the crime scene and at least one at the bottom of the drive. With only seven constables, we're spread pretty thin.'

Karen nods.

'Yes, this is going to take a while. I'll start by talking to all the members of the Groth family, but I really need at least two—'

A familiar voice from the doorway cuts her off.

'So, Eiken,' says Karl Björken. 'Here you are, stuffing your face. I thought we had a murder to solve?'

36

The relief Karen feels at seeing the tall, dark man who seems to fill the entire doorway is overwhelming; it's an effort not to run over and hug him.

Once Detective Inspector Karl Björken from the National CID has been properly introduced to Thorstein Byle, they agree Byle will go down to the hotel to help the officers there, while Karen and Björken tackle the Groth family.

'But before I do anything else, I want to see the body. What's taking Sören and Kneought so long?' Karen snaps impatiently.

'Calm down, Eiken,' Karl Björken says and steals a piece of serrano ham from her plate. 'They were on the same ferry as me. They probably went straight to the scene.'

As they walk over to the spot where Gabriel Stuub's body was found, Karen tells Karl everything Byle just told her, then briefly sums up the Fredrik Stuub case.

'I've done my homework,' Karl says. 'Smeed emailed me your summaries and I skimmed them on the ferry. They made for a pretty unpleasant read . . .'

Karen gives him a surprised look.

'I didn't realise you were so sensitive.'

'I was referring to the language. Why suddenly so formal? I almost dozed off.'

'It serves Smeed right,' she replies airily. 'How come you're here, anyway? I thought you were on parental leave? And I heard you managed to catch the flu, too.'

'Fever-free since yesterday morning. Smeed called me right after talking to you, asked if I would consider deferring my parental leave for a few weeks – and let's just say I was happy to oblige.'

'I take it you have relatives staying over the holidays?'

'Mine and Inger's. And a sober New Year's Eve on top of that. But yours was more fun, it seems . . .'

Karl Björken shoots her clothes a significant look.

'Are you aware your hair is full of sparkly stuff? And you're limping,' he adds after a second look. 'How much pain are you really in these days?'

'Sometimes none at all. Right now, a lot. I made the mistake of dancing last night, in heels, no less, and trudging around in these boots isn't helping either.'

They stop at a strip of red-and-white police tape flapping in the wind. Two floodlights have already been set up and two more are being installed in the last two corners of the cordoned-off area. This time, Larsen has been given reinforcements, too, Karen notes as she spots five men in white protective clothing carrying heavy equipment cases. Larsen himself looks grim and focused as he orders the uniformed officers to aim the lights better.

Outside the cordon, Karen spots another familiar figure looking equally grim. The coroner is struggling to zipper his overalls around his massive gut and replies with a grunt when Karen says hello.

'We're not going to get in your way,' she says. 'I just wanted a first sense of what the scene looks like.'

Without responding, Kneought Brodal bends down to pick up his big black bag, lifts up the police tape and lumbers off.

'Our own little ray of sunshine,' Björken says with a grin. 'I reckon there's a better view from over there.'

He nods toward a hillock on the other side of the cordoned-off area, and after walking over to it, they conclude that he was right. From up here, they have an unobstructed view of Stuub's body. He's lying on his side with his knees pulled up and his arms extended along his sides.

'He was probably sitting with his back against the tree when someone slit his throat. Then he toppled over sideways,' Karen says, shading her eyes with her hand.

'Or he collapsed when the cut was made. No, strike that, I think you're right. He must have died instantly, or his arms wouldn't be in that position. I assume they haven't found the weapon?'

Karen shakes her head slowly without taking her eyes off the dead man. Wincing, she watches Kneought Brodal, who has got down on his knees next to the body and is starting his preliminary examination. If having to come out here for Fredrik Stuub put the coroner in a bad mood, it's probably nothing compared to how testy he's going to be now.

'No,' she says, 'according to Thorstein Byle no weapon was found anywhere near the victim, and I assume we won't find it, either,' she says, nodding toward the edge of the cliff. 'They're probably doing the autopsy as early as tomorrow,' she adds, raising her eyebrows questioningly and firing off a smile she hopes comes across as innocent.

'And I assume you want me to attend it so you don't have to? Want me to placate Brodal to the sound of the bone saw?'

'Yes, please, since you're kind enough to offer,' she replies quickly. 'I had my fill of that the other day. Do you want to head back up? How about I start with Björn Groth and his wife and you drive over to talk to the daughter, Madeleine, and her husband? Apparently, they live over in Gudheimby, so it's only five minutes away. I'll try to get to Jens Groth as well.'

'What about William Tryste and his wife?'

'I think they're going to have to wait until tomorrow. Oh, you need a lot of time on your hands when you talk to that bloke. He enjoys waxing lyrical about malting and mashing. And he has an alibi for the murder of Fredrik Stuub.'

'And we're sure the two murders are connected?'

'For the moment, I choose to believe they are.'

Karen grits her teeth against the pain as she struggles down the hillock in her oversized wellies. As soon as she reaches level ground, she shoves her frozen hands in her jacket pockets and pulls her shoulders up against the cold. Right now, she wouldn't mind a strong shot of whiskey. Single malt, matured in a sherry cask, or American bourbon, either one. Come to think of it, anything would do.

37

When Karen knocks on the front door of the eastern wing of the house, which serves as the couple's private residence, Björn Groth himself comes to open it with a large cloth napkin in hand. Like his son, the man before her is powerfully built, almost fat. But there's none of Jens' stockiness here; Björn Groth's tall and broad-shouldered figure carries every last pound in a way that calls to mind his namesake, the bear. The similarity is underscored by his nut-brown mane, which, though he must be well past sixty, doesn't seem to contain so much as a streak of grey. The contrast with his furrowed face is so stark Karen has to wonder if the hair colour is real.

'We haven't been able to eat a bite until now,' he explains. 'Would you mind if we finish while we talk? Or maybe you'd even like to join us?'

After declining politely, she follows him through the hallway. Despite his size, there's something graceful, almost coquettish, about Björn Groth's movements. His heels barely seem to touch the floor when he walks, and Karen has to cough to cover a sudden fit of mirth when the image of a dancing bear suddenly pops into her head. He leads her into a room dominated by a massive mahogany dining table and eight matching chairs under an enormous crystal chandelier. A woman just north of sixty is sitting at one of the long sides of the table. When Björn and Karen appear in the doorway, she immediately puts down the glass of red wine she was holding, stands up and comes to meet them.

'Laura Groth,' she says with a smile, extending a slender hand. 'Welcome. Inspector Eiken, I presume?'

'Detective Inspector, if we're being pedantic,' Karen replies with a smile. 'Are you sure you wouldn't prefer for me to wait somewhere so you can finish your meal in peace?'

'We're done,' Laura Groth says, and Karen notes Björn's longing look at his half-eaten plate.

With surprising efficiency, and without once coming across as dismissive, the graceful Laura Groth in her tweed skirt and jumper set ushers them out of the dining room.

'Why don't we go into the parlour?' she says. 'We'll be much more comfortable there. Did my husband offer you a drink? Coffee, perhaps, or a cup of tea? I don't suppose there's any point asking if you'd like something stronger?'

'Sadly, no.'

'Maybe another time.'

The so-called parlour turns out to be a living room with oat-coloured sofas and an impressive art collection on the walls, while the rest of the décor looks like it's from the late-nineteenth century. The Groths have indulged in a few modernisations, Karen notes, looking around, but most of the features seem to have been preserved from when the house was first built. The architecture exudes the same fin-de-siècle spirit as William Tryste's office in the distillery building.

They sit down, the Groths in one of the two sofas, Karen in the other.

'Do you live alone in this wing?' she asks.

'Yes, and really, it's much too big since the children moved out,' Björn Groth replies. 'But it's tradition for the owner of the distillery to live here.'

'We're actually the third generation,' his wife adds. 'Björn's grandfather started the company.'

'But I believe your daughter lives in Gudheimby, is that right?'

'Yes, but Madeleine is a silent partner. She and her husband Elias run a real estate company in Ravenby, so there's no point in them living out here. And a modern house would undeniably be more comfortable than this draughty old manor for us, too. But, tradition is tradition.'

Laura Groth speaks very clearly but sounds a bit forced.

'And your son, Jens? His title, is it Head of Sales?'

Björn Groth nods. 'That's right. He and his wife live here, in the other wing. Sandra is probably asleep, but I think Jens is in his office.'

'Sandra has come down with a fever and a terrible headache,' Laura Groth explains in a worried voice. 'I'm afraid she's caught the flu and I honestly don't know if she's in any state to talk . . .'

She trails off.

'We'll see,' Karen replies evasively. 'We're probably going to have to talk to some of you more than once. But right now, I just want to ask you and your husband some basic questions.'

She's met with solemn nods and continues.

'Let's start with the reason you threw such a big party.'

Björn Groth clears his throat and runs a hand through his brown hair.

'Well, with everything that's happened, I feel weird saying it, but we wanted to celebrate, simply put. The company is going to see a lot of changes this year and it's important to us that our employees feel part of that.'

'As you know, this is a family business and loyalty is important to us,' Laura Groth adds. 'Several of our employees have been with us for over twenty years.'

'How many employees do you have?'

'Whiskey-making is largely seasonal, at least if you do it in the traditional way. At peak times, we employ fourteen people in addition to Jens and myself.'

'And I'm told a number of those employees were here last night with their partners.'

'Feel free to say wives, or in some cases girlfriends. All our employees are men,' Björn Groth says. 'It's not that we wouldn't welcome women, but—'

He breaks off at the sound of his wife chuckling.

'As usual, my husband forgets that one of our most pivotal employees, Eva Framnes, is a woman. She works as a secretary and is also in charge of invoicing and payroll.'

Björn Groth looks momentarily sheepish; Karen turns to him.

'You mentioned upcoming changes to the business. Can you tell me more about what they will entail?' she asks and notes that the question seems to make him feel more relaxed.

'Well, in a nutshell, we're going to put Noorö on the map,' he says with a pleased smile and leans back, pulling one leg over the other with some difficulty.

'Is that right?' Karen says. 'I don't seem to recall any difficulty locating it in my school atlas.'

The sarcasm is wasted on Björn Groth.

'Sure, sure, but what are we known for? Aside from the whiskey, I mean. What draws people here?'

230

Karen forces out a smile but says nothing. She hates rhetorical questions.

'Exactly,' Björn Groth says triumphantly. 'Nothing! Tourists simply don't come here. Even though we have Northern Europe's most beautifully situated golf course and an ancient ship setting. People should be flocking to this part of Doggerland! The problem is that we're not trumpeting what we have. We don't market ourselves.'

No, Karen agrees inwardly, you certainly don't. She knows about the old golf course, though she's never been. And now that she thinks about it, it must be beautifully situated out on the promontory, surrounded by the sea on three sides. But she has never heard it spoken of as an attraction worth flocking to. If she'd had to guess, she would have said it was closed down years ago.

'And how can we, unless we also offer potential visitors somewhere to stay?' Björn Groth continues his game-show host act.

Karen can feel her impatience growing and discreetly glances down at her watch. Laura Groth notices.

'What my husband is trying to say is that we're planning to build a conference facility that capitalises on its proximity to the golf course and the distillery.'

'A conference facility? Is there really demand for that up here?'

Karen makes no effort to hide her incredulity.

'Not yet,' Björn Groth admits. 'Though we've actually already hosted our first international guests. And they weren't just your ordinary golfers, let me tell you.'

He pauses for effect.

'I can't tell you their names, we'll save that for the marketing, but I can tell you two of them count among the world's leading businessmen and another two have close connections with the British royal family.'

Karen recalls the air quotes Thorstein Byle put around the word 'hotel' when he mentioned the place up by the golf course, where a group of most likely annoyed and hungover people are currently waiting for the police to take their statements so they can finally leave. She briefly wonders if Björn Groth is sober. That famous businessmen and people close to the British royal family would choose to spend even five minutes there is completely unthinkable.

The explanation comes in the form of a delighted chuckle from the sofa across from her.

'You don't believe me, I can tell,' he says, 'but they really did come here recently to play the course. Flew in on a helicopter and stayed longer than you'd think. The course is as tricky as it is breathtaking. But you're right; they obviously didn't stay the night.'

'I didn't even know you owned the golf course.'

'Yes, my late father was a major golf enthusiast and had grand plans once upon a time. Unfortunately, he was never businessman enough to make anything of it.'

'So it's still playable?'

'Absolutely. We actually have a small number of golfers who come back year after year, but without the revenue from the distillery, we wouldn't have been able to keep it open. That being said, we don't offer any club activities and since there's nowhere to stay, maintenance has been limited to keeping the course itself playable and a few of the boys from the mash house take care of that as a side gig.'

'And the hotel?'

Björn Groth laughs.

'A grand word for that dilapidated shack. The only time it makes any money is when we rent it out to school classes or pensioners' associations visiting the ship setting in Gudheim and looking for something basic. And we let our employees use it when they work late.'

'Only the distillery is profitable. We keep the golf course for nostalgic reasons, I suppose,' Laura Groth explains. 'And to be honest, we've considered letting nature reclaim it once or twice.'

'But then we were asked if we would rent out the entire course for a day to a group of eight golfers and whether there was anywhere for a helicopter to land nearby,' Björn Groth says.

'Did they explain why they wanted to come here to play?'

'From what I gathered, word of the course's unique location had somehow reached one of the businessmen. As I mentioned, it's breathtakingly situated and very challenging, especially when it's windy, and, as you know, that's more rule than exception up here.'

Karen nods. I'm never going to understand golfers, she thinks to herself.

'Also, our single malt is starting to draw attention internationally and we were able to offer them the opportunity to sample some of our more exclusive barrels,' Björn Groth continues. 'Long story short, they were very happy with their visit and it set us to thinking maybe we should invest in something that will benefit all of Noorö.'

Karen forces out another smile. William Tryste's gushing praise for the distillery had been annoying, but at least it had felt like it came from a place of genuine interest in whiskey production. Björn Groth's bombastic bragging is gauche. He could probably just as easily have decided to build an amusement park, she reflects.

She decides to bring the conversation back to the reason she's there. She can find out the exact details of the Groths' expansion plans later, should they turn out to be relevant.

'Great,' she says. 'I'd love to hear more about that some other time, but let's go back to yesterday.'

'Yes, of course, what would you like to know?'

Increasingly discouraged, Karen notes down the Groths' account of the previous night. Yes, it had been a lovely party from start to finish, aside from an incident involving one of the female guests, who had overindulged and been taken home by her husband no later than half past eight. And yes, of course almost everyone had been inebriated to some extent, not least Gabriel Stuub, who had been three sheets to the wind. There had been an unpleasant altercation just before midnight when Gabriel insisted on setting off the fireworks and Jens Groth and the foreman of the mash house, Ingemar Bergvall, had been forced to intervene. Gabriel had lost his temper, yelling and cursing at his employer, but in the end, he'd staggered away with a can of lager in his hand. Neither Björn nor Laura had any idea where he had gone after that. Everyone's attention had been on the fireworks.

The rockets soaring up from the plateau next to the edge of the cliff and exploding over the sea had been a spectacular sight to behold. They had served champagne and drunk a toast to an exciting year ahead. Soon thereafter, Laura had retired, while the others had gone back up to the warehouse, where the party continued. A while later, when Björn realised no one had seen Gabriel, he had worried there might be unexploded fireworks lying around. But Ingemar Bergvall had assured him all the fire-works had been set off as planned and told him Gabriel had probably staggered back to his room and passed out. And no one had seen him after that.

'To be completely honest, I was grateful he'd left. It wasn't the first time Gabriel had had too much to drink at an office party.'

'Are you telling me he had a drinking problem?'

'I'm not really in a position to say; I didn't know him very well. From what I've heard, he had marital problems, so that might be why he drank too much last night,' Björn replies in an attempt to take the sting out of his words.

'And of course he'd recently lost his grandfather in a tragic accident,' Laura adds.

As though suddenly struck by a thought, Laura Groth fixes Karen with a level stare.

'Or . . . it was an accident, wasn't it?'

Karen considers being evasive but dismisses the notion. The truth is going to come out any day now anyway.

'I'm afraid it wasn't,' she says. 'It looks as though Fredrik Stuub was murdered as well.'

Silence engulfs the parlour. Laura is still staring at Karen but Björn's eyes suddenly dart toward the tall windows, as though he has spotted something. Karen quickly turns around, but all she can see is the room reflected in the black glass.

'Can either of you think of any reason someone would want to kill Fredrik and Gabriel?' she asks.

Her words seem to rouse Björn Groth from his torpor.

'Us?' he says in a tone of outrage. 'What could we possibly know about something like that?'

'Well, you've known Gabriel for years. Maybe you knew his grandfather, too?'

'No,' Laura replies, her voice steady. 'We were not acquainted. We had obviously heard of him, but that's all.'

'That's all,' her husband agrees, somewhat less steadily. 'This has absolutely nothing to do with us.'

38

Just like last time, Karen finds Jens Groth behind the cluttered desk in his office at the back of the distillery's warehouse. His wife Sandra is, as Laura Groth informed her, in bed with a high fever. The locum provincial doctor has strongly discouraged but not explicitly forbidden Karen from talking to her, not so much out of concern for Sandra as the risk of contagion.

'Some of the other guests are likely to start experiencing symptoms in the next twenty-four hours,' he'd told her, adding, 'Keep your distance and wash your hands,' before snapping his black doctor's bag shut and departing.

Now, Karen studies the tumbler on Jens Groth's desk and ponders whether sampling is part of his job description or a sign that he needed something to calm his nerves. And, for a moment, she wonders whether it's the alcohol or a nascent flu infection that's making Jens' eyes look slightly glassy in the light of the desk lamp.

At least he seems sober enough to give a statement, she concludes ten minutes later. By and large, Jens Groth confirms his parents' account: there are a lot of exciting changes in the works for the company and the family wanted to throw their employees and their partners a big party. No, not entirely selflessly: because many among the staff will be asked to take on more duties, it was deemed important to 'get everyone on board' and the thinking had been that 'a bit of lubrication tastes more than it costs', as Jens Groth put it.

'Our employees are our most precious resource,' he adds and Karen resists an urge to roll her eyes.

After patiently listening to this and various other nuggets of wisdom, she steers the conversation to the 'resource' that has just been lost.

'I've been told you and Gabriel Stuub got into a fight at the party. Is that correct?'

'Yes, he was absolutely shitfaced and determined to ruin the mood. Bergvall and I had to physically stop him from getting at the fireworks.'

'How physically?' she asks.

Jens Groth shoots her an annoyed look.

'We each grabbed an arm and pulled him back. Tried to talk some sense into him at first, but that was completely pointless. He got angry and shouted a bunch of nonsense. In the end, Bergvall had had enough. He dragged Gabriel away, gave him a shove and told him to fuck off until he'd sobered up.'

'And you didn't give him a hand with any of that?'

'I would have loved to, but as a co-owner, I can't afford the luxury of telling people to go fuck themselves. Not even when it's called for.'

'What time was this?'

'Quarter, maybe twenty to twelve. Bergvall and I had gone down to set up the fireworks and, after a while, Gabriel came out and started making trouble.'

'And when was the next time you saw him after that?'

'I didn't. Well, not until this morning when one of the cleaners came running, screaming that we had to come with her. We had just sat down for breakfast and at first we didn't understand what she was on about, but then we realised something serious must have happened.'

'So you went down to where Gabriel was found. Who came with you?'

Jens looks like he's searching his memory.

'I definitely remember Bergvall and Elias being there. My sister's husband,' he adds. 'I'm sure they weren't the only ones, but I can't say exactly who went with us. It was just mayhem after we saw him lying there in his own blood. And that slash across his throat . . . fuck me.'

Jens Groth reaches for his glass of whiskey but puts it down again after a glance at Karen. She has time to notice his hand trembling.

'I'm going to ask you a question now and I would like you to answer honestly,' she says. 'Was Gabriel stealing from the warehouse?'

Silence.

'I saw the marking on the wall the last time we were here,' she goes on after a while. 'A one followed by a per cent sign, and I know what that stands for. And we know Gabriel had connections in the OP.'

Karen silently studies the man in front of her for a while, then looks down at her notepad, pretending to check something, flipping through the pages, waiting. The silence lasts for eight long seconds.

'OK, fine, but I didn't kill him!'

Jens' voice breaks and this time he picks up the glass and downs the contents.

He's afraid, Karen thinks to herself. The question is whether he's worried about becoming a suspect or about how the OP will react to Gabriel's death.

'Are you sure? Because from where I'm standing, it seems you have a lot to gain from his death, don't you?'

For some reason, the question seems to make Jens Groth relax. Or maybe it's the whiskey.

'Think about it,' he says. 'How stupid would you have to be to kill one of the OP's guys? If I had the guts to do that, I would have put my foot down a long time ago, wouldn't I? The fucking prick stole whiskey to the tune of several thousand a month and I couldn't do anything about it. He told me the OP would come here and burn down the entire warehouse if I didn't keep my mouth shut.'

Karen watches silently as Jens gives in to the urge and tremblingly reaches for a bottle wedged in between a landline telephone and one of the stacks of documents. Something her cousin told her the other day flashes through the back of her mind like a fuzzy memory. No, she realises, not something Odd said, but the way he'd reacted. The look on his face when she'd mentioned the marking.

'Who here knows Gabriel was threatening you?' she asks after a pause. 'Your parents, your sister?'

'Officially, no one. But I assume a few of the guys on the floor must be wondering. I usually get rid of that bloody tag right quick, but someone's bound to have seen it at some point. You need to understand, though, that people up here go about their business and pretend they've seen nothing. Especially if the OP's involved.'

'And not your parents?'

'They don't come down to the warehouse much and I doubt they'd know what the tag means even if they saw it. Besides, they wouldn't notice a few litres disappearing here and there anyway.'

'A few litres?' Karen exclaims in surprise. 'That's it?'

If the OP were behind the thefts, it would have involved a lot more than a few thousand marks a month. Gabriel must have done it on his own initiative and pocketed the profit, as she'd suspected. And then he'd used the OP brand to keep Jens from going to the police. It was probably true that he did odd jobs for the OP, but they didn't have anything to do with stealing whiskey.

Jens Groth doesn't seem to have come to the same conclusion.

'It adds up to quite a lot of money over the course of a year,' he says. 'But the threats were the worst part. Gabriel was very clear about what they would do if I didn't keep my mouth shut. What the fuck do you think is going to happen to me now? I assume the police can't do anything, as usual.'

'I don't think you need to worry about the OP,' Karen tells him. 'I'm pretty sure Gabriel was acting on his own.'

And maybe you knew that all along, she ponders, studying the man on the other side of the desk. Maybe that's why you did have the guts to slit his throat.

'Can you think of anyone who would want to see Gabriel dead? Or his grandfather?' she adds, her eyes fixed on Jens Groth's face.

The revelation that Fredrik's death wasn't an accident is met with a complete absence of surprise. In fact, Jens shows no reaction at all, just shrugs his shoulders.

'How the fuck am I supposed to know? Ask Gabriel's wife,' he says harshly. 'I hardly think it's a coincidence she left him. But I certainly have no idea who would have wanted the old man dead.'

'It almost seems like you already knew Fredrik Stuub was murdered.'

Jens Groth leans forward with a sigh, puts both his hands on his computer monitor and turns it so she can see.

'People are talking. And I know how to read,' he says as she stares at the screen:

KVELLSPOSTEN REVEALS: DOUBLE MURDER ON
    NOORÖ
GRANDFATHER AND GRANDSON VICTIMS OF THE
    SAME KILLER?
NO WORD FROM THE POLICE

Karen curses furiously under her breath all the way back up to the main building. Not because of the *Kvellsposten* headline – she'd been expecting that since the moment Thorstein Byle called to tell her there had been another murder – but because of her meeting with Odd. Because of what she'd seen in her cousin's face the moment after the initial surprise – a split second of disbelief and then a glint of something else, something strange she'd never seen in her cousin's eyes before. That was the moment Odd realised Gabriel had been using the OP's name for his own gain. And just a few days later, Gabriel was found with his throat cut.

And she's the one who gave Odd that information.

39

'All right, who's going first, you or me?'

They're in Karen's Ford Ranger, on their way back to Lysvik. To make the best use of their time and have a chance to go over their impressions and information, they've asked one of the constables to drive Karl's car back. The snow has temporarily stopped falling and the motorway has been ploughed and salted, but the smaller roads they pass are still blocked by deep drifts.

'You start,' Karl says. 'Who did you speak to first?'

'Björn and Laura Groth.'

She sums up their account of the evening and then segues into telling Karl about the Groths' conference centre plan. When she gets to the part about the prominent guests who came in a helicopter, Karl Björken lets out a snort of laughter.

'Isn't that just bloody typical,' he says.

'What? I think it sounds unlikely enough to have been made up.'

'Not at all! More like a textbook example of the global elite's desperate attempts to alleviate their ennui, if you ask me. Apparently, it's the new thing, you know, slumming it. A retreat in some poor remote mountain village, adventure travel to places no one has ever heard of. Anything, so long as no one has done it before.'

'I hardly think a visit to a golf course on Noorö qualifies as adventure travel,' Karen retorts sceptically.

'Sure, but maybe as the one per cent's latest pastime – living like the common people for a couple of hours. My brother-in-law is the master of the hunt in Hammerfors. You know what the manor owners want when they invite their mates to go hunting these days? They want to sit around in simple little huts and eat sausage sandwiches and drink Heimö liquor!'

'Not caviar and champagne?'

'Nope. And they want nothing to do with modern hunting clothes. Nowadays, they either wear nostalgic nonsense from the 1930s or stuff a UN soldier in Afghanistan would be jealous of. They obviously change into their regular penguin suits for dinner, but first they want a little journey into the unknown.'

'Like a helicopter trip to Gudheim?' Karen says, still not convinced.

'Yes, that's exactly the kind of thing that would attract that type. A virtually impossible golf course that none of their friends has ever played. Haven't you heard Smeed and Haugen talk about how difficult it is?'

Karen shakes her head. When golf comes up in conversation, she usually stops listening.

'Well, they do. The Gudheim golf course is apparently ridiculously difficult as well as uniquely situated, with a sea view on three sides. I can see why that might sound tempting to bored businessmen looking for a kick.'

'Fine, but surely that kind of demand is pretty limited? Not really something to build a business on.'

'I wouldn't be so sure. When news spreads that the upper echelons have been there, people will be lining up. Not people in helicopters, perhaps, but regular people. And they'll need somewhere to stay. Add a tour of the distillery, a whiskey sampling and a trip to the stones and you have a concept.'

'You're starting to sound like William Tryste. Are you considering going to work for Groth's?'

'Only if they'll make me a sampler. Tryste's apparently a big name in the business. I'm looking forward to meeting him.'

'Yes, according to Byle, he's one of the best. But back to Björn Groth. I get the impression he knows more than he's saying about both Gabriel and his grandfather. I think he's afraid, or at least worried. Same thing with Jens, his son. They're hiding something.'

'And you have no idea what?'

Karen hesitates.

'In Jens' case, it might have something to do with the OP.'

'The motorcycle gang? Odin Predators or the One Percenters, whichever one it is.'

She nods and tells him about the mark she saw on the warehouse wall and about Gabriel habitually stealing whiskey and threatening Jens to silence.

'Did he take a lot?'

'No, and that's the thing. Maybe a few thousand marks' worth a month.'

'Doesn't sound like the OP. Do you reckon Gabriel was working solo?'

'That's exactly what I think. And if that's true, the boys in the leather pyjamas won't be best pleased.'

She hesitates again.

245

'One of my cousins is apparently a member.'

Karl Björken turns to Karen with raised eyebrows. She meets his eyes for two full seconds before turning her attention back to the road.

'You never cease to surprise, Eiken. Any other criminal relatives?'

'Probably. One aunt, three cousins and only the devil knows who else. And none of them eats sausage sandwiches when they want to let loose between collecting long-term disability cheques and poaching, I can tell you that. But they probably do drink their fair share of moonshine.'

'What is it they call them in the States? Rednecks?'

Karen shrugs. 'Sure, or maybe hillbillies. They all live up near Skalvet, just north of the county border.'

'Not too far from the OP headquarters, in other words. Have you talked to your cousin?'

'Yes, but only over a pint. He seemed genuinely surprised when I told him about the mark on the warehouse and insisted Gabriel wasn't a member. But Byle's boys have apparently seen him up there more than once. God damn it, I don't want to go up there, but I suppose it can't be avoided.'

'I think we can hold off on that, for now at least,' Karl says. 'If the OP had wanted to off Gabriel Stuub, they would hardly have snuck into Groth's on New Year's Eve to slit his throat. A bullet between the eyes in his own living room would be more their style.'

'Yes, that's what I keep telling myself,' Karen replies grimly.

'I also have a hard time seeing a connection between a retired biology teacher and a criminal motorcycle gang. Or is there something there too, something you haven't told me?'

246

'Not that I'm aware of.'

She glances up at the rear-view mirror.

'And now this,' she says with a sigh. 'We're being followed by the *Kvellsposten* car.'

They had left the distillery without stopping, passing exasperated journalists and photographers who were still waiting for a comment.

'I talked to Johan Stolt,' Karen says. 'He's probably going to issue a press statement tomorrow and will be handling all media enquiries for now. But, sooner or later, I suppose we're going to have to bite the bullet and hold a press conference. Stolt said he'll contact Haugen and discuss it with him.'

If she's lucky, she won't have to participate. Chief of Police Viggo Haugen has been clear about not wanting Karen Eiken Hornby talking to the media. The fact that they'd have to go back twenty years to find the newspaper article with the critical comment she'd made as a freshly minted graduate of the College of Policing makes no difference.

After a number of female police trainees had dropped out of the programme, a journalist from *Doggerska Tider* had asked her about gender equality in policing. Her spontaneous, and by today's standards fairly tame, answer about 'persistent resistance to women on the force' and 'the need for a fresh approach' had not been kindly received. Her female peers had supported her, but only in private, safely out of earshot of their superiors. Because it had coincided with an unprecedented dip in the public's confidence in the police and because it had been an election year, Karen's comment had prompted the country's political parties to practically fall over themselves proposing various reforms. The worst-received among the top brass had

247

been the mandatory leadership course in gender theory and equality. Some of them still seemed traumatised by it. And Viggo Haugen has definitely not forgotten; he will never trust Karen Eiken Hornby.

Karen slows down to make the *Kvellsposten* reporters pass them, but their only response is a flash of the high beams.

'Wankers!' Karl says, sounding annoyed. 'We'll have to find some other way to shake them once we get to Lysvik. What else did Jens Groth have to say?'

'Not much. His story matches his parents'. Gabriel was drunk, there was a dispute involving the fireworks and after that he didn't see him again, or so he claims. Not until this morning after some poor cleaner found the body.'

'Unfortunately, I don't have a lot to offer, either,' Karl says. 'What you told me is exactly what the daughter, Madeleine, and her husband, Elias, said. The only thing I can add is that Elias said several people went all the way up to the body when they found him. At least five or six people, he reckoned. I find it a bit odd that they felt the need to get that close. It was perfectly obvious from several feet away that his throat had been cut.'

'OK, so who was it?'

'Elias himself, Jens Groth, Ingemar Bergvall and at least a couple of guys from "the floor", as he put it.'

'Right, so they lined up for a peek at the crime scene. Sören Larsen's not going to be pleased. Let's just hope they didn't poke the corpse.'

'Apparently some idiot suggested CPR, but at least Bergvall had enough sense to nix that. From what I was told, he was the one who took charge and told Jens to call the police.'

'Is that it?'

'Yep, their version of events is pretty much identical to everyone else's,' Karl replies. 'It's almost like they've compared stories.'

'Sure – or maybe it's just what actually happened.'

'Aside from the tiny detail that someone must have slit the poor sod's throat. Surely someone saw or heard something? Even with all the bubbly and fireworks and whatnot.'

'We'll find out tomorrow what Byle and his gang managed to get out of the other guests. And we have to talk to William Tryste and his wife.'

They park outside the police station in Lysvik and are let in just as the *Kvellsposten* car pulls up behind Karen's Ford. The constable who lets them in instantly grasps the situation and shuts the door in the face of the fastest reporter. A moment later, there is a sharp, persistent ringing as the reporter leans on the doorbell.

'Byle's not here,' their colleague says loudly to make himself heard over the racket. 'No one else is, either, everyone's up at Groth's.'

'We're not staying. But we don't want a media escort to Rindler's. Is there another exit?'

Karl shoots Karen a surprised look but bites his tongue when she frowns warningly. The more people who think she's staying at Rindler's, the better.

'Sure, take the lift down and exit through the garage. The ramp comes out on Lotsgatan, just a stone's throw from the hotel. You should get going; I'm legally required to let anyone who rings the bell in.'

Five minutes later they're trudging through the snow down one of the narrow side streets with their hands deep in their pockets.

'Up for a pint at the pub I'm staying at?' Karen asks. 'I imagine all the reporters are staked out by the hotel by now.'

'Do they have any more rooms? I don't exactly relish the idea of walking over to Rindler's later and taking on the assembled forces of *Kvellsposten* by myself.'

'No idea, but it's not exactly tourist season,' Karen replies and stops next to a loading bay.

She fumbles around her pocket for her cigarettes, finds them and lets out a curse.

'Fuck! I meant to ask to borrow some clothes at the station. Now I don't even have the stupid cardigan with me, I left it in the car. God fucking dammit,' she mutters, then manages to light a cigarette and takes a deep drag.

'Are you done?'

'Bloody hell,' she adds.

'I can see why Haugen doesn't want you talking to the media,' Karl says with a grin. 'He doesn't like women who curse. Or smoke, I imagine.'

'Aren't I lucky he's not here then,' Karen snaps and takes another drag, holding the smoke in her lungs and feeling her pulse slow. 'Cursing is actually a sign of intelligence,' she says. 'I read a study about it the other day. That and being messy. Apparently, there's some sort of correlation with creativity.'

'And heart attacks. Feeling calmer?'

She nods and they trudge on.

'Have you talked to Kneought about when the autopsy is going take place?' she asks after a while.

'Eight o'clock tomorrow morning. You'll have to handle the morning meeting by yourself. Or the bone saw, take your pick.'

'I should really swing by Ravenby, too. I need to buy something to wear. And deodorant. I didn't even bring a toothbrush. Do you have any gum?'

Ellen Jensen is on the phone behind the small reception desk. When the door opens, she looks up and waves Karen over. They wait until she has finished the call.

'I think you have a visitor,' she says with a nod in the direction of the pub.

So they found their way here after all, Karen sighs inwardly. She's really not in the mood to fend off reporters tonight. All she wants is a pint of ale.

And while Karl stays behind to ask if Ellen has a room for him, Karen glumly pushes open the door to the pub. Scans the room in search of hungry journalists and bulky camera bags. Then her heart skips a beat.

At one of the window tables, a young woman is reading a paper. A young woman with long black hair and a nose ring.

40

Fear hits her like a hammer. Karen covers the distance to Sigrid's table in four long strides.

'What are you doing here? Did something happen?'

'Hi, Karen. Yes, I'm just fine, thanks for asking. Aren't you happy to see me?'

Karen makes no reply and Sigrid adopts an offended expression.

'No? Well that's *extremely* disappointing,' she says with a pout. 'After I drove all this way . . .'

Then she bends down and pulls a large overnight bag out from under the table. She picks it up with both hands and drops it next to her pint glass with a thud.

'How about now? I bet you're happy to see this, at least?'

Again without replying, Karen opens the zipper and starts rummaging through the contents, finding clean T-shirts, a pair of navy trousers, underwear, socks, her winter coat, her tartan scarf and her fur-lined hat with ear flaps. Hideous, but warm. At the bottom, she discovers her toiletry kit and black winter boots. Speechless, she pulls out a chair, sits down across from Sigrid and stares at her, shaking her head slowly.

'But, how the hell . . . how did you know?'

'Marike called. Said you'd probably die of exposure or get fired unless you could get your hands on some appropriate clothes.'

'And you drove all the way up here in this weather. Which is actually an idiotic thing to do when you know we're about to be snowed in.'

Sigrid's raised eyebrows and affronted silence makes Karen aware of her admonishing tone.

'But thank you!' she adds. 'You're a lifesaver, Sigrid.'

'No worries. You can buy me another a pint to show your gratitude. And get one for yourself, too. You look like you need it.'

Karl is standing by the bar, punching in the pin to his bank card.

'Did you get a room?' Karen asks.

'A closet. Apparently, it was all she had. She warned me she only rents it out in emergencies. Would you mind telling me what the boss's daughter is doing here?'

'She drove up with a bag of clothes for me.'

'She must like you.'

Karen orders two pints of ale without commenting and Karl shoots her a look.

'It's OK, you know. Having people like you.'

'So now you're a psychologist.'

'I'm a man of many talents. And I can read you like an open book by now.'

'Then please close it. I'm not in the mood for therapy tonight.'

They get their pints and sit down at Sigrid's table. Karen takes a sip of her ale and gazes silently out the window, listening to the other two making small talk about the state of the roads. The snow has stopped and the lights from the ferry port look like the last safe outpost against the dark sea beyond it. As a wave of relaxation and weariness surges through her, she sluggishly tries to sum up her day. As recently as this morning, she'd woken up in Marike's studio in Dunker – it feels like a week ago.

Then Sigrid's voice breaks through.

'Is it true there's a *mass murderer* on the loose in these parts?'

'You mean serial killer,' Karl corrects her. 'But no, two murders actually isn't enough to qualify for that epithet either.'

'Oh, *whatever*. It's some kind of lunatic, right? He might be in here now . . .'

Sigrid nods conspiratorially at the other tables and Karl turns around. A flat New Year's Day mood reigns among the sparse regulars in the pub. Two men in their seventies are playing backgammon at one table and three girls in their twenties are fiddling with their phones, holding them up for the others to see at regular intervals, which invariably draws laughter and groans and exclamations of 'that's so embarrassing!'. A few lonely patrons by the bar seem engrossed in reading yesterday's evening paper and others are staring dully at the TV, which is showing a rerun of a Stoke–Newcastle game.

'I don't think you need to worry,' Karl comments drily. 'None of them looks particularly lethal to me.'

'Lethally boring, possibly,' Karen quips. 'And yet, apparently you're planning to stay the night here in Lysvik,' she adds with a nod to Sigrid's pint. 'You can't drive back after drinking that.'

Sigrid sighs.

'Yes, I can. I'm an excellent driver after I've had a few,' she says and grins impudently at Karen. 'Oh my God, I'm *joking*. Is that illegal now, too?'

'Not if you're funny,' Karen mutters. 'Either way, it's too late for you to drive home.'

'Oh my God, relax, I *have* a room. It's actually really nice. The woman at the bar said it was the last decent room she had.'

Karen notices Karl's disgruntled look and decides to change the subject.

'Have you decided what you're going to do, now that the start of term's approaching?'

A few weeks previous, Sigrid had told her she'd been accepted to law school, but that she didn't know if she really wanted to go. Karen had done her best to hide her surprise at Sigrid apparently having finished secondary school with good grades, despite quite a bit of truancy. But to her horror, Sigrid had started asking about applying to the College of Policing next autumn. The mere thought of Sigrid's future being filled with drunkenness, narcotics, domestic disturbances, assault and all the other things that come with the job fills her with dread.

Sigrid shrugs.

'I told you, I don't know.'

'Law is always a good choice, no matter what you decide to do afterwards,' Karen puts in. 'Isn't it, Karl?'

He raises his hands defensively.

'Don't drag me into this. I see you've found yourself a new mother, Sigrid,' he adds and grabs his pint.

Dead silence follows.

'Bollocks,' Karl says after three interminable seconds and slams his glass down so hard it spills. 'I wasn't thinking . . . all I meant was . . . I'm sorry.'

'It's OK,' Sigrid says. 'It's not your fault Mum died.'

Karen says nothing. Her pulse is thudding in her ears, and she feels like she's under water, has carelessly stepped out onto thin ice and immediately plunged into the frigid depths below. As if from a great distance, she can hear the sound of the TV and voices, Karl's saying something contrite and Sigrid replying reassuringly. They are so close, yet so infinitely far away.

Not daring to breathe, she sits stock-still while she sinks toward the bottom. She's afraid to reach out and grab her glass, afraid to move, because she would break if she did. Any movement right now and she will dissolve, wither and blow away like flakes of ash on the wind.

Through the chaos she can hear a voice murmuring about lines that must not be crossed, reminding her about the invisible barbed wire encircling her existence. Inside it, Mathis and John still exist. Outside it, there's nothing. Nothing that's yours, the voice tells her.

Even though she had known better, she had lowered her guard when Sigrid unexpectedly marched into her life, broken, angry and full of pain. And without a thought to the consequences, she had once again allowed herself to take care of someone, to blow on the injured places and make it all better.

She's not your daughter, don't ever forget that.

And now Karl's voice cuts through the noise. He's leaning forward, trying to catch her eye.

'Are you OK, Karen?'

She slowly rises back up toward the surface, breaks through and takes a panting breath. She has done this before, knows how to quickly put on a reassuring smile.

'I'm just tired,' she says. 'It's been a long day; I actually think I'm going to turn in.'

And with that, she stands up, avoiding Sigrid's worried eyes, and retreats to her room. Takes off all her clothes and gets in the shower. The tears don't come until after she has opened the toiletry bag Sigrid has packed for her and squeezed out a dollop of toothpaste, when she catches sight of her own face in the bathroom mirror.

41

She has no idea how long she's been walking for. Slightly hunched over in the wind, she has followed the winding gravel path north along the coast from the ferry port in Lysvik, passing houses and grey sheds crouched between the mountain and the sea. She has walked along bays of frozen meadowland dotted with snow covered junipers and the remnants of net pens. Forlornly, she has studied the remnants of communal efforts to protect the fishermen's nets from grazing animals, a collective struggle to keep the nets in one piece until they go back into the sea – until the seals chew them to pieces again. She can hear her father cursing angrily, remembers the sharp undertone of worry.

Grimly, she has pressed on while the sky above her has paled, sensing something swelling inside her, something lurking under the surface like a crocodile in a muddy river, ready to pounce.

Without speaking to anyone, she had snuck out of the hotel as soon as she woke up. Just got dressed and left. Down to the ferry port first, where she watched one of the yellow steel behemoths slowly approach from the other side of the sound. When the ferry came too close, she'd turned around and walked away, had passed the cutters and trawlers in the fishing harbour and continued through the ugly old container port where only icebreakers and custom ships are berthed these days. She had put one foot in front of the other and kept moving, her mind racing and her lungs burning with the cold air.

Now she stops and checks her watch. Twenty to eight. Karl Björken is probably already halfway to the Centre for Forensic Medicine in Ravenby. She's going to have to call him in a bit.

And Sigrid. Instead of knocking on her door to say goodbye, Karen had sent a text. She had typed, erased, fretted over the words, and, in the end, sent it.

Thank you for coming! Had to head off early. X K

Sigrid hasn't replied. Maybe she's still asleep.

Karen stops and gazes out across the leaden endlessness, absorbing the stillness while her breath sends out white smoke signals. If she wants to make it to the morning meeting on time, she has to turn back now, try to eat something and have a cup of coffee somewhere. She has to focus on work now, squash all other thoughts and that thing that's rumbling inside her.

Just then, her phone rings.

'Hi, Sören,' she says after checking the screen.

'Where the fuck are you? I went by that place you insist on staying at, but the lady at reception said you'd left already. Are you on your way to Ravenby?'

'No, Karl and I decided he'll do this one.'

'Coward. But that's not why I'm calling. The Fredrik Stuub results are back from the lab. You'll have the report in your inbox soon, but if you want I can go over the salient parts while it's still fresh in my memory.'

'Great. So, what did you find?'

'Starting with the crime scene, we managed to secure a set of partial footprints that don't belong to Byle or any of the emergency services guys. They're Timberland boots, size nine, and

259

the right is unevenly worn. We have tyre tracks galore from the turning area at the end of the road, so don't get your hopes up about that. There was nothing on Fredrik Stuub's body. Not so much as a hair that didn't belong to him or the dog. In his house, on the other hand . . . what the fuck! Fucking idiot!'

Karen gives a start and moves the phone away from her ear while Sören Larsen continues to curse. Then she hears the sound of a car door closing, quick footsteps and angry voices. Apparently, Larsen is still holding his phone because Karen can make out words and phrases like 'watch where you're going', 'supposed to yield', 'insurance company', 'bloody lucky' and 'police'. Then a few more searing oaths from Larsen, angry footsteps, and a car door opening and closing again.

'What's going on?' she says after a while.

'Nothing. Where were we?'

Karen bites back the sarcasm. It's common knowledge Sören Larsen thinks he's an outstanding driver even though everyone else considers him a menace. Rumour has it the cost of his insurance policy has steadily gone up over the years, reaching astronomical levels. I'm probably making myself an accessory to reckless endangerment just by talking to him while he's driving, she muses.

'Fredrik Stuub's house,' she says, pushing the thought away. 'Tell me you at least found something useful there.'

'I'm not sure about useful, but we do have two sets of fresh prints that don't belong to Fredrik Stuub or his sister. One set I can help you out with right now: they belong to Gabriel Stuub.'

Karen sighs quietly. She's aware Gabriel Stuub had a criminal record. Two counts of minor assault and several speeding tickets, according to Thorstein Byle. Finding his prints at

260

his grandfather's house might, but only might, have been of interest. If it weren't for the annoying little detail that Gabriel himself is dead now.

'What about the other set?' she asks.

'No match in the database, but if you come across an interesting candidate, I suggest you get out your ink pad.'

'Is that it?'

'I'm not finished. Watch out, will you!'

A sharp honk on the other end has Karen snatching the phone away from her ear again.

'Bloody hell, Sören,' she says. 'There are courses you can take . . .'

'Me? He was out of control. Must have bought his licence online.'

'Just tell me what you found so we can hang up and save some lives.'

'The laptop. The one you and Byle found. They haven't gone through everything yet but the old man had a lot of documents about Noorö history, runes, cod levels, fishing quotas, expansive cement and whatever else. And then some stuff from the university, an employment contract, parts of his research on mould and other crap like that. You'll get copies so you can have a look for yourself. There was nothing of interest in his browser history so far as I could make out. Aside from the aforementioned subjects, Fredrik Stuub apparently spent most his time researching genealogy and mushroom picking. Oh, and he did a search for a dewormer for dogs.'

What the hell is expansive cement? Karen thinks to herself. But this is not the time to ask Sören Larsen to explain; the sooner he can get back to focusing on driving, the better.

'OK, Karl and I will have to go over everything with a fine-tooth comb and see if we can unearth anything interesting,' she says. 'Is that it?'

'Hold your horses, this is the best part. Fredrik Stuub sent some emails that might be worth having a look at. Or, to be more precise, one email. To Björn Groth, on 22 December.'

Larsen pauses for effect. Karen stands stock-still with the phone pressed to her ear, waiting for him to continue.

'Come on, Sören,' she snaps after a few seconds. 'What did he write?'

Sören Larsen sounds decidedly pleased with himself when he replies.

'Verbatim, it says: "I have information that can put an end to your expansion plans. Contact me asap." Signed with Fredrik Stuub's name and mobile number.'

42

'Would you mind holding on?'

The scraping of chairs being pushed drowns out her question, so Karen puts a hand on Thorstein Byle's arm instead as he, too, starts to get up.

He sinks back onto his chair.

'I'd like a word in private,' she says quietly.

The morning meeting at the Lysvik police station is over. Before Röse, Andersson and Svanemark leave the room, they knock back the last of their coffee and reach out for fistfuls of biscuits.

The run-through of the distillery guests' witness statements had been depressingly repetitive. Like the Groths and their children, they all agreed it had been a great party. Sure, people had got drunk, but it was New Year's Eve and the Groths had spared no expense. Gabriel Stuub was the only one who had made trouble. Luckily, Jens Groth and Bergvall had handled him. Two people claimed to have seen Gabriel shuffle off in the direction of the hotel and assumed he was planning to hit the hay. Then everyone had turned around to watch the fireworks and they all agreed it had been a spectacular display. The Groths really had gone all out. And no, no one had seen Gabriel Stuub after he left the party.

Ingemar Bergvall had admitted to being pretty rough when he dragged Gabriel away from the fireworks. Yes, he had pushed him into the snow near the warehouse and told him to go fuck himself. But then he'd had gone straight back to join to the others, a claim that was backed up by at least two people.

A single guest, the wife of one of the warehouse workers, said she'd seen Gabriel after the firework display started. Lyanna Drage, a nurse, had turned around a few times to look for Gabriel. Because although he'd been on his feet, if noticeably unsteady, she hadn't felt confident he'd make it all the way to the hotel by himself. If nothing else, he might slip and fall in the snow. That was why Lyanna Drage had been somewhat reassured to see him turn off toward the warehouse just as the first fireworks exploded overhead. Better that he stay nearby, she'd reasoned, drunk and troublesome though he was. Then she had turned back to the fireworks and she hadn't seen him again.

'So the question is: where did he go after the altercation and who did he meet there? Because he did meet someone, that much we know. Which means at least one of these people is lying,' Karen had summed up, noticing Röse's lips twitching out of the corner of her eye.

'Sure, unless the killer wasn't one of the guests,' he'd countered. 'How do you know it wasn't someone else entirely? Anyone could have got in to Groth's without anyone there noticing.'

'That's true, of course,' Karen had replied, forcing herself to stay calm. 'But before we bring everyone on the island in for questioning, I suggest we focus on the ones we know were at the crime scene. Pretty much everyone had an opportunity; the question is, who had a motive?'

*

264

Björn Groth has to be brought in today, she reflects while the room empties, and that's a task she can't delegate. In fact, she wants Karl Björken with her when she talks to him. But what can I trust Byle's people to do? she wonders and glances down at her notes. Her to-do list includes following up with the party guests, especially Lyanna Drage and Ingemar Bergvall, and the Groths, talking to the Trystes and going through the contents of Fredrik Stuub's laptop. I should really talk to his sister one more time, too, she thinks to herself and feels her pulse rise at the thought of trying to get everything done. And I need to talk to Odd again. Röse had been right about one thing: anyone could have got into the distillery grounds without being detected.

Karen closes the door and turns to Byle. Then she tells him what Fredrik Stuub wrote to Björn Groth.

'Blimey,' he says. 'But you have to ask yourself whether he really had something or whether it was just bluster. He was widely known as a bit of an eccentric old crank. He wrote some irate letters to the editor of the local paper and to various local politicians about the vandalism up at Gudheim. Demanding round-the-clock police surveillance. Can't you just see it, a three-shift operation to protect the ship setting!'

'It might be nothing, but we need to follow up on it. I'll start and see what shakes out. I'm going to try to make the time to at least skim the contents of Fredrik Stuub's laptop right now.'

She flips through her notes.

'Karl and I will talk to William Tryste and his wife as soon as we're done with Björn Groth. And someone needs to talk to the secretary . . .' Karen scans her notes for the name. 'Eva Framnes. Can you do that?'

Byle nods.

'Absolutely. But we need more help. As you know, no one up here has any experience of murder investigations.'

'I talked to Smeed just before we sat down and I made it very clear to him we need more hands on deck. But we can't sit on our hands while we wait for reinforcements to arrive. I want to talk to Björn Groth as soon as possible, and this time I'm not driving up to the distillery. Do you have anyone who can bring him here this afternoon, at, say, three o'clock?'

'I'll have one of the boys go pick him up if necessary. I think he'll be grateful it's Saturday.'

'Why is that?'

'I don't imagine he'd appreciate running into the members of the provincial board, what with the decision on his expansion pending. I'm sure they would have some questions and their offices are right across the street.'

'From what he told me he's already been given the go-ahead. I thought it was a done deal?'

'In theory, sure, but there won't be a formal decision until after Twelfth Night, when the board convenes for its first meeting of the year. If people start talking, they might defer the vote. Politicians do have a tendency to get cold feet once the media get involved.'

'Well, I wasn't going to have him dragged here in handcuffs or anything. And as you know, news of the murder up at Groth's broke yesterday.'

When they're done going over the day's tasks and Byle has left, Karen steps into the office she has been assigned. It's a small, windowless space normally used to store confiscated personal effects and still half taken up by an enormous safe. She sucks her stomach in and squeezes past, puts her laptop down on the desk and logs into the network.

43

The summary of the contents of Fredrik Stuub's laptop is one of the shortest Karen has ever seen. The links to the various documents and websites only take up a couple of pages. And Larsen was right, both the documents and the search history seem focused on a handful of subjects. Karen decides to save the mushroom picking and dog deworming for later. Instead, she opens a horizontal Word document labelled 'The Huss Family' and finds herself staring at a painstakingly constructed family tree. To make the tree fit on a single page, the text is absolutely tiny.

Karen zooms in and starts skimming through the names from left to right, noting that the Huss name doesn't appear until the early nineteenth century. Until then, Scandinavian heritage and patronymics seem to have dominated – box after box of Anderssons, Nielssons and Karlssons, who apparently made their livings as crofters, fishermen and, in a few cases, customs agents. In 1867, however, a Gerhard Huss moved in from somewhere and married a Hilda Andersdotter, she notes before letting her eyes move on to their son, Albin Huss, mine owner.

As Byle has told her, Old Huss and his wife had apparently not been blessed with a son and had instead been forced to make do with two daughters. Both had married and kept the family genes alive, but it had been the end of the Huss line. With a growing lack of interest, Karen continues to peruse the family tree, confirming that Fredrik Stuub was indeed William Tryste's father's first cousin. Both members of a family that was once Doggerland's richest. And yet, Fredrik's earthly possessions at the time of his death had amounted to just 70,000 marks, a house, and sizeable tracts of essentially worthless land.

The question is whether familial relationships have anything at all to do with the case, Karen thinks. William may be related to both victims, but he won't inherit a penny. And he has an alibi, at least for Fredrik's murder, she reminds herself.

The person who does stand to gain from killing first, Fredrik, then his grandson, is Gabriel's wife, Katja. Since their divorce is not final, she's going to inherit both the house she and Gabriel shared and the things he inherited from his grandfather before he died. But Karen is far from convinced a mother of two would kill, or hire a hitman to kill, two people for nothing more than 70,000 marks and a couple of houses on Noorö.

Karen closes the family tree and clicks on the next link. Fredrik Stuub has collected a large number of random documents and facts about ship settings, burial mounds and megaliths around the world, along with photographs and various theories about their function and dating. One of the folders also contains a map of the north-eastern part of Noorö, with roads marked in red. The last document is a PDF entitled *Environmental impact assessment. Expansion of Gudheim Hotel and Conference Centre.*

She sighs and starts to skim the report, registering words like exploited area, cultural impact statement, eastward relocation of road, significant costs, development plan and minor impact. I'm going to have to ask someone else to look at this, too, she realises and leans back in her chair. From what she can gather, the report's conclusion is that the expansion can be approved on the condition that the original plan for the building of a new road can be amended. More expensive than planned, but still possible, in other words.

If this was the document Fredrik Stuub was planning to use to sink the Groths' expansion plans, he was probably barking up the wrong tree, she muses and stretches out her stiff neck. A slight headache is beginning to make itself known.

She continues to plough through document after document, alternating from time to time with Fredrik Stuub's search history. When she gets to the folder entitled 'Work' she suddenly sits up straighter. The document she's staring at is entitled *Employment following retirement* and is a contract between Ravenby University and Docent Emeritus Fredrik Stuub.

Karen googles the university's website and reaches for the phone.

44

'Jenny speaking!'

The voice sounds cheerfully winded, as though the rector of Ravenby University is in the middle of an Instagram-worthy workout and would love to tell whoever's calling all about it but as soon as Karen introduces herself and says why she's calling, Jenny Older's tone loses some of its eagerness.

'Yes, of course I know Fredrik Stuub,' she says, still slightly out of breath. 'Though only by name, to be honest. He hasn't worked for us in years. Can I ask what this is about? I'm not allowed to give out information willy-nilly.'

Karen explains as blandly as she is able that Fredrik Stuub was found dead near his home and that it's her job to 'gather all relevant information'. Strictly 'routine'.

'Oh dear, I'm sorry to hear that,' Jenny Older says distractedly. 'But he was retiring when I started working here, so, like I said, I don't know him personally. What did he die from? No, of course you can't tell me, but I suppose he must have been fairly old.'

Granted, the media haven't released the names of Fredrik or Gabriel Stuub, but the identity of the people behind the headlines are an open secret on Noorö. Jenny Older, however, doesn't seem to have intuited any connection between the double murder and Fredrik Stuub. Karen can see no reason to help her along that path.

'I don't want to take up too much of your time,' she says. 'What I was really looking for was someone who could tell me briefly about Fredrik Stuub's work.'

A short hesitation on the other end. Then Jenny Older seems to decide that information probably isn't confidential.

'He taught and did research within the biochemical field,' she replies. 'That is to say, he taught here until 2012, when he retired. After that, we signed an agreement that gave him continued access to our facilities and equipment for a further five years so he could conclude his research. I remember because Fredrik Stuub was one of the last to enjoy an agreement of that kind. Our policy vis-à-vis former employees has changed since.'

'Why is that?'

'At the end of the day, it's a matter of prioritising. There was some discussion back and forth with our emeritus community. Knowledge transfer on the one hand, a reorientation of the university and resources on the other. In the end, the leadership decided we would no longer allow retired colleagues to remain associated with the university.'

'And what was Fredrik Stuub's research about?'

'Mycotoxins. By which I mean different types of toxins that occur in mould. He was, among other things, regularly consulted by the media as an expert. Like when we had that aflatoxin scare a few years ago, for example.'

Karen searches her memory of alarmist evening news headlines screaming that what you've happily been eating all your life is going to kill you.

'But he only took advantage of his right to stay on for a couple of years, until the end of 2015, if I remember correctly,' Jenny Older continues. 'From what I understand, he

271

gave up his research and hopefully found something else to do with his time. A lot of people resist retirement, but that usually sorts itself out in due course. I suppose it's the same in all walks of life.'

She says that last part with a conspiratorial chuckle that seems to signal an unspoken understanding. When Karen does nothing to join in, Jenny Older continues in a tone that says that, as far as she is concerned, this conversation has run its course.

'We haven't seen or heard from him in a few years, but I'll let everyone in his department know about his passing. Do you know when the funeral is going to be? It would be good if I could put that information in the email. It's possible someone might want to attend.'

Karen ends the call with a sigh.

Getting old really sucks, she reflects and resumes ploughing through the links to the contents of Fredrik Stuub's laptop. As Jenny Older indicated, Stuub's professional interests seem to have revolved around different types of toxins found in mould; there are links to a few newspaper articles where he was quoted as an expert on the subject of mycotoxins in apple sauce and cold-pressed apple juice. She skims through impenetrable terms and stats from comparative measurements of aflatoxins, ochratoxin, patulin, Baudoinia, trichothecenes, zearalenone and fumonisin, without finding any connection to Groth's distillery.

She has never heard of mould being found in spirits, but what does she really know? She's going to have to look into that somehow. Mould in conjunction with shoddy construction sounds more plausible. Those things tend to blow up into big scandals, depending on the extent and consequences, she thinks to herself. Maybe there's a connection there to the Groths' expansion plans. Not likely, granted, but perfectly possible.

I'm going to have to ask someone to go through all of this, too, Karen notes ruefully and checks her watch. Already quarter past one; she should really make sure she has something to eat before her headache gets any worse. The moment she turns off the computer, her phone rings.

Karl Björken appears unperturbed by the autopsy he just witnessed.

'I'm on the ferry now and bloody ravenous,' he says. 'Did you already have lunch?'

273

45

'Nothing?'

'Nope. Björn Groth never responded to Fredrik Stuub's threat, or whatever that was supposed to be. The IT guys checked all deleted emails, too, even the ones that had been removed from the trash folder. No idea how they do it, but Larsen swears there's no other correspondence between Fredrik Stuub and Björn Groth.'

They are sitting in a restaurant near the ferry port. Karen went down to meet Karl and now they're the only guests at something that is probably best described as a dive. Simple wooden tables and aluminium café chairs and, on the walls, the compulsory fishing nets and 'oil paintings' of ships on stormy seas. Here, the faith, hope and love symbol looks carved from a big chunk of driftwood, ominously suspended above the door to the kitchen.

Karl Björken shrugs.

'He might have called or gone to find Stuub in person instead of emailing him back. That actually seems more likely, if it's true the old geezer had information that could threaten the expansion.'

'It's possible; we'll have to ask him, I guess. OK, so what did Brodal learn from the autopsy?'

'You really want to hear about that now, while we wait for our food?'

'Sure, go ahead.'

'All right, but don't get your hopes up,' Karl says and takes a sip of his beer. 'Gabriel Stuub had his throat slit with a serrated knife. Probably a double-edged hunting knife, according to Kneought. The kind with deeper notches on one side and shallower ones on the other. Damn effective whichever way you turn it, so to speak.'

'Right, one of those,' Karen says sarcastically. 'Either way, it's probably at the bottom of the North Sea now.'

'Be that as it may, the killer stabbed Gabriel in the side of his neck and then sliced clean through the larynx from the inside out.'

'Delightful. What else?'

'Well, you know what our beloved Brodal is like, always full of caveats, but he was fairly certain Gabriel was sitting on the ground with his back to the tree where he was found when the killer attacked him from behind. That would apparently explain the marks on his trousers and the mild frostbite on his buttocks.'

'A swift execution, in other words.'

'The knife entered from the left, so in all likeliness we're dealing with a right-handed killer.'

'How unusual. Anything else?'

Karl shakes his head.

'Not as far as the murder is concerned, but there were a number of half-healed bruises on the body, indicating Gabriel had been on the receiving end of a couple of hard punches to the face twenty-four to forty-eight hours before his death. The bloodwork also revealed traces of cocaine and liver values even Kneought Brodal considered unusually poor for a man his age.'

'We know he liked to drink, but he looked remarkably fit. Steroids?'

'Exactly what Brodal said, but we're going to have to wait for the lab results on that one. Well, I suppose that was the gist of it. We'll see what Sören comes up with.'

'I'm working on the assumption that he found piles and piles of DNA that explicitly and unequivocally identifies our killer. And his mobile was still neatly tucked into his pocket, too, I presume?'

Karl grins.

'Of course. No, I'd bet a lot of money his phone went the same way as the murder weapon. At least we should be able to get call lists from his service provider in due course. Finally,' he suddenly exclaims and turns his attention to their waiter.

Karen studies the steaming bowls being set down in front of them. This may be a dive, she muses, breathing in the smell of clams, cod, sugar kelp and garlic, but they certainly seem to know their way around fish soup. Before the waiter has even left, she has torn off a piece of black bread and shoved it into her mouth. They eat quickly and voraciously, burning their tongues on the soup and cooling them back down with small sips of lager. Ten minutes later, Karen leans back in her chair and looks out the window.

'So what did you get up to while I was in Ravenby?' Karl asks. 'And what was the matter with you last night?'

'I've started going through Fredrik Stuub's computer,' Karen replies, ignoring the second question. 'There are some documents and old emails I'd like you to have a look at.'

Karl mops up the last of his soup with a piece of bread and puts it in his mouth.

'Oh yeah? What are they about?' he replies without swallowing first.

'He seems to have been a querulant, our good old Mr Stuub. Be that as it may, he has, as Byle informed us, spent a lot of time writing letters to newspapers and local politicians. He was unhappy about the ferry's weekend timetable, he objected to the decision to instate a fee for using the recycling station in Valby, he complained about the police's inept efforts to curb the resulting fly-tipping – and then there was a large number of rambling jeremiads about speeding and vandalism, particularly the vandalism of the Gudheim ship setting. There are some older emails, too, addressed to his daughter, as well as some of her replies.'

'Ulrika? Gabriel's mother who died of hepatitis?'

'Yes, and they make for pretty sad reading. I haven't had time to go through all of it, but Fredrik was clearly beside himself about her illness and suggested all kinds of alternative treatments. It's odd that he and Gabriel don't seem to have been close. But maybe Gabriel was right. Maybe Fredrik went a bit doddery when Ulrika died.'

'Or maybe losing his child made him scared to let people in. That happens, doesn't it?'

There is a long pause.

Could Sigrid have told him? Karen wonders while she casts about for something to say. Last night, after I went up to my room. No, she would never . . .

The only sound is the clattering of plates from the kitchen. Time stands still.

'What do you know?' she manages after a while.

'Nothing, really,' Karl replies calmly. 'But I'm neither deaf nor blind and being a detective, I know how to put two and two together. And I noticed the reaction last night when I put my foot in it.'

'Well, no wonder. She just lost her mother.'

'Not Sigrid's reaction. Yours. Officially speaking, I know you were married when you lived in London and that you moved back after getting divorced.'

'Then you know everything you need to know.'

Karl leans back and seems to contemplate her.

'How long have we worked together?' he says.

Karen shrugs.

'Five, six years, I guess.'

'Seven,' Karl corrects her. 'Do you trust me?'

'You know I do.'

'Don't you think it's time you told me the truth, then?'

She feels like she's literally being torn in two. Her instinctive reflex is to keep lying. No one can know, not at work, only her closest friends. She had made that a condition of accepting the job offer from the CID ten years ago. Her boss at the time, a friend of her mother's, knew her story and had made sure Karen's lie became the officially recorded truth. Divorced, no children. No questions, no talking about her past, ever. It was the only way she had been able to carry on. If she sticks to that version now, Karl will never ask her again, that much she knows.

But on the other hand, the unrelenting weariness. The exhausting vacuum the lies leave in their wake. Karen swallows hard. Opens her mouth and closes it again.

Then she feels the warmth of Karl's large hand as he puts it over hers, and in the next moment, she hears her own voice speaking. It sounds robotic and strange, she reflects, as though it's coming from a great distance. It says:

'You know I lived in England for many years?'

Karl nods and the voice continues.

'I had a husband and a son there. John and Mathis. They died in a car crash.'

Karl looks like he's about to say something, but he stops himself when Karen takes a deep breath.

'I was driving,' she says and looks him straight in the eyes.

He holds her gaze. Steadily, without looking away. Calmly waiting.

Then she tells him. Talks about the things that can't be put into words. About the lorry driver suddenly veering, about John and Mathis both dying instantly, while she had been cut out of the car virtually unharmed. About the police officer who told her the lorry driver had been using amphetamine to get through the long hours on the road. About how she hadn't been able to stay in London, that the only way forward had been the one that led back. Back home. To Doggerland, to Langevik and to the house she grew up in.

She tells him all those things. But she says nothing about her fight with John that morning, or about the anger that made her decide to drive, even though he was supposed to. Nothing about the fact that she never did manage to get used to driving on the left, despite so many years in London. Nothing about the guilt that has eaten away at her every day since.

But she does tell him about the other things. Matter-of-factly, as though she were talking about someone else.

And she doesn't sink.

279

46

At exactly quarter past four that afternoon, it happens. Unexpectedly, like when a window is thrown open by a sudden gust of wind and threatens to slam shut just as suddenly. A way out.

A big bag, nothing else, just the bare necessities. Thinking about the large sports trunk hidden behind the garden furniture in the storage space at the back of the garage makes Aylin Ramnes' heart race. She packed it less than forty hours ago and lugged it to the one place she could think of where he might not find it. With dazed efficiency she had moved as silently as she could between their wardrobes, the bathroom and the kitchen, straining to pick up the slightest change in the sound of his snoring. When she was done, she'd put Tyra's wet pyjama bottoms to soak.

Now she goes over the contents of the bag yet again while staring vacantly at the tiled wall in front of her. Two changes of clothes each for the children, one for herself, underwear, medicines, painkillers, a bag of sweets, two thin books of fairy tales, an unused pay-as-you-go SIM card, an extra charger, cash. She has to remember to get the passports, hers and the children's, from the safe. She read that on the internet, wouldn't have thought of it herself. Of course she needs their passports. Why didn't I think of that? And Teddy and Bunny, if I forget them, the children will . . . Her mind seizes up.

I can't do this, she whimpers inwardly. He's fucking right; I can't do anything anymore.

She tears off a piece of toilet paper, wipes and checks her watch again. Seven minutes since Bo got in his car and went to the office without warning. On a Saturday afternoon. For some reason, she always pictured this happening on a workday, if it ever happened at all. A regular workday when she would have plenty of time to get it right. Now, he's just picking up some papers and could be back in an hour if he leaves straight away, maybe even sooner if he drives fast.

No, it's not enough time, she tells herself. It's too risky. Safer to wait for another opportunity. He might leave her alone for a few days now – he usually does after an explosion like the one last night. Better to wait until after the holidays, too, when he's back to working regular hours. When I can plan better, make it easier on the children.

She pulls up her trousers, stands up and flushes. Her nether regions feel like they're on fire. She turns the tap on and washes her hands, watching the water flow over her wedding ring and into the wide sink, twisting down the drain. Then she looks up, meets her own eyes in the mirror and studies the right one that is almost too swollen to see out of, the black crack where her lip split, the fresh thumb marks on her throat. This time, there was no point getting out her many shades of concealer. Even Bo realised as much.

'Mum slipped on the stairs,' he said at breakfast yesterday and was met by silence. She had smiled reassuringly at Mikkel but had been too afraid to look Tyra in the eyes.

Another quick glance at the watch; it's already been eleven minutes. If I . . . no, I won't have time; I have to wait. For the children . . .

Her thoughts are interrupted by images flashing before her eyes: Tyra's teddy, the puddle of pee on the stairs. She had known even before she opened the door to the children's bedroom. Mikkel was still asleep and as blissfully ignorant as she has been telling herself he is. But Tyra . . . She had found her curled up under her duvet with wide, staring eyes and soaked pyjama bottoms.

That's an image she will never be able to erase from her memory.

'It's OK, sweetheart,' she'd murmured while she pulled off her daughter's wet bottoms and helped her put on dry ones.

Tyra had made no reply.

'Everything's going to be all right again, Mummy promises,' she'd repeated over and over again, stroking her hair. 'Mummy promises.'

With gritted teeth, Aylin Ramnes pumps out a dollop of hand soap, rubs it around her finger and starts pulling on the big diamond ring she has worn every day for almost six years, even though the big rock always gets in the way. The engagement ring that has always been just a little bit too small for her finger, but that she has had resized. It doesn't budge, just digs into her finger as she starts to panic and more and more memories flash before her: Bo's frustration when he struggled to put it on her finger, his wounded pride when she suggested an adjustment or possibly even a simpler ring, that first glimpse of his rage. How she had desperately bent over backwards to appease him.

How she'd assured him she loved the ring, she loved him and finally, deliberately ignoring her inner alarm bell, that she had been mistaken. No, the ring was perfect the way it was, a perfect fit. He was right, she was just being silly.

She tugs so hard at it that, for a split second, she's worried her finger is going to come off – and when the ring finally falls into the sink with a dull clatter, she jumps. In that moment, as she instinctively puts her hand to her mouth and the pain in her finger is followed by the one in her lip, something stirs inside her. Something strange and hard that has been simmering for two days; an unfamiliar feeling that drives away all the others. Not courage, not grief, not even rage. She figures it must be hate.

She quickly picks up the ring and shoves it into her back pocket. Then she turns off the lights before closing the door behind her. Seventeen minutes.

She already needs to pee again.

The door to the storage area doesn't stick for once and the bag is still where she left it, hidden behind the big tarpaulin, under the grey faux-wicker garden table, wedged behind the storage chest and the rolled-up canvas of the giant umbrella. A safe place in the middle of winter. She wonders at how light it feels when she lifts it up to put it in the boot of her car and wonders if she hasn't packed enough; she must have forgotten something important.

Twenty-seven minutes.

Tyra is watching TV on the sofa. She obediently goes out to the car and climbs into her seat when Aylin cheerfully announces that they're going for a drive. She doesn't ask where they're going, but Aylin keeps talking anyway.

283

'It's going to be a fun surprise, but we have to hurry or we won't make it.'

Mikkel has taken off the clothes she put on him that morning and is now sitting on the kitchen floor in nothing but underwear, playing with his cars. He doesn't want to get dressed. He doesn't want to go for a ride. The howl he lets out when she finally picks up his writhing body gets her adrenaline pumping until her hands shake uncontrollably. In the end she gives up her attempts to dress him and carries him to the car.

Thirty-nine minutes.

'I don't want to!'

Mikkel tries to twist out of his car seat. Their eyes tear up with frustration. His and hers. Only Tyra is calm. She is sitting quietly in her seat with Teddy in her lap, staring out the window. With a final effort, Aylin manages to buckle her son in, wrap the blanket from the back seat around his naked body and close the door on the primal scream that follows. Two breaths before she opens the driver-side door. As she climbs in behind the wheel, she realises their passports are still in the safe. A quick glance at her watch and for a moment her mind goes blank and she panics when she realises she can't remember the code. Oh my God, I'm losing my mind, he's right. Then her brain catches up and she opens the door again. Makes up a lie to buy the time she needs.

'We're going to go see Grandma and Grandpa,' she says. 'They have a surprise for you.'

The code is 1872. She repeats it like a mantra all the way upstairs, 1872, 1872 – please, dear God, let him not have changed the code. With trembling hands she manages to get the safe open on the second try. They're sitting inside in a neat stack, held together with a rubber band. She quickly rips that off and puts Bo's passport back. Just then she spots the cream-coloured leather jewellery box. She quickly pulls it out and empties it out onto the desk, snatching up the things that belong to her: birthday and Christmas presents from Bo, the gold bracelet her parents gave her when she graduated, the pearls she inherited from her grandmother, her grandfather's old Rolex, shoving them into her jeans pockets and bra before starting to put the rest back. Then she stops herself. What does it matter now? With one last look at the mess, she runs back down the stairs.

When Aylin Ramnes once again climbs in behind the wheel six minutes later, sweat is running down her back and her heart is pounding so hard in her throat she has trouble swallowing. Without saying a word, she reverses out of the driveway much too fast and turns out onto the street, drives faster than she really dares to, sees the houses flash past and a neighbour stopping dead at the edge of the pavement, raising a fist in protest.

The back seat is quiet now. Not an excited silence, she notes and glances at her own manic face in the mirror. A frightened silence. Mikkel is sucking his thumb and running his tiny fingers along the raggedy ear of his blue terrycloth bunny. As though he can sense her watching, he meets her eyes.

'Sweetheart, I'm sorry I yelled at you,' she says and pulls the corners of her mouth up in a stiff smile.

Mikkel takes his thumb out of his mouth and says in a voice high and fragile from crying, 'Do you think they got us a dog?'

Tyra says nothing.

*

Another half-mile down the road, Aylin warily approaches the intersection, terrified of Bo's black Mercedes suddenly appearing. She tells herself that if she can just get through the intersection and turn right onto the main road before he gets back, she will make it. He's on his way back from town, he's coming from the other direction and won't see her if she can just get to the spot where the road curves. Please, God, she pleads silently, feeling her sweaty palms slip on the steering wheel. Just give me a few more minutes. She doesn't need to check her watch again; she knows time must be up.

A great wind is blowing now; the window is going to slam shut any second. And it will never open again.

47

Björn Groth studies his fingertips with a look of astonishment on his face, examining the ink on them as though he still can't fathom why someone has put a black inkpad and a sheet with ten blank squares in front of him. And then, as if suddenly overcome with revulsion, he starts rubbing his hands against his trouser legs.

'I'm sorry we haven't been able to get more modern equipment up here yet,' Karen says, 'but it comes out with soap and water. Thank you for agreeing to talk to us on a Saturday.'

'Did I have a choice?'

'Not really,' she says with half a smile. 'Can I get you anything, by the way? Coffee, tea?'

The room is small; the small table with the recording equipment and the four chairs barely fit. Annoyed, Karen glances up at the ceiling where one of the fluorescent lights has begun to flicker. If this is going to take long, her headache is definitely going to come back.

Her conversation with Karl at the restaurant intrudes on her thoughts. He hadn't asked any more questions, just listened as she told him. No details, nothing about the before or after, just the facts. She'd had a husband, she'd had a son and both were gone now. No racing heart, no dizziness, she was still in one piece, even though she had spoken their names out loud. I'm still here, she thinks and glances up at the ceiling in the cramped room. I'm going to conduct an interview in a room with flickering fluorescent lights, and my head is still above water.

'No, thank you, what I want is to know why I'm here,' Björn Groth replies and takes a seat on one of the chairs. 'I've already told you everything I know.'

He runs both his hands through his thick mane, as though to reassure himself it's still there.

'Not quite everything, I'm afraid,' Karen says. 'Are you sure you don't want a lawyer present?'

'Get to it. I have nothing to hide.'

Karen waits while Karl starts the recording equipment, then says:

'Interview with Björn Groth, in connection with the murders of Fredrik Stuub and Gabriel Stuub. The date is Saturday 2 January, the time 3.04 p.m. Present are Björn Groth, lead investigator Detective Inspector Karen Eiken Hornby and Detective Inspector Karl Björken.'

'Let me cut to the chase,' Karen says. 'The last time we spoke, you said you didn't know Fredrik Stuub. Is this still your claim?'

'Yes, it's my claim,' Björn Groth replies stiffly. 'Why?'

'OK, let me rephrase my question. Were you ever in contact with Fredrik Stuub? At any time, in any form, for whatever purpose?'

'We've obviously crossed paths over the years, it's a small island. Exchanged a few words about the weather and such, I suppose, but nothing beyond that. What is this about?'

A hint of uncertainty has seeped into his tone, barely perceptible, but Karen knows Karl has caught it, too. Without taking her eyes off Groth, she can see him leaning forward out of the corner of her eye and she lets him ask the question.

'Then how come Fredrik Stuub emailed you?'

He slides a printout of Stuub's email across the table while reciting the words in it verbatim, from memory.

'"I have information that can put an end to your expansion plans. Contact me asap." Not exactly a few words about the weather and such.'

The transformation is instantaneous. The man in front of them seems to deflate before their eyes. Once more, he looks down at his ink-stained fingertips, his head bowed. He says nothing.

'What did Fredrik Stuub know that could put an end to your expansion plans?'

'Nothing.'

'Nothing? And you want us to believe that?'

'Believe whatever you want.'

'Fine, but our job isn't to believe, it's to *know*. And we're going to find out, sooner or later, so you might as well come out with it. Did you contact Fredrik, as he asked?'

'No. And I want a lawyer. I've changed my mind.'

Karen sighs.

'Please, just answer the question.'

'I have no further comment. I don't know what this is about and I never contacted Stuub. I want a lawyer.'

'OK, then we'll resume this conversation tomorrow. Or, actually, let's make it Monday morning. I hear this neighbour-hood is practically teeming with local politicians on Monday mornings, though, so I guess you'd run the risk of bumping into people who have a lot of questions for you. You can tell us now or you can come back on Monday, if you prefer. But, sooner or later, you will have to answer our questions.'

Karen leans back and waits, watching Groth as he wrestles with his options.

'Fine,' he says eventually. 'I called him.'

'You're saying you called Fredrik Stuub? When?'

'On the nineteenth, the day I had the email. I figured it was about the damn road again.'

'Would you mind telling us a bit about "the damn road"?' Karl asks gently.

'The old git was doddery,' Björn Groth says with a shrug. 'He'd got it in his head that the new road we're building posed a threat to the bloody ship setting. He was always running around up there, acting like it was his private property.'

'And was he right?' Karl asks. 'A new road and a conference centre – that does sound like it would have a significant impact on cultural heritage sites.'

Björn Groth snorts derisively.

'Those rocks have stood there for two thousand years so they can probably survive a road passing by almost a mile away. Yes, we had originally planned to build it closer, but the culture and environment authorities went against us on that one, so we submitted a revised proposal, which was approved. As Stuub was well aware.'

'So what did he say, when you called?'

'Nothing.'

Karen can feel herself getting annoyed and opens her mouth, but Groth beats her to it.

'I told him he would be in real trouble if I took his email to the police. I said it sounded a lot like blackmail.'

'And he had nothing to say to that?'

'Well, he said I was full of lies and that he had never threatened anyone, but if he wanted to, I'd better believe he could.

Then he hung up before I could get another word in. Like I told you, the old git was doddery.'

'OK, so, what do you make of all that?' Karen says after Björn Groth has left.

She wearily pushes a strand of hair out of her eyes and squints at the flickering lights.

'I think I need a pint and a bloody strong shot of whiskey,' Karl replies with a sigh. 'Any kind but Groth's.'

48

'Oh my God, what is that?'

Karl Björken leans forward and cranes his neck to see out the side window. They've turned off the motorway, just before the sign marking the border between Skreby and Gudheim counties. The house Karl is studying with a mix of fascination and disbelief is a four-storey building of pale yellow sandstone that looms up ahead, rising higher and higher the closer they get. The main body of the house is, aside from its size, relatively unremarkable, like a vertical rectangle. What makes the building reminiscent of a postcard from the German alps, rather than the windy moors of Noorö, are the four turrets at each corner, reaching toward the leaden sky. Each is topped with something akin to medieval battlements.

'The old mining baron, Huss, had it built it at the start of the last century,' Karen replies. 'A physical manifestation of his delusions of grandeur, I suppose.'

'Or compensation for a bloody tiny cock,' Karl retorts with a wicked chuckle.

'Could be. The locals call it The Complex. Legend has it he never picked up on the double entendre.'

Karen slows down and turns onto a dead straight gravel road lined by bare horse chestnut trees.

'Of course he had to put in a fancy driveway, too,' she comments, peering up at the house while she slowly drives up the tree-lined road. 'It must be beautiful in the summer.'

'You've never been here before?'

'No, just driven past it on the main road. I used to love this house as a child, I thought it looked like something out of a fairy tale.'

'Not so much anymore,' Karl replies drily. 'Check out the façade.'

They round a flower bed with something that looks suspiciously like a carp pond at its centre and park in front of the wide stone front steps. Karen kills the engine, bends down and looks up through the windscreen at the crumbling sandstone. From afar, The Complex may still look like a palace, but up close like this, she can make out both façade damage and a thin layer of soot.

'Damp,' she says, 'and coal dust. Impossible to get off, apparently, and it's particularly bad up here, what with all the coal mines everywhere. So, shall we get this over with?' she says with a glance at her watch.

A couple of minutes to five. With luck, they can be out of here before six.

They are only halfway up the stone steps when one of the wide double doors is thrown open and William Tryste steps out to welcome them.

'I assume you had no trouble finding this place?' he says with a grin and extends a hand. 'I didn't exactly inherit a discreet house.'

'As a child, I loved seeing it,' Karen says. 'Back then, I thought it looked like a castle. But, well, it's still . . . imposing.'

William Tryste chuckles.

'No need to be tactful. Unlike my forebear, we get what people meant when they named the thing "The Complex".'

'Must be expensive to heat,' Karl says, looking around the enormous hallway.

'We only use a quarter of the living space. Half the ground floor and as much again on the first floor is plenty for our little family, the rest is closed off. The Groths do pay well, no complaints there, but keeping all of this warm would probably require three times my salary. Shall we go in? My wife is waiting in the living room.'

They enter the hallway, where a wide staircase with a leather banister leads up to a landing and then splits into two smaller, steeper staircases.

'We live in the southern part of the house,' William Tryste explains, pointing to the staircase on the left. 'Our bedrooms and bathrooms are up there. Please, come this way!'

He leads them past the stairs and a door revealing a glimpse of what appears to be a study. Karen spots the kitchen at the other end of a long butler's pantry as well as another set of stairs, going down this time.

'In all honesty, we've annexed the part of the house that used to house the servants in the good old days,' Tryste explains. 'That staircase over there leads down to the laundry room, food cellar and the old wine cellar. I have some truly fine specimens down there, but I assume I can't tempt you, since you're on the job and all.'

'I'm afraid not,' Karl replies. 'So it's not all about whiskey then? Not even for the head of a distillery?'

'No, I have all kinds of vices,' William Tryste says with a laugh and opens the door to a long, narrow living room. 'May I introduce my wife, Helena, and these are Detective Inspectors Karen Eiken Hornby and Karl Björken.'

A middle-aged woman with long dark hair in a ponytail gets up from one of the armchairs. They shake hands and Karen notes that Helena Tryste doesn't exude any of the natural confidence her husband has been so abundantly blessed with. Instead, there is a hint of uncertainty, almost shyness about her when their eyes meet.

'Welcome,' she says with a tight smile. 'Can I offer you anything? Coffee, tea?'

Karen quickly declines without waiting to hear what Karl might want. She knows from their last encounter that while William Tryste's verbosity may be charming, it's also time-consuming and she doesn't want to drag this visit out any more than necessary.

'Thank you, but we're not staying long,' she says.

After an inviting gesture from William Tryste, they sit down on a dark blue sofa and look around the room. The décor is pleasantly free of the crystal chandeliers, oak furniture and dark brown leather that dominated the Groths' parlour, and Karen notes that the bookshelves actually look as though they contain contemporary titles. But, just like at the Groths', Helena fetches glasses and bottles of mineral water from a serving cart without asking and places them in front of her guests, mindful of Doggerian custom. A host may reluctantly accept not being allowed to serve coffee or tea – at least if their guests are from the police, customs or tax authorities – but not serving them even water is unthinkable.

'So,' William Tryste says, hiking up his trouser legs and taking a seat in one of the armchairs across from them, 'I assume you want to talk about last night, but what exactly is it you want to know?'

Ten minutes later, William and Helena Tryste have confirmed the account given by the Groths and their guests about the previous evening. They themselves had left the party just before one. Helena Tryste had refrained from drinking and they'd given Eva Framnes a ride home. The only point at which the Trystes' version diverges from the others' is that they claim Björn Groth left the table during dinner to take a call.

'But he can't have been gone for more than five minutes and it was long before midnight,' William Tryste stresses.

'And you don't know what that call was about, I assume?'

'No idea. But I thought it was odd for anyone to be calling at that time of night, and on New Year's Eve, too. His family was there, and it can hardly have been work-related, either.'

'Do you recall if he seemed upset when he returned?'

'No, slightly worried, maybe. But I have to say, I'm not comfortable speculating about it. You should just ask Björn directly.'

'We will,' Karen says, noting that William Tryste looks like he's sorry he mentioned the call at all.

She exchanges a quick look with Karl, leans back and lets him take the reins.

'We would like you to tell us about any threats that may have been made against the distillery or the Groths,' he says.

Suddenly, the room is dead silent. Their host slowly leans forward, reaching for an opener and one of the bottles. The hissing sound when the cap comes off seems to fill the entire room. He doesn't seem surprised, Karen reflects, but he's playing for time.

'Threats against the Groths?' he says eventually. 'What would that be about?'

'That's what we're trying to find out. For example, what might Fredrik Stuub have known that could have threatened the expansion?'

'Threatened the expansion? Nothing. We've already gone through the process with all the requisite reports and planning permissions. The matter is up for discussion at the meeting of the provincial board next week and all the parties will unanimously cast their votes to approve our plan. At least, according to what I've been told.'

'How can you be so sure? Doesn't the opposition always vote no? Just for the sake of it, if nothing else.'

'Maybe in the national parliament, but not out here in the provinces. Sure, political debates get heated up here, too, but not about things like this. No local politician with so much as an ounce of survival instinct would ever vote against something that could both create jobs and—'

'Put Noorö on the map,' Karen finishes with a sigh. 'Yes, that's exactly what Björn Groth told us. But apparently Fredrik Stuub was opposed to the expansion for some reason. I believe he felt it would constitute a threat to the Gudheim ship setting.'

William Tryste leans back with a heavy sigh and out of the corner of her eye Karen notes that his wife mirrors his movements. I guess there's only enough oxygen for one strong personality in any relationship, she thinks.

'That's true,' he says. 'We had to reroute and widen the new road. In practice, it will be almost like an extension of the motorway and in the original plan it would have passed relatively close to the stones, which the environmental agency took issue with. But all that has been worked out. Granted, it's going to be a lot more expensive and it has already caused considerable delay, but there can be no doubt the board will approve it.'

'So the proximity of the Gudheim stones is no longer of concern? No protests against the site being exploited?'

'No, not that I'm aware of.'

'Perhaps Fredrik was worried increased tourism would lead to even more vandalism?' Karen suggests. 'The last instance was pretty serious, from what I hear.'

William Tryste stiffens. Then he frowns and seems to search his memory.

'That would explain . . .' he says hesitantly. 'No.'

'What?'

Karl's voice is sharp and Karen notes that Helena Tryste has gone rigid, too.

'Nothing, it doesn't mean anything. Not in practice.'

They wait silently, watching as Tryste once more seems to be inwardly cursing his loose tongue and looking for a more appropriate way of phrasing what he now has to say.

'Out with it,' Karl says impatiently.

'The drill holes,' William Tryste says darkly. 'I thought it was odd. Not exactly the kind of thing you'd expect from bored teens. Besides, those stupid brats wouldn't have the wherewithal to plan something like that themselves. I mean, graffiti is one thing, but . . .'

'Plan? Bringing a hammer drill doesn't require much planning, does it?' Karl says.

Karen has kept quiet. Now she studies their host, watches him cast about for any explanation other than the one that has just occurred to him.

'You're thinking the Groths had something to do with the vandalism, aren't you?' she says. 'And that Fredrik Stuub was onto them.'

'No,' Tryste says, looking like he's still searching his memory. 'Fredrik Stuub never set foot inside the distillery, as far as I'm aware. He couldn't have known.'

'All right, it's time for you to just tell us plainly,' Karl Björken says. 'What have you seen up at the distillery that could connect the Groths with the drill holes?'

William Tryste seems to be arguing with himself while they silently wait for him to continue. At length, he takes a deep breath.

'Self-stressing cement', he says softly and exhales.

Helena Tryste gasps, like a delayed imitation of her husband.

'Self-stressing cement?' Karen says, looking queryingly from Karl to Tryste and back again.

'The kind you fill drill holes with if you want to crack rock without dynamite,' Karl explains. 'Very practical if you're looking to destroy an entire ship setting, no?'

William Tryste nods.

'I suppose so. But that's unthinkable.'

'And this self-stressing cement is stored up at the distillery?' Karen asks.

'Yes, I found a few bags of it in a storage cupboard behind my office. I didn't give it any thought at the time, though I couldn't see what use we would have for it.'

'You didn't ask anyone?'

'I believe I mentioned it to Björn. But he said he had no idea how the bags had ended up there. Said he hadn't bought them, at any rate.'

'And Fredrik Stuub never visited the distillery? Are you absolutely sure?'

Tryste meets Karl's level gaze and nods.

'As sure as I can be. And even if he had visited, he would hardly have been rummaging through a storage cupboard. I honestly don't know why it came to mind. I suppose it was because you were talking about threats and those drill holes and my brain put the two together. But no, Fredrik couldn't have known about those bags.'

But Gabriel Stuub might have, Karen thinks to herself. And he might have told his grandfather.

49

'What do you know,' Karl says as he buckles himself into the passenger seat. 'The question is whether this was Björn's clever plan or if someone else in the family was behind it.'

'I'm not sure it was so very clever,' Karen says. 'Think about it, what did they hope to gain? The road had already been greenlighted.'

'Well, I assume not having to move the road because there's nothing left but a pile of gravel would save them a few million.'

'A few well-placed holes, a bit of self-stressing cement and boom! – all their problems are solved, you mean? I find that hard to believe.'

'I don't think it goes boom. It takes at least twenty-four hours from when you fill the drill holes to when the stone cracks. Perfect if you don't want to be anywhere near the crime scene.'

Karen starts the car and lets her mind wander while she drives back down the tree-lined driveway. That a member of the Groth family would have vandalised the ship setting sounds implausible. After all, the stone ship must be an important component of their pitch to attract tourists to Noorö. On the other hand, Fredrik Stuub may well have thought they'd be willing to go to such lengths to save a few million and acted accordingly. The question is why he would decide to email Björn Groth rather than go to the police. Or the media. If he had really wanted to stop the expansion, either would have been a more effective way of spreading rumours and tainting the project.

'Maybe he wasn't such a dyed-in-the-wool idealist,' Karl puts in, apparently thinking along the same lines. 'Maybe the old man was trying to squeeze money out of the Groths.'

'If he even knew about the bags of cement. It might have been about something else entirely.'

Karl makes no reply. Just as Karen turns on her indicator to merge onto the motorway, the memory that has been lurking at the back of her head resurfaces.

'Expansive cement,' she says, slapping the steering wheel. 'Of course! It must be the same thing.'

Karl has pulled out his phone and is writing a text. To Ingrid, Karin assumes. Their twins hadn't even turned two when a third child joined the Björken family and Ingrid is no doubt less than pleased that her husband has been called back to work before finishing his parental leave. I wonder what Smeed said to talk him into it, she thinks to herself.

'It goes by different names,' Karl replies distractedly while he types. 'Some call it Type K, but I think that might be a particular kind. Why?'

'Fredrik Stuub's browser history. He did a search for expansive cement.'

Karl slowly puts his phone down and turns to Karen.

'So, bingo, then, I guess,' he says. 'We'll have to talk to Groth again. Do you want to head straight there?'

'No, let's hold off on that. He's won't talk to us again without a lawyer.'

'Can it really wait until Monday?'

Karl fails to hide a note of hopefulness in his voice.

'You go home,' Karen replies calmly. 'The Groths aren't going anywhere. I can bring Byle in if it becomes necessary to talk to them tomorrow.'

'So you're staying?'

'To be honest, I'm too tired to drive home. I rack up enough miles driving up and down this damn motorway.'

'It's a beautiful island,' Karl says with a grin. 'But bloody long.'

Just then, Karen's phone rings.

'Probably Smeed,' she says with a glance at her watch.

It must be the late evening in Thailand, so he's unlikely to be sober, Karen realises with a sigh. She adjusts her earbud, pushes the button on the cord and answers in a formal tone.

But instead of her boss's drawling inflection, she hears a voice so tense she barely recognises it.

'Hi, Karen, it's Leo. I think you need to come back. Right now.'

50

Without knowing how, Karen manages to keep the car on the road. All her instincts are screaming at her to rip out the earbud. She doesn't want to hear it. Whatever it is, she doesn't want to know.

'What's wrong?' she says and wonders if her voice can be heard over the loud buzzing in her ears. 'Is it Sigrid?' she breathes and knows the worst must have happened. Leo wouldn't call otherwise.

Her words draw an instant reaction from Karl Björken.

'Pull over there,' he says, pointing to a pole with the bus company's logo on it. 'Do it, Karen.'

His authoritative voice compels her to obey. She slams on the brakes and turns into the bus stop.

'Hello?' Leo's voice says in her ear. 'Are you still there? You're breaking up.'

'What's wrong?'

'She's been beat up pretty bad. And she's scared. She's here in the kitchen now, but she's in a bad way.'

'Who hit her? If it's that bloody Sam, I'm going to—'

Memories of Sigrid's ex-boyfriend flash before her eyes. It's been three months since they broke up, but she knows Sam still calls to badger Sigrid about getting back together. She pictures the gangly young man: even more tattoos on his arms than Sigrid, even more piercings and the same long black hair. Samuel Nesbö may look dangerous, but Karen never thought he'd be violent.

While her mind races, she absently notes that Karl is taking the keys out of the ignition and opening the door on his side. Then Leo's voice is back.

'Sam? What the fuck are you talking about? It's her husband, obviously. Bo, or whatever the fuck his name is.'

Everything stops. Then fear morphs into unadulterated rage.

'Aylin,' she says quietly. 'Bo beat her?'

'To within an inch of her life. She has the kids with her and says it's only a matter of time before the bastard turns up here.'

'I'm on my way,' Karen says. 'But it's going to take me a few hours to get there. Call the police right now and—'

'She won't,' Leo cuts in. 'Says she'll leave if we contact the police. Sigrid and I have both tried to convince her.'

'Does she need a doctor?'

'That's off the table, too. She claims nothing's broken.'

'Have you talked to Marike?'

'No, I called you first.'

Karen grits her teeth and thinks furiously while Karl firmly leads her over to the passenger seat. If Bo suspects Aylin might have gone to Karen's, he could turn up in Langevik any minute. And if they leave, they risk meeting him on the road.

'Stay where you are. Lock all the doors and windows and make sure Aylin and the kids stay upstairs. Did she drive there or take a taxi?'

'She drove here. No idea how she managed it, but—'

'You're going to have to move the car,' Karen breaks in. 'Go down the gravel road past my house and continue past the turning area. You can make a left across a rocky patch and go down a gully on the other side of the ridge.'

'Cliffs?' Leo asks dubiously.

'My dad turned a trailer around there once, so I know it's possible as long as you're careful. And no one will be able to see the car if you park it down there.'

'All right,' Leo says. 'Anything else?'

'Close the curtains upstairs. All the better if he can see you and Sigrid downstairs, though. But keep Aylin and the kids upstairs until I get there. And go move the damn car right now. Call me when it's done.'

'What's going on?' Karl says after climbing in behind the wheel.

'A friend of mine has been assaulted by husband,' Karen says darkly. 'Damn it, I should have seen it coming!'

She punches the glove compartment so hard it pops open. Then she checks her watch.

'The ferry from Lysvik leaves in twenty-eight minutes. Can we make it?'

Without replying, Karl speeds up.

They just make it. They're the last car to drive onto the ferry; Karen stands powerless on the stern deck, watching the lights from Lysvik retreat into the darkness with excruciating slowness. She takes a deep drag on her cigarette, picturing her house in Langevik. Her home, where she has always felt safe, despite its remote location. The last house of the village, at least two hundred yards to the nearest neighbour, she thinks and touches her keys in her pocket.

For the first time in years she thinks about her service gun, which is locked in a safe on the first floor. She has only fired it once, and a warning shot was enough that time.

'I would call in a few of our colleagues, if I were you,' Karl says, waving away the smoke.

'Leo says she'll take off if I do. I don't even think she's going to report it.'

'Why not? Is she afraid of the police?'

'She's afraid of him. He has contacts in high places.'

'"Contacts in high places"? Who is this guy, the good Lord himself?'

'Hardly. Just Bo Ramnes.'

'*The* Bo Ramnes? The big-shot lawyer?'

'That's the one. He's standing for a parliamentary seat for the Progress Party this autumn. Rumour has it he'll be a candidate for the post of Minister for Justice if the opposition wins.'

'The Progress Party? Aren't they the ones who want tougher policing, law and order, longer prison sentences and mandatory lifetime incarceration for reoffenders? Wouldn't be bloody surprised if they wanted to reinstate the death penalty, too.'

'Not quite, but close enough. Their main demand is for more police on the streets, so a lot of our colleagues are bound to vote for them. And Ramnes will use all his experience from court to win over frightened voters.'

'He must have had a change of heart then. From what I recall, he's usually very successful at keeping criminals out of prison.'

'Only wealthy criminals. Economic crimes, mostly.'

'Fine, but I still think you should call the police.'

'I *am* the police,' Karen says and flicks her cigarette overboard. 'And we don't know that he's going to show up. I can hardly call officers out to Langevik if the prick is sitting at home, happy as a clam. But I'm going to do everything I can to persuade her to report him,' she adds. 'He's not going to get away with this again.'

When the ferry finally reaches Thorsvik, Karen is back behind the wheel. This time she ignores the speed limits. Just two hours later, she drops Karl off outside his terraced house in Sande, and forty minutes after that she slows down to enter Langevik. She keeps her eye out for movements or headlights as she follows the narrow gravel road along the seashore, passing the increasingly sparse row of stone houses on her left and their boat sheds on the right. Snow creaks under the Ford's tyres when she turns off her headlights and slowly rolls toward the last driveway. She leans forward and peers up at the house. The light from the ground-floor windows illuminates a few feet of the yard around the house, the rest is shrouded in darkness.

Even though she spoke to Leo twice during the drive from Thorsvik, and even though he assured her both times that everything was quiet – not a sign of Bo Ramnes – Karen briefly regrets not taking Karl up on his repeated offers to come with her.

'Call me if anything happens,' he'd said. 'At least promise you'll do that.'

Just as she is about to turn into the steep driveway, something moves on the front steps. Someone is standing there, stock-still now, trying blend into the shadows. Her heart begins to race, pumping adrenaline into every muscle.

Then she takes a deep breath, turns on her high beams and floors it.

51

Ingrid Björken doesn't turn around.

'Did you mean what you said?' she asks and puts the frying pan down in the sink with a bang.

Karl is standing in the doorway between the hallway and the kitchen. Instead of going up to his wife and wrapping his arms around her, he has instinctively stopped and started to take off his scarf instead. Something about Ingrid's back is worrisome. Maybe that's it, actually, that she hasn't even turned around even though she must have heard him stomping the snow off his boots on the front steps and then felt the cold gust of air when he opened the door. One look at his wife's rigid back made him stop on the threshold to the warm kitchen like a tramp. No, this is not going to be the calm, loving evening in the warm embrace of his family Karl Björken had envisioned.

He lingers in the doorway, scarf in hand, searching for the right words. He briefly considers saying something like 'Hi, love, it's good to see you, too', but he can sense that wouldn't be well received.

'What are you talking about?' he says instead in a weary voice, deciding to try to play the martyr. 'I've just come home after an extremely tough . . .'

He trails off when he hears how half-hearted he sounds. Ingrid is staring at the puddle of melted snow spreading from his boots. Karen drove him all the way to the roundabout, but the short walk from there to the house was enough to cover his hat and shoulders in a layer of white and pack snow into the deep tracks of his boots.

'Did you mean what you said?' Ingrid asks again. 'Tell me you at least meant it when you said it. That you were going to stay home with the kids until we could sort out a childcare solution. That I would be able to go back to work. It's important for me to know.'

He doesn't ask why it's important for her to know. They've had this conversation before and he remembers it almost verbatim.

You have to do your share this time, promise you will.

That's what Ingrid had said after finding out she was pregnant again, less than two years after their twins, Arne and Frode, were born. They hadn't planned on having more children, not when they already had two. Not when they'd finally found a childminder who could take them and Ingrid was going to be able to go back to work. It had been a very inconvenient surprise.

But no use crying over spilled milk, a new life was on its way. And he had promised: this time they were going to take full advantage of Doggerland's recently expanded paternity leave. Ingrid was going to stay home the first ten months, then Karl would take over until their childminder was able to accommodate all three kids. They were going to make it work; they were going to share the burden.

He really had meant it. In fact, he'd been looking forward to spending six months at home with the children, taking it easy. Yes, that was how he thought about it, even though he'd never been stupid enough to say it out loud, that it was going to be really nice to take it easy for a while.

But then everything had gone wrong at the CID. First, Karen had been put on long-term sick leave, then Evald Johannisen, who had heart problems, had gone down to part-time. They'd needed Karl to stay on. Would it be possible to delay his parental leave, just a few weeks, just until they could figure things out? But the start of October had turned into December before his parental leave became reality. And then Smeed had called the other day. Karl was really needed at work now, could he possibly . . . ?

He'd been home less than a month. More like three weeks.

'Three weeks over Christmas,' Ingrid had said. 'And you were ill most of that time so I had to take care of you *and* the children.'

'It's an emergency, what am I supposed to do? And besides, it's only a few more months for you. Worst-case scenario.'

What was she so upset about? he'd wondered. The childminder had told them she'd be able to take all three children after Easter. Fine, so an extra three and a half months at home for Ingrid.

'That's more than *six months* longer than we agreed. I was supposed to go back to work in October. Or did you forget that?'

Now he walks back to the hallway, bends down and undoes his boots, then yanks down a hanger, drops it on the floor, picks it up and hangs up his coat. What the fuck did he come home for? He might as well have stayed on Noorö. He could be sitting at a hotel bar right now, enjoying the peace and quiet and a nice glass of whiskey, instead of coming home to get yelled at for something he can't do anything about. The laws may be progressive, but reality isn't. If he had refused to pitch in during a crisis like this one, he wouldn't stand a chance of ever being promoted.

He takes a deep breath before returning to the kitchen and lets out a searing oath as his foot lands in the puddle of melted snow he'd already forgotten. His sock is instantly soaked.

'God fucking dammit!' he exclaims and holds on to the door frame while he lifts up his dripping foot and catches a glimpse of Ingrid's smile before she turns away.

'Nice of you to clean up after yourself, at least,' she says, and isn't that a suppressed giggle he hears in her voice?

Without knowing why, he steps into the puddle with both feet. Tramps about in it while Ingrid looks on in disbelief. Driven by a mix of exasperation, weariness and an urge to coax out that smile he glimpsed, he uses his socks to mop up the water. And as he looks up at his wife to gauge her reaction, he slips, landing hard on the linoleum. Dejectedly slumped on the floor, he realises he didn't even manage to wipe it all up – the seat of his jeans is soaking up the last of the melted snow.

'Yes,' he says with a sigh. 'I meant what I said. And that's how it's going to be. This is just . . . a temporary setback.'

He regrets his words the moment they leave his lips. He watches his wife gear up to point out the obvious, that this 'setback' is only a setback for her career, not his. But then she hesitates, studying her six-foot-five husband and his soaked socks on the floor.

'Very mature,' she says after a pause.

And there it is. The smile she can no longer suppress, the smile that transforms her plain face into the most beautiful thing he's ever seen.

'Are you in pain?' she asks.

He nods.

'Good!'

He holds out his hands to her in a silent plea for both reconciliation and help to get back up and feels the warmth of hers as she grabs them and pulls. With a groan he gets back on his feet and wraps his arms around her before she can object.

'My God, I'm stiff these days,' he says, with his mouth against his hair. 'Are the kids asleep?'

'What do you think? It's half past ten. Are you hungry?'

'Mmm. Do we have any wine?'

He can feel her nodding against his chin.

I'm going to talk to Smeed, he thinks to himself. As soon as this damn case is solved.

52

'Bloody hell!'

Leo shields his eyes with his arm and Karen kills the engine. With her adrenaline still pumping, she angrily stomps up the stone steps.

'What were you thinking, prowling about out here?' she yells at him. 'I thought you were him.'

'I went outside for a smoke,' Leo yells back. 'And just as I was closing the door behind me, I heard a car, but I couldn't see anything. Why were you driving with your lights off? I was convinced it was that sick bastard. You scared the shit out of me.'

They glare furiously at each other for a few seconds. Then, at exactly the same time, they both relax and let out a chuckle. Sheepish, relieved.

'Can I bum a cigarette off you before I go inside?' Karen asks. 'I'm out and I need to calm my nerves.'

'Sure thing, freeloader.'

'How is she?' Karen asks after taking a deep drag.

'Not great. The physical injuries are bad enough, but the worst thing is how scared she is.'

'And the children? Do they understand what's happening?'

'Don't know. They're so little and Aylin seems to be in the habit of hiding the truth from them. You know, like, Mummy fell down and hurt herself . . .'

'And they pretend to believe her, to not make her even more sad. Children understand more than we think.'

'Yep. But at least they're asleep now. Sigrid showed them a bunch of new video games, stuffed them full of leftover Christmas chocolate and kept them distracted. They seem to think she's the bee's knees.'

'They might be right about that,' Karen says with a smile.

Before she can react, Leo puts his arm around her neck and pulls her close. He holds her tight for a few seconds before he lets her go.

'I've never been so happy to see the fuzz,' he says.

Aylin is lying on her side with her arm around her two children, and Karen is struck by how long it's been since she's seen them. Mikkel must be four by now and Tyra five. With a sad smile she remembers how desperately Aylin had wanted to become a mother after countless miscarriages in her previous relationship. How Bo Ramnes had turned her world upside down and knocked her up in less than six months. And how his appearance on the scene had meant Aylin gradually disappearing from their daily lives. They'd watched her struggle to keep in touch with them. They'd listened when she pleadingly explained that Bo did want to see them, but he was just so busy with work. Then she had stopped calling, stopped coming out for coffee or drinks, stopped going on weekend trips to Copenhagen or Edinburgh. Party invitations were politely turned down and more and more calls went straight to voicemail.

Even so, no one could have mistaken Aylin's joy when Tyra was born and Karen, Eirik, Kore and Marike had visited her in the hospital without asking permission. That time, even Bo had been friendly, proudly showing off his daughter.

There had been other attempts at keeping their friendship alive after that. A couple of coffee dates in Dunker with Tyra in her pram, a harbourside lunch. And one dinner party at their house in Glitne, an awkward affair during which they all made polite conversation while pretending not to notice Bo's disapproving looks at Kore's tattooed arms against the white damask tablecloth. They had tried. And then Mikkel was born, an unexpected bonus just a year later. At thirty-nine years old, Aylin finally had everything she'd ever wanted.

Now, as she wakes up with a start, she looks as if she's lost everything.

She instinctively scrambles out of bed to stand with her back against the wall, eyes wide with terror. Then her legs seem to give up and she slowly sinks to the floor and buries her face in her hands. Karen rushes over to her.

'Oh, sweetheart,' she says as she squats down next to Aylin, 'we're going to fix this.'

53

Just looking at Aylin hurts; Karen has to steel herself not to look away. One eye is nearly swollen shut and dried blood paints a black line along the crack in her lower lip. And yet, Karen now knows the worst of it was hidden under the thick dressing gown.

They had stayed on the bedroom floor for almost half an hour. Karen had rocked her friend back and forth and gently stroked her hair while silent sobs racked her thin body and tiny gasps slowly turned into regular breathing. Whispering, so as not to wake the children, Karen has managed to make Aylin come with her to the bathroom, helped her take her clothes off and gritted her teeth at the sight it revealed.

She has seen it all before: black and blue backs, shields of last resort against violent husbands and boyfriends. Upper arms with marks from hard fingers, earlobes split by earrings being pulled out, dried blood on the backs of heads smashed against walls. Yes, she has seen it all before: on the estates in Gaarda and Moerbeck, in the neat terraced houses in Sande and Lemdal and in the big fancy villas in Thingwalla and Glitne.

But she has never seen it in her own bathroom.

'We have to,' Karen had said, pulling out her phone.

And aided by her acquired ability to shut down her feelings, learnt from working countless crime scenes, Karen had done what needed doing. Quietly, and as quickly as possible, she had taken picture after picture of Aylin's injuries while the bath filled up. Aylin had stood there in her underwear, passively letting it happen. Then Karen had left, making sure to leave the door open a crack.

And when she heard the soft whimper Aylin let out as she stepped into the warm water, she had leant back against the wall outside the door, both hands pressed firmly over her mouth.

Now, they're in the kitchen. The curtains have been carefully closed and the overhead light turned off. The only light in the room comes from the brass Christmas candelabra. Leo and Sigrid have tactfully withdrawn to the living room; Karen can make out the sound of something that sounds like an American action film through the door. She suspects they're watching it with unseeing eyes.

Aylin, too, is staring vacantly into space with her hands around a mug of hot chocolate fortified with a stiff shot of whiskey. Karen has poured herself two fingers of the latter in a regular water glass.

'Do you think you can tell me about it?'

Aylin slowly shakes her head, then looks up and meets her eyes for a second before averting them again.

'I'm so ashamed, Karen. And I know what you want me to do but reporting him will only make it worse. I'm to blame too, you know, for things having ended up like this.'

'I'm not going to force you do anything,' Karen replies gently. 'From now on, you make all the decisions. Except for one.'

Aylin stares mutely at her mug.

'I never want to hear you say this is your fault again. I don't want you to even *think* it. Am I making myself clear?'

Aylin still doesn't respond, just sniffles and wipes her nose on her wrist.

'I've seen this before,' Karen says, 'so I know what's going to happen if you change your mind and go back. It's only a matter of time.'

Aylin slowly shakes her head.

'He's never going to let me get away.'

'You did get away. You've already left him; the hardest part is behind you.'

Aylin lifts up her head at that, looks Karen straight in the eye and gives her an almost pitying smile.

'This is only the beginning,' she says. 'Don't you see that?'

Karen waits for her to continue.

'You've tried before?' she asks eventually.

'Twice. Once just after Mikkel was born and again early last year.'

'What happened? Drink some of your hot chocolate before it gets cold,' she adds and watches as Aylin obediently raises her mug and grimaces when it bumps against her split lip.

Karen doesn't touch her own glass.

'The first time, I made it a few blocks down the street. I just took the children and walked out the front door without any idea where I was going. Stupid, obviously; he noticed within five minutes and caught up before we had even crossed Kaupinggate.'

'What happened afterwards?'

'He actually calmed down for a while after that, as though what he'd done had scared him, too. He promised it would never happen again, but, well, you know...'

'Was that the first time he hit you?'

'It was the first time he drew blood. Before then, it was mostly grabbing and the occasional slap. I think maybe that was what made me walk out that time, seeing the blood on the sofa. He accidentally got my nose,' she adds. 'I don't think he meant to.'

Karen closes her eyes briefly and forces her anger down. Not now, not yet.

'And the time after that, what happened then?'

Aylin raises her mug again but puts it back down without drinking.

'That time was planned. I had packed a bag with things for the children and took the car. I took off the moment he left for work and drove all the way to Frisel. Dad's parents left him a house down there. A small cottage they used to rent out. Bo and I had never talked about it and I was sure he didn't know it existed. Even so, it took him less than twenty-four hours to find us. He'd had help, he told me. He's always going to find me, he said.'

She runs a hand across her forehead. Then she freezes and stares at the window.

'The rowan tree,' Karen says gently, trying to hide the fact that she, too had jumped. 'The branches scratch against the windows when it's windy.'

'Do you think your parents might have told him?' she continues once Aylin tears her eyes away from the window. 'About the cottage down on Frisel?'

'They were abroad when it happened. I asked them later if Bo had called them. Lied and said something about Bo having mentioned wanting to ask Dad something. But they said he hadn't. He must have found out about the cottage some other way. I assume there are property registers.'

None Bo Ramnes should have access too, Karen thinks to herself.

True, it's relatively easy to find out who owns a certain property, but Doggerian law has long been restrictive about going the other way. Only police and prosecutors have access to the registers and databases that list individual residents' income, assets, debts, fishing rights and properties. In other words, only a police officer or prosecutor could have helped Bo Ramnes find out about Aylin's father's cottage on Frisel.

Maybe she's misremembering, Karen reflects. Maybe she had mentioned the cottage at some point. The alternative is so alarming she prefers not to contemplate it. Out loud, she says, 'Do your parents know Bo hits you?'

Aylin listlessly stirs her mug with a spoon and shakes her head.

'Dad asked me once, but I denied it,' she says without looking up.

Silence falls between them while they both recall the previous summer, when Karen had asked the same question. Neither of them speaks.

'And since then, you haven't made any other attempts to leave him?' Karen continues after a while. 'Until today, I mean.'

Aylin takes a deep, trembling breath.

'I'm going to fail again,' she says shrilly. 'You don't understand. He's going to find me, sooner or later.'

'Yes, he probably will,' Karen says calmly.

'So you think I should just go home?'

Aylin's tone is a mix of resignation and surprise. Karen leans forward and puts her hand on hers.

'Quite the opposite. You should *never* go back to Bo. What I mean is that we're going to make sure you're safe, that he can't hurt you, even if he finds out where you are. You're not alone anymore.'

'He's going to take the children. He says I don't stand a chance of winning custody.'

'No one is going to take your children away from you. Are you sure he's never hit them?'

'Never. He's a good dad. He really is.'

Karen clenches her jaw shut.

'He's probably going to get partial custody, maybe even half the parenting time,' she says. 'But he's never going to lay a finger on you again.'

There's a wet, sucking sound as Aylin tries to pull air in through her nose.

'He can turn up here any moment. Don't you get that?' she says. 'He could be standing outside right now.'

'He can't get in,' Karen says with feigned conviction. 'Now drink up so we can get you to bed. We're going to stand watch all night and tomorrow we're going to come up with a plan.'

54

They go through the available options, one after the other, while hopelessness settles like a heavy blanket over the living room where Karen, Leo, Sigrid and Marike, who has joined them, have gathered to deliberate. When Karen called to tell her what had happened, Marike had ignored all attempts to persuade her to wait until the morning and had instead immediately jumped in her car and driven all the way from her house in Portlande to Langevik. Probably much too fast, too, since it had only just gone half past eleven when she stomped through the front door. And maybe it was knowing that four people were now guarding the house that finally made Aylin feel safe enough to doze off. Or maybe it was sheer exhaustion.

They sat down in the living room and are now slumping deeper and deeper into the sofas and armchairs with every rejected suggestion. In the long run, Aylin won't be able to hide from Bo, they realise; sooner or later, he's going to figure out where she is. What they need to focus on now is getting through the next few weeks; they need to create a calm space amid the chaos, to give Aylin time to heal and muster the strength required to start divorce proceedings.

Karen's house in Langevik and Marike's house in Portlande are both too isolated. Kore and Eirik's house in Thingwalla is better, but not an option until they get back from New York next week. The suggestion that Aylin simply take the children and leave the country for a few weeks is rejected. Even though she has their passports, Bo would probably be able to exploit that kind of behaviour in a future custody process.

They're stuck.

'Would her parents be willing to take the children for a week?' Marike, who has been listening silently to the discussion, suddenly asks.

'For a week? Probably, if we can get Aylin to agree. She hasn't told them about any of this. And they're on holiday. London, I think.'

'Then I might have a suggestion.'

'What?' Leo snaps impatiently. 'Spit it out already, if you're sitting on a damn solution.'

He looks tired, Karen notes, glancing at the dark circles under his eyes and his clenched jaw.

'He's dead,' Marike says and is met with blank, weary stares. 'The owner of the building my studio's in, I mean,' she adds quickly. 'The old man who lived upstairs. Made it to ninety.'

Karen doesn't give a toss how old the owner of the building in which Marike's ceramic studio is housed was when he popped his clogs. She glances down at her watch.

'It's mine now,' Marike continues unhurriedly. 'All of it. His son was eager to sell. Et voilà! I own the whole thing,' she clarifies in perfect Doggerian.

The room goes completely silent while Karen, Leo and Sigrid stare at Marike in disbelief, unsure whether they've interpreted her garbled mix of Danish and Doggerian correctly.

'What are you saying? You bought it?' Sigrid says at length. 'The entire building?'

'Yep. I was just a tenant and I didn't want to risk someone else buying it and kicking me out. There's a one-bed flat upstairs. I figured you, Karen, could use it as a hideout, but I guess we're going to have to put a pin in that for now.'

It takes them a while to process. Follow-up questions are asked: yes, she has purchased the whole building. Yes, there is a small, vacant flat upstairs. It's just a one-bed and a bit run-down at that, but on the other hand it's fairly spacious and centrally located, which should be a plus, right? Lots of people around all day and most of the night. Maybe not great for sleeping, but safe. Not an ideal place for the children, perhaps, and definitely not a permanent solution, but Aylin can stay there until she is back on her feet, if her parents are able to take the children. Also, Karen observes, the purchase won't have been registered in the property database yet.

It's only after Leo and Sigrid have gone to bed, bone-weary, leaving the first watch to Karen and Marike, that her friend's words register fully.

I figured you could use it as a hideout.

An overnight flat in town, a place to spend the night after working late, or when she's snowed in. A place to retreat to on days when the house in Langevik feels crowded. When she needs a break. A place that might make it possible to avoid having to ask Leo to pack up his things and leave. To say the words Sigrid had wanted to hear: 'Yes, of course you can stay here.'

A safe haven for Aylin for as long as she needs it, but then . . .

Karen regretfully snaps out of her reverie. It's not possible.

'I can't afford it, Marike,' she says.

'I don't want your money.'

'You could probably earn three, four thousand marks a month renting out that flat.'

Marike pushes her reading glasses down and gives her a weary look over the rims.

'Seriously, Karen. I have more money than I know what to do with.'

55

They spend all of Sunday morning getting Aylin settled in the flat above the studio. And after a lot of persuading, she eventually agrees to two things: to tell her parents the truth and to report Bo to the police.

Knowing a skilled defence lawyer would ruthlessly exploit any overlap in her roles, Karen takes no part in the police side of things. Friend or officer of the law, not both at once. Instead, she stays with Tyra and Mikkel in the flat while Marike accompanies Aylin to the station. With the help of sweets, a well-worn book of fairy tales Karen found at her house in Langevik and her mobile phone, she does her best to keep the children occupied and distracted. But their anxiety is palpable. And when she meets Tyra's mute gaze and sees something in those eyes that shouldn't be there, she suddenly feels sick. Something stirs restlessly inside her, growling threateningly, tearing at its moorings.

'Mummy will be back soon. Everything's going to be all right,' she tells them.

And when she can tell they no longer believe her, she brings them down to the studio and lets them take their clothes off and go wild. They play with the clay, shrieking with laughter when their little bodies, fingers, hair and faces get covered in blueish-green smears and their worries are briefly forgotten. Even their angry protests half an hour later when Karen makes them get in the shower and pulls their clothes back on are like music to her ears compared to that wide-eyed silence.

But when they get back from the police station, Marike goes straight to the fridge and fetches three glasses, gin, vermouth and olives. Karen can tell she is furious but trying to control herself for Aylin's sake. Apparently, whoever took down Aylin's report didn't live up to Marike's expectations.

'I'm driving,' Karen says and shakes her head when Marike queryingly holds up the bottle of gin. 'But I made coffee.'

Aylin checks her watch.

'I'm good, too. I need to stay sharp, at least until Mum and Dad pick up the kids.'

Aylin's parents had promised to come straight from the airport, blindsided on their way home from a shopping trip to London. Aylin had managed to reach them just as they were about to leave their hotel in Bayswater and get into a taxi. Shocked, they had listened to her and promised to come straight away. Of course they were happy to look after the children. Just for a few days, Aylin had stressed, maybe a week until things calm down and we find somewhere better to stay. She wouldn't hear of going with her parents to their house in Rakne, knowing Bo might show up there. But the children should be safe; he could hardly take them until he'd sorted out some kind of childcare. Or found Aylin.

'It's me he's after. Not the children.'

She looks calmer now, Karen notes. Or maybe it's resignation she sees in her friend's slow movements as she raises her cup to her lips. Just then, a phone rings, making Aylin jump so badly she spills her coffee. Karen quickly pulls out her phone and checks the screen.

'It's just Sigrid,' she says soothingly and stands up.

'Hi, Sigrid, hold on a second.'

She quickly walks out of the living room, pressing the phone to one ear and sticking her finger in the other to block out the sound of Tyra and Mikkel running screaming in their stocking feet across the wooden floor, unperturbed by their mother's attempts to calm them down.

'Let them have fun,' she hears Marike say. 'There's no one downstairs.'

'Hi, Sigrid,' she says again.

'Oh my God, Karen, he's a fucking lunatic!'

The voice on the other end is shrill. A mix of worked-up fear and disjointed words that sends an icy shiver down Karen's spine. Still with the phone pressed to her ear, and the curious eyes on her back, she slips into the bathroom, pulls the door closed behind her and sits down on the toilet lid.

'Calm down, Sigrid, I can't hear you. What happened?'

'He was here. Just now. Tried to force his way in. He's a fucking *mental case!*'

'Are you talking about Bo?' Karen says, even though she knows the answer.

'Like I know his fucking name! Aylin's husband, he was looking for her.'

'Has he left?'

'Yes, I heard the car drive off, but Leo's covered in blood.'

'Leo's hurt? Does he need a doctor?'

Karen is surprised to hear her own voice. Calm and effective, as though her insides weren't on the verge of dissolving.

'No, he says it's just a nosebleed, but you need to come back here, Karen.'

'I'm on my way. Stay calm, I'm leaving right now.'

56

Bo Ramnes kills the engine and leans back. That had gone better than he'd dared to hope. Granted, he had assumed Karen would be home, not that some bloke would open the door and get physical with him. But that will definitely be useful ammunition. He has no doubt Aylin will come crawling back, though he's surprised she has stayed away this long. Twenty-four hours now – and if she's not with her parents, and not hiding at Karen's, she must be with that Danish cunt. Or possibly with the faggots up in Thingwalla. She doesn't have anyone else.

He runs both hands through his hair and feels his knee throb, exhaustion spreading through his body. Whatever, he'll let her sweat until tomorrow. She can just sit there and wait for him to find her. Because he's going to find her. They both know it.

A wave of rage drives his pulse back up. What the fuck does she think she's doing? She's constantly provoking him and then she acts like it's all his fault. Doesn't she understand what a terrible position this puts him in, both professionally and politically? She knows she has no chance of winning. She can cause trouble, yes, but she can't win. Hasn't he made that abundantly fucking clear by now? There isn't a court anywhere that would give her custody after hearing his version. He could probably get the police to bring them back to him right now if he was willing to play all his cards. On the other hand, he won't be able to look after the children on his own, and no one can force her to come back. No, better to wait until she gives up of her own accord.

Bo Ramnes unbuckles his seat belt and opens the car door. There's a stabbing pain in his knee when he twists his leg. Maybe he should just call the police right now and tell them what happened up at Karen's house in Langevik? It's hardly illegal to ring someone's doorbell to ask about one's dear wife and children. Assault, on the other hand . . . Hadn't it been the same guy he'd seen at the faggots' New Year's party? The one who had performed even though he was clearly a bag of nerves going up on stage. Some fucking junkie, no doubt, and now he's staying with Karen. No shock there.

When he slams the car door shut, the garden furniture at the back of the garage suddenly catches his eye. That's not how they're usually stacked, is it? They've been moved and the protective cover has been pulled aside. Aylin must have . . . Then the penny drops. The fucking whore planned this! Not like that time she just took her coat and left. Or when she was stupid enough to go to her parents' old hovel down on Frisel. And then a tiny pang of worry. Could she be stupid enough to actually report him this time? Could that fucking police bitch have talked her into it?

Bo Ramnes pulls out his phone. Might as well bring out the big guns.

Twenty-four hours, he thinks to himself. I'll be damned if I let her get forty-eight.

331

57

Forty minutes later, Karen is eyeing the cotton ball in Leo Friis's left nostril and the bloodstains on his T-shirt. My T-shirt, she corrects herself, noting that Leo has once again helped himself to her clothes. This time, he's gone for a white T-shirt with a print advertising boat engines that must be at least twenty years old. Her dad's T-shirt, she corrects herself again and reflects that Leo must have dug deep into the boxes in her attic to come across that one. And when he asks if she would like a glass of wine and takes out one of her best bottles from Alsace without waiting for a reply, she doesn't have it in her to protest.

'Are you sure we shouldn't get you checked out?' she says and picks up her glass.

'Give it a rest, will you. The bleeding already stopped. Look!' he says and pulls the cotton ball out of his nose.

'Fine, but you're going to have to go in to the station tomorrow and report this.'

'There's no way I'm going to a police station voluntarily. They've dragged me in enough times against my will.'

'Things are different now, Leo.'

'Not really. They know who I am. Besides, I don't want them to know I live here. And I don't think you do either.'

He's probably right. Leo Friis has been nicked a few times for vagrancy and public drunkenness, and once for simple assault. It hadn't led to a formal charge, but it would likely be held against him now. A recently homeless person's word would not hold much weight compared an established lawyer's anyway. And they can't claim Bo was trespassing; he'd rung the doorbell and had certainly tried to force his way inside, but Leo had shoved him back and then been punched in the face. It was probably the profuse bleeding that had given Bo Ramnes cold feet and persuaded him to get back into his car and drive away. According to Leo, who was far less rattled than Sigrid, the whole thing had been over in seconds. She had come running down the stairs when she heard their angry voices, but she hadn't made it in time to witness the fisticuffs.

'Are you sure you shoved him first?' Karen says, studying the dry blood around Leo's nostril.

'I'm afraid so. He tried to get a foot in the door, so I shoved the bastard. He would probably have fallen over backwards if he hadn't been taking a swing at me at the same time. Instead, he landed with one knee on the stone steps. He's probably in more pain than I am,' he adds smugly.

'Here's hoping.'

'Has Aylin reported him?'

Karen nods.

'Yes, in the end, she did. Marike went with her to the station. Aylin has talked to her parents as well, and they're going to look after the children for a few days, so at least they can get some peace and quiet.'

'Have you called Kore and Eirik yet?'

'Yes, Aylin called them herself and asked if she and the children could stay with them for a while after they come back from

New York. She made up some story about remodelling and Bo being away for work.'

'Why didn't she just tell them the truth?'

Karen shrugs.

'She said she didn't want to tell them over the phone, and I think it's important that we let her set the pace. Either way, they'll be back Thursday night. Apparently Eirik was talking about going home earlier, but she didn't want to hear of it. I think he suspects what this is really about.'

'Probably. Didn't you? Ever wonder if he was beating her, I mean.'

Karen looks down at her wine glass. Should she have insisted last summer, even though Aylin denied it? Or had she accepted the answer she got because it was easier that way?

'I've obviously sensed that things weren't good between them and yes, I've had my suspicions. But it's hard to tell real red flags from imagined ones when you dislike someone as much as I dislike Bo.'

Leo nods.

'And when I asked her, she laughed at how ridiculous I was being,' Karen continues. 'But sure, deep down inside, I suspected she was lying. Dammit!'

She abruptly falls silent and claps her hand to her mouth.

'What?'

'She called me a week ago, asked if she could come by, but I was up on Noorö. I remember being surprised; it's been years since she wanted to have a coffee or a pint, but then I forgot all about it. Bloody hell, I'm such an idiot! I of all people should have known . . .'

'You, of all people?'

'I'm a police officer,' Karen says. 'I've met both the men who hit and the women who report them and then take it back. "He's really sorry. He's a good person deep down inside, when he's not drinking." And I've met the children who stick their fingers in their ears every night.'

'The problem with that is that it's impossible to fall asleep with your fingers in your ears,' Leo says and stands up. 'And it's impossible to fall asleep if you take them out. It's a catch-22.'

Karen watches him walk over to the sink and fill up a glass of water. He knows exactly what he's talking about, she realises.

'Your dad?'

Leo shrugs.

'Stepfather. And not just when he was drunk, either. I hated him.'

When Karen climbs into her bed a few hours later, she knows what she has to do. She had planned to get an early start tomorrow. Get to Noorö well before the morning meeting with Thorstein Byle and his team, but they're going to have to wait for her.

Enough is enough.

58

She waits outside in her car, watches the stream of tired men and women in suits stream by. Sees some of them stop in front of the entrance to Idungatan 72 in central Dunker, sees them punch in the code, push open the glass door and disappear toward lifts and stairs that will take them up to marketing firms, import companies and law firms.

When she spots Bo in the distance, it's already half past eight and she decides to give it another fifteen minutes. Tells herself she should drive away, that it would be the wiser choice. Then she unbuckles, opens the door and climbs out of the car.

The law firm Ramnes & Ek has its offices on the fifth floor, according to the board by the entryphone. She rings the bell and waits until a high-pitched voice answers, thinking that being able to introduce yourself as a detective inspector has its advantages. The door opens with a soft buzz without any further questions about who she wants to see or why.

The young woman at reception smiles with a mix of aloof politeness and curiosity when Karen pushes open the frosted glass door and enters.

'How may I help you?' she says.

'I'm here to see Bo Ramnes,' Karen replies curtly and quickly looks around to get a sense of the layout.

Toilets and a waiting room with white leather sofas to her left and a short hallway that ends in another glass door on her right.

'Do you have an appointment?' the receptionist asks and puts her hand on the phone on her desk.

'No, this is an emergency. In there, right?'

Without waiting for a reply, Karen continues toward the glass door and hears the young woman say something about 'from the police . . . I couldn't stop . . . coming in now' behind her.

As she opens the door, she hears a phone being slammed down in the room immediately to her right, so she quickly walks over and pushes down the door handle. Bo Ramnes is getting up out of his tan leather office chair when Karen slams the door shut behind her. If she had bothered to look around, she might have noticed the impressive size of the room, the plush Persian rug and the view of the park. Now, all she has time to register is a tiny glint of uncertainty in Bo Ramnes' eyes and a shadow of rage passing across his face, before he hides it all behind a wide smile.

'If it isn't Karen,' he says and sinks back into his chair. 'Or should I call you Detective Inspector Eiken? To what do we owe the honour?'

Without replying, she pulls up a chair and sits down across from him. She fixes Bo Ramnes with a level stare before calmly telling him:

'It's over.'

'I'm afraid I really don't know what you—'

'You know *exactly* what I'm talking about,' she cuts him off. 'You won't set foot on my property ever again and you won't lay a finger on Aylin.'

'I don't think my wife would appreciate you barging in here to meddle in our marriage.'

'Marriage? You mean frozen hell. But it ends now; she has told me everything.'

Bo Ramnes leans back in his chair with a smile.

'She has, has she?'

'Aylin went to the police yesterday to file an official report saying you've been assaulting her for years.'

'And you went with her, I assume? Helped her concoct this little story?'

'No, I'm afraid you're out of luck on that one. A colleague of mine took her statement. You're not going to be able to play that card in court.'

Bo Ramnes tilts his head to the side and studies his visitor with a kind but concerned expression.

'Is that right?' he says, nodding slowly after she's done speaking. 'Court, you say. So I allegedly assaulted my wife and I'm also guilty of trespassing. Any other accusations you'd like to throw at me?'

'Sure, that you're a big, fat coward, but I'm guessing that's not a charge that will hold up in court. But I imagine the other ones will get the job done.'

'Charges?' he says with a small laugh. 'I don't think so, Karen.'

'Your contacts may have saved you before, but this time—'

'—she has retracted her report,' Bo Ramnes finishes her sentence. 'Late last night, to be precise.'

Silence fills the room.

'She called me herself and told me about her little misadventure. Full of remorse, of course. But it's like that sometimes with overwrought womenfolk. Hormones and whatnot. I'm sure you know that from experience, don't you, Karen.'

For a moment, time stands still. Aylin had sounded so determined last night before they left. Determined and relieved about finally having plucked up the courage, about finally having taken charge of her own life. This time, she was going to see it through. And now she has backed down. And Karen intuitively knows why.

'So that's why you went to my house. You knew Aylin wouldn't be able to bear you attacking her friends. You fucking prick!'

'You certainly have a lively imagination for an officer of the law. And a terribly foul mouth for a woman, if you don't mind me saying. Because you are a woman, aren't you, Karen? Despite failing to keep a man happy and not having any children.'

She is stunned to realise his words have no effect on her. Her head is still above water, her heart is beating regularly, she's not falling apart. In fact, everything is coldly clear.

'She's not going back to you,' Karen says calmly. 'Even if she has recanted her statement, she's never going back.'

'Maybe not just yet, but sooner or later she will,' he replies just as calmly. 'You know what? I actually think my beloved wife just needs some alone time, to think things through. Aylin has always been a bit, how to put it . . . neurotic. You do know she takes antidepressants, don't you? Happy pills. She's been taking them for years.'

'She's not going back to you,' Karen repeats. 'You're going to get divorced and you're going to leave her alone.'

'Is that right? And what happens if I don't?'

Karen gets up slowly and looks at him.

'I will make your life a living hell.'

When she opens the door, she can hear muffled voices. Further down the hallway, a man in a suit and a middle-aged woman with her slate grey hair in a French roll are bent over a copying machine. They're standing with their heads close together, looking like they're studying a document. The clacking of a keyboard is escaping through the cracked door of an office down the hall. When another woman, exhibiting all characteristics of a stressed young jurist, steps out of the room across from Bo's, Karen reaches a decision.

She turns around and says loudly and clearly:

'If you assault your wife one more time, Bo Ramnes, I'm personally going to make sure you pay the price. I have pictures on my phone I think would interest the media.'

Eleven seconds later, Karen Eiken Hornby pushes the button to call the lift and hears the door to the law firm gently close behind her.

59

She drives all the way from Dunker to Thorsvik with her hands-free earbud in her increasingly sore ear. She tries to reach Aylin first, but she doesn't pick up. Then she calls Marike. Tells her about her visit to Bo Ramnes' office and lets her know that Aylin has recanted her statement to the police. As expected, Marike reacts with an unintelligible stream of Danish curses, peppered with a number of four-letter words Karen, to her surprise, has actually never heard before, and then promises to head over to the studio immediately to talk to Aylin.

'Do you think she'll go back to him?'

'I don't think so, not when so many of us know. But promise me you'll call her if you can't find her?'

'I'll be there in half an hour.'

'Well, at least his colleagues know he's a wife beater now,' Karen says grimly. 'Maybe that will persuade him sit on his hands for a bit.'

'Aren't you going to get in trouble?'

'Yes, probably.'

Jounas Smeed calls before she has even reached the Ravenby exit.

'Have you completely lost your mind?' he roars. 'I just spent twenty minutes of my holiday time on the phone with Viggo

Haugen. If I hadn't been able to talk him down, you would have been fired.'

'He's a prick.'

'Haugen?'

'Bo Ramnes. But yes, Haugen, too,' she adds. 'Are you aware Attorney Ramnes tried to force his way into my home last night and assaulted a friend of mine?'

'I'm aware he rang the doorbell to ask to speak to his wife. And I'm aware Ramnes claims he never entered the house. That he was shoved and injured his knee. Count yourself bloody lucky he's not reporting it. There's no law against ringing people's doorbells.'

'I'm telling you, he tried to force his way inside. Leo stopped him.'

'You mean the homeless bloke who has an assault arrest on his record? I'm given to understand he's living with you now? Pretty unprofessional, Eiken.'

'Well, at least he's not homeless anymore, right?'

'He's hardly a star witness, either, and from what I gather, you weren't there, so you don't actually know what happened, do you?'

'No, but—'

Karen stops herself. Telling Smeed his daughter was present won't help matters. And Leo is still refusing to report what happened to the police. She'd made another attempt to persuade him before talking to Bo Ramnes, but had quickly realised she was wasting her breath.

'I have a good mind to take you off this case,' Jounas says.

'Of course you do. But you won't because . . . ?'

'But,' he continues, 'I realise that the further you are from Dunker right now, the better. You're going to stay up there until this case is solved. And you will not contact Bo Ramnes again. Understood?'

Karen makes no reply. Instead, she changes the subject.

'When are you going to get me some more help? Karl and I won't be able to get this done on our own. We're talking about two murders now, and people are in bed at home instead of out here, helping. Or sitting on a beach,' she adds and instantly regrets it.

Her boss has saved her, if not from being fired then at least from a suspension. This is not the time to push his buttons.

'Björken and Loots are both up there right now,' Jounas Smeed replies frostily. 'The only one who's not where she's supposed to be is you.'

And when Karen steps through the doors to the local police station in Lysvik, she realises her boss was right. Detective Sergeant Cornelis Loots is sitting at the conference table with Karl Björken, Thorstein Byle and local constables Röse, Andersson and Svanemark.

'What time do you call this?' Karl says and receives an anxious look from Byle.

He would apparently never even contemplate speaking to a superior that way. Karen takes a seat and reaches for the coffee urn.

'All right,' she says, 'are we going to solve this thing, or were you planning to sit around and gossip all day?'

Ten minutes later, Röse is still looking sour, but he seems to be keeping his feelings about the growing CID contingent to himself. Maybe Thorstein Byle has had a talk with him. Andersson and Svanemark seem more at ease with the situation. They're happily chatting away with Cornelis Loots, which reminds Karen that he actually grew up on the island. It's also clear that while the team took a break, they didn't entirely waste their time. They have been bringing Loots up to speed about where the investigation stands.

She lets Karl Björken and Thorstein Byle continue their summary while she furtively rubs her knee under the table, but when Byle moves on to an account of his conversation with the distillery's secretary, Eva Framnes, she sits up straight and pays attention. With everything that's happened, she hasn't had time to read the written report he sent her. A few minutes later she leans back with a disappointed sigh. A wonderful party, Eva Framnes had said, though she felt people had had too much to drink, but amazing fireworks and yes, she had been dropped off at her door by the Trystes and no, she had neither seen nor heard anything out of the ordinary involving Gabriel, other than that he was very drunk. Well, she had noticed him tapping away on his phone during dinner, which she had found very rude. But apparently that's what people do these days.

Karl Björken also fails to suppress a deep sigh.

'Well, we're unlikely to ever find that phone, but when is the service provider going to have call logs for us? And when are we getting the forensic results from Gabriel's house?'

'Today, I hope,' Karen replies. 'I'll talk to Larsen as soon as we're done here. Would you mind going over what we found out on Saturday?'

She allows her mind to wander while Karl Björken recounts their interview with Björn Groth and their conversation with the Trystes. She realises Thorstein Byle is taking notes and feels a pang of guilt. She hasn't had a chance to talk to him since leaving so abruptly on Saturday night. All she had time for was a text saying she had a family emergency and would be back on Monday. For a moment she considers apologising, but decides against it.

Instead, she listens while Karl Björken wraps up his summary and then starts handing out assignments.

'We still haven't talked to the party guests who didn't spend the night,' she says. 'Among them, two couples that left before midnight. They may have heard or seen something of interest. Would the two of you mind handling that?'

Thorstein Byle and Cornelis Loots nod.

'Karl and I are going to talk to Gabriel's wife, Katja. Have you been able to reach her?' she says, addressing Björken.

'Yes, she said she's off work today, so we can stop by any time.'

'Great. And then, if we get the go-ahead from Larsen, I would like us to have a look at Gabriel's house. Who knows,' she says with a conciliatory smile in Thorstein Byle's direction, 'maybe there's a concealment Larsen and his team missed.'

60

Katja Stuub comes to the door of her parents' yellow wooden house in central Thorsvik. Her blonde hair is pulled back into a ponytail and a light swelling around her eyes reveals she has been crying. A girl of about four with her thumb in her mouth is clinging to one of her jeans-clad legs, while a boy who looks to be a few years older is peering out suspiciously from behind her back. A grey-haired woman is standing further down the hallway. She nods to them from afar but makes no move to come to greet them.

'Welcome,' Katja says and holds out her hand. 'Mum has promised to keep an eye on the kids so we can talk without disruptions. Would you mind if we sit in the kitchen, so they can watch TV?'

'Of course,' Karen replies and smiles at the children. 'Loke and Lava, right?'

An image of Aylin's children flashes before her and suddenly there's a knot in her stomach. It takes considerable effort to bring her focus back to the present. Right here, right now, there's nothing she can do.

Once they have seated themselves around the kitchen table and been served coffee and apple crumble, despite half-hearted protests, Karen gets straight to the point.

'So, as you already know, we're here to ask you some questions about Gabriel's death. From what I understand, you filed for divorce but are still formally married. Is that correct?'

Katja Stuub nods and quickly runs the back of her hand under her nose.

'Yes, the divorce won't be final until the end of the year,' she says. 'Or . . . well, I don't know how it works now. I suppose I'm technically a widow.'

'Yes, according to Doggerian law, divorce proceedings are automatically terminated if one party passes away,' Karen tells her. 'But you can let them know if you want to complete the process,' she adds. 'Since the divorce has already been initiated, it's your right.'

And sure, there have been examples of a people insisting on making the divorce official even after their spouse passed away. But it's highly unusual. And almost always involves domestic abuse. Women who don't even want to be the *widow* of the person who assaulted them.

'But that would entail giving up any claim to the inheritance, of course,' Karl puts in.

Katja Stuub looks uncomfortable, but doesn't rise to the bait. Karen realises direct questions will be required if they want to get anything out of this conversation.

'We're trying to get a sense of what Gabriel was like as a person. Can I ask why you were getting divorced?'

'I wanted to,' Katja replies tersely. 'Gabriel wanted us to carry on.'

'And why did you want to get divorced? Did he beat you?' Karl asks bluntly.

347

Katja shoots him a quick glance and then sighs.

'That's probably what people think, but no. Gabriel never laid so much as a finger on me. Or the children.'

'So why, then?'

They wait while she seems to search for the right words.

'He was . . . impossible,' she says eventually and sniffs.

'Impossible?' Karl asks.

'Yes, impossible. He lived in some kind of fantasy world, dreaming about having money and power. Without ever having to work for it, of course.'

'But he did work at the distillery, didn't he?'

'Yes, he had to make enough to pay the mortgage, but other than that his entire life was about finding ways to make a quick buck. His job up at Groth's was just a necessary evil.'

She looks down at the table, hesitates and seems to steel herself.

'He stole from them,' she says and looks up quickly to gauge their reactions.

Karen nods and Katja looks surprised.

'You knew?'

'Yes, that much we've puzzled out.'

'I don't think it was a lot. But he did steal from the warehouse and sold it to some of the bars down on Heimö and Frisel. He didn't dare try it up here.'

'Tell us about his connections with the OP.'

Another sigh. Heavier this time.

'That's the reason I wanted to get divorced,' Katja Stuub says, and the moment the words leave her lips, the tension seems to drain out of her. 'I suppose he was some kind of *hanger-on*, no more than that, but he was working on becoming a *prospective member*.'

She says the words mockingly, as though to protect herself from their significance. And just as Karl opens his mouth to tell her to go on, Katja continues of her own accord.

'He fawned over them, especially the big boys, Kenny, Allan, Odd and whatever their names are. I think he did some small jobs for them, provided alibis, threatened people . . . Oh, and he went and bought himself a Harley, of course, even though we couldn't afford it. But he was an idiot,' she adds, 'thinking he could run his own schemes on the side.'

'Stealing from Groth's?'

Katja nods.

'That was his own little racket and I know he worried about the guys finding out. But that was Gabriel in a nutshell, always looking for new ways to con people. His employer, the insurance company, the bookmaker at the dog races, the tax authorities . . .'

'And the OP,' Karen finishes her list.

'It scared the living daylights out of me when I realised what he was up to. They would never tolerate something like that, even I know that. We quarrelled about his links with them from the day we started dating. I'm just not the kind of person who . . .'

She falters and seems to be searching for the right words again.

'Look, I know it sounds classist, but we weren't a very good match. Turns out Mum and Dad were right.'

Karen doesn't need to look around the designer kitchen to understand what she means. A warehouse worker from Noorö, and one with links to a criminal motorcycle gang to boot, was probably not the son-in-law Katja's parents had hoped for. After a quick glance at Karen, Katja continues.

'I suppose dating Gabriel was a form of rebellion. Dad's retired now, but he had a pretty senior position on the fisheries board and Mum's a dentist. They wanted me to get an education before I married and had children, but I was in love and too clueless to know all his plans were just castles in the sky. And by the time those rose-tinted spectacles came off and I realised what my future was going to be like, it was too late. We had the children and ... well, I suppose I was too proud to admit I'd been wrong.'

'How long were you married?'

'Almost seven years. It was pretty good at first. Like I said, Gabriel was always sweet to me and the children, even if he was impossible in all other respects. But nothing ever came of his grandiose plans to start his own business. One day it was a garage, the next some kind of import firm, but he never made a move to make it happen, or to leave Groth's. And when he started to try to curry favour with the OP, I realised it was a disaster waiting to happen.'

Katja seems to have a pent-up need to talk. As she teeters between grief and anger, they listen attentively without interrupting.

'In the end, I gave him an ultimatum; it was either me or them. And for a while, I honestly thought he'd cut his ties with the OP. He seemed more settled, worked and made money. In fact, he claimed to have been promoted at Groth's, made foreman or something like that and given a raise. And I believed him.'

'But ... ?'

'But eventually I realised it was just his usual bullshit. When I confronted him, he admitted he hadn't been promoted, that the extra money came from his whiskey-stealing scheme. And he'd found a "foolproof" way of swindling the Groths, he told me. That's when I'd had enough. I took the children and left him that night.'

'And how was he going to swindle the Groths? Do you know?'

Katja Stuub shakes her head.

'No idea, I never asked. It was obviously just a flight of fancy.'

'I'm not so sure about that,' Karl Björken says half an hour later in the car on board the ferry back to Lysvik.

'No, he was probably up to some mischief, but the question is whether whatever it was would have been enough to make someone slit his throat. And if so, what it has to do with the murder of his grandfather.'

'Are we absolutely certain the two murders are connected? I mean, one hundred per cent?'

'Seriously, Charlie Boy, you think it's just a funny coincidence?'

'Not sure it's all that funny. But fine, yes, they're connected. Though that doesn't necessarily mean it's the same killer. Gabriel might have killed his grandpa and then been offed by someone else in turn.'

'It makes no difference if we can't establish a motive. We're not going to be able to rely on technical evidence to solve this. Sören Larsen wasn't exactly a cornucopia of useful information.'

They contemplate their most recent conversation with the Head of Forensic Services. They'd had Sören Larsen on speakerphone in the car a few hours earlier, when he had just finished processing Gabriel Stuub's house.

'I wasn't expecting a big bowl of juicy DNA,' Karl says dejectedly, 'but I was probably hoping for at least a call history from his mobile phone. Who the hell uses pay-as-you-go cards these days?'

'People like Gabriel Stuub,' Karen retorts drily. 'Communications 101 if you want to play with the OP boys. But Sören did say Gabriel had an official email account. We'll have to go through it. And we might come across something at his house that hints at a possible motive.'

Karl shoots her a sceptical look.

'And we're not done with Fredrik Stuub's laptop,' she adds. 'We're going to have Cornelis Loots go over all of it with a fine-tooth comb. He's usually good at finding needles in haystacks, if there are any.'

61

'What a lovely mix,' Karl says, scanning the boxes of whiskey bottles and jars of protein powder and supplements. 'Do you think anyone would notice if I snagged a couple?' he adds with a grin and picks up a bottle of Groth's Smoke from 2006.

They'd started their walkthrough in the two-car garage-cum-workshop and quickly concluded that in addition to a Harley-Davidson and an old Volvo, it contained everything on the list Sören Larsen had emailed over: a set of tools, two cans of petrol, a can of engine oil, a pink inflatable pool, two adult bicycles and a tricycle, a rolled-up green wire fence, eight empty plastic cans and three cans of white primer. And that was it.

Now, they have moved on to Gabriel Stuub's basement and are studying the shelves that cover one of its walls. The items here may be slightly more interesting than the ones in the garage, but hardly more surprising.

Karen picks up one of the jars and reads the table of contents.

'Whey protein, soy, lethicin, flavouring . . . bloody hell, no wonder he needed a whiskey from time to time. But don't bodybuilders try to stay off the sauce?'

'You're thinking about the ones who compete,' Karl says, reluctantly putting the bottle back. 'Most people who pump iron are just regular blokes.'

'Like you, you mean? You keep whiskey and protein powder in your basement, too, do you?'

'I wish. But if his wife is to be believed, he sold most of it. And didn't Brodal say the state of his liver could have been caused by steroids as well? Or a mix of the two?'

Karen nods.

'Unfortunately, we're not getting those results until next week. But the technicians didn't find any growth hormones in the house, for what that's worth. On the other hand, it's probably irrelevant for our purposes. I'm more interested in how Gabriel was trying to con everyone around him than how he treated his body. Ready to do the rest of the house?'

They lock the basement door and walk up the stairs without any great expectations. The walkthrough of the Stuub house seems likely to prove as futile as Sören Larsen had warned it would be.

'Three bedrooms upstairs, living room and a small office behind the kitchen,' he'd said. 'There's a desk with some papers in it, but I have a hard time imagining any of it is particularly interesting. To be honest, it mostly looked like pay stubs and bills, but I leave it to you to find out.'

And he had been right. The house may have looked odd among the traditional Noorö houses surrounding it, but aside from that, Karen is forced to conclude as she walks from room to room with Karl, it's an ordinary home with no signs of illegal activities. A bedroom each for the children and a larger bedroom of which Gabriel had, by all appearances, been the only occupant for the past two months.

The centrepieces of the room Sören Larsen had described as an office are a sewing machine, a computer monitor and a printer, all sitting on a sizeable desk. Baskets of yarn and sewing implements, remnants of children's fabrics and binders full of sewing patterns line a long shelf on the opposite wall. Carefully organised personal papers such as pay stubs from Groth's and the accountancy firm where Katja had started working part-time two years ago, mortgage statements and a few household bills are all neatly filed away in clearly labelled hanging folders. Either Gabriel was far more fastidious than he came across, or this is Katja Stuub's work, Karen thinks and pushes the last drawer shut.

She's not going to bother to look for a concealment; the oversight in Fredrik Stuub's house has prompted Larsen to force his team to scour every square inch of the house for hidden compartments. Besides, Gabriel's computer had been sitting in plain sight on the desk, next to the sewing machine.

'Computer games,' Larsen had summed up his verdict. 'A lot of pirated ones, from the looks of it.'

'Surely there must have been other things?'

'An email account provided by the broadband company. I've only had time to skim it, but it mostly looks like correspondence from authorities, from what I could see. Well, and then there's the browser history, obviously, a few different gaming sites, the sports sections of a couple of newspapers, a handful of obscure gossip forums, porn . . . The usual, in other words. I've just sent you a link to all of it. Enjoy!'

Karen closes the top desk drawer and turns to Karl to see if he has found anything of interest.

'Nothing,' he replies with a shake of his head. 'Do you want to move on so we can get out of here sometime today?'

The living room looks the same as the last time she was in it, relatively tidy, a giant flatscreen TV, sofas and armchairs.

She walks over to the bookcase. Four photographs on the top shelf show the children, Loke and Lava, dressed up in their Sunday best and sitting next to each other on a sofa to be immortalised in some photo studio, a picture of a young Gabriel straddling a moped, a graduation picture of a blonde girl, presumably Katja, and a wedding picture with the two of them smiling happily at each other. As always when she looks at photographs in a victim's home, Karen is overcome with unease. The young man in the picture with his suit and poorly tied tie and wide smile may have been guilty of God knows what, but he didn't deserve to end his days sitting in the snow with his throat slit.

On a sudden impulse, she scans the shelves and spots what she's after. A photo album. Every photograph is neatly tucked into a plastic sleeve, making her once again suspect the involvement of Katja Stuub. The order is chronological and Karen only has to flip to the third page to have her suspicions confirmed.

The photograph must have been taken thirty-five years ago. A young, emaciated woman with dark circles under her eyes stares listlessly at the camera, looking as if she's about to collapse under the weight of the infant she's cradling in one arm. Ulrika Stuub looks uncomfortable with the situation. Standing next to her is a Fredrik Stuub in his forties, with one arm around his daughter's frail shoulders and the other raised to shield his eyes from the sun. The old man with lanky grey hair Karen remembers from the autopsy table is still years away.

The sunlight sets Fredrik's hair ablaze. It's as flamingly red as Odd's.

'Have you found anything or can we get out of here?' Karl asks from the kitchen.

'Nothing. We're done.'

Cursing under her breath, she puts the photo album back.

62

Karl Björken is staring blankly at the screen even though it's been several minutes since he stopped taking in the information about the contents of Fredrik Stuub's computer displayed on it. His thoughts are on Ingrid and the children in their terraced house in Sande.

He'd thought he'd managed to dodge the bullet when he was last home, narrowly avoiding a big row. And the fact is the weekend had been everything he'd hoped for; the children had been unusually well-behaved, and he and Ingrid had both made an effort to avoid The Subject.

But late on Sunday night, right after they'd made love for the second time that weekend, he'd made his first big mistake. After setting the alarm on his phone, he had sighed and said something about how he wasn't going to get much sleep before he had to get up again.

'Unlike me, you mean?' Ingrid had snapped. 'Fine, you try staying home with the kids by yourself and we'll see how many hours of sleep you get.'

The way she jumped down his throat and the fact that she didn't mind ruining what had been two frictionless days, had made disappointment crowd out caution. And that was when he had made his second mistake.

'I don't know why you're in such a hurry to go back to work – you don't even like your job,' he'd said. 'Every night when you got home all you did was complain and say how much you disliked it and wanted to quit.'

It was the truth. Ingrid's job in the public relations department of the Provincial Board in Dunker had been a constant source of frustration as she was tasked with spinning desperate, economically motivated or simply idiotic decisions as success stories in the media through 'proactive informational efforts'. And Karl had been genuinely appalled when Ingrid was twice passed over for promotion in favour of men in their early twenties with CVs that might have been believable for someone twice their age. Ingrid had increasingly taken to venting over dinner and had started reading the job ads more frequently.

And now their childminder had called Ingrid to tell them she was moving to Amsterdam to live with her sister. And, as his wife had frostily pointed out on the phone, they're no longer on the waiting list for state-provided day care. Karl had felt the annual fee of 300 marks was an unnecessary expense since they'd found a private childminder they were happy with.

The caseworker Ingrid had talked to had apparently told her the wait was at least eight months. At a minimum. But something might open up after the summer, if they were lucky.

'How am I ever supposed to find a new job, if I'm trapped at home?' Ingrid had said, her voice dangerously calm.

He would have preferred yelling.

I'm going to talk to Smeed the minute this investigation is over, Karl thinks to himself and slowly tears his eyes away from the screen. He's going to have to deal with me not being here for a while. Karen is back now and he's going to have to find a permanent replacement for Johannisen as well; the man's well past sixty.

But what's really eating at him, what has Karl Björken genuinely worried, is what Ingrid didn't say. Why hadn't she pointed out the obvious? That Karl has been complaining about all the idiots he has to work with for years. He has griped about Viggo Haugen's spineless sycophancy vis-à-vis the political leadership, about Jounas Smeed's obvious lack of leadership skills, about Karen's mood swings and lack of social grace, about Johannisen's insufferable bitterness, which brings the whole team down. If anyone has been complaining about their job, it's him.

But Ingrid had said nothing. Hadn't wrenched the weapon out of his hand, even though it would have been so easy. Worry ties knots in his stomach.

Has she given up?

His dark thoughts are interrupted when something about what Karen and Cornelis Loots are discussing catches his ear.

'Toxins, sure, I know what they are. But what exactly have they got to do with anything?'

'Well, he might have figured out some flaw in the production process up at Groth's. That would certainly be a threat to both their current business and the expansion.'

'It would have to be mould toxins,' Karen says. 'Because that's what his research was about, different kinds of mould. At least that's what that woman from the university told me.'

'They say mould can be bloody serious.'

'Maybe in houses and food. Fredrik Stuub was quoted in the newspapers a few years ago, talking about aflatoxins in rice. But

I've never heard of mould in spirits. Besides, all the documents related to Fredrik's research are several years old.'

Karen sounds sceptical and Karl has already pushed aside his thoughts about Ingrid's ominous silence. He has read the documents on Fredrik Stuub's laptop, too.

'And what's the connection with Gabriel Stuub?' he puts in. 'Mould in his protein powder?'

Cornelis shrugs sullenly.

'I still think we should let someone who knows about these things have a look. Maybe a doctor.'

'OK,' Karen replies. 'You're right. I'll ask Brodal. It's possible Fredrik was onto something, but how it could be connected to Groth's is beyond me. And as Karl just pointed out, how does Gabriel come into it? He and his grandfather hardly had the kind of relationship where they discussed old research results. But it's past eight. Let's pack it up for today.'

'What are your holiday plans? Are you going home for Twelfth Night?' Karl asks, trying to sound casual.

He fails. Karen shoots him a searching look. Though he hasn't said a word about it, she knows her sick leave has thrown a spanner in his parental leave plans. Ingrid can hardly be happy he's back on the job again.

'Trouble at home?' she says.

He nods.

'Then you're definitely going home,' she says. 'Do it right. Dress up and put on a fake beard and shower your wife and children with gifts. That's an order.'

'OK, I'll head off tomorrow after lunch and I'll be back early Thursday morning. What about you? Are things OK with your friend?'

'OK might be overstating it, but it seems things are pretty calm for now.'

'Has she reported the bastard?'

Karen sighs.

'Yes. And then she recanted her statement, but I don't think she'll go back to him this time. And Marike and Leo have promised to call me straight away if something happens.'

'So you're staying here over Twelfth Night, all alone?'

'Cornelis is sticking around, too, so I suppose the two of us will have to make what we can of it. I'm probably going to be invited to a family get-together, and the thought of driving all the way back to Langevik is very nearly more off-putting. Besides, things didn't go so well the last time I left the island,' she adds with a wry smile. 'We wouldn't want to risk a third murder.'

63

The sound is almost imperceptible; it's a deep vibration rever-
berating from downstairs that makes her sit bolt upright in bed,
a light rattling of the windows that's not caused by a passing
lorry or the wind or some clomping neighbour. There are no
lorries driving around here at one in the morning, the snow
is falling silently outside, and she is alone in the house. Even
before she hears the sound again, louder this time, she knows
someone has grabbed the door handle and is trying to push
open the door to the studio.

She has known he would come, sooner or later. He is going to
methodically check every place he can think of, one after the other.
Karen's house, Marike's, the studio. And Kore and Eirik's house,
too, of course. He's already been to her parents'. Her mother hadn't
wanted to tell her yesterday, hadn't wanted to upset her daughter,
but eventually, when asked directly, she had admitted Bo had been
there. He'd sat in his car outside their house for almost an hour.
In the end, her father had gone out and shouted at him that there
was no point hanging around. Aylin wasn't there. Her mother had
reluctantly told her what Bo had said back.

'He asked us to tell you he's heartbroken and just wants you
to come home. He doesn't understand why you've left him.'

He had declined to see the children. Didn't want to confuse
them 'before things are back to normal'. He hadn't even asked

where she was. He'd probably realised they wouldn't tell him. Or he hadn't needed them to. Sooner or later, he's going to figure it out. She had thought it would take a bit longer. She had hoped.

Now she's sitting frozen on the edge of the bed while her mind spins like a white load in a tumble dryer and blood throbs in her skull. She looks at the half-full glass of whiskey on the bedside table, the unread book, the bread knife she had fetched last night when she couldn't sleep. For some reason, it had made her feel safer at the time. Now, it seems like a bad joke. I don't stand a chance, she thinks to herself. How could I ever have thought I'd be able to hide here?

And that thought finally makes the tumble dryer stop spinning. Slowly, a realisation sinks in: he's tugging at the wrong door. He doesn't know about the flat above the studio. And then she recalls Marike's exasperated response to Karen's question. 'Do you really think I don't have a burglar alarm?' Of course there's an alarm; the studio is full of valuable art. Apparently, yanking the door handle doesn't set it off, but if someone were to actually break in . . . and then that thought is cut short by the next one.

Maybe it's not him.

Infinitesimally slowly she slides down to the floor and crawls over to the wall by the window. The closed curtains are heavy and don't move in the draught when she stands up. The gap between them is too small; she hesitates briefly before gingerly pushing one of the curtains aside. Reluctantly, she presses her face to the glass and peers down at the street.

The light from the street lamps is dimmed by the falling snow. The dark figure that has just taken a step back to stare at the studio could be anyone. No one would be able to pick him out of a line-up. No one but her.

Then time stops. Bo Ramnes takes another step back and looks up at the first floor. She is paralysed. She stands there motionless, unbreathing, watching his eyes scan the row of black windows. Then he abruptly turns away and walks back toward his car. When she hears the door slam shut and the black Mercedes drive away, Aylin lets out a gasp of relief and collapses onto the cold floor.

64

Twenty minutes past four, Karen Eiken Hornby startles awake so violently the bed creaks. At first, she thinks something on the street outside woke her, or maybe a sound from the hotel corridor, and she lifts her head off the pillow to listen. The only sound is the faint keening of the wind against the window and a soft rushing of water through the pipes in the bathroom.

She lets her cheek sink back onto the soft pillow and feels sleep gently pull her back down into oblivion. But some part of her brain is resisting, making her closed eyelids flutter anxiously. Disjointed images flash before her in quick succession: Thorstein Byle's worried face, Odd's long, grey plait and the OP logo on his back, the photograph of Fredrik Stuub with flaming red hair, Leo stubbing out a cigarette on the railing, sweeping panoramas of mountain ridges and houses blackened by coal dust, Aylin's voice saying 'I'm to blame too, you know', the whiskey boxes in Gabriel Stuub's basement, the jars of protein powder, the sound of Sigrid's bright laughter, Karl's grateful look when she ordered him to go home, Cornelis wearily looking up from his computer and rubbing his eyes, Björn Groth's pale face in the flickering fluorescent light, Leo's back when he reluctantly got up on stage and picked up the guitar, Bo Ramnes raising his glass in a toast, the list of contents of Fredrik Stuub's laptop: his email exchanges with the local paper, the bus company, the fisheries board, the hopelessly impenetrable documents, incomprehensible words like interleukins, neurodegenerative, acetylcholine, Baudoinia compniacensis, the drill holes in the blackened stones up by Gudheim, a wall with the shadow of a one followed by a per cent sign.

Suddenly, she's wide awake.

She spends a few minutes slowly rewinding the film, searching for the right image. She's looking for a word, a single word from the documents on Fredrik Stuub's computer. A word she has come across somewhere else long ago, in a completely different context. An elusive little word that has burrowed into her subconscious and is now refusing to reveal itself. A bloody annoying little word that's going to make it impossible for her to go back to sleep.

And now I need to pee, too, she thinks and sits up with a sigh. I'm going to have to get my laptop and go through it all again.

The toilet seat is cold against her buttocks and Karen studies the unhygienic wall-to-wall carpet while she answers nature's call. Unlike the pub culture, the carpeted bathrooms are a part of Doggerland's British heritage she could do without. On the other hand, she considers, there's probably not a single person under sixty who still insists on having these hotbeds of mould in their bathrooms anymore.

And before she can say how or why the roulette wheel suddenly stops and the ball magically settles into the right slot with a faint rattle, she hears herself say the word she's been looking for.

'Baudoinia.'

*

Forty minutes later, Karen Eiken Hornby leans back against the wall and looks over at the window. It's dark outside and will remain so for another – she glances down at the numbers in the bottom right-hand corner of the screen – three hours at least. She carefully puts the laptop down on the duvet and stretches out her legs. Her right foot has gone numb and she wiggles her toes to get rid of the pins and needles.

She closes her eyes and runs through what she has managed to find out online. Baudoinia compniacensis, a sac fungus known to cover buildings and trees with a black film reminiscent of soot and commonly found in places where distillation and storage of spirits take place. Prevalent near whiskey distilleries as a result of ethanol vapours escaping during maturing, an evaporation process often dubbed the angels' share.

Angels' share. She has obviously heard the poetic term before. The small volume of precious spirits that finds its way out of porous wooden barrels every year and rises into the heavens.

Or rather, she realises now, stains every surface around a distillery black. Impossible to get rid without a pressure washer and known to persistently return anyway. The images online of sooty façades, tree trunks, lamp posts and cars near whiskey distilleries in Scotland and the US. And the same thing near French cognac warehouses.

The articles about local residents' attempts to bring class action lawsuits against distilleries for the impact on their property values. Hadn't John told her once about a case his firm had been considered for but ended up not getting? Hadn't he described his colleagues joking over an after-work pint about how they were glad they weren't going to have to wage war against the whiskey industry because winning would have been a decidedly mixed blessing?

But Karen can't recall ever hearing about anything like that on Noorö. There are no property values to maintain here. The growing number of vacant properties on the island can hardly be blamed on sooty exteriors. And the people who have stayed are used to it.

A thick, black film.

'It's the coal,' Karen can hear Aunt Ingeborg say, back then. 'The black gold. Without it, we'd have nothing.'

And that was a truth neither Karen nor likely anyone else had thought to question. Noorö houses were black because of the coal. But no one seems to be asking why certain parts of the island are still shrouded in a mourning veil, decades after the last mine was closed and the last coal piles removed.

No one, except Fredrik Stuub.

Not soot. Mould. Baudoinia compniacensis. A fungus. A mould which, while black, is nowhere near as dangerous as black mould, from what Karen has been able to make out. *No adverse effects on the health of humans or animals have been recorded*, one site had informed her. *Unlikely to be a health hazard* another one had proclaimed.

With a shudder, she thinks about what the internet showed her when she searched for some of the other words in Fredrik Stuub's document; interleukins, neurodegenerative, acetylcholine, neurofibrillary tangle . . . Could Fredrik Stuub really have been trying to prove that there was a connection?

Could he have been right?

65

Kneought Brodal picks up after the sixth ring. Impersonally, giving his title and both his first and last name, even though he can obviously see it's her calling. As soon as she hears the hostile tone, she can tell this isn't going to be an easy conversation.

After patiently listening to the coroner's tirade about how his Christmas was ruined and then his New Year's, too, and then sitting through a lengthy outburst about how murderous Noorlings have apparently found a way to ruin his Twelfth Night as well, she manages to get a word in.

'No, no need to worry. No new murders. At least not yet. That's not why I'm calling.'

A slurping sound on the other end. Evidently, Brodal is taking the opportunity to moisten his throat in preparation for another jeremiad. The brief pause gives Karen enough time to gently approach the real reason she is calling.

'Have you had a moment to look at those documents I sent over?' she says, bracing herself for the answer while listening to the harsh clatter of china as Kneought Brodal puts his cup down.

'What bloody documents? Would you mind being a bit more specific, my inbox is full of all kinds of crap.'

'It's a few documents from Fredrik Stuub's computer that I can't make heads or tails of. I could really use your expertise. A lot of medical research terms.'

'Oh, that. No, I haven't had a chance yet. But it's hardly medicine. More like biochemistry, unless I miss my guess.'

So you did look at it, she thinks to herself.

'No,' he says as though he could hear her optimistic thought, 'I haven't read it. I opened it to see what it was about and then I closed it and marked it as unread. That's what I do with all my emails in order to triage all the idiotic questions I get.'

'Fine, but this could be important,' Karen says. 'And urgent.'

She pauses for a few seconds to think, decides on the strategy she think will yield the fastest results and continues, 'The thing is, I think I've found a connection between Fredrik Stuub's research and his murder. And probably Gabriel's, too,' she adds, as a sweetener.

There's not a sound on the other end. She knows that's a good sign. Kneought Brodal's interest has been piqued, though he would never admit it. A deep, quiet breath, then she presses on.

'When I did a close read of the documents we found on Fredrik's laptop, I came across some terms I wanted to know more about.'

'So you googled them?' the coroner groans. 'This ought to be good . . .'

'It's about something called Baudoinia.'

'Go on,' Brodal says tersely.

'Apparently, it's some kind of fungus that spreads—'

'I know what Baudoinia is,' Brodal cuts in. 'Get to the point.'

'So I looked up some of the other recurring terms Stuub seems to have been examining in conjunction with Baudoinia. At least, that's what I think he was doing, but that kind of research jargon is completely impenetrable to me. I don't even know if my interpretation of what little I've found is correct.'

'And what is your interpretation?'

'That Fredrik Stuub was trying to demonstrate that the Baudoinia fungus isn't as harmless as we think. That there are links to . . . I mean, I could be completely wrong about this . . .'

'Are you telling me you called me at quarter past six in the morning on Twelfth Night to inform me that you have a hunch, but you think you're wrong about it?'

'Alzheimer's,' Karen says. 'And I don't think I'm wrong. But I would be very happy to find out I am.'

A booming laugh on the other end.

'Alzheimer's? Are you serious?'

'I don't know, Kneought. To my eyes it looks like Stuub was trying to link Alzheimer's or some other disease like it to the shit leaking out of the distillery.'

'And now you want me to verify this insanity?'

'Not the results themselves, of course. Just if that was, in fact, what he was researching. And I don't really care if Stuub was right or not. What's important is to find out if he was in a position to make others believe he was. If he managed to scare someone badly enough for that person to want to silence him.'

'One of the Groths, you mean.'

'Too early to say, but sure. If Fredrik had enough to make people even suspect such a link, it would threaten their entire company.'

Not to mention their expansion plans, she adds silently. The provincial board would certainly get cold feet and even if Stuub's results were proven wrong in due course, it would still throw a spanner in the works for the Groths and lead to costly delays.

'I need a few hours,' Brodal says curtly.

'Thank you.'

'But like I said, don't expect me to be able to cover all of this so-called research. And if he was in fact on to something, unlikely as that may be, we must be talking about old data. Didn't Stuub retire years ago?'

'He did, but apparently he had access to the university's equipment and facilities for five years after leaving. Docent emeritus, according to the woman I talked to at the university.'

'I see. But that's still several years ago. Why would he have sat on his results until now? No, never mind, don't answer. That's for you to figure out.'

'So you're going to take a look at it straight away?' Karen says as meekly as she is able.

'I intend to eat two slices of toast, drink one cup of coffee and read the newspaper first, unless you mind.'

'Thank you, Kneought. Call me as soon as you know anything. And like I said, I'm not expecting—'

Kneought Brodal has already hung up.

66

Karen studies the flat grey stone marking her father's place in the family tomb.

Fisherman
Walter Eiken
1939–2002

Third row from the top, second marker from the left. To the right of it are two more flat grey stones: Aino Eiken, who survived her son by four months, and Johannes Eiken, who held on for three more years. Dad, Grandma and Grandpa, to date the last people to be interred in the Eiken family tomb. But there's room for more in front of the large iron anchor standing guard over the generations. Fishermen, fishermen's wives and a pilot related by marriage. It could have been any one of the countless anchor-topped family tombs here at Gudheim Cemetery.

Karen straightens up and lets her eyes follow the gently sweeping slope of the promontory. A handful of visitors are moving between the headstones, seeming to talk quietly with one another. At the far end, before land gives way to sky and sea, she can just make out the monoliths of the ship setting, forty-two ten-foot stones in a semicircle facing the east. Perhaps that imposing sight is what made the Noorlings decide not to bother with upright headstones; there's not a single one in the Gudheim Cemetery, only rows of anchors of varying sizes, watching over rows of horizontal, flat stone markers engraved with the names of lost sons and daughters. Names and dates, no poems such as those on the headstones on Heimö and Frisel. No 'loved, missed'. Why waste words on stating the obvious?

'Don't for a second think I'm going in there,' Eleanor Eiken had told her daughter after her husband's marker had been installed. 'You go wherever you want, but I plan on being buried in Langevik. Or in Ravenby with Mum and Dad, but not on Noorö. Promise me!'

Karen smiles at the memory. 'You go wherever you want.' That was probably her mother's tactful attempt to make it known that she didn't expect Karen's eternal resting place to be on the Doggerian islands. Maybe she would prefer to be buried next to John and Mathis in Haslemere in Surrey or scattered at sea. Eleanor Eiken had never felt compelled to control other people and was definitely not interested in being controlled herself.

Karen notes that she still feels the same; she doesn't care where she's buried when it's her turn. Graves mean nothing to her. This is only her third visit to her father's final resting place. She has never been back to Haslemere. Karen Eiken Hornby doesn't believe in heaven or hell, or maybe she believes in both. But one thing she knows for certain: John and Mathis are with her every day, she doesn't need a grave to remember them.

Dad, on the other hand. His soul might be lingering in these parts, she muses. Somehow, Walter Eiken had been the embodiment of Noorö's barren landscape with his furrowed, weather-beaten face and his pragmatic relationship with laws and

375

regulations. He's with her, too, of course. The smell of brine and tar, diesel and sweat. The quick shifts of those ice-blue eyes with the yellow ring around the iris, which could turn in a second from frightening and wolflike to mischievous and playful. She remembers the days when he was out at sea, Mum and Karen alone in the house. The quiet worry when the weather was calm, the rumbling fear when the weather changed and the relief when his boat came in. The sound of her dad pulling off his boots in the hallway, his broad back bent over the kitchen table, his big, tanned hands firmly gripping his glass. A moment free of worry before the boat went out again. A never-ending cycle of worry and relief, as natural as the ebb and flow of the tide. All of it is still part of her.

Suddenly sensing a different kind of presence among the circling gulls, skuas and petrels, Karen's eyes are drawn upward. She watches the white-tailed eagle as it majestically and seemingly effortlessly rides the updraughts. Well, Dad, she thinks to herself. Who am I to say?

Then her thoughts return to the phone call she had a few hours previous. The phone call that brought her here. Ingeborg had been firm on two points: now that she had finally come home, she had to go visit her father's grave and she had to come to dinner that night. Celebrating Twelfth Night alone was out of the question.

'I don't know if I can make it,' she'd said. 'Work comes first.'

'You have to eat either way. There will be salmon with juniper and golden neeps. And apple pie with cardamom, your favourite. All three boys are coming. Einar is on shore leave and dying to see his cousin.'

She hadn't promised, and yet Karen knows she's going to be sitting there with a heaped plate of diced, honey-glazed turnip and salmon baked in a thick protective layer of salt and juniper branches. And she knows she's going to have to answer questions about her work and plans for the future, grateful everyone is tactful enough not to mention her past. She's going to pretend not to notice the looks exchanged when they realise Karen is still living alone and seems disinclined to change that. And she's going to ignore Ingeborg's derisive tone when she asks if Eleanor still likes it down in the tropics.

Oh yes, Karen will be there.

The eagle lets the winds carry it out to sea. She reluctantly looks away, pulls her collar up and realises she's alone in the cemetery. The sky has grown overcast and the clouds that have scudded in from the west are heavy with snow. Everyone else has already noticed the change in weather and hurried off toward the car park. The cold wind and the desolateness send a shiver down Karen's spine.

She makes a slight bow to the grave, turns around and freezes. The man standing at the edge of the cemetery is staring straight at her.

67

'What are you doing here?'

He's standing less than twenty yards away and yet Karen is unsure whether her words reach him before they're snatched away by the wind. Odd tosses his head, takes a drag on his cigarette and starts walking toward the car park. She hesitates briefly before following. That her cousin has come to find her here probably means he has bad news.

Karen's green Ford Ranger and Odd's Harley-Davidson are now the only vehicles in the small gravel lot. He reaches her car first, flicks the butt of his cigarette away and plants himself next to the passenger door with his arms folded. He looks cold despite his leather trousers and jacket.

'How do you drive a hog in this weather?' she asks as she gets closer and digs around her jacket pocket for the car key.

Odd doesn't return her smile.

'We need to talk,' he informs her curtly. 'Could you hurry up?'

She unlocks the car and they climb in.

'My God, I'd almost forgotten how quickly the weather changes up here,' she says and pulls the door shut behind her with both hands. 'Have you seen the forecast?'

'Storm this evening, but I guess they were off by a few hours, as usual.'

Odd leans forward and peers up at the leaden sky.

'I have fifteen minutes, tops, before I have to get out of here,' he says.

'All right. The ball's in your court. How did you know I was here, by the way?'

'I was home when Mum called you. I hear you're coming over tonight,' he says darkly.

'Probably. I hear you're going to be there, too. And Einar is apparently home from the oil rig. I haven't seen him in ten years, so I'm looking forward to it. But you don't seem thrilled?'

'I don't want any trouble. No fucking fuzz crap at Mum's house. Or anywhere else. No trips to the clubhouse.'

'I can't promise not to go up there, you know that. But fine, no trouble tonight. Was that all you came here to say?'

'How much is information about Gabriel worth to you? Enough for you to back off the OP?'

So that's how it is, she thinks to herself, and feels her pulse make her arms tingle. So that's how important it is to you that I don't come barging into your headquarters, introducing myself as your cousin. You might even be aspiring to the top job now that Allan Jonshed is in the nick. Having a copper in the family probably doesn't look good on the CV.

'I guess that depends on what you have for me,' she says, feigning indifference.

'Information about who slit his throat.'

Karen is momentarily taken aback.

'If you know who did it, you need to testify.'

'Forget it. Then the deal's off. Take it or leave it.'

'You really care that much about your mates in that little scout troop finding out we're related? Because you're not going to convince me you're doing it to keep your family out of this.'

Odd pulls out a rumpled packet of cigarettes and Karen waves her hand impatiently when he makes no move to share. He hands her the packet and leans back with a heavy sigh.

'It's up to you,' he says. 'I'll tell you what I know if you promise to keep me out of it.'

She takes a moment to weigh her options. If she does make that promise, she will have a hard time breaking it. Or at least it will mean never speaking to Odd again. Or anyone else on her father's side of the family. No one would take her side in that kind of dispute.

'OK, deal,' she says after taking a deep drag. 'On the condition that you're not involved.'

He shoots her a wry smile.

'Come on, Kay-Kay, you really think I could kill a man? Does that sound like me?'

'What do you have?' she demands curtly.

'All right, it's like this. Gabriel talked a big game. Mostly bullshit.'

'Yes, that much I've gathered.'

'And he whored around.'

'"Whored around"? You mean because he was stealing from Groth's?'

Odd nods and Karen feels her stomach tighten at the memory of Kneought Brodal's report about the two-day-old signs of assault on Gabriel's body. She had been the one who revealed his side hustle to her cousin.

Odd shoots her a sidelong glance.

'I didn't tell the boys. Couldn't reveal where I got the information from, but I also couldn't let Gabriel get away with it, so I took care of it myself.'

Karen briefly considers her cousin and wonders whether he has ever thought about it, the way she has. Has he ever wondered why he's the only one in the family with red hair? Has he ever suspected that the same blood that flows in his veins flowed in Gabriel's, too? Was that the real reason he chose to 'take care of' Gabriel himself, instead of leaving it to the OP boys?

And she thinks about the cigarette butt Odd dropped before getting into the car. How easy it would be for her to get a definitive answer.

She pushes the thought aside, shrugs and fixes her cousin with a disapproving stare.

'I can probably guess how you took care of it . . .'

'What do you expect? He knew what he was doing and he got off bloody lightly, let's be crystal fucking clear about that. And I talked to him afterwards. Or, to be more precise, he started talking.'

'And what did he say?'

Odd takes a last drag on his cigarette, opens the door a crack and flicks the butt out. A freezing gust of wind finds its way into the cab, making the tip of Karen's cigarette flare. She pulls out the ashtray and stubs hers out.

'Look, he'd been bragging for a while about this grand scheme he'd come up with. Something that would hand control of Groth's distillery over to the OP. The boys didn't believe him and neither did I. The guy was a tosser, a useful idiot who thought he was halfway to joining. We got some use out of him, sure, but admitting him as a full member was never on the table.'

Karen decides to refrain from asking what use the OP got out of Gabriel Stuub – at least for now.

'But when you told me he was using our mark, I decided to have a chat with him, like I said,' Odd continues.

'When was this?'

'The day before New Year's Eve, or the night, I should say. In this very spot, actually. A good place for a serious chat, this.'

Close to Gabriel's work, not too far from Odd's house. And yet remote and deserted. At least on a dark December night when no one is visiting the cemetery. Like right now. Probably an ideal place for 'a serious chat' Karen thinks to herself and suppresses a sudden shudder of uncertainty. Surely Odd would never hurt her?

'Fine,' she says curtly. 'Would you mind cutting to the chase; what did Gabriel tell you that might be of use to me?'

'He told me who killed his grandpa.'

Karen stares at her cousin. Is this a trick to send her off on a wild goose chase or does Odd actually have a key piece of information?

'I assume you have a name?' she says with feigned disinterest.

Odd pulls out another cigarette with his lips and spins the metal wheel on his lighter. He studiously lights his cigarette, inhales deeply and holds the smoke in his lungs. Then he leans back and exhales.

'Björn Groth.'

'Björn Groth,' Karen says, successfully hiding a tiny thrill of excitement. 'So he supposedly killed Fredrik Stuub. And how did Gabriel know that?'

She shakes her head at Odd's offer of another cigarette. The smoke is making her nauseous enough as it is, but she doesn't want to risk asking him to throw his out. Instead, she rolls down the window on her side an inch or so. A few snowflakes find their way in through the gap and land on her cheek.

'Apparently, the old man had information that could harm Groth's. According to Gabriel, they have big expansion plans and Björn would have lost all the money he'd already invested if Fredrik Stuub had started blabbing.'

Baudoinia, Karen thinks to herself. Out loud, she says:

'So he might have had a motive, but that's hardly enough.'

'Yeah, thanks, I'm not an idiot, Karen. The thing is that Gabriel actually saw Björn right when the murder took place, or so he claimed. Apparently, he was on his way to drop off his kids with his ex when he spotted Björn's car.'

'Where?'

'The turning area where the road ends near Karby Quarry. Where people dump their rubbish when they don't want to pay to get rid of it. Gabriel apparently swung by to get rid of some stuff on his way to the ferry. Said he was taking his kids to his ex-wife's place in Thorsvik.'

'And he saw Björn Groth there?'

'Or at least his car. It was parked, but Björn himself was apparently not in it. Gabriel didn't give it a lot of thought at the time, though he thought it was strange that Björn had parked his car there and gone into the woods.'

'But he never actually saw Björn?'

'No, he drove away after dumping his rubbish. He had the kids in the car and besides, at that point he had no idea his grandpa was going to be found dead in the quarry just a few hours later.'

'And how sure was he it was Björn Groth's car?'

Odd gives her an incredulous look.

'He was his bloody boss. I assume he saw it every day.'

'And why didn't he tell the police about this?'

'Well, some people are less than keen to have anything to do with you people. Besides, he was planning to use it against Björn.'

'So, blackmail?' Karen says doubtfully. 'He was going to use his grandfather's murder to extort Björn?'

'Look, I don't know and, to be honest, I don't give a shit. But he did say he was going to drop the bomb at the party unless Björn did as he was told. "I'm going to break the bastard" were the exact words he used.'

Just then, Karen's phone buzzes and the coroner's name lights up the screen.

'Hiya, Kneought,' Karen says. 'Could you hold on for just one moment?'

Odd has already opened the door and is halfway out the car. Then he turns around and fixes her with a level look.

'Keep me out of this,' he says. 'I never forget a promise.'

384

68

'You're not as dumb as you look,' Kneought Brodal says.

Karen can feel her pulse quicken. She forces herself to listen patiently while Brodal expounds on the deficiencies of the material he was sent and explains that it must be a mere fraction of the documentation Fredrik Stuub had available to him and that what he'd read should rightfully be viewed as little more than a very rough summary.

'All right, all right, I get it!' she exclaims finally. 'But you're saying I was right about what it implies? Some kind of link between mould at Groth's distillery and damage to human nerve cells?'

'Yes, you were right about that part. The results are hardly statistically significant, but it does look like Fredrik Stuub found – or at least *thought* he'd found – a link between the stuff leaking out of the warehouses and a disproportionate number of certain medical diagnoses.'

'Alzheimer's?'

'Among others. Apparently, he was able to show a small but measurable increase in the number of diagnosed cases in populations living near distilleries.'

'Near Groth's, you mean? Because I don't think there are any other distilleries in this country, are there? Well, except down on Frisel, but they make gin and snaps. Did he find the same pattern down there?'

'No, they don't use barrels. Baudoinia requires spirits maturing in wooden barrels to form and contaminate the surrounding environment.'

'But he did find a correlation on Noorö?'

'Sadly, yes, and not only there. According to Stuub's documentation, he found the same statistical increase in degenerative dementia in other countries in areas where spirits are matured in barrels. And at a younger age than in the control groups, too, I'm afraid.'

'Are you sure?'

'Of course not,' Kneought Brodal retorts brusquely. 'And neither was Stuub. The only thing I can confirm is that this was the potential link he was investigating, and it looks as though he found *some* data to support his hypothesis. But you have no idea how many scientists claim to have found all kinds of correlations that turn out not to hold up to rigorous scrutiny. Not least in order to drum up new research funds.'

I may have some idea, Karen muses, picturing the alarmist headlines in the evening papers.

'On the other hand, Stuub apparently had enough sense to not publish this half-baked,' Brodal continues. 'If he'd been sure, he would have made his findings known.'

Or used them to blackmail the Groth family, Karen adds inwardly. She thanks Kneought Brodal and ends the call. Ten seconds later, she is dialling Dineke Vegen's number. The prosecutor listens to Karen's summary without interrupting.

'All right, you can arrest Björn Groth. But a motive isn't enough. We're going to need more to charge him.'

'A *strong* motive,' Karen points out. 'And we have the email from Stuub to Björn Groth as well.'

386

'Sure, but you need more if you want it to hold up in court. How on earth is it possible that no one saw or heard anything? Are people blind as well as deaf up there in hinterlands?'

Not entirely, Karen thinks to herself, but she says nothing. We actually have a statement from someone who is refusing to testify about something that was said by someone who is no longer able to verify it. Completely unusable unless I can get Odd to change his mind. Or I break my promise.

'You have three days,' Dineke Vegen says. 'Make them count.'

Her conversation with Cornelis Loots is almost as brief. She quickly explains that the prosecutor has given them the green light; Björn Groth is to be arrested and they have warrants to search both his business and his home. They have three days before they have to charge him or let him go.

'Go up there right now and take Byle with you; I'll meet you there to make the actual arrest. I'm going to call Larsen and ask him to send up technicians to do a first sweep before we go in.'

'OK, but what about Groth's wife?'

'We're going to cordon off the whole place, so she has to find somewhere else to sleep tonight. And make sure you bring a couple of uniforms to drive Björn Groth to the station.'

'We're going to keep him in Lysvik for three days?' Cornelis says in disbelief. 'I don't think the station's holding cell is up to standard, is it?'

'No, it's only approved to hold people for twenty-four hours. We're going to have to take him down to Ravenby. You and I will do that tomorrow.'

After finishing the call, she stays in the driver's seat with her phone in her lap. Three days until charges have to be brought. Seventy-two hours to find something to strengthen the case against Björn Groth – or dismiss it entirely. We're going to have to talk to every member of the Groth family again, but that can wait, she decides. What I absolutely have to make time for today, if I want to interview Björn Groth tomorrow, is another chat with William Tryste. He might know more about Fredrik Stuub's threat than he was willing to admit before. When he finds out we already know about the research and that it will eventually be included in the public investigative file, he might stop protecting his employer and realise he'd be better off telling us what he knows. It's more likely than getting someone in Björn Groth's family to talk, at any rate. It's certainly worth a try, she tells herself, carefully avoiding what she doesn't want to think about.

She needs to talk to Odd again. Convince him to testify.

She might as well do it tonight. After dinner. Or maybe before is better. More upfront. Once the rest of them find out I made a promise and went back on it, I won't be welcome to dinner ever again. On the other hand, I'm not going to have a job if it gets out that I prioritised protecting my relatives over solving a murder case.

'Fuck,' she says loudly and punches the steering wheel.

Then she turns the key and starts the engine. She might as well drive over to the distillery and wait for Loots and Byle at the bottom of the driveway.

69

Karen watches the hot dogs glistening with grease on the steel rack behind the glass counter with a mix of fascination and disgust. The young man with the petrol station's logo on his shirt pocket notices and holds up a pair of tongs with a querying look.

'No thanks, I'll have a couple of those instead,' she says, pointing to the pizza slices in the fridge next to the grill. 'And a Coke. And this guy,' she adds and takes a chocolate bar from the shelf by the counter.

The guy puts two slices of pizza on a paper plate and pops it into a microwave, then turns around and checks the petrol receipt before punching in the total cost.

'That'll be two hundred and seventy-six marks. If you want coffee, it's included,' he adds with a nod toward the vending machine.

Karen looks around and spots a few barstools next to a counter with a view of the pumps. There are CCTV cameras in two corners of the room, and a TV playing on mute in a third. She glances up at a commercial for one of the countless online betting firms, pulls off her hat and scarf and is putting her handbag on the counter when the microwave dings. Just then, the advertisement ends and the news comes on.

'Your pizza's ready. Would you like salad with it?'

'No thanks, but could you turn the TV up?'

'Sorry, someone nicked the remote,' the guy replies glumly.

The second she takes the plate from him, he puts on headphones. Then he sits down on a chair behind the counter and turns his attention to his phone.

Another glance at the TV shows Karen an unflattering picture of the police press officer, Johan Stolt, alongside a map of Noorö with the two crime scenes marked with red crosses. Then they show a video from several days ago, of the Groth's driveway. Karen heaves a sigh of relief.

So far, Stolt has handled all press queries and, according to him, media interest has been unexpectedly low the past two days. That is because, as the TV now confirms, their attention has been on a plane crash off the coast of the Philippines that claimed the lives of 232 people, of which five were Doggerian citizens. Speculation about whether the pilot deliberately crashed into the sea, whether it might have been a terrorist attack, or whether it was simply a technical failure, fills front pages and news broadcasts. But Karen knows the tragedy only buys them a short reprieve. Once the media catch wind of Björn Groth's arrest, interest in the investigation will be rekindled and this time, the journalists are unlikely to give up so easily.

Karen turns her attention to the cheese that has stretched into a two-foot string from the pizza to her front teeth. She severs it with two fingers, wipes her hand on her napkin and stares vacantly out the window while she chews. She remembers Björn Groth's deflated form in the back seat of the police car half an hour before. His surprise when Karen read him his rights and explained what the next few days had in store for him had seemed genuine.

He had been alone at the distillery when they drove up, had come to greet them with a mix of politeness and mild exasperation. All employees had left after lunch since it was Twelfth Night. Laura was shopping in Lysvik and Jens had gone with his family to visit his in-laws on Frisel, Björn Groth had explained. Pale but composed, he had listened to Karen's answers to the handful of questions he'd asked. Yes, he had a right to a lawyer but no access to phones or computers. No, he was not going to be allowed to call anyone before leaving.

'We will inform your wife as soon as she can be reached and we will also make sure a lawyer is contacted immediately. Do you have representation or would you like a lawyer to be appointed for you?'

Björn Groth had given them a name and Cornelis Loots had noted it down along with the phone number he had also provided.

'But you have to tell William straight away. We had arranged to meet here tomorrow morning for a planning session, to talk about the expansion. There's a lot of work that needs to be done, even when production is at a standstill,' Björn Groth had said.

'We'll inform William Tryste as well,' Karen had assured him with a nod. 'I'll speak to him myself.'

And then the two constables had put him in the car and driven off. Karen had informed Cornelis Loots and Thorstein Byle that, aside from visiting William Tryste, she also had another matter to deal before the end of the day. Neither one seemed to notice to the slight hesitation in her voice at the word 'matter'.

Now, she wolfs down the rest of the pizza, washes it down with a couple of sips of Coke and checks her watch. Half past five. First Tryste, then Odd, she thinks to herself, and feels gorge rising in her throat along with the taste of oregano. At least it's going to be an early night; I'm hardly going to be welcome to Twelfth Night dinner after saying what I have to say to Odd. It might be for the best anyway; I need a good night's sleep before interviewing Björn Groth tomorrow. She and Loots had agreed to meet at nine o'clock at the Ravenby detention facility.

Why the hell did I have to go and send Karl home? she berates herself. Cornelis is good, but they've never interviewed a suspect together and she would really have liked to have Karl with her tomorrow. Or at least discuss it with him. Just a short call maybe, then she's going to let him tend to his family. He picks up after the first ring and with a statement instead of his name.

'So you've arrested Björn Groth. Can I ask on what grounds?'

'Good ones, of course. But how do you know? Did Cornelis contact you?'

'There was no need. I was sitting next to him when you called.'

'You're still in Lysvik?' Karen exclaims in surprise. 'I thought you'd be home by now.'

'Plans changed. But tell me about Groth. I've been sitting here waiting for you to call.'

Karen gives a brief account of her suspicions after reading Fredrik Stuub's research and Brodal's confirmation of them.

'Well, that does sound like a clear motive. Whether Stuub was on to something or not, the suspicion alone would surely be enough to put the expansion on hold.'

'And it provides leverage for extortion,' Karen replies. 'I actually think that was Stuub's intention, otherwise he would have gone straight to the provincial board. And it explains the email.'

'What about the son? And the wife, come to think of it. Can we be sure Björn acted on his own?'

'We're going to have to bring them in, of course, but I want to talk to Björn first.'

'The question is how Gabriel fits into this,' Karl says. 'Could he have been closer to his grandfather than he claimed and had some part in the blackmail? Or did he know something about the old man's murder?'

'Maybe,' Karen replies evasively. 'We're going to have to try to find out.'

I have to tell him about Odd, she thinks to herself, but not yet. Not until I've at least tried to persuade him to testify voluntarily.

'Well, this isn't going to be enough on its own,' Karl says. 'I'm surprised the prosecutor let you make the arrest. Who was it?'

'Dineke Vegen.'

'Ah, then I take it back,' Karl says with a dry laugh. 'She's probably still feeling guilty about not backing you up last time.'

His comment irks Karen. True, last year, Dineke Vegen had steered an investigation in a direction that had ultimately placed Karen in lethal danger, but Karl's insinuation that guilt was the basis for her decision to let them arrest Björn Groth offends her.

'I resent that! I had good reason to nick—'

'Calm down, Eiken, it was a joke. All right, three days . . . I guess we have our work cut out for us.'

'Not you. At least not for the next twenty-four hours. Cornelis will sit in on the initial interview with Björn Groth tomorrow and we'll catch you up on Thursday. Why haven't you left yet, speaking of which? I seem to remember giving you an order.'

There's a brief pause as Karl hesitates.

'I talked to Ingrid again and she has invited her parents over for the weekend,' he says darkly. 'She thought I was working.'

'Oh, come on. You can't let your in-laws drive you out of your own home.'

'I'm *not*. If I hadn't heard about the arrest I would have been on my way.'

'Good. Then I'll see you the day after tomorrow. Early! And say hi to Ingrid from me, my respect for that woman grows with every passing day . . .'

I should get going, she thinks to herself after they hang up. She checks her watch and then glances up at the TV again. Even without sound, the message is clear; she has seen the weather map enough times to recognise the symbols for low pressure, storm and heavy snowfall. Karen squints at the screen. Does it really say minus seventeen?

Reluctantly, she runs through all the reasons why she can't stay just a little while longer, have a cup of coffee and enjoy the warmth. Might as well get it over with. Tryste might even have something useful to say and then I really do have to talk to Odd. Surely he'll understand that I simply *can't* keep him out of this. What Gabriel told him will be crucial in tomorrow's interview.

After that, I should stop by the distillery and talk to the technicians about the warrant, she reminds herself and feels her heart race in response to her stress level. Then her phone buzzes.

Jounas Smeed is calling.

I didn't send him a report last night, she realises as her boss's name lights up the screen. I can't believe I bloody forgot. Suddenly dizzy, she grabs hold of the counter with both hands. Not now, she thinks and declines the call. I'll call him back later, just not right now. With a sigh, she pulls on her hideous hat and stands up. And is struck by another unwelcome thought.

I should call Ingeborg and tell her I won't be able to make it tonight. I don't actually need to explain, I can just tell her I have to work. Or maybe I don't call at all. I never promised to go.

Then a memory of warm hands, rough like fish scales, and a voice saying, 'If you fetch four eggs from the henhouse, Kay-Kay, I'll get the flour.'

Goddammit, she curses inwardly and pulls out her phone.

70

The headlights are barely able to cut through the swirling snow and point the way up the tree-lined drive, and Karen can't make out the lit windows of The Complex until she's almost on top of it. The memory of her aunt's voice on the phone is still ringing in her ears. Her disappointment when Karen told her she couldn't make it, the hard edge in her voice when she asked if Karen was planning on making trouble.

'Why would I do that?' she'd replied, wondering how much her aunt knew about her meeting with Odd.

'You know what I mean. Let sleeping dogs lie.'

And with those words, she'd hung up, leaving Karen with the question that's still nagging at her as she drives past the last few trees: is it her own secrets or her son's Ingeborg Eiken doesn't want brought to light?

She parks as close to the grand entrance as she dares, jogs up the wide stone steps and rings the bell. The wind is howling around the massive building, tearing at her scarf while she waits to be let in. It's Helena Tryste who pushes the heavy oak door open a crack a few seconds later and peers out.

'Yes . . . ?' she says queryingly. 'Oh, it's you,' she then adds quickly. 'Come inside, hurry!'

She opens the door wider, but only just enough to let Karen slip in without bringing too much snow with her.

'I'm sorry to come by unannounced like this and on Twelfth Night of all days,' she says and stomps off the snow on the hall rug. 'But I need to talk to your husband.'

A look of concern passes over Helena Tryste's face, and as though worried she has revealed her anxiety, she pushes her dark hair from her forehead.

'I hope nothing's the matter?' she says. 'Another murder, I mean.'

'No,' Karen replies quickly with a reassuring smile, 'but I would like to inform him of something that will affect his work up at Groth's. Is he home?'

'William is in the wine cellar,' Helena replies. 'I'll let him know you're here. Please, make yourself comfortable in the living room.'

Karen follows her to the room she and Karl had sat in . . . was it just a few days ago? she wonders wearily. The same day Leo called. The same day she had sat in her kitchen with a battered Aylin. It feels like an eternity ago. Now, a fire is crackling on the hearth and, instead of taking a seat, she puts her handbag on the floor in front of the blaze and holds her hands out to warm them.

'Yes, this is terrible weather we're having,' Helena says. 'Can I get you anything? Coffee? Or maybe you would prefer tea?'

'A cup of tea would be lovely, thank you,' Karen replies.

It's easier to say yes than no, she reflects. She'll probably be out of here sooner if she downs a cup without waiting to be cajoled. Just then, she hears an outraged voice. A young voice.

'What the fuck! Dad has stolen my phone again!'

'Please, Alvin, we have company,' Helena says, and Karen catches her embarrassed smile just as a gangly teenage boy appears in the doorway, poised to continue his indignant outburst.

He stops when he spots Karen and closes his mouth.

'Hello,' she says and introduces herself. 'I'm just here to talk to your dad.'

'Yeah, you and me both,' Alvin Tryste mutters and shakes Karen's hand. 'Where is he?'

'He's in the wine cellar,' Helena replies. 'If you turn on the kettle, Alvin, I'll go and get him.'

'Tell him I'm in a hurry. And make sure he brings my phone so I can go.'

'Are you working tonight?' Karen asks after Helena leaves.

'No, I'm going out with some friends. But I can't leave until I have my phone. This is the second time this has happened. We have the same kind,' he adds and holds out the iPhone. 'Except mine is new, obviously.'

Something about what he just said makes Karen go cold. Suddenly, her mind is rewinding the past few days. Every meeting, every conversation, every piece of information. And everything points to the same conclusion.

Impossible. And yet.

When she asks the next question, the howling of the wind outside and the crackling of the fire seem to subside. The world goes quiet to make sure she doesn't miss a word, not a nuance of Alvin's answer.

'So he took your phone by mistake,' she says as casually as she is able. 'That sucks. When was the other time it happened?'

'Christmas Day,' Alvin says with a sigh. 'Dad accidentally took mine and then, as if taking it wasn't bad enough, he dropped it in the toilet right before we left. He let me borrow his but spending all day at work without my phone was a proper drag. I sit vigil at the nursing home in Lysvik,' he adds.

'Wow, well, I can see why you'd want your own apps. But at least you could still call your friends.'

'We only use text.'

'You didn't call anyone? Not even your mum?'

'Maybe, I guess. Actually, yeah, I did do that ... Dad made me promise to call Mum to wake her up at eight. But how did you know ... ?'

Alvin looks confused and then the sound of William Tryste's voice reaches them.

'Here's your phone, Alvin. Now get going, your friends are waiting for you outside.'

And as Alvin snatches up his phone and makes a beeline for the door, Karen notices Helena looking helplessly from her husband to Karen and back before turning and following her son.

William stays in the doorway with his arms folded. Their eyes meet briefly. Neither one of them is happy about this unexpected revelation, she realises. And yet, there it sits, like a stinking pile of truth in the middle of the floor. William Tryste wasn't the one who called Helena from Lysvik at the exact same time the murder of Fredrik Stuub was taking place. Alvin was.

You fucking prick, she thinks to herself. You used your own son to make up an alibi.

'Why?' she says calmly.

He makes no reply. Just stands there, studying her thoughtfully. And it isn't until that moment, when she notices the regretful, almost sad smile on William Tryste's face, that her astonishment morphs into fear. She slowly backs away, then turns around and bends down quickly to pick up her handbag from the floor in front of the fireplace. She almost makes it.

As the sound of the front door slamming shut reaches her ears, she spots a movement out of the corner of her eye. Then a hand closes like a vice around her neck and the mantelpiece comes closer and closer, as though in slow motion.

Then everything goes dark.

71

When she opens her eyes, she can't see anything. She closes them again, fighting hard to keep the panic at bay.

Then her other senses engage. A faint smell of damp, the realisation that she's lying on something hard. Without daring to move, she touches what's underneath her with her fingertips. Rough, cold. A rock? No, smoother than that ... rectangular slabs. The stone markers at Gudheim Cemetery? Am I dead?

No, these are smaller, all the same size and grouted together. She traces the thin lines with her fingertips. I know this, I know what this is, she thinks. Bricks. With an effort, she tenses her neck muscles and raises her head. Pain. Dull and throbbing across her forehead. And there's a light, she realises now. A faint, flickering light somewhere. Nausea and relief wash over her simultaneously. Not dead.

She runs a hand over her forehead and feels wetness against her palm. Hesitates, then holds it up to her mouth, licks it gingerly and tastes the iron. Just as her mind registers that it's blood, her memory returns in short, brutal snippets. The fear, her futile attempt to escape, the hand around her neck, her forehead being slammed into the sharp corner of the mantelpiece. And suddenly she becomes aware of a presence.

She's not alone in the room.

As quickly as she is able, Karen pushes up onto all fours and from there into a squat. She pauses for a few seconds, then stands up, sways and fumbles for something to hold on to.

William Tryste is sitting in an armchair with his legs crossed and his hand around a tumbler that is resting on his knee. Half his face is illuminated by the seven-armed brass candelabra on the table next to him.

'So, Karen. What shall we do with you?'

She stares at him mutely. Then her eyes quickly dart left and then right, registering shelves lined with wine bottles and glasses, an oak table and six chairs, wooden barrels over by the wall. She instinctively turns around, looking for the exit.

'Forget it,' Tryste says. 'You're not getting out of here.'

'What are you going to do to me?'

Is that really her voice? Faint, rough, unfamiliar.

'I'm genuinely sorry, Karen, but you brought this on yourself. You shouldn't have dragged my son into this.'

You're the one who dragged him into this, she retorts inwardly. You manipulated your own son into creating an alibi for you. 'Accidentally' dropped his phone into the toilet so he had to borrow yours. Made him promise to call his mother from Lysvik while you were at the quarry. And your visit to your poor old dad can't have lasted more than five minutes, rather than the hour you claimed you spent with him. Fucking psychopath. How did I bloody miss it? The grandiose self-image, the feigned humility, the charm. The ability to dupe the people around you, the compulsive talking. It was all there.

And with mounting horror, she recalls the number one characteristic of a psychopath: the inability to feel empathy.

Out loud, she says, 'Why did you do it? What's in it for you?'

'What's in it for me? Everything, obviously. The Groths don't stand a chance of getting the expansion approved in time to pay their creditors. The provincial board won't stand for it. Alzheimer's is the bogeyman of our time, well, Alzheimer's and cancer. The slightest hint of suspicion will be enough to make the politicians pull the emergency brake.'

Suddenly light-headed, Karen staggers slightly. Without asking permission, she walks over to the table and sits down on one of the chairs. William watches her impassively.

'But why kill Fredrik? He was the one who did the research.'

'Because he refused to publish, of course, said the results hadn't been verified. I just wanted him to go public with what he had, it would have been enough. But the old git refused.'

'But he did send Björn Groth a threatening email,' she says, hoping he'll take the bait.

Pretend you don't understand, she tells herself. Play dumb, stoke his vanity. Make him feel smart. Stall.

He chuckles.

'Wrong again. Technically, Gabriel sent that email. He knew where the old man kept his laptop – Lord knows I looked everywhere before I asked for his help. But Gabriel wasn't exactly difficult to persuade.'

And then you put the laptop back in the concealment to make us think Björn Groth had been there to look for it but hadn't found it, she thinks to herself. You have no idea how close we came to missing it ourselves.

'When did Fredrik figure out what you'd done?' she says instead.

'When Björn called him. Fredrik was furious, of course, since he knew he hadn't sent any threatening emails. But eventually he put two and two together and realised it must have been me. I'd been trying to talk him into publishing for months. On Christmas Eve he pulled me aside at Gertrud's house, demanded that I talk to Björn, or he would. It was an unsustainable situation.'

'Did he know you'd dragged Gabriel into it as well?'

William sighs. Then he takes a long sip of his drink.

'Would you like a glass?'

Karen shakes her head. The small movement makes her skull throb.

'If you want me to tell you the whole story, I demand that you have a drink with me.'

He gets up and walks over to a barrel sitting on a wooden stand. Puts a white rag over the wooden bung, wiggles it gently and pulls it out. Then he picks up something that looks like a skinny soup ladle with a long handle and dips it into the barrel through the hole. Scoops up a few centilitres and pours them into a tumbler along with a few drops of water from a small glass pitcher sitting on the table.

'Savour it. Do you know how old this whiskey is?' he says.

She takes the tumbler from him without responding.

'Try it,' he says. 'Try it and tell me what you think of the 1947 Huss & Groth.'

72

The sound from the handbag makes Helena Tryste jump and spill her whiskey. One glass, he'd told her, just one to calm her nerves, no more. With shaking hands and an iron grip on the bottle, she pours herself a third glass.

She checks her watch again. Fifteen minutes until they have to go if they want to make it, ten minutes until she has to go down to the basement to tell him everything's ready. Just one more thing to see to before it's time. She takes a deep swig and opens the handbag sitting in front of her on the kitchen table.

Something inside her is hoping there's a password, that she won't have to do this, that it can't be done. But the moment she picks up the phone, the screen lights up: *4 missed calls, 2 voicemails*. There's a red six at the corner of the text message app. Everything inside her is screaming at her not to do it. Don't look, it pleads, it'll only make it harder. With her lips pressed tightly together, she taps the speech bubble and scans the list of unread text messages and their first words.

Leo	*Call me. Now! 6.03*
Marike	*Where the hell are you??? Call me . . . 5.54*
Marike	*He's found her. We're in the stud . . . 5.37*
Leo	*BR is at it again. Aylin terrified. Have . . . 5.14*

Mum	*14+ and sunny here. Harry says hi. Lov . . . 4.59*
Sigrid	*Picked up the books. Happy now? XX . . . 4.41*

And one that has been opened:

Jounas	*Still waiting for today's report 4.27*

She closes the app and puts the phone down, rubs her trembling hand against her jeans as though to wipe off the revulsion, repeats the words under her breath, the message William told her she has to write now, before she forgets.

'But don't hit send until the ferry is docking in Thorsvik. Check who her most frequent contacts are and send it to them.'

Another sip, just to stop the shaking. She looks down at the phone, leans forward and studies the lit screen, the red number next to the green phone receiver showing missed calls. Impatient, annoyed people, friends whose irritation will soon be replaced by concern. And then something worse.

Her most frequent contacts.

Presumably the people who love her.

'We're going to have to wait for the seven-thirty ferry,' he'd told her. 'There will be too many people if we go earlier. I'll drive you down to Lysvik, but after that you're on your own. And pull it the fuck together – everything's riding on you.'

She checks her watch again. She needs to go down there now if they want to make it. Just do what he says, she tells herself. Write the damn message and then go down to the basement.

Stop thinking!

Without picking the phone up off the table, she opens a new message with a trembling index finger and starts to type.

73

Karen stares at William Tryste, then down at the glass in her hand and then back up at Tryste again. She raises the glass to her lips. Tastes the distinctive flavour: whiskey, smoke and oak barrel. A peculiar mix of strength and mildness.

'The post-war first vintage,' he says. 'My great-grandfather got twelve barrels as part of his deal with the Groths. Worth their weight in gold now. I found eleven of them in a tunnel leading down to the mine.'

He inclines his head toward the other end of the room and smiles.

'What deal?'

'The Groths forced Albin Huss out of the distillery they owned together. You didn't think the Groths were always the uncontested whiskey kings of this country, did you?'

Karen ponders that for a moment. She's pretty sure Byle never mentioned that Albin Huss, the old mining baron, had also co-owned the distillery.

'So how come he gave up his share?'

'Extortion,' William Tryste replies curtly. 'Albin Huss and Jocken Groth started the company together almost a hundred years ago. But Albin was in cahoots with the Germans during the war and when Jocken found out he saw his chance of seizing the distillery for himself. Albin had his mines and his seat on the provincial board and would have lost everything if it got out so Jocken Groth promised to keep what he knew to himself if Albin signed the distillery over to him. Otherwise, half of it would have been mine, you see. Instead, I work for those sanctimonious pricks.'

Karen is reminded of what her aunt told her. If Albin Huss had, in fact, been a Nazi collaborator, that would undeniably have been solid leverage for blackmail. His position as the strong man of Noorö would have been gone for sure, and the government would have seized the opportunity to expropriate his mines for a pittance. Something similar had happened to the owner of one of the lanoline factories outside Ravenby right after the war when some unpleasant truths were revealed. To William Tryste's forebear, relinquishing the distillery had probably seemed a low price to pay.

'So the Groths made off like bandits and kept mum about what they knew,' she says. 'I imagine it would hurt their brand if that became public knowledge.'

'Probably. Which suits me just fine. But we're going to keep that a secret between the two of us.'

The significance of his words sends a shiver of fear down her spine. I need to play for time, she tells herself again. Keep him talking. Play dumb, let him brag.

'Gabriel,' she says quickly. 'How did he get involved?'

'When I couldn't persuade Fredrik, it made sense to try my luck with him instead. Convincing Gabriel that we ought to take back what should rightfully have belonged to our family wasn't much of a challenge. You met him, right?'

Karin nods mutely.

'Then I'm sure you believe me when I say it didn't take much. The mere thought of ousting the Groths and taking over their expansion plans had the poor sod drooling with anticipation. The prospect of money and power, without having to lift a finger to get it. Well, that and a few words about how the Groths blackmailed Albin Huss back in the day. You know, I'm not sure he even knew he was related to Old Huss until I told him.'

'So, did he figure out that you were the one who killed his grandfather?' Karen says sceptically and thinks about her impression of Gabriel Stuub. Granted, he had hinted that his grandfather was doddery and troublesome, but he'd also expressed a kind of respect for him.

'No, he was dumb enough to think it must have been Björn Groth. And I got lucky. Gabriel actually drove past the quarry on Christmas Day and saw one of the Groth's company cars parked there. I'd obviously made sure to take the one Björn normally used, so it wasn't hard to convince the stupid git it must have been Björn driving it.'

It can't have been that easy, Karen thinks. And after a look at her sceptical face, William Tryste continues, 'The fact that he felt guilty helped, I'm sure. After all, Gabriel was the one who sent the threatening email to Björn from Fredrik's computer and a few days later the old man was dead. It was relatively easy to convince him Björn must have killed Fredrik. He was more than happy to believe it, put it that way. Just like you. Laura called a while ago and told me you'd finally arrested Björn Groth. She was in tears, poor thing.'

Karen shuts her eyes as a wave of shame mingles with her rage. William Tryste has been controlling them like puppets, pulling their strings and watching them obey, methodically working to incriminate the Groth family, while playing the role of the dedicated employee, unsuccessfully pressuring Fredrik Stuub to publish his incomplete research, making Gabriel send threatening emails in Fredrik's name, bringing him on board with his plan to destroy the Groths and, in the end, making him believe Björn Groth killed his grandfather.

Replaying her own conversations with William Tryste now, the patterns are even more obvious. He had put in a very convincing performance as a dedicated whiskey connoisseur who had everything to gain from the continued success of the Groth family but, in reality, he had been working to undermine them all along. The way he had dismissed all questions about threats against the Groths and their expansion plans, the contrite expression on his face when he'd 'let slip' about the expansive cement he'd found in the storage room. Karen doesn't doubt for a second Tryste was the one responsible for both the drill holes and the planting of the cement. An ingenious plan, she admits. He had turned Fredrik's house upside down to make sure it would look like the killer had searched it and used the police investigation to make Fredrik's research public. Then he had calmly watched as the noose tightened.

How could I have missed it? she berates herself again.

'But why did you kill Gabriel? He was doing your dirty work for you.'

'Yes, that was my only mistake,' Tryste says with a small sigh. 'My plan was to lie low and let the police investigation run its course. As soon as you found the research it would become public knowledge and Björn Groth would never be able to clear his name, even if he did manage to avoid conviction. Rumours about the threatening email and the drill holes would do the rest; the Groth's brand would be destroyed and I would buy the whole company for a song and a dance and rebuild it under my own name. And Gabriel actually believed I would make him a co-owner. It's almost sad, isn't it?'

'But why did you kill him?' Karen asks again.

'Two reasons. When I first brought him on board, I didn't know about his links with the OP. When I found out he was stealing from the warehouse in their name, I confronted him. I didn't take me long to figure out the OP had nothing to do with it, but Gabriel still posed a serious security risk.'

'You figured he would try to con you, too?'

William Tryste doesn't seem to hear her question.

'He was getting nervous,' he continues. 'Apparently one of the OP boys had found out about the stealing and beaten him up. There was an imminent risk he would start blabbing about our plans to get back in their good graces. Or even worse, he might promise to get them involved in the company.'

Karen says nothing.

'And as if that wasn't bad enough,' Tryste continues, 'he'd also got it in his head that he had to confront Björn Groth about killing Fredrik. I explained to him that the best thing we could do was to lie low, that it was only a matter of time before Björn was caught, that all the evidence pointed to him and that we should let the police do their job. But I could tell at the New Year's party he wasn't going to be able to keep his mouth shut. Simply put, the guy was a ticking time bomb.'

So you had to act quickly, Karen thinks to herself. If Gabriel started to talk, there was a significant risk your name would eventually come up.

She stares at him, unable to hide her revulsion.

'You forgot something,' she says. 'If Fredrik's research becomes public, won't it be just as hard for you to get the expansion approved? Then the provincial board's concern about Baudoinia would be your headache, right?'

'Au contraire, my dear. I'm going to swoop in and save the day. I'm going to be the one who rescues the company, creating jobs and making Noorö famous in the process. That's the best part.'

'And how are you going to pull that off?'

'The mines, of course. We're going to be renowned for maturing our whiskey underground.'

William Tryste gestures toward the barrels by the wall.

'The fact that I've discovered seventy-year-old whiskey in one of the mines won't hurt our finances or marketing one bit, either. You would have been able to vouch for the quality of it, right?'

Would have been.

The sound of the door opening startles her. She turns around. William Tryste empties his glass and stands up.

'Finally. Are you ready?' he says.

The question is addressed to Helena Tryste, who is standing in the doorway. She's holding Karen's handbag in one hand and her tartan scarf and the hat with the earflaps in the other. She nods mutely.

'Where are we going?' Karen asks.

Tryste makes no reply. Instead, he turns to his wife.

'Are they in the bag?' he asks. Helena shakes her head.

He turns to Karen and holds out his hand.

'Give me your coat.'

412

She hesitates briefly. Stares at him until she realises there's no point resisting. Then she slowly takes off her coat and hands it to Tryste who quickly digs through the pockets. Her car keys catch the light from the candelabra when he triumphantly holds them up. Karen turns back toward the door. Confused, she tries to catch Helena's eye. But she keeps her head bowed, her dark hair hiding her face.

And then, the penny drops.

74

When the door closes behind the Trystes, Karen's knees nearly buckle. Maintaining a conversation with William Tryste while her mind reeled with thoughts of what he's going to do to her had taken extreme effort and now she can finally relax. The release of tension is so intense it makes her whole body shake. She grabs hold of a chair arm and stands still, breathing deeply.

She had been convinced they were going to take her with them. Drive her somewhere, kill her there and then dump her body in the sea, she'd figured. It had given her a sliver of hope; taking her out of here would have introduced an element of risk for Tryste. Someone might have seen, someone might have heard. I'll find a way to escape, she'd told herself. All I need is for him to be distracted for a second and I'll be gone.

And then that other thought. That he might succeed. That these might be her last moments.

Sooner or later, the tracks will lead them here, she'd thought to herself. Enough people knew where I was going. I did tell Loots and Byle I was going to talk to Tryste, didn't I? And Karl, too, right? They won't make here it in time to save me, but eventually, someone's going to look for me here. He won't get away with it; sooner or later, they're going to figure out what he's done.

The moment she saw Helena Tryste in the doorway, she'd realised she'd been mistaken.

No one's going to look for me here, she thinks and feels her relief at being alone slowly morph into panic. When they talk to Tryste, which they will, he's going to say I was here for a little while and then I left. He's going to mention that I said something about the ferry, he might even name a specific departure.

Karen looks at her watch and in her mind she can hear William Tryste's voice, 'I think she said she was going to try to make the seven-thirty ferry.'

They're going to speak to the ferry company, check if my car was on that ferry. And if they take a look at the CCTV footage, they'll see me sitting behind the wheel. My head will be down, maybe I'll look like I'm on my phone. But they're going to recognise my long dark hair and that ugly hat. They're going to recognise my coat and tartan scarf.

They'll find my car somewhere on Heimö, probably near the sea, and my handbag will be on the front seat. They'll find my phone, check if I made any calls. I won't have, but I might have sent a text to someone, maybe Mum. Probably something about how I can't take it anymore.

She screams at the top of her lungs.

The sound rebounds from the arched ceiling and the brick floor, underlining the fact that she is trapped. Sheer desperation makes her stand up and walk over to the door. But William Tryste was right not to worry about leaving her here; the door is new and made of steel, carefully selected to protect the fortune contained in the eleven whiskey barrels.

I'm going to pour out your precious booze, she hisses under her breath. Break every last wine bottle and empty out the barrels. Let the millions seep out through the cracks in the floor. That will be my revenge. There won't be so much as a fucking

415

drop left. He's going to kill me anyway. Besides, I can drink myself into oblivion before he comes back. I won't feel a thing.

She walks over to the barrel on the wooden stand. Picks up the white rag and grabs hold of the bung. Feels how easily it comes out. The others are bound to be wedged in tighter, she muses and glances over at the ten barrels lined up against the wall. Just then, the memory of how smug William Tryste had looked when he told her about the barrels he'd discovered in the tunnel leading down to the mine flashes through her mind. She recalls the involuntary movement of his head. A nod toward the wall behind him, hidden behind a shelving unit holding row upon row of wine bottles.

The shelving unit is solidly built and very heavy, but it's not bolted to the wall. When Karen finally feels it topple and hears the crash of about fifty wine bottles hitting the brick floor, followed by the sound of the massive shelving unit itself landing in a mess of broken glass and wine, she lets out another scream. Not because her jeans are wet, not because she has cuts on her face and hands from ricocheting shards of glass, but because she feels like her prayers have been answered.

The door is wide but low. She has to bend over to examine it and feels her spirits plummet. A padlock. She should have known Tryste would never leave it unlocked, even if it was hidden. And she won't find the key in the basement. On the other hand, the lock feels old when she touches the rough surface, maybe even as old as the door itself. She quickly walks over to fetch the brass candelabra and holds it up so she can have a better look at the rusty padlock. Yes, definitely old, she confirms. I could probably break it if only I had the right tools. Or

416

any tools. She looks around, holds the candelabra up above her head to try to find a thin, sharp object she might be able to use, but can't see anything.

He could be back any minute, she thinks frantically and feels the sharp pounding of her pulse in her throat. He's probably going with Helena to make sure she does what she's told. Puts on my coat, my hat, my scarf and drives my car onto the ferry. But then he'll be back. If Helena manages to catch the seven-thirty ferry, he'll be back within the hour, she realises and feels her hands go cold with desperation. I'll never make it.

Her eyes dart around the shadowy room, looking for something, anything. She stares at the steel door, imagining it opening and seeing his outline in the doorway. A new idea comes to her. Maybe I can barricade myself in here, draw things out? The door opens in, so if I pull up the table and topple the rest of the shelving units . . .

And just as she's thinking that, something on the bottom shelf on the wall across from her catches her eye. Or course!

It's impossible, she realises after a few futile attempts to angle the tip of the corkscrew into the keyhole. In frustration, she tugs at the rusty padlock and lets out a stream of curses. So close. So God damn fucking close! She punches the lock and feels pain radiate through her hand – and something else. She reaches for the heavy brass candelabra again, holds it up and leans forward. This time, the sudden surge of hope doesn't draw a scream. The lock may be impossible to break, and it's securely fastened to the door. All the screws are still there, but the wood around them shows signs of age. She pushes on the lock again. Yes, there is a slight movement there.

417

Worried that using the corkscrew as a lever might end up breaking it, she scratches at the wood around two of the screws with the tip instead, wiggling and pulling the lock as she goes. She keeps at it, refusing to check her watch, hacking, carving, wiggling.

When the first screw lands on the brick floor with a faint jingling sound, Karen Eiken Hornby is dripping with sweat, wine, tears and snot.

When the second screw comes out, she stands up, grabs the brass candelabra and kicks open the door.

75

Karl Björken angrily drums his fingers against the steering wheel. Normally, he wouldn't care about the ferry being delayed by snow and high winds. Any other day, he, like most of his countrymen, would stoically accept that man must bend to the forces of nature.

But today, he knows every passing minute is stoking Ingrid's fury. For every passing minute, she is going to ask herself again why her husband didn't leave work at a reasonable hour when he'd been told he could go home for Twelfth Night. Why would he have stayed at work well into the evening instead of coming home? And with every passing minute, she's going to grow more convinced that it's the news of her parents being invited that's keeping her big coward of a husband away. And with every passing minute, there's an increased risk Ingrid Björken might ask herself if she's married to an arsehole.

Maybe she is, Karl thinks ruefully and resists the urge to honk his horn in frustration. Instead, he leans forward and looks up at the digital noticeboard above the on-ramp. The text that until twenty minutes ago had announced *Severe delays. Irregular traffic* is gone. The board is blank.

He could have been home now if he'd left half an hour earlier. But the irregular ferry service had caused the line to grow so long the car ahead of him had been the last to get on the previous one. His contention that it would be possible to fit one more car if everyone just moved over a little had fallen on deaf ears.

'It's full, you're going to have to wait for the next one,' a guy in an orange vest with the ferry company's logo on it had told him.

He had considered flashing his badge but had stopped himself at the last second. They were all in the same boat here, so to speak, and he refuses to behave like the provincial doctors scattered across the islands, who invariably get out their passes and bypass the queue, whether they're on their way to see a patient or going to the supermarket for their weekend shop. Everyone knows they do it but no one ever speaks up. Because one day it could be you lying there, grateful there's a doctor in your town at all.

Karl looks at the ferry that's finally coming in, then glances up at the rear-view mirror. The line behind him is so long now only half of the cars are likely to make this departure. Another glance at the ferry, which has now docked and is pitching wildly in the choppy waters, and then one at the staff waving their arms at the cars disembarking. Through the window, Karl can see them shouting at each other and pointing up at a part of the ferry hidden behind the noticeboard.

Just then, it lights up again:

Service cancelled until further notice. Technical problems.

Abuse of power or not, Karl opens the door and climbs out. The snow has stopped, but the wind has picked up more than he realised. The gusts are powerful enough to take his breath away.

'How long?' he shouts, approaching one of the orange vests with his police badge held out in front of him.

'No bloody idea. See for yourself,' he replies and points. 'The whole thing's coming apart.'

And when Karl turns around and looks at the ferry, he realises it's going to be a long time before Ingrid forgives him. The bridge is listing visibly, buffeted this way and that by the wind, looking as though it's about to topple.

'They've redirected one of the Frisel ferries, but it's going to take hours to get here in this weather. You're all going to have to turn around.'

Karl turns to look at the queue; the people at the back have given up and are putting their cars in reverse. With a sigh, he walks back to his car, climbs in behind the wheel and stares up at the rear-view mirror.

Nothing happens. None of the cars behind him are moving. But he can hear an increasingly strident chorus of horns and angry voices. With a stream of curses, Karl Björken opens his door and climbs back out. This time, his badge receives a warmer welcome.

'Great, can you get some of your people over here to help out?' one of the orange vests asks.

'What the fuck's going on? Why can't people just back up?'

'Because there's a big bloody Ford blocking the way. Some woman lost it and just took off, apparently. And she took the keys with her. I guess we're going to have to call someone to come tow it.'

Karl peers down the line of cars, but he can't see a Ford from where he is.

'Or hot-wire it,' he says. 'It'll be a lot faster.'

With a sigh, he starts walking toward the back of the queue, picking his way down the narrow space between the steel railing, open car doors and annoyed drivers.

Thirty seconds later, Karl Björken freezes mid-step. At the very back of the queue, effectively plugging the space between the steel railings, is a green Ford Ranger. The driver-side door is open and the dent is clearly visible even from where he's standing. He has been badgering Karen about fixing it for six months now.

76

Helena Tryste walks straight ahead, unseeing. Voices had yelled at her, cursing, asking what the hell she was doing, but no one had tried to stop her. She hadn't said a word. What could she say? She doesn't know what she's doing. Doesn't know where she's going, doesn't know what's going to happen now. She has never known; William is the one who knows.

He always knows what's going to happen next.

He had dealt with that detective – Karen something-or-other – turning up at the house without missing a beat. Well, maybe one beat, just at that moment when he came up from the wine cellar and heard her talking to Alvin, that moment when Karen turned around and gave him that strange look. Yes, he'd been rattled there for a few seconds, she'd seen it. Just for a few seconds, then he'd known what to do.

William always knows what to do.

I think he enjoyed it, she muses. That brief moment when he was forced to rethink, that little shudder of fear he must have felt at the risk of being exposed, of everything falling apart. And then the thrill of finding a way around the problem. Yes, he had enjoyed it. That's who he is, I've always known that. I walked into his life with my eyes open.

'You fit together like two pieces of a puzzle,' his mother had said. 'William is the opposite of his father; he has ambition, reaches for the stars. But he needs someone to ground him.'

Her own parents had not been as delighted. Even though William had been so charming the first time they invited him over for dinner, kissing both her mother's and grandmother's hands, bringing a bottle of eighteen-year-old whiskey for her father and singing the food's praises, they had seemed awkward and uncomfortable. But so what? William's mother thought they were made for each other, and she if anyone should know her son, right?

But her grandmother had taken her aside, gently put her hand on hers and given her a look full of concern.

'Be careful, sweetheart. Or he will gobble you up.'

She had laughed, then.

Now she keeps her eyes on the ground and walks on without knowing where to. It doesn't matter anymore. It's over, she's ruined everything. He's never going to forgive her.

What was I supposed to do? something inside her screams. I couldn't stay in the car, not with the ferry service cancelled. Someone would have recognised Karen's Ford eventually and they might have decided to come over to say hi. And they would have seen it wasn't her behind the wheel.

You could have gone back, another voice inside her replies. William's voice. You could have just turned the car right around and driven back home. I told you to call me straight away if anything went wrong. Why can't you ever do what you're told?

Because I'm at my breaking point. You should have known that.

Maybe she says that last part out loud, maybe she shouts it into the wind, she doesn't know. I don't know anything, she thinks to herself and feels her mind racing faster and faster until she can't hold onto her thoughts anymore. It makes no difference now. All she can do is keep walking.

She slips on the packed snow and staggers into the road. A car honks loudly as it narrowly misses her. She has time to feel frightened before the realisation sinks in, before a single irrefutable truth cuts through the chaos.

Somehow, William is going to come out on top. He always does. It's who he is.

77

She is greeted by a solid wall of darkness. Complete and utter blackness and the smell of stagnant damp. And something fusty. She hesitates for a second. Surely there must be another exit somewhere? Maybe more than one? She had come across tunnel entrances in the woods all the time as a child when her aunt took her mushroom picking. Sometimes hastily boarded up, sometimes meticulously sealed with bricks. She can still hear Ingeborg's warning. *No one who goes in ever comes out again.*

Karen looks back over her shoulder at the wine cellar, at the devastation of smashed wine bottles and the steel door at the far end. She might be safer staying there than aimlessly wandering around an abandoned mine. Not a mine, she corrects herself, a tunnel that leads to the mine; the mine proper is several hundred feet further down.

Then she squares her shoulders and takes a first step, raises the heavy brass candelabra and stops. It's too heavy, it's going to slow her down. She checks to make sure her lighter is still in her pocket. Then she blows out six of the seven candles and pushes them into the waistband of her jeans. Holding the seventh candle, she drops the candelabra, which lands on the floor with a heavy thud. A few more steps, then she notices the flame flickering. She stops again to think. Unless she wants the candle blown out by the draught every few feet, she needs to find a way to shield the flame; a cupped hand won't be enough. A screen, or a shade of some kind. She steps back into the wine cellar.

Ignoring the cuts to her hands, she rummages through the piles of broken glass. Eventually, she finds something that will have to do. The top of the bottle is in one piece, but the edge where the bottom used to be is razor sharp. She needs something to protect her hand, like a piece of cloth. My T-shirt, she thinks. I can wrap my it around my hand. Walking around in just my bra will be cold, but I can do it. I can do it.

'Goddammit!' she screams in helpless frustration. 'I'm just going to stay in here where it's warm and drink myself into a stupor. I can't take anymore!'

Just then she spots the white rag on the whiskey barrel.

Karen wraps the thick cloth around her hand and up her forearm, gently lowers the broken bottle over the candle. Moves her hand back and forth a few times. It works; the flame is steady.

With the candle in one hand and the other on the rough stone wall for support, she takes a few steps into the tunnel. With an effort, she forces down her fear and moves forward. One step at a time, she tells herself. Just keep moving forward; this is as bad as it gets.

Twenty minutes later, she realises it wasn't.

Karen Eiken Hornby has never been claustrophobic. Until now. The compact darkness in front of her, behind her; the sudden realisation that she can feel one wall against her shoulder while touching the other with her outstretched hand; the certainty that she could reach the ceiling if she reached up. There is impenetrable rock all around her, layers of soil and snow on top of that.

She wants to flail her arms about, scream. But terror at the way the narrow tunnel envelops her and the thought of the stagnant air seeping even deeper into her lungs stops her. Instead, she presses on – moving forward is the only way to keep the panic at bay. There has to be an exit, she tells herself over and over again. There has to be.

Then the wall comes to an abrupt end and she fumbles around blindly.

She holds up the candle and realises she has come to a fork in the road. She carefully reaches around the corner, hesitates. The tunnel she's in looks as if it continues straight ahead, but further down there's another passage branching off to the left. With mounting panic she tries to figure out in which direction she has been walking. The entrance to The Complex is east-facing and she saw the stairs down to the wine cellar on her first visit – they must have faced north. But they might not be straight. They probably aren't. Or . . . ?

I have no idea, she admits to herself and feels her throat burn with held-back tears. And what fucking difference does it make anyway?

With her hand on the wall, she rounds the corner and sets off down the perpendicular passage. It seems wider than the first one and for a while her claustrophobia subsides slightly. Moments later, she pulls up short. Even with the candle, she almost walked straight into a wall in front of her. It's a dead end.

Then the candle goes out.

78

Karl Björken peers into the front seat of the abandoned car and whatever hope he'd had of being mistaken is instantly dashed. It's definitely Karen's car – her handbag is on the seat.

But there's no sign of Karen herself. He straightens up and looks around.

Without taking off his gloves, he opens the handbag and digs around, without finding what he's looking for. He pulls out his phone and dials Karen's number. Two seconds later, he hears the familiar ringtone from somewhere inside the car. As he fishes Karen's phone out from the space between the seats, he hears an annoyed voice behind him.

'Fucking bitch just opened the door and left. She didn't seem right in the head.'

Karl turns around.

'What did she look like?' he asks the man who is standing behind him, craning his neck to see inside the car.

He's dressed in a dark blue down jacket that looks like it's puffed itself up in the strong wind. His eyes express a mix of anger and curiosity.

'I don't know,' he says slowly. 'Dark, I think. Long hair, yeah, she had long hair. I remember it whipping in the wind.'

'Did you see which direction she went in?'

'Are you simple or something? Isn't there just one possible direction unless you're planning to go for a swim?'

The man nods toward the terminal building.

'I meant after that,' Karl says, gritting his teeth. 'Did you see which way she went after that?'

The man shakes his head and Karl turns away. He slams the door shut and turns to the young man in the yellow vest who has now joined them.

'You're going to have to call a tow truck. I'm not letting anyone into this car.'

'I though you said we were going to hot-wire it?'

'No one's allowed in it,' Karl repeats. 'Consider it a crime scene.'

The guy stares at him in disbelief.

'A crime scene? It's just some lady who cracked up.'

No, Karl thinks to himself. This is something else entirely.

Half an hour later, Karl Björken leaves the police garage in Lysvik in a patrol car. While running the half-mile back to the station, he'd called Cornelis Loots, cursed when he got put through to his voicemail and then moved on to the next number.

Thorstein Byle had picked up immediately.

'I'll send some guys down there right now,' he'd said when an out-of-breath Karl was done explaining the situation, 'but I'm not sure what you think might have happened.'

'I have no fucking idea!' Karl had bellowed. 'But something's wrong. Karen would never just up and leave everything.'

Ellen Jensen had been absolutely certain when Karl burst into the pub. There had been no sign of Karen since that morning. If he wanted to, he could go upstairs and check her room

430

himself, of course. And he had, climbing the stairs two steps at a time. Where the hell was she? Definitely not in her hotel room, that much he knew for sure.

Now he's methodically driving up and down the streets of Lysvik, using the car's headlights to illuminate every nook and cranny. He goes down the same back street he and Karen used to escape a pack of reporters just a few days ago. No Karen. The blustery streets are deserted.

Karl doubles back, pulls over outside Rindler's Hotel and runs up the front steps with snow building up under the thick soles of his boots. The receptionist looks up in surprise when a tall man bursts into the lobby, loses his footing on the slippery floor and only just manages to right himself before taking a pratfall. Wasting no time, Karl urgently fires off question after question and feels hope fade with each answer. No, no one by that name has checked in. No, no other dark-haired woman either.

'No woman of any description has checked in today. Not a single one,' the receptionist tells him eventually in a tone that reveals her patience is wearing thin.

When Karl climbs back in behind the wheel of the patrol car, he forces himself to acknowledge the thought he has been doing his best to stamp out. Karen wouldn't do something like this. Just get out of her car and walk away. Not normally. But then he remembers her face at the lunch restaurant in the harbour when he cajoled her into telling him about her past, forced her to talk about something she had wanted to keep to herself.

'Consider it a crime scene,' he'd told the guy at the ferry. But the truth is that, deep down inside, that's not what he's worried about.

Karl Björken jumps when his phone rings. A second later, he feels his throat contract with relief.

'We've found her,' Thorstein Byle says. 'A car heading south picked her up on the motorway. They're bringing her in now.'

79

Karen pulls another candle out of her jeans. It's cracked and wobbles ominously when she carefully lowers her improvised shade back down over her hand, but the flame burns bright. Then she turns around and starts retracing her steps. Stops, suddenly unsure: I'm supposed to turn left, aren't I? Or is that where I came from?

Oh my God, I don't know.

Just think, damn it!

Fear is making her brain foggy; she clings desperately to reason. Any attempt to breathe slowly and think positively is immediately swallowed by a maelstrom of terror as she keeps moving forward, step by step, inch by inch. Hour after hour? Or has it only been minutes? All sense of time and space seems to have been devoured by the darkness.

And now the dam bursts and the forbidden question forces its way through. How long can I survive in here if I don't find an exit? What is it they say? Three days without food? Three days without water? And suddenly, it's no longer a fear of dying that's making it hard to breathe, it's the thought of what awaits her before then. Three days in hell before she finally succumbs.

Horror sets her heart racing and her arms and legs seem to go numb. Losing control of where she's putting her feet, she trips and falls to her knees. She instinctively catches herself with her left hand and holds her light up with the other. The impact sends a jolt through the candle, which goes out. In the darkness, everything becomes a tangle of pain without beginning or end. Everything hurts now there's no light. This plan was doomed to fail from the start; she shouldn't even have tried. Aunt Ingeborg was right.

I'm not going to make it out of this mine alive.

The realisation hits her like a cudgel. The thought of lighting one of the candles, getting to her feet and carrying on is drowned in a flood of liberating resignation. I've reached the end of the road, she thinks and pulls her legs out from under her. She leans back against the wall and carefully puts the broken wine bottle down, feeling its sharp edges against her fingers and the hard outline of the corkscrew in her back pocket. Hard, sharp objects – a way out, after all. William Tryste is not going to kill her. She's going to take care of it herself.

I can slit my wrists, she reflects. Or my throat. The thought is unexpectedly reassuring; she lets out a sob of relief. Suddenly, she can breathe again. Knowing that she has a means of escape is enough to make her heart stop racing. There's a way out. Not a tunnel entrance in the woods, but still, a way out. It'll be quick, she tells herself and closes her eyes so she won't have to look at the darkness. Then, only my body will be stuck in this hell.

I'll be free.

And from somewhere inside her, she hears her mother's voice: *You go wherever you want, but I plan on being buried in Langevik*, and feels the faint caress of a breeze against her cheek. Mum . . .

Karen smiles and lets her head fall back against the stone wall.

Then it sinks in.

Slowly, almost reluctantly, she opens her eyes and turns her head to the side. You must have imagined it, she berates herself, don't start to hope again. It's almost over, it's going to be quick.

Then she feels it again, a faint draught against her face.

She gets up too quickly and lets out a yelp of pain when she inadvertently puts her full weight on her bad knee. Pain and hypotension makes her so unsteady she has to lean against the wall. Did she imagine it? Now that she's standing up, she can't feel anything. Desperately, she fumbles around the waistband of her jeans, but finding only greasy lumps of wax and exposed wicks she realises her fall must have broken the candles. Determined, she digs deeper and suddenly her fingers find something. She carefully pulls out an unbroken piece of candle about the length of her finger, gets out the lighter and watches as the flame catches. Then she defies the pain and sinks into a deep squat.

A moment later, the incontrovertible proof draws a strange sound from her throat. The flame is bending toward her and she can feel the draught on her face again.

Somewhere up ahead there's an exit.

80

'OK, I'll be right there. Make sure you call a doctor, too,' Karl shouts at Thorstein Byle before throwing the phone down on the passenger seat.

The tyres spin in the snow when he roars off toward the police station. The relief of knowing Karen has been found mingles with a sudden surge of irrational anger. How dare she fucking do something like this?

Eight minutes later, Karl Björken stares uncomprehendingly at the woman in front of him. She is sitting with her head bowed on one of the sofas in the waiting room and her long dark hair is hiding her face. Karen's coat, Karen's hat and scarf, and yet one look is enough. This is not Karen.

It takes him another ten seconds to put his finger on where he has seen her before.

'Helena Tryste?' he says incredulously. 'What on earth are you doing here? Where's Karen?'

She looks down at her shoes without responding. The female constable squatting next to her puts a protective arm around her drooping shoulders just as Karl hears the sound of Thorstein Byle's voice behind him.

'What the . . . ?'

'Yes, I know,' Karl says. 'It's not her. But she's wearing Karen's clothes. And was driving her car.'

Byle walks over to Helena. He stops in front of her and something about his presence compels her to look up.

'What the fuck is the meaning of this?' he says, his voice hard.

Helena Tryste stares back at him apathetically.

They keep at it for twenty minutes. Twenty minutes without any kind of result. Nothing seems able to break her paralysis, not hot tea, not kind questions, nor harsh ones. No one manages to make Helena Tryste utter a single word. Not Karl Björken, not Cornelis Loots, not Thorstein Byle. She doesn't touch the tea, doesn't cry, her hands in her lap don't move. Twenty minutes, and Helena Tryste doesn't even seem to blink.

Then the doctor arrives.

'She needs to be taken to the hospital,' Sven Andersén determines after a quick look at her pallid face and seemingly lifeless dark eyes.

'No. She has to talk to us first,' Karl says and turns back to Helena Tryste.

'Where the fuck is she?' he bellows. 'Open your goddamn mouth!'

'Having much luck?' Andersén asks coolly and opens his bag.

He takes out a syringe and a glass phial. Draws the liquid, flicks the syringe and squirts out a small spray. Then he squats down next to Helena Tryste.

Karl is furious.

'Has it occurred to you that while you're treating this woman, Karen is out there somewhere? She's likely in grave danger and we need to find out where she is.'

'I understand, but this woman is my patient now,' Andersén replies calmly, pulls the needle out and applies a tiny white compress to Helena Tryste's arm.

There's no visible reaction. Nothing in her ashen face seems changed by what the doctor injected.

'Is William Tryste still not answering his phone?' Karl demands.

Byle shakes his head.

'I've sent a patrol up to Tryste's house, but they're not even halfway there. Conditions are pretty difficult,' he adds.

'Send everyone we have, half of them to Tryste's and the rest up to the distillery – he could just as easily be up there. The three of us will have to split up and get a move on. Now!'

Karl picks his coat up off the floor.

'You're going to have to open the gun locker, I didn't bring anything,' he says to Byle, who nods.

Karl shoots Helena Tryste a final baleful glare and turns to leave.

'Come on, let's go! What are you fucking waiting for?'

Cornelis Loots, who has kept his coat and hat on since rushing over from the hotel, grabs hold of his arm to stop him and Karl turns around.

'What was that?' Cornelis says.

He is addressing Helena, whose face seems to have regained the faintest tinge of colour.

'The wine cellar,' she says weakly. 'He locked her in there until . . . I was supposed to . . .' She falters.

438

'You were supposed to *what*?' Karl roars and is blocked by Andersén when he, too, takes a step forward.

But Helena meets his eyes.

'It's too late now anyway,' she says. 'He's probably back already.'

81

She takes twelve steps at a time, stops and raises the shade to check the draught. It's getting colder by the minute now and she can feel the wind clearly on her face without bending down. Another set of twelve steps. Then another. Her hand disappears around a corner, signalling another fork in the road, but this time she knows which way to go.

Without asking herself why, she continues to count her steps, twelve at a time, then a pause, straining with all her senses. Listening for noises, looking for a lessening of the darkness and feeling the wind on her face, each time more strongly. She no longer bothers to raise the shade. Walk, pause, continue. Walk, pause. And suddenly, she hears something. A faint, keening sound. Another series of steps and then another. Now she can make out the keening clearly – and something else as well. The gusts of wind outside are making something move just in front of her with a deep, trembling sound.

She knows what it is before she sees it.

The colour shift is almost imperceptible. But the candle finally picks up a grey rectangle just a few feet away. The opening has been carefully boarded up from the outside. Eight six-inch boards with one going crosswise on the inside and probably another on the outside. Relief makes her heart skip a beat. Nails, not mortar.

The boards are set close together, but the millimetre-wide gaps between them is all she needs. She kneels down and puts her eye to one of the gaps. Another gust of wind makes her pull back abruptly, but she saw enough. It's dark outside and very windy, likely a full-blown storm. And yet, the night is not completely dark, not that solid, merciless black that fills the tunnels behind her. The snow must be reflecting the lights from the TV tower in Skreby, she reasons and shudders. Then she can't have far to go. Half a mile, one at most. Close enough that the cold won't kill her. Or will it? As an icy wind pushes through the gaps between the boards and swirls around her body, she recalls the map from the forecast. Seventeen below and she's in a T-shirt.

I'm going to get through this, she tells herself and takes a deep breath to steel herself against the pain, raises her foot to kick. And freezes mid-movement. A sudden gust of wind rushes past her down the tunnel. She instinctively knows what it means. This time it's not just the storm outside. It's a cross breeze. William Tryste must have come back and opened the door to the wine cellar.

She tries to figure out how much time she has. Tryste knows the tunnels and will probably be able to cover the same distance she has in a fraction of the time. And he will likely make sure to bring a torch, so she won't be able to hide. Panic floods her body, leaving room for only one single thought: I need to get out. Now.

Pain radiates all the way up to her neck when she kicks out. She grits her teeth and takes a few quick breaths. Kicks again. Throws herself at the opening shoulder first. And again. Puts her back against it and kicks out backwards.

441

Why didn't I bring the damn candelabra? she rebukes herself as the impact reverberates through her body. Something, anything to beat at these boards with. But she only has her own strength, her own ability to ignore the searing pain of old injuries reopening and new ones being inflicted. Panting, she forces herself to rest and digs through her pocket for the lighter. Shielding the flame with her hand, she can tell a couple of the gaps are slightly wider now. And aren't a couple of the boards looking ever so slightly warped as well?

She resumes kicking, focusing on the same two boards every time now, pushing with her shoulder and then changing over to horse kicks, while the feeling that she's going to hear Tryste's voice behind her any second grows stronger and stronger. Fear floods her system with adrenaline, giving her the strength to keep going, but she realises she's being carried by a temporary wave of strength that will run out very soon. She knows that's how it works. Eventually, fear wears itself out and turns into capitulation.

But when she hears the creaking of a board finally giving way, her body goes all in for one last push and she suddenly feels invincible. She almost bursts into hysterical laughter when her next kick snaps the board in half. Two more kicks and another one breaks.

She tugs and pulls on the sharp stumps, twisting them back and forth, forcing them outward. Another piece breaks off. She straightens up and studies the hole; it's barely large enough, but it has to do. Carefully, she puts her head through, eases out her right arm, turns sideways and slowly starts pushing the rest of her body through the opening. She can feel her T-shirt snag on something and rip, absently notes when her back and shoulders scrape against the splintered wood. It doesn't hurt, all pain is gone now. She will feel it later, she knows, and the cold, too. Right now, all she can feel is triumph flowing through her like champagne and she lets out a shout of relief as she lands in the snow after a final heave.

Karen Eiken Hornby never gets a chance to wonder what's lighting up the snow, what's making the night outside less dark than the black hell she just escaped. She doesn't have time to realise it's not the lights from the TV tower in Skreby, doesn't have time to notice the lights of the car parked just sixty feet away. She's too exhausted to think, she just instinctively registers the presence of another person.

When she hears him breathe in, she realises he didn't follow her through the tunnels, after all. He knew where the exit was all along and drove over here to wait for her. A last wave of hatred crashes over her. The bastard must have stood right next to the opening, watching her kick and claw her way out.

The voice comes from behind her.

'Don't you think it's time we end this charade now?' William Tryste asks.

82

The long caravan of cars that were turned away from the ferry port is slowly making its way north. The snow has almost stopped, but the wind is making the most of the foot that has fallen, blowing in flurries from nearby fields, packing the snow into drifts against the asphalt.

'The road's fucking straight here, you could at least try to overtake,' Karl Björken snaps, noting with frustration that Thorstein Byle is ignoring his request yet again.

This time, he doesn't even respond. The straight stretch of road Karl is referring to ends in another sharp bend less than a hundred feet from where it began. Taking no notice of the lights from the oncoming car that vindicate Thorstein Byle's caution, Karl curses himself for having climbed into his colleague's car instead of getting his own. It has already taken them almost forty-five minutes to cover a distance that under normal circumstances wouldn't have taken half that. At least not with sirens on. They're not even using their hazard lights. Byle turned them off the moment the road began to meander, making overtaking impossible. There's no point adding stress to an already hazardous traffic situation, he had reasoned.

'Calm down, lad,' he'd added. 'Better to get there safely than not at all.'

Karl glances over at the mirror and reluctantly concludes that Byle might be right. There is a police car with its disco lights on ahead of them and another behind, both unable to gain so much as an inch of ground on the narrow road. The patrol that had been near Gudheim when the call went out had probably adopted the same puppy-like enthusiasm, and with lights flashing and sirens wailing, they'd skidded into a ditch before they'd made it two miles. 'No injuries, but it's going to take us a while to pull the car out,' dispatch had informed them. Three cars remain, two men in each, and Cornelis Loots, whose personal vehicle had been parked outside the police station and who had consequently been able to set off slightly earlier than the rest of them. He's probably just a few hundred yards up the road, Karl thinks darkly.

The question is: where is William Tryste?

It had taken them eight precious minutes to get enough out of Helena Tryste to convince them they should direct all available units to Tryste's residence north of Skreby. They had been unsure how to interpret her disjointed words and incomplete sentences like 'borrowed Alvin's phone', 'barrels from after the war', 'didn't use to belong to the Groths'. But the rest had been crystal clear.

'He's going to kill her. As soon as I call, he's going to kill her.'

Karl still has no idea how she managed it, but somehow, Karen Eiken Hornby has apparently figured out that William Tryste committed both murders and now she's locked up in Tryste's home. That had been enough to send all available units to The Complex.

All available units, Karl thinks bleakly and checks his holster and the Glock he signed out. Actually, 'signed out' might be overstating it. More accurately, everyone had snatched up guns and ammunition from the gun locker like it was a post-Christmas sale, before racing down to their cars. Byle had shouted to the on-duty officer to 'make sure you bloody well call Vrede in right bloody now!' before the station door slammed shut. Once they were on their way, he had explained to Karl that Olaf Vrede is a retired canine officer who lives outside Skreby. No longer active, but hopefully home – and he still has his dog.

Eight men, six guns and a dog. Stuck in traffic on a snowed in road.

We're never going to make it, Karl Björken thinks to himself.

Just when he opens his mouth to point out that the road has straightened out again, he realises Thorstein Byle apparently agrees that it's finally time for lights and sirens.

A moment later, he puts his foot down and turns into the oncoming lane.

83

'I'm sorry, but you're going to have to go back in there.'

William Tryste nods toward the splintered opening with an apologetic smile. Karen turns over in the snow, tries to stand up but slips and ends up on her bum with both hands flat on the ground behind her. Anything, just not back in there, something inside her screams while she stares at Tryste's hand. In the dark, she can't quite make out what he's holding, just that it's some kind of rifle.

He gestures impatiently with the barrel.

'Get up,' he says.

'No!' she yells at him. 'I'm not going back in there. You're going to have to shoot me out here.'

'Sorry, can't do that, someone might hear. And think of all the blood . . . I'm sure you can see why I can't risk leaving any traces out here in the open.'

'No one's going to look for me here. I know what you're planning.'

'Oh, you puzzled that out, did you? Now, up we go.'

'They're not going to look for me here,' she repeats frantically. 'Helena must have brought my car over to Heimö by now.'

Tryste's seems to stiffen at that and he glances down at his watch while keeping the rifle trained on her. He's worried about something, she realises. It doesn't take her many seconds to figure out what.

'She hasn't called?' she says slowly. 'You're still waiting for the signal.'

'Shut up and get on your feet,' Tryste barks at her.

Karen refuses to move. Deliberately provoking him. He's going to have to shoot me out here, she thinks to herself. I'm not going back in there.

'Well, if she hasn't been in touch by now, something must have gone wrong,' she says. 'It's been a long time since she left. Maybe you should have waited down in Lysvik, to make sure she really did board that ferry . . .'

Tryste takes a few steps forward. Karen holds her ground.

'Maybe you can't make your wife do whatever you want after all. Helena might be at the police station right now, telling them everything she knows. Have you considered that?'

'Up,' he says, his voice like ice.

He bends down and tries to grab Karen's arm, but she tucks and rolls, and he misses. Fumbling in the air, he looks as if he's about to topple over, but then he regains his balance. She scrambles up onto her feet but it's too late, she doesn't have the strength to stop him. The force of the rifle butt against her jaw sends her staggering. With Karen in a one-arm choke and the rifle in his other hand, he drags her toward the opening.

William Tryste is tall and his arm is like a vice. Karen's flailing attempts to twist free have no effect whatsoever. Instead, she can feel her throat being squeezed shut. Desperately, she fumbles behind her, trying to reach the only thing that can save her, but when Tryste starts kicking at the boards to make the

448

opening larger, the arm around her neck tenses up and she can feel the blood throbbing in her face.

Knowing it's almost over, she makes one last attempt to reach her back pocket . . .

It could have ended very differently. If William Tryste hadn't managed to break a few boards just then. If he hadn't been forced to adjust his hold on her to pull her through the opening. If that hadn't allowed her the one gasping breath she needed to stay conscious. If she hadn't managed to turn the long cork-screw around to get the tip facing the right way. If her arm had been too short, or the angle wrong, or his reflexes too quick.

She knows she has failed when there's no scream. She didn't feel any resistance from skin or cartilage. She didn't hear the faint crunching sound that was swallowed by the wind.

She doesn't understand until the arm around her throat goes limp and Tryste collapses. Panting, she gets up and turns around.

He's lying on his side, one arm still twitching. As though making one last attempt to reach the corkscrew sticking out of his eye.

84

The cold overcomes her the moment she notices William Tryste's blood is melting a hole in the snow under his cheek. The icy wind scatters the last remnants of adrenaline and makes her sweat-soaked T-shirt cling to her back. Her mind races like an express train. I can't die now, not when I've made it this far. And then another voice that casts about for answers but finds none: how long can a person survive in seventeen below and storm-force winds without appropriate clothing? How is she going to make it through a dark forest full of gaping windthrows and tall pines that can splinter like matchsticks at any moment? The cold makes her lungs ache; she takes short, shallow breaths. Like a silent mantra, she repeats what she does know: I need to get warm, I need to keep moving, I mustn't go into shock.

And then the unavoidable conclusion: I need his coat.

It's not until she once again forces herself to look at Tryste's body, at the blood still gushing out of his eye socket, turning the snow red, that she notices. The snow is red. It should be dark; she shouldn't be able to see colours. She quickly turns around and blinks at the lights of the car parked just sixty feet away. The relief is so overwhelming she almost loses her footing.

He has left the door unlocked and the keys in the ignition. She manages to close the door behind her and tries to start the engine but is forced to stop. Her hands are shaking uncontrollably and despite the relative warmth of the cab she can feel that her body is starting to give up. She's shivering so violently her head bangs against the headrest. Helplessly, Karen Eiken Hornby realises she can no longer make her body obey. All her strength is used up, all her resources exhausted.

And she thinks to herself that she's so terribly tired now, so tired that she just has to have a little rest. Not sleep, just close her eyes for a minute . . .

Olaf Vrede is the one who finds her. Or, more accurately, his nine-year-old German shepherd is. Or, even more accurately, the dog finds William Tryste's body, drawn by the warm blood. It's another few seconds before Cornelis Loots discovers that Tryste's car, which is parked sixty feet away, isn't empty. When Karl Björken and Thorstein Byle arrive, Loots has wrapped his coat around Karen and is trying to make her open her eyes.

'It's her! She has a pulse, but it's weak and rapid!' he shouts.

They lay Karen down on the back seat with her head on Karl's lap and Cornelis Loots climbs in behind the wheel and puts the car in reverse.

Thorstein Byle watches the tail lights of William Tryste's car disappear as the lights from an approaching police vehicle turns the snowy scene blue. Then he turns around and studies the German shepherd, which is sitting on the ground, panting, with her owner's firm grip on her collar. The dog hasn't taken her eyes off the body in the snow for so much as a second.

They waste no time on changing vehicles, just drive on in Tryste's company car with the Groth logo painted on both front doors. Karen's hands are ice-cold, but she's awake, Karl realises when they turn back onto the motorway a few minutes later.

'How are you?' he asks when she opens her eyes. 'Are you in pain?'

Her eyes dart around the dark car and Karl is caught off guard when she tries to sit up. He fails to grab her arms when they begin to flail and he pulls back when she hits him in the face.

'I need to get out,' she says in a strangled voice. 'I can't breathe.'

Karl notices that her chest is heaving far too violently, hears her short, gasping breaths, sees her fingers clawing at the door, fumbling for the handle.

'Turn the fucking lights on!' he shouts at Cornelis.

Then he rolls down the window, letting in a blast of frigid air. Watches the panic slowly drain out of her. Then Karl Björken gently puts his arm around Karen's shoulders.

85

Leo Friis wakes up and winces at the sharp light from the bedside lamp. The sound of breathing coming from the other side of the bed is calm and regular, but the duvet is bunched up at the foot of the bed and the forehead under the long, dark fringe looks damp with sweat. He checks the clock radio. Quarter past seven. In an hour, he'll be able to turn the light off. If she wakes up then, it won't be completely dark.

It's better now, he reflects. The bedside lamp is enough, she doesn't need the overhead light, too, and it's enough to keep the window open a crack, so the room isn't as frigid as it was every night back when she first came home and during the weeks that followed.

Back then, when Karen had been unable to sleep at all without drinking herself into a coma, she wouldn't doze off until dawn, on the sofa, with all the lights on. Eventually, she had felt ready to move back into her bedroom, so long as the ceiling light was on and all doors and windows were open. Under those conditions she had been able to close her eyes and fall asleep, so long as he or Sigrid stayed with her and kept guard against the dark. She would wake up in a cold sweat, panic in her eyes, every night and they would gently talk her back to reality. It's better now, Leo reflects and slowly pushes the damp hair away from Karen's forehead. Just me and the bedside lamp and the window cracked. And she's asleep.

And something has happened to him, too. He's no longer eyeing the nearest exit or keeping constant track of how small the room he's in is, how close the walls seem to be. He no longer reacts – well, he doesn't outright panic – when he hears the sound of a door closing behind him. Last week, he'd barely noticed how crowded the bar was down at Repet, and in the bathroom, he'd gone into a stall when there was no room at the urinal. Fine, so he hadn't locked the door, but still.

Leo Friis knows exactly why the memory of the cupboard under the stairs has suddenly lost its power over him. It's not because it's been almost thirty years since his stepfather last locked him in there. Not because the bastard fell down the stairs and died two days later. Not because Leo had stood panting at the top of the steps, thinking it was finally over. He'd been wrong. The memory of the abuse had survived his stepfather's fall. His fear of locked spaces had retained its iron grip on him. Until, suddenly, it had let go and slouched off into the background.

He'd known it the moment he stepped into the hospital room in Ravenby almost six weeks ago. Karl Björken had called and given a quick account of what had happened, told him Karen had been taken to the hospital in Ravenby.

'She's not badly injured, but she's not doing well,' he'd said. 'Can you come?'

They had run to the car, driven in complete silence and much too fast. Out of breath after running up seven flights of stairs, and arriving just behind Sigrid, who had taken the lift, Leo had opened the door and seen Karen by the window, the back of her light blue hospital gown dark with sweat, the air in the room crackling with panic.

She's more scared than I am, he'd thought.

Another quick glance at the clock radio: almost half past seven, no point trying to go back to sleep. But no point getting up just yet, either, he decides and turns to look at the face on the pillow next to his. He watches Karen's eyelids twitch, listens to her light snoring, studies her bare feet that are sticking out of a pair of tartan flannel pyjama bottoms. The scars are still there, a pale line along her ankle, a pink worm wreathed around her left knee. Old scars; there had been no need for surgery this time. She got lucky, her injuries are superficial, the doctor had said.

Not all of them, Leo had thought to himself back then, at the hospital, when he had looked into Karen's terrified eyes and suddenly felt completely calm.

But they will heal, he thinks now.

She's going to wake up soon and everything will be back to normal. She's going to yell at us for not having descaled the coffee pot, point out that leaving towels in a pile on the bathroom floor won't make them clean, sigh about the amount of time Sigrid spends staring at her phone instead of studying.

But she's not going to say anything about them moving out.

86

Annoyed, Bo Ramnes gets up off the sofa.

Is a little bit of peace and quiet too much to ask? he thinks and turns the TV up. Bad enough I have to sit here all alone on a Saturday night like some loser. Now I have my evening ruined by some inbred hayseed kids who have nothing better to do than to drive their fucking mopeds and outrageously expensive ATVs around?

Truth be told, he shouldn't have turned the TV on in the first place; he should be reading up to prepare for the autumn, shouldn't have poured that second whiskey. Or is it his third? Whatever. After everything he's been put through, he has a right to unwind.

The conversation with Yngve Kroon had been challenging; it had taken him over an hour to convince the party secretary it was all a big misunderstanding, that he is still both willing and fit to be a candidate. It had been an hour of being questioned like a schoolboy. Of answering meekly and appropriately. Yes, Aylin has been having a hard time lately, but she's doing better now. Just stressed, she's had a lot on her plate with the children and her mother being sick, cancer, actually, yes, terrible, but it looks like she's going to pull through. And now Aylin and her mother have gone away together to rest up and recover. Yes, the kids went with them, of course.

Yes, of course they've had some problems, especially over the past six months, what with Aylin having such a hard time. Yes, that's correct, she had filed a police report against him. She had been confused, of course. She feels so very bad about it now. And she had recanted the next day, hadn't she?

In fact, this might be a good thing for the party. If you had any idea how many men this happens to daily, not to mention how many have been wrongfully convicted. True, there are some bad eggs out there who hurt their wives and girlfriends, but it's far from everyone who gets accused. Yes, he still feels minimum sentences need to be raised. Yes, generally speaking, of course, but above all for serious crimes like murder and drug dealing. Yes, and also in cases of genuine domestic abuse, of course. But they also need to protect innocent citizens from spurious charges.

Yes, he and Aylin are staying together. Of course. Right now, she just needs some time to rest up. Absolutely, she's going to support him at home and in the media, if necessary. Their home and children have always been her top priority; she would never put herself before her family. No, not before the party either, of course.

A fucking interrogation is what it had been.

'You fucking bitch,' Bo Ramnes mutters under his breath as he goes out to the kitchen.

She has held out for more than six weeks this time. Digging her heels in, intent on keeping up her little charade. Even when he has sought her out to talk some sense into her, she has refused to back down, despite almost wetting herself with terror every time she sees him. He has explained, apologised, slapped her around and threatened her, but nothing has worked. She has just stood there and taken it. And then moved again. To a small one-bed flat in Sande this time, apparently. Thank God for loyal friends who keep him well-informed.

Aylin's friends, on the other hand, have never known what's best for her, Bo Ramnes ponders and tops up his glass. They don't know her, don't understand what she really needs. And yet, they've been able to manipulate her for over a month now, that police cunt, the Danish hag and the faggots. She seems fucking brainwashed. At least she hasn't gone back to the police, she hasn't dared go that far. Probably realises she doesn't stand a chance.

Or maybe it was what he had told her the last time he found her, the thing that had made Aylin's face go rigid with terror. Maybe he shouldn't have said it, but he'd meant every word.

A dead wife is better than no wife at all, Aylin. You're running out of time to make this right.

There's a roar outside his window. It's so loud he jumps and drops his glass.

'Fucking enough already!' he announces and marches out into the hallway.

The moment he opens the door, he realises these are not local teens with souped-up mopeds and expensive ATVs. But by then, it's too late.

Bo Ramnes doesn't even have time to protest before he's pushed back inside by a wall of muscles and leather.

He doesn't move when he hears the rumbling of motorcycles revving up fifteen minutes later. He stays curled up on the kitchen floor with the smell of his own vomit in his nostrils.

458

He doesn't open his eyes and sit up until long after the noise has subsided. He's not hurt; they hadn't hit him even once, that wasn't why they'd come. Not this time. The warning had been crystal clear.

For the first time in his adult life, Bo Ramnes feels fear creeping up his spine, immobilising his arms and legs, leaving him paralysed on the floor. A raw, merciless, stomach-emptying fear. He retches again, but this time, nothing comes up. The world spins and he puts his hand down in something wet. Another warm puddle. He doesn't need to look down at his light grey trousers to know there's a dark stain of urine on them.

EPILOGUE

Outside, the February dusk is falling, soft and grey. Settling over the sea, the cliffs and rocks, the bare branches of the rowan tree and the thin layer of brittle snow on the ground, blurring contours, urging patience. It's not time yet. Perhaps the light has already changed, perhaps the shadows are not as long as just a few weeks ago. Perhaps the first lapwing has already returned, but the old song is right: 'It's long yet before lambs and codlings play.'

A hissing sound from the kitchen breaks the stillness, but no one moves. Leo is sitting in one of the armchairs with his guitar in his lap and a notepad on the table next to him. Big black headphones hide his ears and his lips move silently as he marks down chords. Sigrid is sprawled on the sofa with one leg hooked over the back, looking just as focused, but on a different medium; she is staring intently at her phone while her thumbs move ceaselessly across the screen.

'For God's sake!' Karen exclaims, lowering her book. 'Can't you hear it boiling over?'

She can't remember whether it's Leo's or Sigrid's turn to cook. Just that it's not hers. There's another loud hiss from the hob. With a deep sigh, she stands up and walks out into the kitchen, stomping her knitted socks a little bit harder than she really needs to as she crosses the wooden floor.

In addition to the smell of starchy rice water burning, she is greeted by a fragrant mix of garlic, thyme and lamb. She quickly takes the wildly bubbling pot off the burner and turns down the heat. Lifts the lid off the other pot and stirs the stew to make sure nothing is burning or sticking. Then she turns around and studies the kitchen table with a sigh. Whoever had the ambition to lay the table for some reason changed their mind halfway through the process. A stack of plates is sitting at one end of the table, crowned by a pile of cutlery, but the crumbs from breakfast are still scattered across the rest of it.

Sigrid, she thinks and opens one of the kitchen cabinets. She reaches for the everyday glasses but changes her mind and looks up at the top shelf. Red wine. You can't have lamb stew without red wine.

'Sorry, but Hanne from the club texted and then I forgot . . .'

Sigrid has apparently roused herself from her phone-induced stupor and followed her to the kitchen. Instead of finishing her sentence, she starts to set out plates, knives and forks.

'Fine, but no wine for people who neglect their chores,' Karen says without turning around. 'That's the rule, you know. Who the fuck put the glasses up there where no one can reach them?' she adds, pushing up on tiptoe.

Sigrid is staring at her back with a look on her face like she has just found out the last of the polar ice caps melted.

'She's kidding. Just play along and pretend she's funny.'

Leo has joined them and moves in behind Karen. Tightly pressed against her back, he casually takes the glasses down, puts them aside and leans forward with both hands on the counter and his chin on her shoulder.

461

He knows she's smiling. Knows Sigrid is rolling her eyes behind them.

'Which wine would you like?' he says with his lips against Karen's right ear.

'*I'll* get it,' she says pointedly and wriggles out of his embrace.

Leo has been going through her wine collection like an indiscriminate bulldozer, and she's not about to waste the few bottles of Brouilly she has left on a regular Thursday.

She's halfway down the basement stairs when there's a buzzing in her back pocket. She freezes mid-step. One glance at the screen and her heart is racing. This is the call she has been waiting for with a mixture of dread and anticipation for two weeks.

The call she has been waiting for ever since she decided to put it all on the line.

For hours she had paced around the kitchen before making her final decision. She had listened to the tempting voice saying she didn't have to, the stern voice saying she shouldn't. Really shouldn't. And then her own voice, saying she already knew she was going to do it. That all the handwringing was just a means of delaying the inevitable. She was going to pick her phone up from the kitchen table and make the call she neither has to, nor should, make. The call that's going to cost her her job if anyone ever finds out.

They would try to understand. Maybe they would make excuses for her, saying she had still been in shock after everything that happened, that she had been fighting for her life in that tunnel only two weeks earlier, that she hadn't been herself, hadn't been able to grasp the consequences. Yes, that was probably what they would think.

And they would be completely mistaken.

Karen Eiken Hornby had known exactly what she was doing that day almost two weeks ago when she made the phone call that would cost her much more than her job if the person on the other end betrayed her.

Now, he's calling her back.

She turns around and goes out onto the front steps before picking up. This conversation is not for Leo's or Sigrid's ears.

'Yes?' she says bluntly.

'It's done,' Odd tells her.

'He's alive, though, right?'

'Yes, since that's how you wanted it. But he's not going to bother her again.'

'Are you sure?'

'Let's just say we made it very clear to him what would happen if the thought ever even so much as crossed his mind. So, are we even now, Kay-Kay?'

'Absolutely, Odd Boy,' she replies.

And with a barely perceptible smile, Karen Eiken Hornby ends the call and goes back inside.

463

Keep reading for an exclusive look at the next case for
DI Karen Eiken Hornby

CRUEL TIDES

THE GLOBAL BESTSELLING SERIES

A secluded island. A missing woman. An impossible choice.

Detective Inspector Karen Eiken Hornby is not the only person to have returned to her native Doggerland after years abroad. Following a ten-year hiatus, Luna has chosen to secretly record her comeback album where she was born and raised. Spirits are high among her team at the wrap party, though Karen is less than impressed with the simpering singer. The next morning, Luna is nowhere to be found.

Hidden between the UK and Denmark in the North Sea, nothing goes unnoticed in the tight-knit island community – certainly not the arrival, or disappearance, of a world-famous singer. So, while the rest of the force is frantically searching for a suspect whose brutal attacks on women are increasing in intensity and frequency, a reluctant Karen is tasked with discreetly looking into Luna's whereabouts.

As time ebbs away so does the possibility of finding Luna alive, while Karen faces seemingly impossible choices, ones that could spell life or death, both for herself and others.

PROLOGUE

A rushing sound in his ears. A torrent draining his arms and legs of strength. Hot blood surging to his head, making his face boil in the cold light from the TV.

It's a short segment, the image of her face flashes by. Naked, serious. The quick glance into the camera. Just a few seconds, four, maybe five. Then it's over.

But long enough for him to see.

The smugness, the self-righteousness. The hypocrisy. The big fucking lie. The face of a person who knows her worth. As though she actually imagines she has any.

As though she were something other than a stupid bitch.

The remote hits the wall as his roar fills the room.

Is he the only one who sees it? Is he the only one who sees through the charade? Is it really his fucking responsibility to put things right?

His body is heavy in the armchair, pulling him down, and for a moment, he thinks he just can't do it. Not again. He should give up, let her get away with it. There are others, there will be others like her, others he won't be able to sort out. He has done his fair share; it's someone else's turn now.

He could let this one get away.

Could.

Could have.

If she hadn't pushed herself on him, invaded his home through the TV. Yes, maybe he could have let her get away if she hadn't forced his hand. But she's asking for it. Begging.

And he's going to give it to her.

He's going to turn on his computer, watch the segment again. Stare at that face, again and again, until his strength returns. One last time.

FATAL ISLES

A remote island. A brutal murder. A secret hidden in the past.

In the middle of the North Sea, between the UK and Denmark, lies the beautiful and rugged island nation of Doggerland.

Detective Inspector Karen Eiken Hornby has returned to the main island, Heimö, after many years in London and has worked hard to become one of the few female police officers in Doggerland.

So, when she wakes up in a hotel room next to her boss, Jounas Smeed, she knows she's made a big mistake. But things are about to get worse: later that day, Jounas's ex-wife is found brutally murdered. And Karen is the only one who can give him an alibi.

The news sends shockwaves through the tight-knit island community, and with no leads and no obvious motive for the murder, Karen struggles to find the killer in a race against time.

Soon she starts to suspect that the truth might lie in Doggerland's history. And the deeper she digs, the clearer it becomes that even small islands can hide deadly secrets . . .

Available now